More praise for
S. K. Wolf
and
THE HARBINGER EFFECT

"Fast and fun."

The Kirkus Reviews

"Hair-raising . . . a hard-edged, taut story."

Detroit News

"One looks forward to future mysteries from Wolf."

Publishers Weekly

Also by S.K. Wolf:

LONG CHAIN OF DEATH

THE
HARBINGER
EFFECT

S. K. Wolf

IVY BOOKS • NEW YORK

Ivy Books
Published by Ballantine Books
Copyright © 1989 by S.K. Wolf

This book is a work of fiction. Names, characters, places and
incidents are either the product of the author's imagination or are
used fictitiously. Any resemblance to actual events or locales or
persons, living or dead, is entirely coincidental.

Library of Congress Catalog Card Number 89-21659

ISBN 0-8041-0710-6

This edition published by arrangement with Simon and Schuster,
Inc.

Manufactured in the United States of America

First Ballantine Books Edition: December 1990

FOR
KATHY,
LAURIE
AND
DAN—
I
COULDN'T
HAVE
ASKED
FOR
BETTER

Acknowledgment

A number of people gave assistance in a variety of ways toward the writing of this book. I would like to thank particularly Neal Shine of the *Detroit Free Press*, who told me more about newspapering than I would have thought to ask; two friends who prefer to remain unnamed, but whose expertise in some areas of sensitive operations has been invaluable; Coralyn Riley, an intrepid traveling companion; and, of course, my family for their continued support and encouragement.

YURI ANDREYEVICH KLEBANOFF STOOD AT THE WIN-
dow, his back to the room. Before him spread the city, its
cement-and-limestone buildings turned nearly to gold as the
sun slid beyond the Atlantic. At another time he would have
been fascinated by the color, would have watched, expecting
the gold to turn to rose, and then to lavender, would have
reached instinctively for a camera, trying once again to cap-
ture the essence of Bodamwe. Instead, he gazed almost without seeing. *Now*, he was thinking, *do it now*. He forced
himself not to think of what could come after.

"I'm not going," he said without turning around. Behind
him, Gregor Bunin cleared his throat. Klebanoff waited, almost impatiently, for Bunin to speak. He's going to say they're
expecting me, Klebanoff thought. He had rehearsed this scene
in his mind so many times that he could have fed Bunin his
lines.

"But Yuri Andreyevich, they expect you."

Klebanoff let the words hang in the air without reply. It
was not right. The time was not right. Certainly the place was
not right. He shook his head, impatient with himself.
Where would be right? Paris? London? Don't be a fool, he
thought. Take what you can. Rafetna would do as well as any
place. Even now, at sunset, the heat was oppressive. He had
expected that Africa would be hot, but even so he'd not been
prepared for the reality. The highlands had been bad enough;
here on the coast it was nearly unbearable. He stubbed his
cigarette against the glass pane. *"Nichevo!"* he said abruptly.
"It makes no difference. I'm still not going."

Behind him, Bunin sighed heavily. And now he's going to
play the martyr, Klebanoff thought.

From somewhere nearby, a muezzin began the evening call to prayer, his voice distorted by a faulty amplification system.

"Stupid noise," Bunin muttered.

"At dawn as well, I suppose," Klebanoff said, turning around at last.

The older man shrugged. "Of course."

"All the more reason, then. It's hot, I'm completely exhausted, and I have absolutely no interest in trying to act friendly tonight."

Gregor Danielovich Bunin stood his ground, his small fat feet incongruously shod in sandals beneath blue serge trousers. Across his belly, his shirt stretched to the limit between its buttons. He mopped his forehead and down the sides of his face with a damp handkerchief. The air-conditioning was not working again. "Yuri Andreyevich, they expect you," he repeated, as if he could think of no other reason to give.

Klebanoff cleared his throat. "Look, Gregor Danielovich, I'm tired and I'm hot. You would be too, if you'd made that trip yesterday. Leave at sunset to miss the worst of the heat, drive all night on roads not fit for donkeys, get in at five this morning. Then only a few hours' sleep and up again and out to be at the airport before seven—that'll mean leaving here by six, or maybe even earlier if the holiday traffic is as bad as they say. I have to sleep sometime. And the heat. It was bad enough in the Dioula, but at least there it's dry. Here you might as well be in a steam bath."

"You have obligations, you know." Bunin was making one last try.

"Don't talk to me about obligations. I'm only here as a photographer, nothing else. The rest is irrelevant. Photographers are nothing; you're not even supposed to notice them."

Bunin sighed again and stared at some point beyond Yuri's left shoulder.

"I really do need the rest," Yuri said more consolingly than he had rehearsed. "I'm going to bed—yes, right now I'm on my way. I'll take a book and in half an hour I'll be asleep. I know it'll be boring for you to have to stay here and miss the party, so go ahead, really; no one here blames you for wanting to go. Have a couple of vodkas for me. Just get back in time to leave by five-thirty or six in the morning." He paused and counted silently to ten. The uncertainty showed on Bunin's face. Not too much, Klebanoff warned himself, give him the line but let him tangle himself. "I

haven't been in this country as long as you have, Gregor Danielovich; you can see that I'm not yet used to the heat. No
one cares about a photographer who doesn't come to a party—
no one will even notice if I'm not there. It's flattering that
you say they will, but I know they won't. Everyone will be
having a good time—I understand that you want to be there,
but it's just one party I'm not going to make." He started
toward the door. "It seems to me it should be no problem
for you, but I suppose you know what you have to do and
what you don't. Just please ask whoever is on duty not to
bother me for the rest of the evening. I'm going to take a
cold shower and go to bed. In the Dioula I've gotten used to
that kind of life—up at dawn and to bed at dark. It's a peculiar
way to fight a war, but at least it's predictable. Good night."
He paused in the doorway and turned around. "Did I hear
Stefan say there were going to be women?"

Bunin nodded, a hopeful smile showing his missing front
tooth.

"Damn," Yuri said, and paused just briefly. "But I'm so
tired I probably wouldn't be able to get it up anyway."

"You'd be surprised what a little vodka can do to revive a
person," Bunin suggested. "If you know what I mean," he
added, grinning in a way that was meant to indicate male
camaraderie, like a nudge in the ribs, but only succeeded in
showing his bad teeth.

Yuri suppressed a smile. He'd tagged Gregor Danielovich
almost immediately. For a man in a job like his, he was
incredibly inept. He wondered who propped Bunin up, how
the man managed not to fall under the wheels. He shook his
head slowly, as if in regret. Then he turned once again and
left, with Bunin staring after him.

In the room that had been assigned to him, Klebanoff removed his shirt and pants and hung them over the chair. He
looked at himself for a long moment in the mirror over the
washstand. He had not washed or shaved in three days, and
he really was as tired as he'd let on to Bunin. For that reason,
it was not a good time. On the other hand, it was the only
time he was going to get. If Bunin cooperated. He was counting on that. It would be against procedure, but Bunin wanted
to go; he'd seen the dilemma in his eyes. "Then do it," he
said softly to his reflection.

He stepped into the enclosure and under the meager luke-
warm spray. It was far from the cold shower he'd told Bunin

he was going to take. His mistake—as if, in this country, he'd
really expected cold water to come out of the tap. Even so,
it was somehow refreshing. Bunin. Gregor Danielovich. At
least he'd been lucky in that one; perhaps he could take it for
an omen. They'd been paired for the duration of Yuri's stay
in Rafetna—that had been evident from the start—a common
practice, each responsible for keeping an eye on the other.
But Bunin could easily make a threesome with another pair;
he was not required to stay at the Embassy residence just
because Yuri chose to. Only the most meticulous of men
would carry his responsibilities that far, and Bunin seemed
far from meticulous. The man didn't seem competent enough
even to know for sure whether or not his shoelaces were tied.
Klebanoff wondered idly what Bunin's connections were—
why he hadn't been sacked long ago. Whatever—or whoever—they were, they'd probably thought he'd be safe in
Rafetna, doing as little harm as possible. It ought to have been
a safe assignment for him. Klebanoff smiled to himself. For
reasons like that, Rafetna was not so bad a place after all.

He turned the water off and shoved the curtain aside. The
mirror over the sink was steamy. He'd shave quickly, and then
get into bed with a book, turn off the light in twenty minutes
or so, and wait. He was not sure enough of Bunin to know
if the man would check. In half an hour it would be dark;
anyone who'd gotten used to going to bed with the sun could
be expected to be asleep.

But Bunin did not check—or if he did, it was with far more
subtlety than Klebanoff would have expected. There were no
sounds at the door, no cautious opening to allow a head to
peer in, nothing. The whole floor was as still as the breathless
air; the duty officer had apparently been warned. And that
ought to mean something; they were all at the party. An hour
and a quarter after he'd turned out the light, Klebanoff swung
himself out of bed and put on his clothes. He'd laid everything out so that he could dress in the dark—his baggiest
pants to accommodate as much film as possible, the nondescript shirt that would not call attention to him, the one camera he dared take laid carefully on the floor by the foot of the
bed. He was ready in less than a minute, and he slipped out
of the room, closing the door carefully behind him.

The hallway was deserted, with only a dim light at the end
where the stairs were. At the bottom of the stairs, sitting
behind a small wooden desk, was the officer on duty—eyes

half-closed from boredom. When he saw Klebanoff coming down the steps he sat up a little straighter. "Comrade?" he asked.

"I was extremely tired and I went to bed early, but I seem to have only slept an hour or so before waking. Everyone's already gone to the party by now, I suppose?"

"I'm afraid so."

"Even Comrade Bunin?"

"Yes. Was he not supposed to go?"

"It's perfectly all right. Can you get a taxi for me? Since I can't sleep, I might as well join them. Do you know the address?"

"Yes, Comrade, of course. It's right here."

"Good. If you'd take care of the taxi, I'd appreciate it. My French is atrocious."

"I'm not so sure . . ."

"Bunin will be delighted I could make it. This way he won't feel so guilty." Klebanoff winked at the sergeant, and the sergeant smiled back knowingly.

"Of course."

He went out the door, Klebanoff following, and walked briskly toward the gate. At the gate both men waited until the soldier on duty opened the small iron-clad door beside the main entrance and then both walked through. The sergeant raised his arm and a taxi made an immediate U-turn in the middle of the boulevard and pulled up at the curb. Klebanoff stepped in as the sergeant gave the address to the driver. "Have a good time." The sergeant waved.

Klebanoff smiled in return. "I'll try," he said.

The cabdriver pulled away from the curb with a vigor that threw Klebanoff deep against the seat back. He waited purposefully until they had gone three blocks. By then they were traveling faster than any other vehicle on the street. "Do you speak English?" Klebanoff asked.

"A little."

"Do you understand this: American Embassy?"

The man shot a glance in the rearview mirror. Surprise and curiosity showed in his eyes. He nodded. "I understand," he said slowly, his eyes still on Klebanoff.

"Good," Klebanoff said. "Take me there. American Embassy."

The driver started to say something, then stopped. Klebanoff caught his gaze in the mirror. "Do not ask me," he said firmly. The man's eyes narrowed, but he nodded solemnly and said nothing for the rest of the trip.

Klebanoff recognized the building while they were still a block away—spotlights shone on the imposing white structure behind its heavy wrought-iron gates. He'd seen it earlier, when he was on the streets scouting shots for the festivities. That had been a perfect cover to move around Rafetna and get his bearings. The driver sped almost to the drive before slamming his foot on the brakes and bringing the cab to a sudden, jerking stop in front of the gate. Klebanoff handed over a couple of bills and stepped out. Now, he thought, now I'm really doing it.

A black man in uniform stood at the gate, and Klebanoff felt sudden confusion. Was this a black American, or was he a Bodamwean? He didn't recognize the uniform. Klebanoff felt a trickle of sweat down his sides and he knew it was not from the heat.

"May I help you?" the man asked in English.

"I . . . will see someone inside," Klebanoff said. Then, more forcefully, he repeated the words. "I will see someone inside."

The man's dark eyes scrutinized Klebanoff for a moment before he stepped back and allowed the Soviet through the gate. "Ring the night bell beside the door," he said. He pronounced the words in a clipped sort of way, and Klebanoff suspected that the accent was not American, but he could not be sure. Without a backward glance, he walked, quickly now, toward the Embassy building. Already he could see another guard, another black man, but in a different uniform this time, staring out at him. He tried to make himself breathe more slowly. He had passed the first obstacle; he had gotten this far. He would make it now.

Corporal Preston Williams watched the man come toward him, and timed his move so as to step out of the small door at the side of the main entrance just as the man reached the top of the steps. "Sir?" he said.

The man hesitated and Williams realized that he looked nervous, and that put him on guard. Every Marine at every embassy in the world knew the lessons of Tehran and Beirut, and every Marine's worst nightmare was that his assignment would turn out to be the next in that little litany of violated embassies. And this was how it had always appeared in Preston Williams' nightmares—a nervous-looking man showing up some night when it was only he and one other guard in the whole building and the fucking local at the front gate would let him walk in just as if he owned the place. "Sir," Williams repeated, taking another step forward, as if he were walking point in Nam or somewhere.

The man stopped now. "My name is Klebanoff, Yuri Andreyevich," he said slowly. "I am Soviet citizen. And I am asking for political asylum."

The Marine's eyes widened in surprise. "Will you repeat that?" he asked warily.

The man glanced quickly around, and Preston Williams' eyes automatically surveyed the area. Traffic seemed normal, no parked cars lurking just out of range, no loiterers. He'd seen the taxi that had brought this man, but it was long gone now.

"I am asking for asylum," the man was repeating. "My name is Klebanoff—"

"Okay," Williams interrupted, catching the urgency in the man's voice. "Come inside." He pulled the door open and stepped aside so that the man could go in first. *Never leave your flank vulnerable.* That had been one of the first things they'd taught him at Parris Island. *Or your backside*, he'd learned long before that, on the streets of South Boston. He clicked the door locked and directed the man into an anteroom to the side of the broad entrance hall. "First, you'll have to give me the camera."

Klebanoff's hand moved protectively to the camera that hung on a strap around his neck.

"I'm sorry, sir," Williams insisted. "No cameras allowed in the Embassy."

"I am photographer," the Russian responded. "I always carry cameras."

"Not in here you don't." Williams extended his hand for the camera.

"But I have film—"

"Nothing will be disturbed," Williams assured him, wondering if that was true. "It'll be returned to you when you leave."

Reluctantly, Klebanoff handed over the camera.

"And I'll need to see some identification."

Klebanoff pulled a leather folder from his pocket and flipped it open. Williams shoved the camera under his left arm and took the ID folder in his left hand. His right hand still rested on the butt of his side arm, which was still holstered, but with the flap unsnapped. Behind discolored plastic in the folder was a card with words in a language Williams took to be Russian. Clipped to the plastic was another card, this one in English and French, and Williams scanned the English part. It was a press pass, issued by the Bodamwean government, and the name on the pass was the same name that the man had given—Yuri Andreyevich Klebanoff.

"You don't have a passport?" Williams asked.

"It is at my embassy. They keep our passports if we are not traveling. What you have should be sufficient."

Williams glanced at the press pass again. "Excuse me, sir," he said. "Will you please be seated." He indicated a wooden chair against the wall. "Can I get you a glass of water, can of soda? Cigarette, maybe?"

Klebanoff moved to the chair but didn't sit. "I would like a cigarette."

"Just one moment, sir," Williams said, backing toward the door. "Please, sit down. Make yourself comfortable. Uh, maybe you'd like to look at a magazine." He pointed at the small table beside the chair. "I'll be right back." He stood uncomfortably in the doorway until Klebanoff had seated himself. Then he hurried back toward the front doors, checking all of them again to make sure they were locked. He strode quickly into the small room on the opposite side of the entrance hall and grabbed an unopened pack of Marlboros from a shelf. With his other hand he punched a button on the intercom on the desk. He looked at his watch: ten thirty-seven. Come on, Longman, he thought, you've got to have the chars out of there by now.

He punched the number again, impatiently, and this time it was answered. "Yeah?" Scott Longman's voice came over the line.

"I need a status report," Williams said. "We've got a seven blue."

"A what?"

"You heard me."

Scott Longman cleared his throat and spoke into the walkie-talkie. "Char force finished and gone. Just one moment." He stepped over to the back door to make sure it was locked. "Back door secure," he said into the speaker. "Mr. Jones working late. I'm checking safes. I'll be right there." Sweet

Jesus, he thought, who the hell thinks he can make a defection case from Bodamwe? His footsteps echoed on the terrazzo floor of the hall as he hurried to the front of the building. There could be a million reasons why someone would want to get out of this place, but making a political asylum case would be something else again. Good luck, he thought, turning a corner in the hall. You'd better have some damn good reason. Or else you'd better be bringing along some very good stuff. Or else, it dawned on him, you'd better be somebody these guys can use.

Preston Williams was back in the anteroom. He handed the Soviet the cigarettes and a lighter. He noticed that the man was still sitting stiffly in the chair and hadn't picked up any magazines. "Make yourself at home, sir," he said. "I'll have someone here to take care of you just as soon as possible." He backed out the door and was relieved that he could hear Longman's footsteps now. He paused in the entrance hall until Scott came into view, and then he nodded his head back toward the room where he'd left the Soviet. Let Longman keep an eye on him, he thought, moving across the hall into the guard office again. He had his own work cut out for him.

He crouched before a small safe and turned its dial. From the safe he took a typed sheet of paper. At the top of the paper, someone had penciled in red: "SECURITY—EYES ONLY." Below that, typed, was the heading: "Defector Instructions." He quickly read through the instructions. Yes, he'd secured the doors. Yes, he'd taken the man out of public view. Yes, he'd tried to make the guy comfortable. Yes, he'd asked for and seen some identification. Yes, he'd called the other guard. All right; he was breathing slower now.

Below the instructions was a typed question followed by a list of names and telephone numbers. He read the first one. Dennis O'Neal. Shit. O'Neal had left less than two hours ago with Tom Little, and they'd been talking about going out to dinner. There was little chance O'Neal would be home yet, but he tried anyway. On the fourth ring, an answering machine clicked in. Williams listened to the message, wondering whether he should just hang up or what. But when the beep sounded he was still on the line. He took a deep breath. "Mr. O'Neal," he said, "this is Corporal Williams. I was just wondering if you'd gotten your tickets for the Marine Ball yet." Then he hung up.

He looked at the next name and dialed the number beside it.

A woman answered the phone after three rings. "Hello?"

"Could I speak with Mr. Hartley, please?"

"Just a minute."

Williams could hear kids' voices coming from the background. Hartley had a couple of daughters.

"Hello?" Hartley's voice came on the line.

"Mr. Hartley, this is Corporal Williams. I was just wondering if you've gotten your tickets for the Marine Ball yet."

"All right. Give me fifteen minutes."

Williams hung up the phone, shaking his head. Dollars to doughnuts, O'Neal would have answered in a less obvious way, but the State wimps thought they were above such things. From where Williams stood, he could see the doorway to the anteroom across the entrance hall. Scott Longman stood in the hall, a discreet distance from the doorway. Williams locked the sheet of paper back in the safe and walked out into the hall. "Everything okay?" he asked.

Longman nodded. "You didn't tell me he was a white guy."

Williams grinned. "What's the matter, he your brother or something?"

"Who the hell is he?" Longman whispered.

"Russian guy, supposedly."

"You seen his ID?"

"Yeah. You think I'm a fuck-up or something?"

Scott Longman edged over so that he could see the man again. He was still sitting in the chair, looking at one of the magazines. He glanced up when Longman looked in.

"Get'cha a drink of water?" Williams asked, raising his voice.

Behind him, Longman whispered, "Water? Shit, Pres!"

Klebanoff licked his lips. "Water would be fine," he said.

"That's what the instructions say," Williams muttered at Longman. "Make him feel at home. Offer him water or cigarettes."

"Hell," Longman said, trailing Williams back into the guard office, "if you're going to offer him cancer, you might as well give him something better to drink than water."

Williams reached for a paper cup and held it under the water-cooler spout. "Letter of the law," he said. "You follow the letter of the law and you don't get yourself into no-o-o-o trouble."

* * *

George Hartley arrived twelve minutes after Preston Williams had called him. And, practically on his heels, Dennis O'Neal came in with Tom Little. Figures, Williams thought to himself. O'Neal and Little both lived in the same building, and Little's name had been added to the bottom of the list shortly after he'd arrived, only a month or so ago. O'Neal probably wants him to see how it's done, Williams thought to himself.

"Got your message," O'Neal said as he came in. "Thanks."

"Mr. Hartley's already here. He just went in with the guy." Williams nodded at the room across the hall.

"That's fine," O'Neal said.

Hartley heard O'Neal's voice and stepped out into the hall to meet him. "You want to handle it?" Hartley asked in a lowered voice.

"Have you seen any ID?"

"Just getting started. I only beat you by a couple of minutes."

"Why don't you do it, then," O'Neal responded. "I'll be woodwork." He turned to Williams, who stood in the doorway of the guard office. "Anybody else in the building?"

"Mr. Jones came in about an hour ago. He's the only one."

"Good," O'Neal said. "Give him a ring, will you? Tell him he might want to hang around. Just in case."

"Yes, sir."

O'Neal turned to Hartley. "It's your ball game. Where do you want him?"

"Second-floor conference room?"

"Sounds good to me."

The room was small, furnished with a wide, formica-topped table with chrome legs. The chairs were also of chrome, with dark-blue fabric seats. Three men sat on one side of the table, facing Yuri Andreyevich Klebanoff. They'd introduced themselves as they came into the room one by one—Consul General George Hartley, tall with graying curly hair, who'd introduced himself before, downstairs; and Second Secretary Dennis O'Neal, freckle-faced with restless blue eyes. At the far end of the table sat Tom Little, who'd introduced himself as an assistant economic attaché. Klebanoff wondered which of them were CIA, or maybe they all were. If the opposite thing had happened, he had no doubt that all three would have been KGB. Two windows, high on the opposite wall, were covered with blinds. In the American Embassy, the air-conditioning was working.

"Your name is Yuri Andreyevich Klebanoff," the Consul began, mistakenly putting the accent on the first syllable of Yuri's last name.

Klebanoff nodded.

"And you have no passport with you, only your press credentials."

Yuri shrugged. "There should be no reason for me to have a passport."

"Because you are not traveling anywhere at the moment."

"Exactly."

"How long have you been in Rafetna?"

"Since yesterday in Rafetna. But I have been in Bodamwe longer."

Hartley raised his eyebrows. "Where?"

"In Dioula—covering fighting."

"You are a photographer, is that correct?"

"Yes."

"Mr. Klebanoff, what exactly are you doing here? How can we help you?"

Klebanoff looked uncomfortable and cleared his throat. "I already said that. I am asking for asylum." He glanced around the table. At the far end, Thomas Little was writing something on a pad of paper.

"For what reason are you asking asylum?"

"Is it so strange that someone would want to leave Soviet Union and live in America?"

There was a sound at the door and all four men turned. A fifth man walked in, well under six feet in height, with a barrel chest supported by a broad stomach. His suit looked wrinkled, as if he had worn it continuously for too many hours. He nodded to the other men and pulled a chair up to the table next to O'Neal.

"Mr. Yuri Klebanoff, this is Mr. Alvin Jones," George Hartley said. Jones nodded at Klebanoff but didn't offer his hand.

"Well, Mr. Klebanoff," Hartley went on, "it's not so strange that you would prefer to live in the United States. But I think we should make it clear at the outset that while we will do whatever we can to help anyone who wants to live in freedom, it is not always possible for people to come to the United States. We would be willing, however, to do whatever we can to help you live elsewhere, if that is indicated.''

"I am interested in living in United States."

"Mr. Klebanoff, who knows you are here?"

Klebanoff looked around the room. "You. The men downstairs."

"And outside of this building?"

"No one."

"How did you get here?"

"Taxi."

"How soon do you think someone will notice that you are missing?"

Klebanoff shrugged. "Who is to say? Maybe already."

Hartley leaned forward across the table from Klebanoff. "You know, Mr. Klebanoff, you could do us a great deal of good if you would think about going back to your embassy before you are missed. And maybe you could do yourself some good as well."

Klebanoff stiffened. "What do you mean?"

Hartley made a slight shrugging gesture. "You're a photographer. I'm sure you could take some pictures that would be quite useful to us. Since you say you've been in Dioula Province, perhaps you already have taken pictures we would be interested in."

Before he had even finished, Jones was leaning toward O'Neal, whispering something. O'Neal responded with a single whispered syllable.

"You want me to spy for you. Take photographs of secret Soviet materials, I suppose."

"For a short time. We would reward you, of course."

"Money? I am not interested in being a spy, for money or otherwise."

"The United States government would look with more interest on the asylum application of someone who had done it some favors," Hartley suggested.

"I am not interested in being a spy. Period. I do not think I can go back to Soviet Embassy in any case by now."

"You mean they will have already noticed that you have gone."

"I mean circumstances under which I left were too unusual."

Dennis O'Neal cleared his throat. "How long were you in the Dioula?" he asked.

"Five weeks."

"Before that?" Hartley asked.

"In Moscow."

"Who were you covering the fighting for?" Hartley asked.

"Tass, of course. This is seen as a people's revolution."

"Have you brought any photographs?"

"I have all my unprocessed film."

"Have you, then, been in the camps with the rebels?"

"Yes."

"And seen who leads them?"

"Yes."

"And you have film of that?"

"Yes."

"And does this have anything to do with why you want to leave?"

"I am photographer—artist. I prefer to photograph what I choose."

O'Neal pushed his chair away from the table, stood, walked several paces away, and then turned. "Instead of . . . ?"

"What they tell me."

"Are you talking about the fighting, or your work for Tass in general, or all your photography work?"

"Everything."

Jones glanced quickly at O'Neal, and O'Neal said, "Then this was not a decision you made as a result of photographing the fighting?"

Yuri Andreyevich waved his hand. "It is all involved."

"Does that mean you'd rather be doing art photography than war photography?" O'Neal asked.

"That is only part of it, anyway," Yuri Andreyevich said impatiently.

O'Neal frowned. "What do you mean by that?"

Yuri Andreyevich stubbed his cigarette in the ashtray and lit another one before he responded. "There are many reasons to leave."

Hartley leaned forward. "I hope we have made it clear that the United States cannot grant asylum to everyone who asks."

"If person is famous you do."

Jones spoke at last. "Mr. Klebanoff," he said, pronouncing the name correctly, "it's possible you may not be famous enough, if that is the yardstick by which you think we measure.''

"I am sure I am not famous at all. But that does not mean I am ordinary person.''

O'Neal, standing, leaned on his palms on the table. "In plain words, Mr. Klebanoff, for what reason should we grant you asylum? Do you have photographs to offer us, or what?''

"I have photographs you may be interested in," Klebanoff said, speaking slowly and deliberately, "but that is not all. It is who I am that may be of interest as well. My father is Andrei Klebanoff, editor in chief of *Pravda*.''

O'Neal stood up straight, his eyes fixed on the opposite wall, as if he were thinking.

"That is not all, either," Yuri Andreyevich went on. "My grandfather . . . my mother's father . . . is Sergei Butakov. I am his only living grandchild.''

For a moment there was utter silence. O'Neal's eyes moved immediately to focus on Klebanoff's.

"*The* Sergei Butakov?" Hartley asked finally.

"Of course.''

At the far end of the table, Thomas Little whispered to himself. "Holy shit. Holy, bloody, fucking shit." But the expression on his face hadn't changed; he was too well trained for that.

"Mr. Klebanoff," O'Neal said, still looking straight at the Soviet, "in what year was Sergei Butakov born?''

A broad grin spread across Klebanoff's face. "You want me to prove who I am? My grandfather was born in 1904. Yes, he is that old, though he doesn't look it or act it. He will bury us all, probably. He was born in Moscow, believe it or not. He was married to my grandmother in 1931; you will learn nothing of her in your reference books. She is one of his best-kept secrets. He has one daughter, my mother, Lidiya, who was born in same year. And my father, Andrei Ivanovich Klebanoff, is indeed editor in chief of *Pravda*. I am sure those things can be verified.''

O'Neal bent over and whispered something to Tom Little, who had been writing furiously. Little rose and left the room.

Klebanoff, still smiling, watched him go. "You will see. I am telling truth. Do you want to hear more about my grandfather, or my father, perhaps? Or have you heard enough?''

"I imagine we have heard enough, at least for now,''

O'Neal said. ''In the meantime, perhaps you will tell us what sorts of pictures you take.''

The smile faded from Klebanoff's face. He nodded as if to himself. ''For my job, or for my own pleasure?''

''For your job,'' Hartley said.

''What I am asked to take.''

''And in the Dioula, what were you asked to take?''

''Photographs of the fighting, naturally. Revolutionaries fighting against the American-backed regime.''

''Is that what is on your unprocessed film?''

Before Klebanoff could respond, Alvin Jones cut in with a question. ''Just one more question about the present situation at your embassy, Mr. Klebanoff. Is it possible that they do not yet know you have left?''

Klebanoff shrugged impatiently. ''Anything is possible. I do not know what they know by now.''

''So it is possible you could go back there with no one there being the wiser,'' Jones persisted.

''I will not go back there,'' Klebanoff said firmly. ''I have already said that.''

''Why do you ask for asylum?'' Jones asked.

''I have right to ask for asylum!'' Klebanoff's voice was raised in frustration.

''Mr. Klebanoff.'' George Hartley spoke quietly. ''Of course you have a right to ask. But you must acknowledge that we have a right to wonder why you ask.''

Klebanoff looked at each man in turn before he spoke. ''You all think that United States is good country, do you not? Best country, even. They why do you think it so strange that someone else wants to live there?''

''We just want to know if your reasons are political or economic or what,'' Hartley said.

Klebanoff looked at him for a long time before responding. ''It is all together,'' he said at last.

Jones cleared his throat. ''How much unprocessed film do you have?''

''A few rolls.''

''We're going to need them.''

Klebanoff looked at each man in turn before responding. ''No.''

O'Neal stepped closer. ''To assess the damage that they could do to the Soviet cause—and therefore the danger you might be facing—we'll need to see the pictures.''

"Fine. But I keep my film with me. You process it with me there."

"It doesn't work that way," O'Neal said quietly. "It has to go back to Washington for the analysts to see. Places you wouldn't be allowed to go."

Klebanoff shook his head.

"Make up your mind," Hartley said. "You can't have it all your way. If you want asylum, you have to give in somewhere."

Klebanoff reached into his pocket and pulled out two rolls and handed them to O'Neal.

"Is that all?" O'Neal asked.

"There's more in my camera. They promised I could have my camera back."

"And you will," Alvin Jones said. "You have to realize how things work, that's all. You can't blame our government for wanting to take what it can get."

Klebanoff nodded curtly, but said nothing.

The door opened then and Tom Little stood on the threshold. O'Neal pocketed the film and walked slowly, almost casually, toward the door. "It checks," Little murmured.

"Call the Ambassador," O'Neal whispered in response.

2

HENRY WILLIS, UNITED STATES AMBASSADOR TO
Bodamwe, was not a career politician. What he had been was
a junior high school social-studies teacher who had become
active in his teachers' union, been elected to state union office, and, in that position, been on hand to run counter to
traditional party allegiances and lead his strongly black union
to support the election of the first black to a state governor-
ship—and a Republican at that. It was a measure of the importance the Washington administration placed on a believable
black constituency that, in recognition of Willis' role as the
most influential union leader to have supported that historic
successful candidacy, the revived Republican leadership in
Washington had granted Willis a political plum usually re-
served for supporters at a national level.

As ambassador, Henry Willis had been expected to do little
more than show the flag at appropriate times. Bodamwe had
had a reputation as the most cosmopolitan and most stable of
all West African nations. The appearance of a rebel group on
Bodamwe's northeastern border—claiming wide support in the
villages, attacking local gendarmes, and carving out areas of
control—had taken the authorities in Rafetna by apparent surprise. Henry Willis, a giant of a man at six feet six and two
hundred and seventy pounds, was not running scared. In his
mind, the fighting in the Dioula Province might as well have
been a thousand miles away. He had unflinching faith that his
government would recall him if the situation became truly
dangerous. In the meantime, it remained his duty to carry
out all formal ambassadorial functions—and to let the professionals at the Embassy take care of the real work.

He stood now behind his desk, looking at the three men

facing him. They've already made up their minds, he thought; and if things went as usual, they'd only tell him what they thought he needed to know. Or what he had brains enough to ask. "Where is he now?" he asked.

"Upstairs," Hartley said. "We've asked him to give us a written statement. He's working on it."

The others were letting Hartley do the talking, which was interesting, given the situation. Willis wished he knew what O'Neal was thinking. He'd given up second-guessing Jones.

"What are the options?" Willis asked.

"Basically, three," Hartley said. "We can refuse; we can let him stay in Bodamwe and let him—or help him—fight it out in the courts here; or we can get him out before they realize he's missing."

"We can't refuse him," Willis said. O'Neal nodded per-functorily—no one else reacted. "What happens if we let the courts decide?"

"Good question," Hartley said. "Actually, the question then becomes what will happen to Bodamwe. They don't need this right now."

"Sit down, please," Willis said, suddenly realizing that they wouldn't until he mentioned it. There were some things so far from how he'd lived his whole life that he'd probably never get used to them. He lowered himself into the leather chair behind his desk. Jones and Hartley sat facing him, but O'Neal remained standing. Willis frowned. "Mightn't this repudiate the rebels—a Soviet defector?"

"It might," Hartley responded. "It could just as easily polarize the situation. President Akinya is walking a tightrope right now. He does not need to be put on the spot. What he needs is proof of who is helping the rebels and to be able to confront the Soviet leadership with that. A defector in his courts is going to make him look partisan. A defector who was taken out of his country without his knowledge or con-sent is a somewhat different thing."

"So we end up being the bad guys?" Willis asked. "I'm not comfortable with that. If you try something funny, and it ends up embarrassing Bodamwe, I'm the one who's going to have to clean up the shit."

"There's a lot of tails on this one," Hartley said. "This guy's a photographer, remember. He's been at the fighting, photographing the camps and everything. So he says at least. If he really has been, he may have the proof Akinya needs to show the Russian connection. If Akinya can get that proof, there'll be a reaction in Moscow.''

Willis frowned. ''But I thought the Soviets were wearing a new face these days, keeping their heavy hands at home.''

''Exactly,'' O'Neal said. ''The question is, is it real, or is it only what they want us to think? Either way, General Secretary Kalishev is not going to like it if proof of Soviet tampering gets into Western hands. If that happens, there'll be a reaction in Moscow. At the very least, the Soviet military will get their hands slapped for letting themselves get caught. And if it really is a matter of an unauthorized military op, it'll almost certainly help Kalishev solidify what has recently been a rather tenuous position.''

''Kalishev's faction wins a round,'' Willis mused. ''And the outside support for the fighting in the Dioula stops, and we end up looking like the good guys.''

''If the pictures show anything,'' Jones added.

''There are a lot of ifs,'' Willis said.

''Not the least of which is if he really is who he says he is,'' O'Neal interjected.

''Not the least,'' Willis agreed. ''How do we know he's not an undercover KGB agent or something?''

Hartley nodded. ''We could get burned; it wouldn't be the first time. And you can almost count on the Tass guys being KGB. But it's not likely he would claim a connection to Butakov if that were the case. No, he's probably real.''

''Does that mean you believe that he wants out for—what did he call it, artistic freedom?'' Willis asked.

''That's unlikely to be all of it,'' O'Neal said, ''but it may be a while before we find out what he's really after.''

''In the meantime,'' Jones said, ''if his grandfather really is Sergei Butakov, we have just been handed the hottest potato we could have gotten.''

''Surely you've checked him out,'' Willis said.

''As much as we can in the limited amount of time we've got,'' O'Neal said. ''We can't exactly call up the Soviets and ask if they're missing former Premier Butakov's grandson. But if he's who he says he is and if he has the right pictures, he can blow the Old Guard right out of the water.''

''I though Butakov's crowd was out,'' Willis said.

''They are,'' O'Neal said. ''Out, but not forgotten. There's been a very quiet revolution going on in the Soviet Union. The technocrats are taking over. It's been quiet, but don't let that fool you. The Butakov faction is fighting back. One indication is what's going on in the Dioula. Everybody's sure the Soviet hard-liners are behind it, even though we haven't been able to prove it. If their people can overthrow the Bodamwean government—which used to be the most stable in black Africa—they will win a lot of credibility and gain momentum. Pockets of them exist, especially in the military. The GRU is full of them. They see the new regime as too accommodating to the West, too willing to make sacrifices—politically and militarily—for what they consider unacceptable economic gains. They want a strong military and they won't give up easily.''

"In short," Willis said, leaning back into his chair, "they're afraid the technocrats are selling the Russian Revolution down the drain."

"Exactly."

Willis stared over the heads of the three men. "And if this Yuri Klebanoff is really Butakov's grandson, and if he has the pictures to prove who's leading the rebels—or even if one of those is true—then I don't suppose it will do the hard-liners any good." He paused, then turned his attention to O'Neal. "Is there any reason why we should want to protect the hard-liners?"

"No."

"Then we haven't a choice," Willis said. "We get him out."

"It's not quite so easy as that," Jones said. "There's a problem."

"In getting him out?" Willis asked.

"That too. But what I'm talking about is the Summit. It's a top priority for the administration. Washington would not like this messing it up."

"But if this guy's pictures repudiate the hard-liners, wouldn't it support Kalishev and his side? Wouldn't it be a nice present for the President to bring to the bargaining table?"

"If," Jones repeated. "As you said, there are a lot of ifs. It could just as easily go the other way."

Willis leaned back in his chair, absently picked up a pencil and tapped it against his lips. "What does Washington say?" he asked finally.

O'Neal stood abruptly, shoved his fists into his pants pockets and strode toward the door. Willis thought for a moment he was going to leave, but he turned around at the door and caught Willis' eyes with his own. "Nothing," he said finally.

Willis licked his lips. "They've had time to respond?"

"Yes."

"Just barely," Jones said. "If they're working it out themselves—"

"We haven't got time to screw around," O'Neal interrupted. "We have to get him out of here."

Willis looked to Jones for a reaction, but there was none. "What do you propose?" he asked.

Jones shrugged and glanced back at O'Neal. O'Neal moved closer to the center of the room. "If it were just a matter of processing the film, it might be worth the risk to keep him here, but we'd still need to have the pictures analyzed. And it will take time to figure out how it would impact both sides. We need time for all that and we don't have it. Once they know he's missing, we'll never get him out of the country in one piece."

"And if the Soviets find out we have him, the Summit gets jeopardized—for perhaps no gain," Jones added.

"Then it's back to square one," Willis said.

"Not exactly," Hartley said. "If we get him out fast— before they know we have him—we can keep him secretly somewhere until we know what we have. In the meantime, we can deny any knowledge—as far as anyone is concerned, he will have disappeared, that's all. We keep him in a safe house, no leaks, until we know the damage that his defection will do—both to us and to Kalishev's side. If it's an unacceptable level, we give him back. If he can make points against the rebels and the hard-liners without disrupting the Summit, we keep him. The key is getting him out fast—and secretly."

Willis looked at each man in turn, wondering if he was supposed to ask how they planned to do it. "I assume you think you've got a way to do that."

Hartley looked at Jones. O'Neal, without glancing at the other two, kept his eyes on Willis. "We think so," he responded.

"And—" Willis began, and then stopped to clear his throat.

"Mr. Ambassador," Hartley said in a suddenly formal voice, "as far as we all are concerned, this conversation never took place. You came to the office tonight to work on the speech you have to give tomorrow afternoon. You have no knowledge of anything else going on in the Embassy this evening, nor do you know what the three of us have been doing.''

"Of course," Willis replied, just as formally.

Hartley and O'Neal rose and followed Jones out of the room. Willis turned and stared out the window into the night. From this height he could see all the way to the airport. He would resist the temptation to stay in the office until the defector had gone. He would not give in to curiosity; he would know nothing about it, not who did what, nor when anything happened. He would put it out of his mind completely.

Once out of the Ambassador's offices, Hartley turned left and strode off down the dimly lit hall toward the Consular Section. O'Neal and Jones watched him go for a moment.

"How soon can the film go out?" O'Neal asked.

"First thing in the morning. Special pouch."

"No sooner than that?"

Alvin Jones chuckled. "They'll be bending over the c-prints at Langley before you even start wondering what you'll have for lunch. If you want to worry about something, try thinking about how many of us were in there with the defector. Four. That's a little out of control, isn't it?"

O'Neal shrugged. "One of those things. You know how it goes—the Marine couldn't reach me but left a message, then called George, who's next on the list. I got back home and there's the message, and Tom, who could use the experience, was just downstairs, so I brought him along with me. That would have been only three, not so bad. Then you show up. That's not the end of the world. It's the silence from Langley that I don't like."

They started down the hall in the opposite direction from that taken by Hartley. "Are you trying to tell me that you've never done anything without Langley's go-ahead before?" Jones asked.

O'Neal shook his head. "That's not it. As Hartley pointed out back there, there's too goddamn many tails on this one. And something about it doesn't feel right—"

"You think he's a plant."

"Not that. Something . . . I can't put my finger on it. Maybe it's the combination; I don't know."

"Makes a naval pickup at sea look better, doesn't it?" Jones asked.

"That the way you want it?"

"I'm not going to insist."

O'Neal let out a deep breath. "I'm just not comfortable with that, Al, and not hearing from D.C. doesn't help. We'd have to run the request through them and then back out to sea . . . back and forth while it's put together. That's too damn many channels for me and God knows how much time. I don't like it."

"The trouble with you is you're scared to give up control. Or maybe it's not that you're scared. Maybe it's that you want it for yourself."

O'Neal gave him a quick, sharp look. They'd come to Jones' office and both men stepped inside, closing the door behind them. "Is that what you think?" O'Neal challenged.

Al Jones shrugged and sat in the leather chair behind the desk.

"Is it?" O'Neal's palms were on the desk as he leaned toward Jones, pushing for a response.

Jones leaned back in the chair, away from O'Neal. "I said I wasn't going to insist."

O'Neal straightened. "The small ones work better, Al, it's always seemed that way to me. You get the goddamn military in there, thinking that if one ship's good, then five ought to be better, and Lord knows what's going to happen."

"A naval pickup at night—it's quick and it's quiet."

"It'd be a circus is what it'd be. Look at Desert One. Look at Grenada. Every goddamn service'd want a piece of it."

"I said I wasn't going to insist. But if you want my *opinion*, taking him out on a commercial flight is asking for trouble."

"The best cover in the world," O'Neal responded. "Hiding him in plain sight. No naval involvement, no flurry of communication with Washington, nothing. He went out into the night and he disappeared. There's nothing to connect him to us. He just disappears and we claim complete ignorance."

"What about the cabdriver who brought him here?"

"We'd have to take care of him either way. We pay him off and send him back to his village for a good long time. No problem."

"Sure," Jones said. "You march him into the airport and onto the plane and nobody's going to notice."

"He doesn't go as a Soviet defector, you know. He's just a passenger. With a fake passport no one will pay him any attention. And I'll be on the plane, but not with him. No, I've got a better one than that." He paused, waiting for Jones to ask, but when he didn't, O'Neal leaned his palms on the desk again. "A girl, a rather attractive girl, in fact, new in Rafetna so no one's likely to recognize her. The two of them. A couple. Tourists. Who will notice him? If they notice anything at all, they'll be looking at her."

Alvin Jones straightened in his chair, the springs squeaking against the sudden movement. "You must be out of your mind! A girl? A goddamn *girl*? Where did you ever drag her up from? Who the hell is she?"

O'Neal grinned. "She's perfect, is what she is. New, like I said. She's with One-to-One; Jay Phillips gave me her name. I had her vetted before she even got here. Clean as a whistle."

"What the hell are you vetting One-to-One people for?"

"You know damn well what for. They get out into the villages. You want to know what the talk is, you get them working for you, and you hear a lot of it."

"Ex-Peace Corps, I suppose," Jones said.

O'Neal nodded.

"She won't work for you."

"She will. On this one at least, she will."

Jones leaned back in his chair again and smiled. "You're going to have to end up doing it my way after all. She won't do it."

"Tell me now, Al. If you're going to veto it, I want to know it now."

Alvin Jones shook his head. "I already told you I won't." He wouldn't have to. She would veto it for him.

3

MOLLY DAVISON WOKE AT THE SOUND OF THE TELE-
phone. "Who on earth . . . ?" she muttered, fumbling her
way out from under the mosquito netting in the dark. "I
finally get to sleep on the hottest night I've ever spent in my
whole life and the phone rings." She felt for the bedside lamp
and managed to knock it off its stand. Ignoring the lamp, she
stumbled in the dark toward the sound of the ringing telephone. "That's all right, wake up the whole world," she
mumbled. "Calling in the middle of the night . . . I hardly
even know anybody in Rafetna yet." And then she thought
of her father. Six hours behind; he would know better than
to call at this time of night, unless . . . God, no, don't let it
be something happened to him. She groped for the receiver
and finally found it. Without thinking, she spoke in English.
"Hello?"

"Molly Davis?" It was a man's voice and she didn't recognize it.

"Davison," she said testily. "If you're going to call me
up at God knows what hour, at least you can get the name
right. It's Molly Davison."

"Sorry. I'm calling from the American Embassy. We have
a message for you from Jay Phillips. I assume you know
him."

"He's my boss." Suddenly her mind was clear. What could
have happened to Jay that they would call at this time of
night? "What time is it anyway?" she asked.

"Twelve-thirty."

Not as late as she'd guessed, then. She could have sworn
that she'd tossed and turned in the heat for hours before falling asleep.

"What's the message?"

"It's a little unclear, I'm sorry to say. He needs you there—he's in St. Jean, I understand?—first thing in the morning. I didn't really get what it's about. Some visiting dignitaries or something. He says you're new in Rafetna and asked if we could arrange transportation for you. It happens we've got someone who's going up there tonight—we travel at night as much as possible here, to avoid the heat of the day. He'll take you up there if you can be at the Embassy in half an hour. If you can't make that, I'm afraid you're on your own. We don't make a habit of arranging transportation for private-agency people. Jay called me because he happens to be a friend and because he's concerned that you wouldn't know your way around yet. If you can make it to ride up with our folks, you'll be doing yourself a big favor. *Car rapides* in this kind of weather will just about kill you."

"Half an hour?" Good God, she thought, what do I take?

"Can you make it?"

"Yes." Was there an option? She'd ridden in enough *car rapides* with goats and chickens among the passengers to know that she didn't want to make that long trip in the heat of the day in one if she didn't have to.

"Our man asks just one thing. There'll be three of you in a Jeep. Bring as little as you can manage. One small bag, if possible."

"Did Jay give you any idea how long he wants me there?" she asked.

"No. Sorry. But I understand it wasn't to be more than a couple of days. If you can be done by Friday, you can come back with the same people you go up there with."

"How do I get into the Embassy at this time of night?"

"Someone will pick you up. We don't advise women out alone on the streets at this time of night. He'll be there in thirty minutes. Try to be ready. And don't forget your passport."

"All right," she said. The telephone clicked in her ear. Great, she thought. She felt for a light switch on the wall. Half an hour to get ready. She'd prepared for trips in less time than that, but it would have been nice if Jay had been a little clearer about why he wanted her. How on earth was she going to know what to pack?

* * *

Thomas Little pressed down the lever of the coffeemaker and watched idly as his mug filled.

"Tom." Dennis O'Neal's voice came from behind him. "How's it going?" O'Neal closed the door to the coffee room.

"Not bad. He hasn't told us anything yet that hasn't checked. Jones is with him now. Want a cup?"

"No, thanks. I'm hyper enough already." O'Neal grinned. "Looks as if we might have gotten ourselves a big one."

"Looks as if." Little sipped his coffee. "Might as well drink it. I won't sleep the rest of the night anyway. This could blow them right out of the water, couldn't it?"

"We won't speculate just yet, but you could be right. We need your passport, Tom."

"Mine?" There was just a moment's hesitation. "Sure."

"You're right." O'Neal nodded. "He doesn't look much like you. But we want to use at least the entry-exit pages. We're going to try to interweave one for him. We don't want a clean one."

"Will it be a diplomatic one?"

"Civilian. No Embassy connection, that's how he should look."

"Is there going to be time?"

"Just barely. Tomorrow, when things have cooled down, Hartley'll have his folks make you a new one. You can claim you lost yours, or it got stolen at the restaurant tonight."

"No problem. I'm not going anywhere."

"We appreciate it. I don't have to tell you again: this is beyond confidential. And, Tom, one more thing. The way things work, you may never hear of this guy again. If he turns out to be a fake, or if his defection is just too hot right now, it's going to be kept quiet for a good long time."

"I understand."

"It's a hell of a way to begin your career."

Little smiled. "I thought it would be interesting. I guess I've gotten what I bargained for."

Viktor Evchenko was a robust man with round, rosy cheeks that made him look more like a Slavic version of Santa Claus than what he really was—the KGB *Rezident* in Rafetna, Bodamwe. Evchenko stubbed out his cigarette and looked at his watch. The caller had said one o'clock; it was twelve forty-five now. Ten minutes to get to the stadium—if he went—two minutes to make his excuses here; he had three minutes to decide. "Urgent meeting," the caller had said, "important to both of us." The wording was curious in its ambiguity. Had the caller meant both our countries or both of us as individuals? He lit another cigarette.

"Viktor!" Anatoly Cherpinsky grabbed him by the arm and ash spilled between them. "Don't look so glum! Or is it because your glass is empty? Why don't you get it refilled?"

Cherpinsky's thin-lipped smile made Evchenko think of a fox. Involuntarily, he pulled back from Cherpinsky's grip. He hated to be touched. He hated any kind of familiarities. "I'm tired," he said, "I'm thinking of going home."

"Not yet, Viktor!" Cherpinsky leaned close and whispered. He was four inches shorter, and Evchenko felt as if Cherpinsky was confiding to his necktie. "I think Anya and Svetlana are loosening up. I wouldn't be surprised to see them begin dancing at any moment. You can't go now."

Evchenko took a step back and blew smoke in Cherpinsky's direction. "Have you forgotten, Anatol? I have to be at the airport by six—the plane comes in at quarter to seven."

"Plenty of time! Plenty!" Cherpinsky's face suddenly sobered. "Is something the matter? Is there a problem?"

"No," Evchenko said firmly and flicked more ash on the floor. "Nothing. I'm just tired." And now he would have to go. If this phone message referred to something important, and if he failed to learn it in time, and if Cherpinsky remembered this conversation, it could come back to haunt him. Even the KGB *Rezident* was not beyond the criticism of a party flak like Cherpinsky. "Perhaps I'll stay for a short time, though. I guess I should fill up my glass." He ambled off toward the bar, hoping Cherpinsky would not follow. Nothing unusual to report here, Cherpinsky. To his vast relief, Cherpinsky turned in the opposite direction. As Evchenko moved away he could hear Cherpinsky's voice growing less distinct behind him. "Anya, what a beautiful dress . . ." Evchenko smiled ironically. Nothing unusual at all, except a meeting with an American counterpart he had never had two words with before this night.

Viktor Evchenko got out of the cab, paid the exact fare—no tip—and stepped onto the sidewalk. He was one block from the stadium and three minutes early. He would make it with time to spare. He had gone half the distance when he heard steps behind him. His body tensed but he did not change his pace. From all outward appearances, he had not heard anything. "Evchenko," the voice behind him said, "I'm glad you came."

Evchenko slowed his pace just slightly. "You said a major problem, an urgent meeting." He walked ten more paces before the man caught up with him.

"I did," the American said.

Evchenko glanced to his left and the American nodded slightly.

"Well?"

The American walked beside him for a while in silence. "Who is Yuri Klebanoff?' he asked finally.

Evchenko lit a cigarette, taking his time before responding. "He is a journalist. Why?"

"A photographer?"

"Yes."

"He's been at the fighting in the Dioula?"

"Why do you ask?"

"Is it true that he's the son of the editor in chief of *Pravda*?"

"I don't know who his father is."

The American didn't even pursue that one. "But you know who is grandfather is, don't you." It was not a question.

"In the Soviet Union," Evchenko responded carefully, "we consider a man on the basis of his own merits, not who his family is."

The American walked in silence for a few moments. "Do you know where he is right now?"

"Should I?"

"He came to our embassy less than three hours ago, asking for asylum."

Because he was a professional, Viktor Evchenko did not react or respond.

"Since then, we've been sorting out the damage such a defection might do—to both sides," the American said.

Evchenko flicked his cigarette toward the street and took out another. "I have no reason to believe you," he responded at last.

"How else would I know what I've already said?"

"It would not be impossible to discover such things."

"If Yuri Klebanoff defected, and if he is the grandson of Sergei Butakov, and if the photographs he has taken in the

Dioula show who is leading the rebels and what kind of help they are getting, it could be very damaging.''

Viktor Evchenko said nothing.

"To the Summit, for example.''

"If all those things were true, it could be.''

"To the Butakov faction.''

Evchenko shrugged.

"To those of us who have vested interests.''

"Meaning?''

"You know, I think,'' the American said.

Evchenko looked at the American squarely for the first time. "What are you proposing?''

"Nothing.''

"Nothing?''

"I am suggesting that it might be to your best interests and mine that this defection attempt fail.''

"You certainly must be in a position to make that happen.''

"Unlike you, Evchenko, I don't have authority that extends that far. I would have to offer an explanation to those who know about Klebanoff's defection.''

"In other words, you want me to do your dirty work,'' Evchenko said.

"Our dirty work. It will be as bad for you if he makes it successfully as it would be for me if I openly aborted it.''

"How do they plan to get him out of Bodamwe?''

"Commercial jet. In less than two hours.''

"Then it is already arranged?''

"Pretty much.''

"You don't leave me much time.''

"You have time,'' the American said. "He's going into hiding until my government can assess the damage he might do. If you already know for certain who he is and what kind of photographs he might have, you'll be one step ahead of us. The plane goes to Rome. Your men can pick up his trail there.''

"It seems you have already planned my actions. How do I know this is not some kind of trap?''

"Go back to your embassy and see if he's asleep there where he's supposed to be. If not, you'll know what kind of trouble you could be in.''

"And if he is there?'' Evchenko said.

"He won't be.''

"Our men in Rome have never seen him.''

"He'll be traveling with a young woman, an American. They will appear as an American couple. Her name is Molly Davison; his passport identifies him as Thomas Little. If you're quick, you can get someone on the airplane with them. Or your people in Rome can spot them as they get off the plane. It's an Air Afrique flight."

"What do you want for this?" Evchenko asked cautiously.

"You take care of it, that's all."

"That's all?"

"Probably."

"I don't like to hear 'probably.' "

"There's one more man in the Embassy who might pose a problem. If I can't handle him, you may have to."

"I owe you nothing."

"I know that."

"Then why would I do your dirty work?"

"Because"—the American stopped walking and turned to face Viktor Evchenko—"as you know, we have some common interests."

Evchenko stared at him without speaking.

"Don't we?" the American asked.

"Perhaps we do," Evchenko said at last. Then he turned and walked away, leaving the American standing alone.

4

MOLLY DAVISON ZIPPED HER DUFFEL BAG CLOSED
and looked at her watch. Just one. A drop of sweat ran down
her forehead and fell off the end of her nose. She shoved
light-brown hair out of her face and fastened it with a clip.
Got to get the hair cut, she thought. It's too much trouble in
the heat. She hadn't believed it could be this hot. Even the
minor exertion of packing a few things into a bag was enough
to make a person sweat. Her two years in the Central African
Republic had been nothing like this. There it was hot but
dry; here, with the humidity, the heat became palpable, an
enveloping presence. No time to take another shower. She
walked into the bathroom and splashed tepid water on her
face. Not even any cold water. At least it was almost over.
She'd heard that June and July were the worst. You'll love
Rafetna, people kept telling her, just wait until the heat sub-
sides.

She already liked it. Rafetna was much more cosmopolitan
than she'd imagined—the French colonials had left deep in-
fluences on the culture. In fact, French was even the unoffi-
cial language of Bodamwe, which otherwise broke down
linguistically into a wide variety of native languages. Although no one had actually told her so, she knew that had
been the reason for her placement in Rafetna. She was fluent
in French, and the agency needed her in the capital to handle
the paperwork and permits that a private aid agency like One-
to-One found essential to maintain its operations. It had been
a disappointment because she'd wanted to get out into the
field—to St. Jean, or even farther into the Sahel, where the
need was the greatest—but she had to admit that it made good

sense to keep the best French-speaker in the capital where she could smooth the way for the field-workers.

That had been one reason why she'd actually been glad for the phone call and the chance to go to St. Jean. It would be her first trip into the Sahel, where the desert was slowly creeping southward. She was eager to see what was happening there. With luck, she might even be able to stay longer than the two or three days that had been mentioned on the phone. She'd watered the two hanging plants she'd brought home from the street market, though she wasn't sure why she'd even bought them in the first place. She'd never managed to keep a plant alive for more than a couple of months even under the best of conditions. Black thumb, she'd always say with a shrug.

She looked again at her watch. They were late. Idly she wondered what Jay wanted that was so urgent. And why he hadn't called her directly. On second thought, she knew the answer to that one. Phone service in St. Jean was undependable at best. He'd probably sent a radio message to the Embassy. Most of the communications in the north country were done by radio.

She heard the sound of a car in the street below and walked over to the window. A man was just stepping out of a white American-sized car. She pulled the window closed. It was the last one—she'd already closed the others. The apartment would be an absolute oven when she returned, but there was no choice. Rains came almost daily during this season, driven by fierce winds that blew the torrent sideways. She'd learned that a window left open even a crack would let enough water in to flood an apartment. Rainstorms were a mixed blessing: temperatures dropped slightly in their aftermath, but humidity rose abruptly. Even so, one could hardly complain—at least the rains came; in the Sahel the land lay parched under an unrelenting sun.

She heard the footsteps coming down the hallway and pause at her door before the knock sounded. Duffel bag in hand, she opened the apartment door and was mildly surprised at the man standing in front of her. He was in his mid-forties, with red curly hair going to gray, and a face full of freckles. He didn't fit her image of a driver who would be sent from the Embassy to pick up a civilian at one o'clock in the morning.

"Molly Davison?" he asked. "Are you ready?" he added before she could even answer.

In response, she half-lifted her duffel bag. "I hope so."

"Okay, then. Let's go."

He stepped back as she closed and locked the door and wordlessly he let her lead the way to the stairs and out onto the street. He opened the car door for her and then walked around to the driver's side.

"Are you the one who's going to St. Jean?" she asked.

"Actually, no," he said. He started the car, pulled out from the curb, made a quick U-turn, and headed back the way he'd come. Traffic was not heavy on this street at any time of day; after midnight, even in summer, there were almost no cars at all.

"You're not the one who called me, are you?" she asked.

He glanced at her, then turned his gaze toward the street again. "I think we should straighten a couple of things out," he said. He downshifted and paused at an intersection, waiting for an oncoming car. She supposed that he was going to give her the usual lecture about her being a private citizen and the Embassy's position that it was not responsible for her well-being, and therefore, not to assume that this would be standard procedure. She'd heard it all before.

When he had turned left onto the boulevard he spoke again. "You will not be going to St. Jean."

A flood of apprehension came over her and she reached for the door handle. Who was he?

"Listen to me," he said urgently, grabbing her other arm. "This is going to be very important." His voice was harsh and overloud in the confines of the car.

"Who are you?" she demanded. "Let go of me. Where are you taking me?"

"My name is Dennis O'Neal," he answered, speaking slowly now, as if to calm her. "I'm from the American Embassy and that's where I'm taking you. We've got a particular problem and we need your help."

Help? Her mind was racing. "Who is 'we'?"

"Embassy staff."

"Meaning who?"

"Just what I said, Embassy staff."

"What do you need me for?"

"Take your hand off the door handle and I'll tell you."

The speedometer was edging toward fifty; it would be crazy

to jump out of the car at this speed. She knew that as long as he was on the boulevard he would not need to slow down, but when he turned off . . . In the meantime, she had little choice. She released the door handle and he let go of her arm.

"You work for One-to-One," he said, without looking at her.

"Yes."

"And you've been in the country for how long?"

Her eyes narrowed. What was he getting at? "Less than two weeks—about ten days."

"So you're quite new here and you're the only One-to-One staff member in town. Right?"

She nodded and he glanced quickly at her.

"We can assume you don't know very many people yet. You have no Embassy connection. You are an American woman and you're very attractive. All of which makes you a prime candidate. You are probably the only person in Rafetna right now with those qualifications and we need you." He turned toward her again.

"I can't imagine what for."

"Shortly after ten this evening, a man appeared at the Embassy claiming to be a Soviet defector," he said, his eyes back on the boulevard. "It doesn't matter to you who he is, but if what he says is true, we have a major defection on our hands. A *major* defection." He glanced at her as if to check her reaction. "We have to get him out of Bodamwe fast. At this moment, the Russians still probably don't know he's missing and there's a very good chance we can get him out before they discover he's gone. But even so, we need to provide him with a cover that will make him unnoticeable. We figure the best way to do that is to pass him off as an American, as part of a couple where the woman is more noticeable than the man. For that, we need a very attractive woman." He looked at her again and grinned. "We need a woman who is clearly American and who will talk to him in English, who will let him say 'yes' and 'no' every now and then so that any casual observer will come away with the impression that the two of them are speaking English. That and the right haircut and the right clothes ought to be enough to do it."

"And you want me to be the woman?"

"Exactly. You haven't been in Rafetna long enough for people to know you—that you're single. But even if someone did recognize you, you could always say he's your boyfriend, or your brother. Or even just a friend. You have no Embassy connection and that's important. What they'd expect is Embassy personnel escorting him. You even have a civilian passport."

"Isn't that convenient for you," she said sarcastically.

"I realize that it's probably not at all convenient for you, but this shouldn't take more than twenty-four hours of your time. Not a bad investment when you consider the gain. Especially since now that you know about it, even if you refuse, we'd still have to keep you at the Embassy until he's safely out."

"You can't do that. I'm a private citizen."

"Miss Davison, believe me, we can do a great deal."

She looked at him more carefully. "You're CIA, aren't you?"

"No, I'm Second Secretary at the Embassy—a rather thankless job that involves mostly taking care of problems."

"But the CIA is involved."

"They know about it, but this is not one of their operations."

"You know perfectly well that legitimate private aid agencies stay as far away from the CIA as they can. There's no way I can do this."

"I told you the CIA is not part of it."

"That doesn't matter. It'll look as if they are."

He stared straight ahead. Half a block ahead, a man dashed across the street, was caught for a moment in the headlights, then faded again into the dark. "So things are that black and white with you?" he asked. "You won't help someone who needs you simply because of how it might look?"

"I can't believe I'm the only possibility."

"You know Rafetna isn't that big. There aren't very many American women around. If you haven't already discovered that, you soon will. I can guarantee that there are virtually none with your qualifications."

At least that part was the truth. Even in the short time she'd been in Rafetna, she'd come to realize how few other American women were there. She gazed absently out the car window, seeing yet not seeing the giant palms that lined the boulevard. Two years in the Peace Corps in the Central African Republic, then two more years in grad school preparing for this. And the whole time her father saying, "For God's

sake, Molly, haven't you gotten that do-gooder spirit out of you yet? Two years is enough; let someone else go this time."
It was not really that he'd objected to her doing the work, she knew, but he hated to have her go so far away again. When she'd been in the C.A.R., her mother had died. She realized he spoke from his own loneliness and she'd thought about giving it up. It would please him if she'd just stay home and settle down, really please him if she got married and had children, but she'd come anyway. And despite what he said, she knew he was proud of her. No, she hadn't given this up for her father; there was no way she would give it up for someone she didn't even know.

"No," she said, "I can't."

"You have to," he responded, not even looking at her. "Molly . . . can I call you that? No one else is in as good a position as you are. You have to, simply because you can, and because there's no one else."

She looked at him, then down at her hands. It was the same argument she had used with her father, the only one that, in the end, had made any sense to him. "Dad," she'd said back then, "those of us who can do these things have to—otherwise no one will at all." He'd understood that, though he hadn't liked it. It seemed unfair for the same argument to be used now against her. "Who is he? Why is he so important?"

"Does he have to be important? Isn't it enough for him to see a chance to get to freedom and want to take it?"

"You said this could be a major defection. They're your words, not mine."

"Because of what he may know, not necessarily because of who he is."

"I'm sure you can find someone else—"

"Believe me, if we could have found someone else, we would have."

"What does he know that's so important?"

"If you agree to do it, and if you need to know that, I'll tell you."

"If I agree to do it, you're going to have to tell me everything."

O'Neal nodded. "What you need to know."

"Not what I need to know. Everything. If I'm going to be responsible for his safety, then I have a right to know everything."

"You would be the cover, but you will not be responsible for his safety. That's my part."

"I suppose you'd be on the plane, too?"

"Who said anything about a plane?"

"Come on, now, I may be naive, but I'm not stupid. If you're going to get him out fast and you're worried about people recognizing him, then you're talking about airplanes. There aren't any buses or trains going where you might want to take him. I don't suppose more than one or two passenger ships come here in any given month. Plus you said twenty-four hours of my time. Unless there's something else I've missed?"

He nodded. "Okay," he said. "The answer is yes, I'll be on the plane with you. Any other questions?"

She looked at him and let out a long breath of air. "How dangerous is it?"

"For you, not dangerous at all."

"Not even if they find out and come after him with their guns blazing?"

"You have a lot to learn, Molly. Blazing guns happen in movies, not in real life."

"Then what happens in real life?"

"Something much more subtle. You wouldn't even notice it and neither would anyone else on the plane."

"I'd be with him. I'd notice."

"That's why I'll be there—to make sure that no one intercepts you."

"And if they 'intercept' you first?"

"It will not be like a picnic at the beach, but you won't be in any more danger than anyone else on that plane."

"But obviously in more danger than if I'd stayed home in bed."

"You can become an earthquake victim while you're home in bed, you know."

"That's not the point, is it?"

He glanced at her in exasperation. "Okay. Yes. There is some risk involved. We think it's minimal or we would have devised another plan. Nothing is without risk." He turned left off the boulevard. She recognized the street. At least he really was heading toward the Embassy. When he spoke again his voice was more earnest. "I already told you that this could be a major defection. No one knows at the moment what effect this could have on American-Soviet relations, because none of us in the Embassy knows what this could do to the government of the Soviet Union. We need time to consider the angles; but we also need to get him out before he's missed. We'll take him to a safe house until Washington can sort out the probable repercussions. We had to think of the fastest and safest way to get him out. This is the plan we've devised. We're not crazy about involving you or anyone else who doesn't need to know, but we think this is the best chance to get him out safely. I'm not asking you to play martyr or heroine or superpatriot. I'm asking you to do this because you can do it, and because we need it. And he needs it. And it won't take that much of your time. That's all."

"I want to meet him first."

"No."

"Why not?"

"Because we haven't time to play games. When I get to the Embassy I have to know whether you will or whether you won't."

"That gives you only a few more minutes to convince me, doesn't it?"

He shook his head without looking at her. "I've given you the argument. You've got only a few more minutes to decide."

She looked at him curiously. "You'd be with us every step of the way?"

"Yes."

"So our lives would be in your hands."

"As his life would be in yours. You're the one who's going to have to pull it off—to make people think he's an American."

She stared ahead. She could already see the Embassy. There was no reason in the world that she should do this, except, as he had said, because she could. Twenty-four hours, he'd said. Less time than it would have taken if she'd really been going to St. Jean as she'd thought. Twenty-four hours. Not much in exchange for a man's life, and whatever it was he had to tell them. "Why isn't the CIA doing this?"

"Because he came to us, not them."

"Are you trying to tell me there aren't any CIA people in the Embassy?"

"I'm trying to tell you the CIA doesn't run the Embassy."

"If I say yes, how much more will you tell me?"

"I already said I'd tell you all you need to know."

"And you'll decide how much that is?"

"You're stalling," he said, turning into the driveway, and nodding to the guard who waved them on.

"In a similar situation, how much would you do for me if I needed it?"

"Am I now going to get a lecture on how embassies should support private citizens? Listen, Molly, in this building is a man who wants out of the Soviet Union. You can choose to help him get out or you can refuse. It's as simple as that. Are you going to help him?" He pulled into a parking space and turned off the engine.

She looked for a long moment at his hand holding the key still in the ignition. "All right," she said finally.

His face broke into a wide boyish grin.

And I hope this is not a major mistake, she thought.

She followed him through a back door and tried to match his stride as he hurried down a long, brightly lit hall. "Is this place open all night?" she asked.

"You'd think so tonight."

"Is this the kind of thing you do all the time? Do you live at the Embassy?"

"God, no. On both counts."

She almost had to run to keep up with him. All the doors on the hall were closed. "Your wife must be one of the American women in Rafetna. I wonder why you don't use her to do this? I suppose she's too well known. Or is she too old?"

"What makes you think I have a wife?"

"Wedding ring."

"She doesn't live here. She stayed in the States."

"Oh?"

"Don't put meanings where there aren't any. This is a short-term assignment for me. It's not worth it to uproot the kids for that kind of time. That's all. And it's actually none of your business."

"Where are we going?"

"For a little indoctrination. Then you'll get to meet him."

"I mean where does the plane go?"

"Rome. It's an Air Afrique flight. You leave for the airport in less than an hour."

"I thought you were going with us."

"In the same plane, not in the same taxi."

"Taxi? Is that safe?"

"Don't worry; it's safe the way we've planned it." He

opened a door and stood back for her as she stepped in ahead of him.

The room was small—a conference room, she guessed—containing a table and a half dozen chairs, and there was already someone sitting at the table. "Molly Davison?" the man asked, rising and coming forward with his hand extended. "My name is George Hartley." He shook her hand perfunctorily, then turned to O'Neal. "How much does she know?" he asked in a lowered voice.

"Enough," O'Neal said.

"And has she agreed?"

"Ask her."

Hartley turned toward Molly. "Well? Will you do it?"

"You don't make it very attractive for me to refuse."

"What's that supposed to mean?" Hartley asked O'Neal.

O'Neal shrugged. "Now that she knows the basics, she either goes along or she stays here in the Embassy until everything's in place. Maybe she doesn't like hanging around us Embassy types."

"Is that what you mean?" Hartley asked her.

"Yes—that, and the way it was put to me: that if I don't do it he might not get out."

"You have your passport?" Hartley asked.

"Yes. Now I know why."

"You have luggage for a couple of days?"

"I packed for the trip to St. Jean. I don't know how appropriate it'll be for Rome."

"Hopefully, for you it will be a quick round trip," Hartley said.

"Hopefully? I might have to stay there longer?"

"We're not planning on it," O'Neal said, then turned his attention to Hartley. "How's his passport coming?"

"It's going to work out fine."

"How many of your people did we have to bring in on this?"

"Just Louise," Hartley said. "She does the lost passports. She's good and she's fast."

"They should leave in half an hour at the most."

"We'll have it."

"Anything else we should know?" O'Neal asked.

"That's about it. Everything's being taken care of."

"Where is he?"

"Upstairs with Jones. He's written his statement and Jones is clearing some things up right now."

"Then I think we should sit Molly down and tell her a few things before they meet." O'Neal motioned Molly to a chair and he sat down on the opposite side of the table. Hartley sat in a chair some distance from the table. "His name is Yuri Klebanoff. He's about thirty years old—"

"Thirty-two," Hartley interrupted.

"He's a photographer," O'Neal continued, as if he hadn't heard Hartley. "He worked for Tass and he's been covering the fighting in the Dioula. He's got undeveloped film that could be very interesting."

"Why is he defecting?" Molly asked.

O'Neal sighed. "We're not really clear on that. He says it's for 'artistic freedom,' whatever that's supposed to mean."

"Could he be in some kind of trouble?" Molly asked.

O'Neal shot a glance at Hartley before he answered. "Not that we know of."

"But he could be?"

"It's not likely, but it's possible."

"Why isn't it likely?"

"I don't think you need to bother yourself about every detail," Hartley interjected. His voice was deep and powerful, as if designed to invoke confidence. "It really doesn't matter as far as you're concerned whether he could be in trouble or not."

"I disagree." Molly turned in her chair to face him. "The more I know the better, in case something unexpected happens."

"Nothing unexpected is going to happen," Hartley said.

"Of course there's always the possibility that he's in some kind of trouble," O'Neal said. "Although in this case we assume that if he were in real trouble, they would have been watching him more closely and he wouldn't have gotten away. But that does bring up something you should be aware of. Sometimes the first reason a defector gives isn't the real reason for the crossover. Sometimes he'll go through three or four different reasons before he gets to the one that really sent him over. You have to understand that a defection is a very traumatic event for the defector. Often he won't even admit the real reason to himself for a long time. Sometimes it's not just one thing, but a combination of things, any one of which by itself wouldn't be reason enough. In this case—who knows?

It's very likely a combination of things. You can help us by keeping your ears open for anything he might say, anything that might provide a clue to what's behind his decision. Incidentally, he doesn't like being called a defector. He prefers to think in terms of asking for asylum.''

"So you want me to pump him for his real reasons?"

"No, absolutely not," O'Neal said. "Leave the pumping to the professionals; you could really mess things up. But if he says something, if he volunteers anything, remember it and let us know later. We're counting on you for that. And one more thing—one very important thing: defectors are special animals. They almost always, eventually, come to regret what they've done. It could happen to him while he's with you on the plane. It could, for all I know, be happening to him right now. On the other hand, it could be several years. When it happens, he's going to be very vulnerable. If it should happen coincidently with an attempt to take him back, he'll go—willingly. While you're with him at the airport and on the plane, it's going to be up to you to notice if he might be falling into that state of mind. If you do notice it, signal me. I'll need to know."

"How shall I signal?"

He looked at her for a moment. "Take your earrings off," he said. "If you're sitting, stand up and take them off. I'll do the rest."

"What will you do?"

"That depends on the circumstances. What's more important for you to know is how to recognize that he's wavering. If he starts being critical about the West, or if he starts talking nostalgically about home, that's a sign. They usually get extremely critical about our side when they begin to reconsider. And they usually try to convince themselves that Russia isn't so bad after all. Look for that."

"What if he starts talking in Russian?"

"He's absolutely forbidden to talk in Russian. Good God, nothing will identify him faster. Absolutely he cannot." O'Neal turned to Hartley. "He's been warned of that?"

"Yes, of course," Hartley said.

"And that's another thing, Molly." O'Neal turned to her again. "You keep him talking, or rather, you keep talking to him. Don't give him time to think. Don't give him time to begin having regrets."

"Is this fair?" Molly asked. "Is it right to keep him from changing his mind?"

"Fair?" O'Neal said in surprise. "Who's talking about fair? He came to us; we didn't grab him off the street. He's made his move; we're just seeing that he sticks with it. Those two things, Molly: you listen for possible reasons for his defection, and you watch for signs that he's wavering. And, above all, you keep talking to him. You're the cover. Never forget that. Without you, he's completely vulnerable."

"Why is he so important?" Molly asked. "If what you're after is the film—if you're thinking that his undeveloped film will show what's really happening in the Dioula and who's leading the fighting—why don't you just take the film and process it? Why worry about him?"

O'Neal looked at Hartley and grinned. Hartley stood and walked to the door, then walked back to his chair. O'Neal straightened some papers on the table. "It's not just the photographs," he said finally, "it's also who he is. His father is Andrei Klebanoff, the editor in chief of *Pravda*." O'Neal cleared his throat before going on. "His grandfather is Sergei Butakov."

Molly looked from one man to the other, and in silence they stared back. "You weren't gong to tell me that, were you?" she asked.

"We debated about it," Hartley said. "It didn't seem something you needed to know."

"Didn't need to know? I'm supposed to talk to this guy for the next how many hours? I'm supposed to look for his reasons, or notice if he's wavering? And you don't think I need to know the most important thing about him?" She raised her hands in exasperation. "What did you think? That I was going to have this nice little conversation with him and sometime he just might mention his grandfather, and I would politely ask his grandfather's name and he would tell me and I would say 'Oh, isn't that nice,' and keep on talking? Are you crazy? Are you absolutely crazy?" She stood abruptly, her chair scraping the bare floor.

"Molly," O'Neal said, waving his hand. "Molly, listen. This is not something that happens every day. There's no procedure for this—"

"No procedure? *No procedure?*"

"Molly, listen. If he were a KGB agent we'd know how to deal with this, but a close relative of someone this important?

Someone whose defection could bring down a whole political faction? Believe me, we're playing this by ear all the way."

"And what makes you think I want to be part of this experiment?"

"You can call it an experiment if you want, but he's still a viable human being, he still wants out. Forget about who his grandfather is—how about him? Does he have a right to get out or not? You were willing to help when he was a nobody, why should you have second thoughts now that you know he has connections?"

"You know damn well! Because they're more likely to come after him than someone who doesn't have any connections."

"All the more reason, then."

"What else haven't you told me?"

"Nothing else. We don't even know for sure if he's who is says he is. And maybe his pictures are nothing either. We have to assume they are, and we have to assume he is, too, until we can prove otherwise. Yes, there's some risk—I told you that already. But getting him out on the first plane minimizes the risk as much as possible. What will be seen at the airport will be a young man and woman, both obviously American. Unless everything is against us, it will be enough to get him safely to Rome. You provide the cover until he gets on the plane. Then all you have to do is keep him from thinking about changing his mind."

She sat back down in the chair and looked from one to the other. "I've heard you guys provide women for defectors, to keep them happy. Is that another part of the plan you've neglected to tell me?"

"What do you mean, 'you guys'?"

"You're CIA, aren't you?"

"I told you we weren't."

"You don't expect me to believe it, do you?"

"If this were a CIA operation, we would not use a civilian like you."

"I notice you avoided the real question."

"No, you are not coming along for anything other than cover. If this guy gets provided with female companionship of the kind you're talking about, it will not be you, you can count on that."

"I don't know why I should believe that."

"I can give you one good reason," Hartley said, leaning

on the table toward her. "By the time you get him to Rome, you'll have talked your head off to him and he won't be able to stand the sight of you. Or maybe I should say the sound of you."

"We only ask one thing of you," O'Neal said, "and that is to talk. If it turns out that a woman is needed for something else, we'll find one who hasn't already talked him to death." He leaned back in his chair. "Would you like to go meet him now?"

"It's about time," she said, rising.

"One more thing," O'Neal said as he opened the door for her. "You may find him a little arrogant."

She paused in the doorway, suddenly overwhelmed. What was she doing? What was she getting into? She could still say no; what could they do to her? Send her back home? Make her stay here in the Embassy for a while—that was what O'Neal had said. No, Molly, she thought wryly to herself, they've done a very good job with you. No matter what you say, you've known all along—and they probably did, too— that you would do it. Twenty-four hours, O'Neal had said. She'd hold him to that. Twenty-four hours was not so much to give up for someone wanting asylum—even if he did turn out to be arrogant. She wondered, cynical now, how much else they hadn't told her.

It was a larger conference room. There were two men in it: one looked overweight and close to fifty; the other was younger, about six inches taller than she, with very short red hair. He was wearing light-tan poplin slacks, a short-sleeved blue oxford-cloth shirt, and scuffed deck shoes. She gazed at him with serious blue eyes. It might work, she thought. They had done a good job; he looked very much like an American.

"What do you think?" O'Neal asked her.

"I think you could introduce us," she answered.

"Sorry. Molly, Yuri Klebanoff. Yuri, this is the woman who's going to be with you on the plane—Molly Davison."

Yuri Klebanoff nodded. He's sizing me up, she thought. He's no more sure of this than I am. "Yuri," she said, reaching out to shake hands. He shook her hand in a firm grip, but his green-gray eyes betrayed no emotion. He's used to hiding his feelings, she thought, or else he hasn't any.

"Molly, this is Alvin Jones," O'Neal said.

Jones nodded perfunctorily, barely looking at her.

"Have you explained it to him?" O'Neal asked him.

"He understands," Jones said.

O'Neal turned to Klebanoff. "I'll be on the plane, too. The two of you will go from here by cab to the Rafetna Palais Hotel. That cab will be driven by an African you can trust. He'll take you to a side entrance. You will go into the hotel, wait ten minutes, then come out the main entrance and have the doorman flag you a cab for the airport. Speak only English to the doorman and the cabdriver. Do not try to speak French to either of them, no matter how good your French is. Keep talking English. Make up things to say, if you have to, Molly. Yuri's name is to be Thomas Little. You call him Tom, not Thomas, and never call him Yuri, even when you're certain that no one is within earshot. Understand?"

Molly nodded. Yuri gazed absently at O'Neal as if no response were required.

"Do you understand, Yuri?" O'Neal repeated.

"Yes."

"That second cabdriver will be an ordinary taxi driver, but someone from the Embassy will be tailing you in a private car. You will be under surveillance at all times. Is that clear?"

Molly nodded and looked at Yuri. Yuri nodded.

"I will arrive separately. I'll be there before you come. You may see me or you may not—as you remember, it's a fairly open airport with no particular areas to wait for specific flights. There will be others as well. George Hartley"—he nodded in Hartley's direction—"will be there with me; he'll have driven me to the airport and will stay to see me off. Alvin Jones here will be there, too. He'll see Hartley and me and act surprised to see us. All this will be for show, of course. You will in no way act as if you know any of us. You will both have civilian passports. There is to be nothing to link you with the American diplomatic post here.

"Yuri," O'Neal went on, "you understand that at no time are you to speak Russian. You are only to speak English, no matter what."

"I have already been told that," Yuri said.

"You are also not to speak at all beyond yes or no unless it is absolutely necessary. While your English is very creditable, you do have an accent that would give you away."

"I know."

"Molly will do the talking. She may talk you to death, but that's her job. You are not to get impatient with her. It is her responsibility to create the illusion that both of you are speaking English. Once the plane is in the air, you may relent and speak more if you wish, but only in English.''

''I do not expect to have need to talk,'' Yuri said stiffly. ''I can manage several hours in silence.''

O'Neal shrugged. ''Whatever you prefer. Then I think everything is arranged. It's time to go.''

''Isn't it awfully early?'' Molly asked.

''You know they overbook. The only way to be sure to get on is to get there early.''

''But doesn't that just expose us for a longer period?''

''The greater risk is in coming in at the last minute. Then it's obvious that you're someone unusual, especially if you manage to get on the plane despite the late arrival. No, you get there in good time, you sit down, and you work hard at blending into the scenery.'' O'Neal moved closer. ''Good luck,'' he said, shaking her hand, and then Yuri's. ''See you at the airport. The next time we speak will be in Rome.''

''You haven't told us what happens in Rome,'' Molly said.

''Go through the motions, just as if you were a tourist. You will both carry on your bags. They're small enough not to be checked through and it'll save you time and hassle. Go through customs. I'll handle the rest. I'll make the first move. You just follow my lead.''

''I'd rather have more concrete instructions than that,'' Molly said.

''Sorry, but I can't give them to you. It depends on who's on the plane with us, who's at the airport, both from Yuri's side and ours.''

''Then you do expect that they might realize what happened to him.''

''Everything's possible. Keep your eyes on me; I'll signal.'' O'Neal looked at Klebanoff. ''Are you going to be okay?'' he asked.

''Yes.''

''Have they gotten you a bag?''

''Yes.'' Yuri pointed to a small canvas duffel bag sitting near the door.

''Then let's go,'' O'Neal said. He led the way along the corridor, down the stairs, and out the front entrance. A taxi was waiting in the drive. ''Good,'' he said, more to himself than to anyone else, ''Sammy's already here.'' He stood aside and followed with his eyes as Molly and Yuri stepped into the cab. "Who's at the hotel?" he asked.

"I will be," Jones said.

"Hadn't you better get going?"

"I'm on my way."

O'Neal and Hartley stood together and watched the cab pull out of the drive and onto the street in front of the Embassy. "Is it going to work?" Hartley asked.

"It's a hell of a question to ask now," O'Neal responded.

"An awful lot depends on her. It seems to me she overreacted back there."

"Not any more than you would have done in her shoes. Or than I would," O'Neal mused. "No, she was a very good choice. She's sharp, she's quick, she notices things. If it can be pulled off at all, I think she can do it."

"*If* it can be pulled off—?"

"It's a big risk. We've known that all along. This is not minimal risk; this is a big risk."

"Then why are we doing it?"

O'Neal turned to him. "Have we got another choice?"

5

THE CAB PULLED SLOWLY OUT OF THE EMBASSY
drive. Five minutes, Molly guessed, to the Rafetna Palais
Hotel in the middle of town. Yuri sat stiffly on the seat beside
her, looking straight ahead. "How long have you been in
Rafetna?" she asked.

"One day," he answered, still staring ahead.

"And before coming here, you were in the Dioula?"

"Yes."

She stared openly at him, and if he was aware of it he gave
no sign. An emptiness in the pit of her stomach warned that
this was not going to work, that there was no way she was
going to be able to carry it off. But he does look like an
American, she reassured herself, and there's no reason we
can't do it. "Is your hair really red or did they dye it?" she
asked.

"My hair is brown."

She nodded approval—it was just the right shade for credibility, not too carroty, not too titian. Someone had done a
very good job. And O'Neal had told her that the Russians
wouldn't even know yet that he was missing. There was every
chance it would work; all she had to do was play her own
part.

"Do you smoke?" she asked.

"Why?"

"Because if you do, you're going to need American cigarettes."

"They already gave me cigarettes."

"Where are they?"

He looked at her and she thought she could read annoyance

in his eyes. "You were not supposed to talk to me like this. Only yes and no questions."

"They said in the cab it would be safe. If we're going to pretend to be married or lovers or whatever, we might as well be on speaking terms."

He shrugged. "As you wish."

"Your cigarettes?"

"I think I left them back there."

She turned away from him and gazed out the side window. For someone in his position he was certainly not very cooperative. "We'll buy some at the hotel," she said finally. "It'll give us something to do. When we get them, put them in your left-hand shirt pocket."

"Why?"

"Because that's where you would carry them."

"I do not smoke very much."

"Put them there anyway," she snapped, not even hiding her irritation.

He said nothing in response and she absently watched the palm trees that lined the boulevard sliding by in the night, trying not to think that she didn't like his attitude. *You might find him arrogant*, O'Neal had said. Or maybe it was that he was just plain obnoxious. Spoiled brat of the Soviet hierarchy, she thought. Half the Embassy goes nuts trying to get you out and you act like it's nothing—like we owe you or something. In a couple of years you'll probably change your mind and want to go back. She crossed her arms in disgust. *Twenty-four hours*, O'Neal had said. Or less. She'd hold him to that. It was probably about twenty-three hours more than the guy deserved, and if the first few minutes were any indication, it was going to be a long twenty-four hours. Or maybe, she thought hopefully, maybe I'm reading him all wrong. Maybe it's just that he's as scared as I am.

"You're a photographer," she said.

He nodded without looking at her.

"For Tass?"

He nodded again.

"Where were you before you came to Bodamwe?"

"Moscow."

"Is this your first time out of Russia?"

"Of course not."

"Where else have you been?"

"Many places."

"For example."

"Warszawa. Bucuresti. Praha. Kabul. Dresden. Others."

"But not the West before."

He looked at her and shook his head. "This is not the West."

The driver slowed to a stop. "They told me to take you to the side entrance," he said without turning around. She wondered briefly if it had also been part of his instructions not to look at them.

"How much is it?" she asked.

"They've taken care of it," the driver said.

"Okay," she said to Yuri, "it begins now." She opened the door and he slid over in the seat to come out the same door. "You'll open the hotel door for me," she said. "In America men hold doors open for women."

"That is not what I have read."

"The kind of man you are supposed to be—the kind of relationship we're supposed to be having—you'll open the door."

He reached around her and pulled the door open. She gave him a smile and walked inside.

The lobby blazed with light and color. Geometric designs of deep blue, rose brick, and rust marched around the walls, provoking at the same time sensations of warmth and spaciousness. Cone-shaped chandeliers of native copper hung on long gold velvet cords, creating circles of light on the gold carpeting. Even at this time of night a few people sat on couches and chairs, deep in quiet conversations or reading European newspapers. Molly strode purposefully across the wide room, and Yuri followed half a step behind. "Have you been in here before?" she asked in a low voice.

"No."

"It's really quite beautiful." She paused in the center of the room and looked around; no one was paying them any attention. "It's not at all what I would have expected; the building looks so plain on the outside. Would you have thought it would look like this in here?" It's stupid, she thought, but at least it's practice.

"No," he responded.

"Neither would I." She continued across the lobby, heading now toward a cigarette-and-candy counter in the corner. "Would you give me a couple of packs of Winstons, please?"

she asked the girl behind the counter. "Oh, darling," she
said as if just thinking of it, "didn't you run out of matches?"

"Yes."

"Matches, too, then," she said.

The girl shoved two packs of cigarettes and a box of
matches across the glass countertop. "One hundred and fifty-
two francs."

"Darling, do put the matches in your pants pocket," Molly
said, laying the bills on the counter. "You know how they
stretch your shirt pockets." She handed the matches and one
cigarette pack to Yuri, and placed the other in her purse.
"Shall we see if we can find a *Herald Tribune*?" She led him
off to another part of the lobby. "We're doing very well, I
think," she whispered, heading toward an empty couch. But
I'm going to have to think of something else to talk about,
she told herself.

Ten minutes later they walked out the front door. The doorman looked at their hand luggage. "Taxi?" he asked.

Molly glanced at Yuri. "Yes," he said. The doorman whis-
tled and a cab drew up beside them.

"Airport?" the doorman asked.

"Yes," Yuri said this time without prompting.

The doorman leaned over and said something to the driver.
Molly looked anxiously at Yuri, but he didn't seem concerned. Relax, she told herself. It's perfectly normal; Americans never speak any language other than English. And isn't
someone supposed to be following us to the airport? She
looked at the cars parked along the street. One of them must
contain someone from the Embassy. Which one? Were they
really there? Don't be paranoid, she told herself, of course
they're there. Even so, she stole a glance out the back window
as the taxi drove off.

It was almost a half-hour drive from the center of Rafetna
to the airport, which sat on a narrow spit of land jutting into
the Atlantic west of the city. It was too long a ride to sit in
silence, she decided. It had seemed so easy when O'Neal had
explained it—just talk to him and let him answer yes and no
occasionally. But what do you talk about at a time like this?
she wondered. She started tentatively with comments about
the hotel, warmed up to what she imagined were typical tourist comments about the city in general, even ventured into
trying to compare Rafetna with Nairobi—where she had never
been. Yuri sat stiffly beside her, nodding now and then,

throwing out a "yes" or a "no" on occasion, but mostly letting her chatter on. It was with an enormous sense of relief that she finally saw the lights of the airport ahead.

The terminal at Rafetna was a long, low cement building, painted dusty rose inside and out. Its single ticket counter ran along the front wall, and at two o'clock in the morning only one ticket agent was on duty, standing beneath the Air Afrique sign, the only lighted sign above an otherwise deserted counter. Molly glanced at her watch. One hour, she thought. *If we can make it through the next hour, we're home free.*

"May I help you?" the young man asked. He was wearing a loose shirt, open at the neck. Even at that hour of the morning, it was uncomfortably warm.

"We're here to check in for the flight to Rome," Molly said. "Tom, you have the tickets, don't you?"

Yuri handed the tickets to the young man.

"That's fine," the young man said, glancing at them to make sure they were in order and then handing them back. "I'll announce when the plane can be boarded."

"We'd like to get our seat assignments," Molly persisted.

"Oh, no." He smiled. "We don't do those things here. You'll get your seat when you board the plane."

"Can't we get them now?"

"But that would be impossible. How would we know what seats have already been taken?"

Of course, she thought, no computers. "But how can we be sure we'll have seats?"

"I think you will have them. I think there will be no problem."

"That's not good enough," she persisted. "We have to catch another plane in Rome. If we don't get this flight, we won't make our connection."

The young man smiled broadly. "Don't worry. I am sure everyone who wants to get on the plane will be able to do so. Just sit down and wait until I announce it." He turned away from her then as if to dismiss the matter.

Molly moved slowly away from the counter, her eyes surveying the place, looking for O'Neal. He was nowhere in sight, and she tried to keep the panic from overwhelming her. *I'll be there,* he'd said, and she'd trusted that. What if he didn't show up? What was she supposed to do? What if they didn't get seats on the plane? She glanced at Yuri and he was watching her. *This is not the worst thing that could be hap-*

pening to me, she told herself deliberately; I could be in his shoes. She forced herself to smile faintly at him and walked toward a deserted area of the terminal.

"When I was living in the Central African Republic, I went to visit a friend," she said to him as they walked. "I was teaching English in a school there and she taught in the same school. Her husband met me at the door of their home and invited me inside. I knew him because he taught at the school as well. I assumed she was in the kitchen—it was in the summer and school was out. He sat me down on the couch—he was a very gentlemanly kind of person, very good-looking and he knew it—and offered me a glass of tea. I could hardly refuse; I was seated in his parlor by then and it would have been highly insulting if I had left. So of course I accepted. It took him only a moment or two to pour the tea; it must already have been made. When he returned with the glasses, he made excuses for my friend, his wife. She was not feeling well and was napping in the other room, he said. Well, we began drinking the tea, and the next thing I knew he was admiring a ring I was wearing, and then he was holding my hand to look at it more closely, and then he was just plain holding my hand. The conversation was perfectly innocuous and so there was no way I could act insulted, and yet it was clear to me what he was trying to do—he was trying to romance me with his wife in the next room, for God's sake. Though of course he was clever enough not to say anything too obvious." She paused.

"And . . . ?" he asked.

"And . . . in the end . . . nothing." She shrugged. "I managed to get out of it finally, but I never felt comfortable around him again. Or around her, either, though I certainly hadn't done anything to be embarrassed about. It was a feeling more than anything, a feeling that all I would have to do was show an interest in him. For a while I wondered if he treated all women like that. Then, not so much later, I began hearing rumors about him and the wife of the school's headmaster. The school staff went on an outing some time after that, and it was clear to me that the rumors were true, though the wife never acted as if she suspected anything at all. I always wondered if she knew, and if she just pretended she didn't see what was going on. I also always wondered why he thought I'd be interested. If I was going to have a lover, it certainly wouldn't have been him. He thought he was so smooth and he was really such a jerk. And he was practically old enough to be my father. Maybe he always acted that way with women. Maybe he was just fishing, and finally, with the headmaster's wife, he caught something.''

Yuri stared off across the terminal.

"I don't mean to bore you," she said.

"No," he responded.

She wondered what that meant, and she wondered what had possessed her to agree to this in the first place. "When one finds oneself in another culture, it's quite possible to convey messages completely unknowingly. I've always wondered about that, if somehow I did that. And I've tried to keep it in mind. You can't always tell how someone from another culture is gong to interpret what you say or what you do.''

He nodded, still gazing into the distance.

She saw O'Neal and Hartley now, walking slowly the length of the terminal, lost in conversation, and relief flooded through her. At least O'Neal was there. It was going to work after all.

"It's not going to be all that easy, carrying on a one-sided conversation for the next hour."

He turned toward her at last. "Yes, I know."

"Well, what would you like to hear about? More of my adventures in Africa? Music? Art? Books? Politics? Religion?" She watched his face for an indication of interest, but it remained passive; she could read nothing in his eyes.

"You decide," he said.

She started out slowly, working backwards—graduate school, Peace Corps, college; talking about what she imagined someone who had lived his whole life in the Soviet Union would want to know. She told him about high school, about the two years her family had spent living in Athens while her father redesigned a major hotel. She touched on her childhood, growing up in a small town in Wisconsin. She told him about the time she was four years old and a neighbor boy had pushed her off a tricycle and broken her arm. She laughed at the memory, and was pleased when he smiled. Then the smile faded and the face was impassive once more. He is bored to death, she thought, but she went on talking because that was what she had agreed to do.

The terminal had filled with more and more people waiting for the flight: families with children climbing over paper-covered suitcases and cloth bundles, businessmen with garment bags slung over their shoulders, a group of black American tourists, lone men standing around in new suits, chatting women in flowing African robes, their hair covered with turbans. O'Neal and Hartley continued walking slowly back and forth. She had not seen Alvin Jones.

An African family—a young man and woman with a small child and a baby—took seats nearby.

"Cute kids," Molly commented.

"Yes."

The little boy, finger in mouth, stared shyly at Molly. "Hi there," she said softly to him. He wriggled closer to his mother and the woman smiled indulgently. "He's adorable," Molly said to the mother. The woman whispered something in the boy's ear. He shook his head and burrowed closer. The mother smiled apologetically to Molly.

"He is shy," the African man said in English.

She sensed Yuri suddenly stiffen beside her and she followed the direction of his eyes. A man was walking toward them, moving in the opposite direction as O'Neal and Hartley. He was of stocky build but not overweight, looking uncomfortably warm in a blue serge suit, the jacket open, the tie pulled loose at the neck.

"Is he . . . ?"

"Yes," Yuri said.

She watched O'Neal's retreating back. Something could happen right here and O'Neal wouldn't even know until it was too late. Suddenly she realized how foolish it had all been—she talking her head off to Yuri, and no one more than ten or twenty feet away could even hear. O'Neal had said she would be his cover, but it was no cover at all. If the Soviets knew they were here, there would be nothing they could do.

Suddenly Yuri stood and pulled the cigarette pack from his pocket. Almost as an afterthought, he stepped over and offered the pack to the African. Smiling, the African stood too, nodded, and took a cigarette from the pack. Yuri drew the matchbox from his pocket and lit the man's cigarette and his own. "You live in Rafetna?" Yuri asked.

"No," the African said. "In Lambé, to the south."

"You speak English," Molly said, standing now too.

"A little."

"And your wife?" she asked.

"No my wife," the young man said, "my sister. No. She only speak French."

"She has beautiful children."

The young man smiled and said something to the woman. She smiled and nodded. "Are you going back to America?" the African asked.

"Yes," Yuri said. He pulled on the cigarette again and looked absently about the terminal. The man in the serge suit had passed them and was nearing the end of the building.

"Are you taking the plane to Rome?" Molly asked.

"Yes," the young man said. "And then to America. I will study at the Michigan State University."

"Really?" asked Molly. "Will you study agriculture?"

"No, economics."

"My name is Molly Davison," she said, extending her hand. "And this is my . . . fiancé, Tom Little."

The African shook her hand and Yuri's. "I am Abdou Ngor," he said formally. "And this is my sister Miryam."

Molly smiled a greeting, and the woman smiled shyly in return. "Is there somewhere that we can get something to eat?" Molly asked.

The African looked surprised. "I think . . . perhaps around the corner."

"Wouldn't you like something to eat, Tom? I don't suppose they'll give us much of anything on the plane."

"Yes," Yuri said. "Okay."

"I will go with you and get something," the African said. He turned and spoke to the woman, then said, "And we will find something for the children. Come, I think they sell things this way."

At the far end of the room, the man in the serge suit had stopped. He was leaning against the wall, watching no one in particular, or perhaps everyone. And were there others, Molly wondered, were there others from both sides? Somehow she felt safer with the Africans, less obtrusive. It was as if O'Neal had arranged for yet another cover. She wondered vaguely if indeed that was what the Africans were.

At last the man behind the ticket counter took a microphone, and, after several attempts to make it work properly, announced the flight. People bent to gather up their things; children who had been sleeping fussed fretfully when awakened. Molly and Yuri hurried toward the passport control, but Abdou turned back to hug his sister and kiss each of the children.

Ahead, Molly could see O'Neal already in line. She watched as the officials looked at each passport, riffled through the pages as if curious which entry and exit stamps appeared in each, then stamped an exit stamp before returning it. Suddenly she wondered if Yuri's passport could endure close scrutiny. She knew they'd made the passport for him at the Embassy, but she hadn't seen it. She was beginning to realize how many things she'd assumed, including that Yuri's disguise, or her cover, would be good enough. If the Russian really was there looking for Yuri—if he really was a Russian—he had not made a move. She hoped that meant something. Just a few more minutes, she said to herself, just a few more minutes and we'll be on the plane and gone. Safe.

She handed the official her passport. He looked at it and looked at her. She smiled at him. "Too short a stay," she said.

He smiled and nodded and stamped the passport.

"Tom, do you have the tickets handy?" she asked, forcing her voice to an even pitch.

"Yes," Yuri said and handed his passport to the official.

"Good. Let's not hold this plane up any more than it has to be. It's already late, and it looks as if it's going to be full of screaming babies all the way to Rome."

Her eyes were on the official as he slowly turned the pages of Yuri's passport. He muttered something in French that she didn't catch, and then looked from Yuri's picture to Yuri. Then with what could almost be described as a flourish, he brought the stamp down on Yuri's passport.

"And that's it," she said as they walked onto the tarmac. She felt like laughing; it had been so easy and she had been so terrified. He walked beside her still so serious-faced that she wondered if he didn't realize that the worst was over. "Whatever your friend was here for, he didn't stop us," she said.

"Did you see other one?" Yuri asked.

"Other one?"

"Yes, one who wasn't wearing suit."

"No. Another—?"

"Yes."

"Are you sure?"

"Yes."

"But they couldn't have seen you. They couldn't have recognized you. They didn't do anything at all. Thank God for Abdou. He was perfect, he made us credible, he spoke English and everything."

Yuri didn't respond. They were approaching the plane. The steward took their tickets, glanced at them, and waved the two of them up the steps.

As they entered the plane, Molly could see O'Neal already seated toward the back. He was wearing earphones and appeared to be gazing absently into space. Molly searched for seats that could be seen easily from his, but almost immediately she realized that the best they could hope for in the crowded plane would be two seats together—anywhere. She moved toward the back and claimed the first two she could find. "Beggars can't be choosers," she said lightly.

"What?"

"We'll sit here. At least they're together."

He looked briefly around the plane, then nodded and sat beside her. She smiled at him. "Home free," she said.

"I do not understand."

"I think we've made it."

He looked at her curiously.

"They can't have recognized you, or else they would have stopped you from getting on the plane."

"I hope you are correct."

"In Rome we have O'Neal."

"I hope so."

She smiled to reassure him. "It's okay," she said. "Believe me, it's going to be okay." She watched the rest of the passengers come into the cabin, saw the looks of dismay on their faces when they realized how full the plane already was, then saw them scramble for the few remaining seats. She waited, looking for Abdou, but he never appeared. The doors were shut, the FASTEN SEAT BELT sign came on, and she leaned back and tried to relax. It was only then that she noticed her hands were shaking. The men in the airport had done nothing, had not even gotten on the plane. But they had come close enough and it had been frightening. *They will not come after him with blazing guns,* O'Neal had said. *If it comes to that, it will be something much more subtle.* She realized now how terrifying something much more subtle could be. She thought again of Abdou and she wondered if he had indeed been O'Neal's man—an extra cover just in case.

* * *

Alvin Jones watched the last of the Rome-bound passengers disappear into the dark outside the terminal, aware that two other men had also been watching. He saw the African man pick up his suitcase and head toward the front doors, followed by the African woman with the two children. Then he went to the airline counter and talked the clerk into letting him use the telephone. He made two calls.

Outside the terminal, Jones stood at the curb, waiting for a taxi that finally pulled up beside him. Getting in, he said, "Thanks, Sammy. I really appreciate your coming for me."

"No problem," the driver said affably.

"Well, it's late and everything."

"Not too easy to find a cab at this time of night, especially one that will take you all the way out where you live."

"I suppose all the drivers are home resting up for the big day tomorrow."

"Big day for sure. Lots of money is going to be made tomorrow, with all the foreigners coming and going from the airport."

"When do they start arriving?"

"Oh, some have already come. But I won't be working tomorrow. I be home with the family. I always take Independence Day off and we go to the parade together."

"You took a couple of people to the Rafetna Palais earlier this evening."

The driver glanced at him in the rearview mirror. "Yes, I did."

"What were they talking about?"

"In my cab? You should know, sir, I never pay attention to what my passengers say."

"You must have overheard something."

"Nothing. Nothing that I can remember."

"Who was doing most of the talking? He or she?"

"She, maybe. A little of both, I guess."

"But you didn't hear what they were saying?"

"No sir. I told you. I never listen to that kind of thing. Isn't that why you people use my taxi?"

They drove for a long time in silence, until Alvin Jones spoke again. "Will you let me off at Chez Papa? Believe it or not, I haven't had any dinner yet this evening. It'll still be open, don't you think?"

"Chez Papa?" The African laughed. "Do they ever close?"

Jones nodded. "I can walk home from there."

The lights of the restaurant blazed into the night as the taxi stopped in front. Alvin Jones got out and bent to pay, and just as he was doing so, another white man emerged from the restaurant. "Taxi! Hey, taxi!" the man called.

Jones grinned at Sammy. "Looks like it's your lucky night," he said.

"Time for me to go home," the driver said.

"And lose a fare?" Jones raised his eyebrows.

But the other man was already opening the back door of the taxi, and Sammy gave Jones a hopeless look. "Well," he said, "I am going to take tomorrow off anyway. Go to the celebration with the family."

Jones stood at the curb and watched the taxi leave. Sammy had already turned off his taxi sign. This would be his last fare of the night. Jones turned away and walked toward home.

In the taxi, Sammy tried to catch the man's face in the rearview mirror. A European, maybe even an American, but he didn't recognize him. Probably a tourist.

"Big celebration tomorrow, eh?" the man said in English.

"You bet."

"Thought I'd take a look at the parade. Got any ideas of a good spot?"

"Not the Square. It will definitely be too crowded. You won't be able to see a thing. Maybe a couple of blocks before, that's what I intend to do."

"Oh, really? Maybe you could show me a good place."

"Sure." The cabdriver made a quick left turn and barreled down some side streets until he was almost at the Square. "In this area," he said, driving more slowly now.

"Could a person stand on that wall?"

"If you could climb up there."

"Want to stop and see if I can?"

"Now?"

"Why not?" the man said, laughing. "When better? No one's around, in case I make a fool of myself."

Sammy wondered if he was drunk, but he pulled to the curb.

The man got out and immediately bent down. "Damn!" he said.

"What's the matter?" the driver asked, leaning out the window.

"I've lost my keys," the man said from the curb. "They fell out of my pocket as I got out. Didn't you hear them?"

"Here, let me back up and shine my lights—"

"No, you don't have to do that. Just open the car door and let the interior light shine. We should be able to pick them up in the light. Can't see a thing in this dark."

The driver opened the door, then got out as the man continued crawling around beside the gutter. "Here, sir, you shouldn't ruin your good clothes. I'll find them." Gently he shoved the other man out of the way and bent down to look.

The man stood quickly and reached into his pocket. With a smooth, practiced movement, he put his left hand over the driver's mouth and pulled the head back to expose the neck. At the same moment his right hand drew a knife blade across the man's throat. As the body slumped, he let it fall quietly to the street. Then he closed the car door and felt in the man's pockets, drawing out a few bills and some coins. He pocketed the money and then he turned and hurried away.

6

MOLLY OPENED HER EYES. SHE WAS EXHAUSTED, BUT it was impossible to sleep. The plane's cabin lights were on, though dim. Somewhere behind her a baby cried, the sound of its fussing muffled, as though the mother was holding it close. A large, heavyset man padded shoeless up the aisle, his pants dragging over maroon socks, the edges of his suit coat brushing the aisle seats. A weary-looking stewardess in the far aisle searched the overhead compartments for yet one more pillow. They had been in the air for almost an hour, and Molly felt the strange, disembodied sense of a disparate group of people flying together through the night sky.

Now, up front, another baby started crying. Molly looked at her watch—seven minutes to four—and tried not to think of the long hours ahead. It's done, she told herself; we did it. Nothing had happened in the airport, neither the sudden attack she'd half feared nor the much more subtle maneuver O'Neal had suggested. Nothing. Despite the men Yuri had seen—nothing. It should have made her feel relieved.

She glanced at Yuri beside her. His eyes were closed, but she felt certain he was not asleep. "I wish I knew about Abdou," she said quietly.

"I told you," he said without opening his eyes. "He was probably too far back in line. There were not enough seats. You can see how it is. You can see plane is full."

"No," she persisted, shaking her head. "It was more than that. He sat with us. He talked with us. When that—that KGB man or whatever he was—came by, he was talking with us. He stayed with us right up until we got into the line for passport control. It was almost as if he were escorting us. Even when we went to the snack bar he went with us. And then,

65

when it came time to get in line, even though he must have known that he'd have to hurry if he wanted to get a seat, he stayed back.''

Yuri turned and gazed lazily at her. "You still think he was one of O'Neal's men?"

"Doesn't it make sense?"

"Why did O'Neal not tell us?"

"I don't know.''

Yuri looked away. "Maybe because O'Neal is stupid.''

"You think that? You think he's stupid? Your life is in his hands, you know.''

"My life has always been in hands of stupid men. That part has not changed.''

Molly shot him a glance. "That other man didn't get on either. Do you think he recognized you?"

"I do not know.'' He was still turned away and he spoke softly. She could barely hear him.

"Doesn't it bother you?" she persisted.

He shrugged. "If they stop me, they stop me.''

"But surely you don't want that. If they take you back, what will happen?"

As if explaining to a child, he spoke slowly. "There is never perfect time to do this thing. One takes one's chances. There are other reasons why he might have been at airport.''

"Do you know him? Did you recognize him?"

"No. Neither one of them. But I recognized who they must be.''

"KGB?" she whispered, as if she needed him to confirm it.

He looked at her but said nothing.

"But they must have been looking for you. Why else would they have been at the airport?"

"Tomorrow—today now—is big Independence Day celebration in Bodamwe, surely you know that. There will be large delegation from Moscow; they arrive at seven this morning. He could have been at airport for that.''

"How do you know when they come?"

"That was what I was doing in Rafetna. I was to meet plane and take photographs of arriving dignitaries. Pictures would have been shown on Soviet television and would be in newspapers as well. It has been decided that our friendship with Bodamwe is very important. Next year fifty Bodamwean students will be at Soviet universities.''

"In that case," she said slowly, "maybe they really weren't looking for you." Somehow the knowledge made her feel better.

"Perhaps not."

"Does O'Neal know this?"

"Do not ask me what O'Neal knows. If you are so nervous, have a cigarette to calm yourself."

"I don't smoke."

He looked at her appraisingly. "You bought two packs of cigarettes at hotel. You put one in your purse."

"If I had bought only one pack, and given it to you, she would have wondered why you didn't buy it yourself. I had to buy two."

"Oh," he said, and stared at her a moment longer. Then he turned away again, gazing out at the night sky. She looked openly at him. There was something about him, something that she couldn't quite grasp. He is not going to say anything to me, she thought, not unless I push.

"Why did you decide to leave?" she asked.

"That is not something you need to know."

"Maybe not, but I'm still curious."

He turned toward her with a wry grin. "You say, I think, that curiosity kills cats."

"I was given a great deal of responsibility for you. It seems only fair—"

"Fair?" he asked harshly. "What is fair? What does fair have to do with it?"

She shook her head. "You sound like O'Neal."

"I do? What does O'Neal say about being fair?"

"Same thing."

He leaned toward her, curious now. "Did you ask him this: why I was asking for asylum?"

"Yes, but he didn't really say."

"Did he tell you who I was?"

"Yes."

"Everything?"

"Your father and your grandfather? He told me that."

Yuri leaned his head back and exhaled deeply, staring straight ahead. "There are many reasons," he said at last. "There are many reasons to leave."

"For example."

He smiled slyly. "Because I could no longer keep myself from

seeing glories of the West—streets paved with gold, poor people
driving in Cadillacs."

"Spare me."

"Race riots. Ghettos. Unemployed starving on Wall Street.
Do you like that version better?"

"Is that why you came? To see which version is true?"

He smiled again, that wry smile that seemed so superior. I
could hate him for that smile alone, she thought. "I did not need
to come for that," he said. "I already know. If you do not
object, now I am going to sleep." He closed his eyes, his head
still leaning against the seat back. "You should sleep also," he
added, his eyes still closed. "Who knows when we will have
chance to sleep again."

She knew he was right, but she could not imagine sleeping
now. There was too much to think about, and she wished she
could have a chance to talk with O'Neal. She'd thought that
delivering Yuri safely onto the plane would be the end of it, but
it wasn't. Who were Abdou and the men Yuri had seen, and
why had they been there? And Yuri himself was no help. If his
reasons for defecting were other than what O'Neal had already
told her, she hadn't been able to discover what they were. And
if he was beginning to have second thoughts, he was giving no
indication.

When they got to Rome, her part would be finished; she could
board the next plane back and be home before she was missed.
She imagined O'Neal would tell her not to mention this little
trip. Someday she would read in the papers that Yuri Andreyevich Klebanoff, photographer for Tass and grandson of former
Soviet Premier Sergei Butakov, had defected to the West, and
when that happened, maybe she would be allowed to tell her
part in it all. If he truly was who he said he was. She studied
him as he slept. There are many reasons to leave, he had said,
as if that were an answer.

The long hallways of Rome's Fiumicino Airport presented an
austere, no-nonsense countenance to the arriving travelers, with
always at least one security guard in view, more often two or
more. These were not the smartly uniformed security guards of
American airports, but rather soldiers in full battle dress, with
·tomatic weapons at the ready. Yuri stared openly as they
passed the first pair, and the soldiers stared back. "Welcome to
the free world," Yuri muttered. Molly gave him a wan smile.
Behind them by ten to fifteen feet—she had glanced back to

make sure—O'Neal kept pace. "People must be very unruly here if it takes soldiers with guns to keep order," Yuri said.

"Why don't you limit yourself to simple yes and no responses in such a public place," Molly suggested.

He gave her a sharp look and without another word he walked on, quickening his pace until Molly almost had to run to stay with him. "There's no rush, you know," she said, but he kept on as if he hadn't heard. "Do you even know where you're going?" she asked.

"No," he said, but he didn't slow down.

Ahead of them now, down the long hall, they could see the signs for luggage pickup and customs. As they neared the signs, Yuri slowed almost imperceptibly and Molly took the lead. By the time they reached the customs line O'Neal was right behind them. He must have been hard put, Molly thought, to keep up with us back there. She did not look directly at him, nor he at her.

The customs agent glanced cursorily at Molly's passport, and glanced at her. "American," he said.

"Yes." She gave him what she hoped was a winning smile.

He opened her bag, lifted a cotton dress, and glanced beneath it.

"We're going to the south, to Naples," Molly said.

"Ah, Napoli?" The customs agent smiled broadly. "Is beautiful, Napoli."

"So I hear."

He moved a few more items, as if looking for contraband, but she had the distinct impression that he was more interested in seeing what kinds of apparel she carried with her. He rezipped her bag and smiled ingratiatingly again. "Have a nice time in Italia."

"Thank you. I hope to."

"And you, sir," he said turning to Yuri.

Yuri held out his passport.

"You are together?" The agent looked from Yuri to Molly and back.

"Yes," Yuri said.

"American too."

"Yes."

"Come from Africa."

"Yes."

"Hot there?"

"Yes."

"Unbearably hot," Molly said. "Naples will seem like heaven."

"How you go to Napoli?"

Molly opened her mouth. "Train," Yuri said.

"Can we take a taxi to the train station?" Molly asked.

"Yes, of course. Right outside." He pointed vaguely with his left hand.

"Good," Yuri said.

The young man opened Yuri's bag. Inside, neatly folded, were another pair of slacks, a few shirts, and, at the bottom, a faded pair of jeans. The customs agent's practiced eye found the jeans at once, and his fingers appreciatively felt the fabric. "Good jean. Levi's," he said.

"Yes," Yuri said.

Without looking further at the contents, the young man zipped Yuri's bag. "Have a nice time," he repeated.

"Thank you," Molly said. "We will."

"Are you two Americans?" called an overly loud voice behind her.

She turned; it was O'Neal. "Yes." She smiled, relieved.

"Going into town? Want to share a taxi with me?"

The customs agent had turned back to handle the next person in line, but, for his benefit, Molly said, "We're going to the train station."

"Fine," O'Neal said, "it's right on my way. We can both save money."

"Tom?" Molly asked. "Shall we?"

"Why not?" Yuri responded.

"Let's go," O'Neal said.

Once in the taxi, Molly settled back, relaxed at last. From now on, it was O'Neal's problem. "I've been wanting to talk with you," she said.

O'Neal frowned and his eyes flicked up toward the driver.

"You got on the plane with us at Rafetna," she recovered.

"Yes." His voice was wary.

"Were you in Rafetna long?"

"Not too long. I was there on business."

"Do you know anyone named Abdou? Abdou Ngor, I think his name is."

"Abdou? Should I?"

"I don't know. I thought you might."

"No," he said slowly, "I don't think I do."

They rode the rest of the way into the city in silence.

The taxi pulled up at the train station and Yuri opened the door. "I'll walk the rest of the way," O'Neal said, getting out the other side. "I'll pay and then we can work out how much you owe me." When the cab had driven off he turned to the others. "What's this Abdou business?" he asked.

"You're sure you don't know him?" Molly asked.

"Who is he?"

"He's the African we were talking with at the airport. He said he was going to the States to study, but he never got on the plane. He stayed with us the whole time—kept talking with us. He even went with us when we walked over to get something to eat. He was with us right up until we got into the passport line; yet he wasn't on the plane. I was sure he was one of your men."

"Did he say he was taking that plane?"

"Yes."

"Is that how you remember it?" O'Neal asked, turning abruptly to Yuri.

"He talked to us," Yuri said. "I do not know more than that."

"He wasn't one of yours then?" Molly said. "Did you see the two KGB guys?"

"I saw one."

"Yuri says there were two."

"The one who leaned against the wall," O'Neal said to Yuri.

"And another. In pants and shirt, not in suit."

"You're sure."

Yuri's eyes narrowed. "Of course I am sure."

"Did that one get on the plane?"

"None of them did," Molly said.

"None of them?"

"Not the two KGB guys, or Abdou."

O'Neal raised his hand for a cab. "Don't say anything important in the cab," he said. "We'll go to a safe place and then we'll talk."

They took two more cabs, and Molly had the feeling that they were doubling back over their own trail. The last cab dropped them off on a quiet street and O'Neal directed them to pick up their bags and follow him. He seemed preoccupied and barely spoke as he hurried along.

When they finally arrived at their destination, Molly found that it was a small hotel on a side street, with a sign so minuscule that it was nearly obscured by detergent posters affixed

to the wall of the building. A door with peeling paint
stood open, green and yellow plastic streamers hanging in the
doorway to discourage flies. Inside, it was dim and cool.
The walls were of chipped yellow plaster; the brown tiles of the
floor were freshly washed. O'Neal pressed a button and a distant
buzzer sounded. Within moments a small woman, gray hair
pulled neatly back into a bun, appeared. She looked at the three
of them, then at O'Neal in particular, but there was no hint of
recognition on her face.

"Do you have rooms?" O'Neal asked.

"Not rooms. One room. It is still early in the day." Her voice
was quiet and firm.

Molly looked at her watch. It was ten o'clock in the morning—no, Rome time it would be eleven.

"Will you have another room later?"

"Yes."

"Good. We will take the one now, and the other when it
becomes available."

"You don't wish to see first?" she asked, pushing the register
toward O'Neal.

"It won't be necessary," O'Neal said, pushing the book back
unsigned.

The woman shrugged, took a key from a rack on the wall,
and walked toward the stairs. "The lift does not work," she
said over her shoulder.

"What floor is it?" O'Neal asked.

"The next one."

She led the way up the stairs and down the hall, unlocked the
door and stood aside so the others could enter. The room smelled
musty; faded chintz draperies covered the windows, which,
Molly realized, were on the front of the building. She walked
over and pulled the curtains back and looked at the street below.
O'Neal spoke a few words to the woman before she left, closing
the door behind her.

"Pull the drapes, please," O'Neal said quietly.

Molly looked at him in surprise, then pulled the draperies
closed. "How long will we stay here?" she asked. "Don't I go
right back?"

"Hopefully."

"What do you mean—hopefully? What are we waiting for?"

"Sit down, both of you," O'Neal said, "and tell me all of
it."

Molly looked at Yuri, who hadn't said a word, and back at O'Neal. "All of what?"

"Why did you think this Abdou was one of my men?"

Molly frowned uncertainly. "I'm not sure why I did. I guess it was just a feeling I had. It seemed like he was staying close to us for a reason."

O'Neal turned to Yuri. "Did you think that?"

He shrugged. "Molly thought it."

"And you didn't?"

"I do not know."

"He was the one with the woman and children," O'Neal said.

"Yes," Molly said. "And he told us he was going to the States to study—at Michigan State."

"Economics," Yuri said.

"When did you get the feeling he might be more than he said he was?" O'Neal asked.

Molly turned to Yuri. "I guess when he didn't get on the plane. Maybe sooner; maybe when we went to the snack bar and he came with us."

"But he never actually said anything to make you think it?" O'Neal persisted.

Molly shook her head. "Nothing that would make you suspicious."

O'Neal turned to Yuri. "What about the other man—the one you said wasn't wearing a suit. You think he was KGB?"

"Yes."

"Why?"

Yuri was standing in a corner, facing the other two. "One gets a feeling. One learns to read the eyes."

"Two of them?" O'Neal asked. "Two KGB?"

"Yuri says they might have been waiting for the Russian delegation to the celebration," Molly put in.

"They arrive this morning?" O'Neal asked Yuri.

"At seven o'clock."

"It seems a little early . . ." O'Neal mused. "Still, one never knows. It could have been."

"It must have been," Molly said. "If they had recognized Yuri, they would have stopped him, wouldn't they?"

"Would they?" O'Neal responded absently.

"Well, wouldn't they have? Why would they let him get away?"

"Why indeed?" O'Neal demanded, looking directly at Yuri. Yuri stared back, his face blank.

"I can think of a few possibilities," O'Neal went on. "One: they were at the airport for the Soviet delegation, as you said, and they knew nothing about Yuri. Two: they were looking for Yuri but your cover worked well enough to fool them. Or three: they knew who he was and chose not to stop him." His eyes were still on Yuri. "Is there any reason why they would have done that?"

Yuri shook his head slowly. "No, I do not think of one."

"In reality," O'Neal said, as if ignoring Yuri's response, "there are only two possibilities. Either they did not recognize him and we got him out safely. Or they knew very well who he is and they let him go."

"But why would they have done that?" Molly asked.

"You tell me," O'Neal said. "But if that's the case, then we've got a whole new ball game."

"You are CIA," Yuri said quietly.

O'Neal hesitated.

Molly turned in surprise. "You told me—"

"I know what I said."

She took an angry step forward. "I asked you twice! Twice I asked you and you told me both times that you weren't!"

"Calm down. And keep your voice quiet. You don't ask a person that kind of question, Molly, if you want an honest answer."

"I wouldn't have come if I'd known that! I wouldn't have—"

"You wouldn't have? Why not? You would have let us take care of it ourselves?"

"Us? *Us?* Who else? Those other two guys—Hartley and Jones—are they CIA, too?"

"It really doesn't matter, does it?"

"It doesn't? The KGB is in this and the CIA is too, and I don't even know who I can trust and who I can't!"

"We don't know the KGB is in this,"

"I can see the look on your face," she said, pointing her finger at him, her voice rising again in anger. "You think they are. You think they let Yuri out knowing full well who he was."

"Don't tell me what I think," O'Neal said harshly.

"I'll tell you more than that!" she said, advancing on him. "You brought me into this, letting me think you were telling me everything, and you were only telling me half!"

"Keep your voice down!"

"I asked you straight out if you were CIA," she whispered

angrily, "and you said you were not. I believed that. How many other lies did you tell me? How much else did you leave out?"

O'Neal stood. "Get your things. We're leaving."

Molly looked at him in confusion, then at Yuri. Yuri hesitated only a moment before hoisting his bag.

"Hurry up," O'Neal urged her impatiently. "Get your stuff. Let's go."

"Where?"

"Out of here." He opened the door and without even looking to see if they were following, he hurried down the stairs. At the landing he paused, looking down the stairwell. Then he took the rest of the steps two at a time, and then another half flight toward the basement to another landing where a dust-laden door led outside at the back of the hotel. He tried the door, but it refused to budge. Impatiently, he took the handle in both hands and tugged until it finally gave way.

Behind the hotel was a narrow lane, bounded on both sides by buildings. Without stopping O'Neal strode to the left until they reached an intersecting lane to the right, and then followed that until they emerged at last onto a busy street. Molly looked about; she assumed they were on the street behind the hotel. "Where now?" she asked.

Ignoring her, O'Neal crossed the street, trailing the others behind, walked briskly to the next corner, and hailed a passing cab. "Trattoria Cervi," he said to the driver.

Trattoria Cervi sat on a narrow side street three blocks from the Trevi Fountain. For that reason, it was open nearly all hours of the day and night, serving the tourists who managed to find it, as well as its customary neighborhood clientele. At this time of day, the sidewalk tables were filled with tourists lingering over their morning coffee and *panini*. Scattered amongst the tourists were elderly neighborhood men who used this most convenient spot as a gathering place to discuss neighborhood politics and to keep a hopeful eye for women passing by in the sunlight, slipless in cotton dresses.

O'Neal shook off the waiter's offer of a table near the sidewalk and headed instead for one at the back, far under a vine-covered arbor. "*Caffè,*" he said, holding up three fingers.

As soon as the waiter had scurried away, O'Neal turned to Yuri. "It's time you leveled with us. Why did you really leave?"

"I told you."

"Artistic freedom? Sorry, I don't buy it."

Yuri looked down at his hands. "It is true."

"Your family is well fixed. You had a good job. Why endanger all that now?"

"It is first chance I had."

"I don't buy it," O'Neal repeated harshly. "There's another reason. As the grandson of Butakov you must have had anything you wanted—including any kind of photographic career you wanted. Ditto for the son of the editor of *Pravda*, if that's who you really are. You could have gotten a cushy job in some research institution where you only had to show up once in a while and collect your pay. And then you could have spent your time doing whatever you wanted, including taking pictures, if that's what turns you on. You certainly are a member of the Party?"

Yuri nodded.

"You could have done that, if you'd wanted 'artistic freedom.' "

Yuri nodded, conceding the point. "That is correct. I could have done that."

"So I don't buy the reasons. The KGB was not there at two o'clock in the morning for a Soviet delegation that wasn't supposed to arrive until seven. They were there for you. Why? And why didn't they stop you?"

"Because they didn't recognize him," Molly said. "You dyed his hair, he was wearing American clothes. And I was there for his cover, wasn't I? We did a good enough job; we fooled them."

O'Neal was shaking his head before she even finished. "Sorry, no. Your cover would have worked for anyone who might have been asked to recall after the fact if Yuri had been at the airport. Or if one of theirs just happened to have been at the airport he probably wouldn't have noticed Yuri. But if they *knew* he was going to be there, and if they knew him by sight, they wouldn't have been fooled. We did not have time to make it that good. And with two Soviets there—and this Abdou, if that's what he was—then they must have known. No, we knew all along that the only way we'd get him out would be if we did it before they found out."

"Of course," Molly said angrily, "of course. There was a great deal you knew all along that you didn't bother to tell me, wasn't there? I talked my fool head off to this guy for nothing."

O'Neal turned his attention to her and was about to say something when out of the corner of his eye he saw the waiter approaching. ". . . and after the Fountain we may as well head over toward the Quirinal, don't you think?" He smiled as the waiter served their coffees. "Would you like something else? How about an omelet?"

Molly shook her head.

"Thank you, then," he said to the waiter. "And thank you both," he added when the waiter had left. "We'll pick something up later. Right now we need to talk uninterrupted. And you're wrong, Molly, you did a good job; you did exactly what we asked you to do. But if the Soviets knew he was at the airport, there was no way we could have sneaked him past them."

"But it looks as if we did," Molly said.

"We got him out, but we did not sneak him past them. They knew what we were doing. They knew so well that they even had your Abdou there."

"He was theirs?" Molly asked.

"He wasn't ours. If he was anything, he was theirs."

"Why did they let me go, then?" Yuri asked.

"You tell me," O'Neal said. "You should know the answer to that better than I."

Yuri leaned back stiffly in his chair, toying with the fork at his place. "I know nothing more than I already told you. I was not lying."

"You may not have been lying, but there is something more than you are telling us."

"I did not go to work for an institute because that was not what I chose to do."

"Meaning?" O'Neal asked, leaning closer to the table.

"I think if one is going to work for an institute one ought to work for them. If one is going to be a photographer, one ought to do that. One ought not to pretend to do one thing while one is really doing the other."

"You may be the only person in the Soviet Union who feels that way," O'Neal snorted.

"Perhaps I am . . . was," Yuri replied coldly.

O'Neal gazed at him, or beyond him for a long moment. Molly took a sip of coffee. Yuri stared defiantly back at O'Neal.

"How much family did you leave back there?" O'Neal asked finally.

"All of them."

"Tell me. Who are they? Are you married?"

"No."

"Okay, and we know about your father and grandfather. What other family?"

"My grandmother . . . but . . . she is in mental institution.

I had sister, but she died at age of eleven. My mother is researcher at Moscow Polytechnic Institute. I have no other relatives. My mother was only child. All my father's family died in siege of Leningrad when my father was quite young."

"So," O'Neal said, removing a piece of lint from his saucer, "only your parents and your maternal grandparents."

"Yes."

"When did you decide to leave?"

"There was no one time. It was gradual."

"What if you don't really like America? What will you do then?"

Yuri shrugged. "I will not have lost anything, will I? I did not like where I was, either."

"But you don't actually expect to like it, do you?" Molly said.

"Why do you say that?" O'Neal said.

"Because of what he said on the plane. Cynical things—about poor people riding in Cadillacs. I don't believe he really thinks things are any better in the West."

"Did you say that?" O'Neal demanded. "Is that how you feel?"

"I have seen schizophrenia on one side," Yuri said slowly. "I am now curious to see it on the other side."

"Curious? *Curious?* Is that why you asked for asylum? Because you were *curious*?"

Yuri stiffened as if he had been slapped. "Life is compromise. You find what you can live with. I want to know if I can live with compromises on your side—and I am well aware there must be some; I am not stupid. I already know I cannot live with ones on other side."

"Great!" O'Neal spat. "Just great. We've gone through this whole goddamned business for your curiosity."

"Not for my curiosity. Not at all. For my life."

O'Neal leaned over the table. "What is that supposed to mean?"

Yuri leaned back in his chair. "Nothing."

"Nothing?" O'Neal pressed. "Nothing? Don't give me that. I brought Molly into this because we thought you were a genuine defector. Yes, I know you don't like that word, but it's about time we stopped pussyfooting around with you. You are not that special here, not to us. We can throw you back to the KGB if we want to, and if you give us enough reason we'll do it and say good riddance. The KGB let you go because they had a reason.

No, Yuri Andreyevich, you would not be the first false defector the KGB sent over. So you'd better open up damned quick, or Molly and I will walk out of this place and let you figure out how to satisfy your curiosity all by yourself."

Yuri stared back at O'Neal defiantly, his eyes angry. Then he shoved his cup and saucer away, stood and looked toward the street. Then, still standing, he looked down at O'Neal, his eyes still angry, but there was something else in them, something Molly could not quite understand. "I have seen things," he said at last. "I have photographed things. They had always assumed I was safe—because of who my grandfather is, and my father— and they did not hide them from me. I have been to Afghanistan and seen things, and now in Dioula. Photographer, you know, is supposed to be invisible. When he is safe person, as I was supposed to be, it is without question, he can take whatever pictures he wishes. Someone, somewhere, looks at them and decides which should be published and which should be destroyed. Photographs, after all, are just . . . raw materials. Someone else decides what they are pictures of and what their importance is."

O'Neal cleared his throat.

Yuri looked first at O'Neal and then at Molly. "I never thought about it one way or another," he said. "It was way world works, I thought; everyone covers his own . . . ass . . . I think you say. Even political parties do it, even countries. It is only logical that government should be shown in best possible light. But in Afghanistan, and even more in Dioula, I began to realize it is more than that. We make reality to be what we want it to be. That is what is called political reality. In Afghanistan we fought for freedom of Afghan people, and yet we did not. In Dioula, we fight against American-backed regime in Rafetna, and yet we are helped by Americans—"

"What?" O'Neal was on his feet.

"Nothing is real, nor what it seems. On both sides, we pretend a reality that does not exist."

"What Americans? What are you talking about?"

"Americans in Dioula."

"Helping the rebels? You saw them?"

"Yes."

O'Neal sat back down. "You took pictures of them?"

"I sent pictures to Moscow, to my superiors, but of course they did not publish them."

"Sit down," O'Neal said.

Yuri Andreyevich remained standing.

"For God's sake, man, sit down!" O'Neal hissed. "Do you want the whole restaurant to notice you?"

Yuri sat.

"On the film you gave us, do you have any more pictures of Americans in the Dioula?"

"I may."

"You may?"

"You must realize, one takes many pictures. They were not there at all times. For that matter, probably even I was not supposed to know about them. But I saw them and I did take pictures from time to time, and send them to Moscow. They publish very few pictures I take."

"I can imagine."

"I take very good photographs," Yuri said defensively.

"But of the wrong things."

Yuri grinned boyishly. It was the first time Molly had seen him look so vulnerable. "Yes," he admitted, "of wrong things sometimes."

"Then why did they let you out?"

"I do not know. It is truth, I do not know."

O'Neal stared at Yuri for a long time in silence. Then he looked at Molly and back again at Yuri. When he spoke finally, his voice was very cold. "You will both stay here. I am going to make a telephone call." He rose abruptly and walked into the restaurant, leaving them staring after him.

7

O'NEAL COULD HEAR THE TELEPHONE RINGING. BE there, he thought, dammit, be there. He looked at his watch—just after eleven Rafetna time. The festivities would be in full swing, the parade set to begin at noon, Bodamwe's biggest national holiday, the Embassy officially closed. The phone clicked in his ear.

"Mr. O'Neal's office," Peggy said. So she'd come into the office after all.

"What are you doing there?" he asked. "I thought you were taking the day off."

"So did I. I got your note. Where are you calling from, anyway?"

"Rome." No point in lying; it was too easy to check. If Peg—or anyone else—was going to try to check.

"Can't you even take a week off without having to call in?"

"Better, probably. Who's in today?"

"Haven't seen much of anyone. Who are you looking for?"

"You haven't seen Hartley?"

"No. You want me to buzz him?"

"No. What about Al Jones?"

"Like I said, Mr. O'Neal, I haven't seen anybody. Oh, yes, I saw Lattimer downstairs. Hey, you know what? He told me—Lattimer did—Sammy's dead."

"Sammy?"

"You know, the cabdriver we use sometimes."

"What happened?"

"Somebody killed him. Robbed and killed him. Right by Independence Square, too. That's how they found him so fast—they were getting ready early this morning for the reviewing stand, and they found him there. His cab was right there, too, but all his money was gone."

"How'd they kill him?"

"Knife. Cut his throat. Pretty grotesque, I think. I always thought Rafetna was safer then Des Moines. I guess you never know."

"I guess not." *Sammy.* His mind was racing. "How much longer do you plan to be there, Peg?"

"Not any longer than I have to. Something I can do for you?"

"No . . . I guess not."

"Look, boss, you call all the way from Rome, you must have had something on your mind."

Sammy. Who? *Who?* "I did, but if no one's around . . . then it doesn't really matter."

"You could leave a message. I might see someone later . . ."

"No, I'm just between planes. Just thought of a couple more things. Nothing important. Have you seen Tom Little?"

"Ha! That's my question. We were going out to Tortun Beach today. He never showed up at my house and he doesn't answer his phone. I thought he might have stopped by here and gotten held up, but there's no sign of him."

O'Neal frowned. "He was there last night when I left. It's not like Tom not to let a person know, is it?"

"All I can say is he's not here today. I've looked all over and I've asked what few people are around. Damned shame, too. It's a perfect day for the beach."

O'Neal's eyes narrowed. Tom Little and Sammy. And who else? He took a breath. "Peg, it looks like you're going to have to do something for me after all."

"Sure. What is it?"

"Get in touch with George Hartley for me, will you? Tell him I've changed hotels. Tell him I'll call him later."

"Changed hotels?"

"He'll understand."

"Um-hmmm." She was too sharp, which was what he liked about her, but she knew better than to ask.

"Catch him as fast as you can, will you?"

"Sure thing. I'll try calling his house, although he's probably gone to the parade."

"And something else. You don't have to mention anything to Al Jones. It won't mean anything to him anyway."

"Sure." She would wonder, he knew. She was just going to have to wonder.

"And one more thing."

"Yes?"

"Where are you going to be at nine o'clock tonight?"

"Where do you want me to be?"

"Somewhere I can reach you."

"Here?"

"Fine."

"That's all?"

"Yes. Thanks. And have a nice holiday." He knew she wouldn't. She would spend the next several hours wondering. "Oh. One more thing."

"Yes?" her voice was wary.

"Give Al a call, will you? Tell him I called. Tell him that you told me about Sammy. And ask him about Tom, but don't tell him I told you to. Just ask him if he happens to know where Tom is. And don't tell him anything about any hotels. Got that?"

"To Mr. Hartley you want me to say that you've changed hotels and you'll call. And nothing about Sammy or Tom. To Mr. Jones you want me to say about Sammy being killed and about Tom not showing up. Right?"

"Right."

She paused just a moment. "Is there anything else I should know?"

"Have a nice holiday. Maybe Tom'll show up after all."

"Thanks."

He hung up and turned away from the telephone. She would do it and she would not ask questions, no matter how curious she got. And in the meantime—he began walking toward the door—in the meantime it was indeed a whole new ball game.

He paused on his way to rejoin the others, turned and hurried back to the phone, fumbling in his pocket for the scrap of paper he knew was there. He pulled it from his pocket and began dialing the number on it. In mid-dial his hand stopped. The number had come from Jones. Al Jones. He held the receiver away from his ear for a moment. Whom could he trust? How did the KGB know? Either Klebanoff was the plant, or someone else had told them. But it was Klebanoff himself who had identified the KGB men. It didn't make sense, unless . . . Slowly he hung up. If Klebanoff was the plant, there was no problem. They would reach home safely; it would be in the KGB's interest that nothing happened. But if the problem was somewhere else, then that would be a different story. Sammy dead. Tom Little disappeared. Maybe the two were connected and maybe not. He'd keep his options open. He would not yet allow himself to think the thought that was seeping into the corners of his mind. He turned away from the phone and started back toward the table.

"Ready to go?" he asked, pulling out his wallet. He laid three bills on the table; then, on second thought, he added a fourth. "This ought to cover it," he said. Yuri looked in surprise at the bills. You've got a lot to learn, O'Neal thought.

"Where are we going?" Molly asked.

Without answering, O'Neal led the way out to the street. Once there, he turned right and walked briskly to the next cross street. Then he turned left and walked halfway down the block before he finally stopped and turned, face to face with Yuri. "Okay, goddammit," he said, "tell me. Who are you really?"

Yuri frowned. "I don't understand."

"Yuri Klebanoff? Grandson of Sergei Butakov? How much longer do you expect us to believe that?"

"I—don't know—" Yuri stammered. "I don't know what you mean."

"The KGB were not at the airport at two o'clock in the morning for a plane that wasn't to come in until seven. You know that and I know that. They were there for you, weren't they?"

"But they did not stop me."

"I noticed."

"You think they knew? You think they want me to . . . to leave?"

"Doesn't it look that way?"

"I suppose it does," Yuri said softly.

"Or maybe they didn't know how to stop him," Molly suggested. "Maybe they wanted to see if he did leave. Or whom he left with."

"How would they even know he was gone?" O'Neal challenged.

"They could have checked my room. They could have found I was gone," Yuri said.

"How would they know to look at the airport?"

"If I was leaving, how else would I get out?"

"As far as they knew, you didn't even have a passport. How could they guess that you'd have gotten one? What good would it do you to go to the airport without a passport?"

"Maybe they didn't guess. Maybe they knew."

"There was no way for them to know, unless you told them yourself."

"Don't be stupid," Yuri said contemptuously. "How many people in your Embassy knew I was there last night?"

"Not that many. We kept it to a minimum for just that reason."

"But nevertheless—you and Hartley and Jones."

"And the taxi driver who took us to the Rafetna Palais," Molly added.

Sammy.

"And the younger man—Thomas Little," Yuri said. "The guards, person who did passport. And Ambassador. Not so few."

Sammy and Tom Little. And Americans in the Dioula. "You know what you're saying?" O'Neal asked.

"I know very well what I say. I also know very well that it was not I who told KGB I was asking for asylum."

"What difference does it make?" Molly asked. "We got out, didn't we?"

"Yes," O'Neal nodded. "We got out of Bodamwe, but if what Yuri wants me to believe is true, we may never get back to the States."

Molly's eyes widened. "Then why didn't they . . . do something . . . there?"

O'Neal didn't even look at her. He was staring at Klebanoff, and Klebanoff's eyes told him that he already knew the answer to that. "Because," O'Neal said softly without taking his eyes from Klebanoff's, "because that might have implicated someone there. If they do it here, it lets someone in Rafetna off the hook."

"Here?" Molly echoed.

O'Neal didn't answer her. "Was there ever a time that you were alone with Thomas Little?" he asked Yuri.

"Yes, of course. When I was writing the paper you asked for. I think you were with Ambassador."

Of course. O'Neal looked at his watch and then at the two people standing before him. He thought again of the phone conversation with Peg. That part was okay; he could leave that for now. "Was there ever a time when you were alone with Alvin Jones?" Even before Yuri responded he knew the answer to that one. "How about George Hartley?"

Yuri thought for a moment. "No," he said finally, "I was not."

Then the damage was done in Rafetna, O'Neal thought, there's no looking back on that. He looked at his watch again. "Let's go," he said.

Almost without thinking, he made his way along the Via del Tritone to where the Via Crispi angles off from it, then followed Crispi northward. He was walking fast, not speaking, his mind almost acting on its own as it sorted through the facts—and the implications—only vaguely aware of his surroundings, or of the other two who hurried to keep up with him. It was not until they'd entered the Pincio that he turned to them.

"Have you been to Rome before?" he asked Molly.

"Only when I was a kid; I hardly remember it."

So much the worse, he thought. He didn't bother to ask Yuri. "Pincio Gardens," he said, waving his hand vaguely. "Plenty of tourists and plenty of Romans around. It's as safe as anywhere right now." His mind was racing now. He needed time to work it out, and he needed space. Molly. *What the hell are you vetting One-to-One people for?* Al Jones had asked. He grinned to himself now. And he'd destroyed his notes of that. He knew, but it would take them time to find it themselves. It was a risk. He let out a quick, short breath. Everything was a risk.

Molly glanced quickly about. A woman dressed entirely in black—probably a grandmother—proudly pushed a baby carriage. In the opposite direction a little boy holding a green balloon tugged impatiently at his father's pant leg while the man remained engrossed in conversation with a priest. A gaggle of tourists strolled toward them, munching on pistachios and strewing the shells behind them. More tourists leaned over the stone railing, taking in the views of the Piazza del Popolo below and the rest of Rome beyond. Everything indeed looked normal and safe. "Who is being protected in Rafetna?" she asked.

"That's the question, isn't it?" O'Neal said.

"You must have an idea," Yuri said.

O'Neal squinted against the summer sun. "For now, Yuri Andreyevich, I am taking you at your word. But I know better than to trust anyone completely. And that," he said, turning to Molly, "is the most important thing you can remember right now." He paused and looked hard at her. "I'm sorry I got you into this, but you're in it and there's no going back."

"I can't just—"

"You haven't a choice," he interrupted. "Neither of us has." He began walking again. As if the thought had just occurred to him, he reached for Molly's bag. "Sorry," he said, "I should have been carrying this for you."

"You have your own," she responded. "I can carry mine."

"Chalk it up to male chauvinism," he said, taking it from her. "Under the circumstances, it's the least I can do. We're going to have to find a place for you two to stay."

"And you?" Yuri asked.

"I'm going to test the waters."

Yuri frowned but said nothing.

"It's Hartley or Jones, isn't it?" Molly asked. "Which one of them is CIA? Or are they both?"

Without answering, O'Neal walked over to a bench and set down his bag and Molly's. "Yuri," he said, "sit here for a while and keep an eye on the bags. I have a couple of things to say to Molly." He didn't even wait for Yuri's response before taking Molly by the elbow and leading her along the path.

"I think he's for real," he said.

"You didn't sound much like it back there."

"The way I baited him? Maybe I didn't. Question everything. That's how you survive."

"Tell me who you think it is."

"I don't know who it is."

"But you have an idea."

"I don't think you were listening. I was serious, Molly. The way you survive is to doubt everybody."

"But one of them is CIA, too. Or are they both?"

"One of them is," he conceded.

"Who?"

"I'm not going to tell you."

"Goddammit it, O'Neal, what do I have to do? We could all be killed and you're still not telling me things!"

He sighed and walked along beside her in silence for a while. "I'm not an ogre, you know," he said at last. "I'm a pretty normal guy with a pretty normal family. I don't go around killing people or doing any of that spy stuff you read about. I collect information; I really don't even do that much collecting—I analyze it mostly. I sit in my office and I read reports and I come to conclusions and I pass them on. Right now we're very interested in the rebels in the Dioula. We've known, but not been able to prove, that the Russians are helping them. If there are Americans there too, that's news that'll blow somebody out of the water. It looks like somebody may not want us to get back with that. Somebody is getting rid of the people who might have heard Yuri talk about it. Somebody is running scared, and because he is, we are, too. Until we know for sure who that somebody is, what I'm trying to tell you, Molly, is the most important thing—the only thing, really. There is no one you can trust. No one. If I tell you who is CIA, what would you do with that? I'll tell you: you would trust him more—or less—than you would if you didn't know. That's not going to help you. No, it's better for you if you don't know, because right now there's no way to tell who the bad guys are. Maybe it's one of them; maybe it's the CIA one and maybe it's not. Maybe it's both of them. Maybe it's neither. Maybe it's nobody; maybe it's all explainable. But if you want my gut feeling, I think we're in trouble.''

O'Neal paused and turned around. Yuri Andreyevich sat stiffly on the bench, out of earshot, watching them. The boy with the green balloon had wandered off by himself and was playing in the gravel at the edge of a footpath.

"We could walk off right now and leave him," O'Neal mused.

"Would you do that?" Molly asked.

"Would you?"

Two nuns swept by and blocked her view of the bench for a moment. "You were right. He can be incredibly arrogant."

"You didn't answer the question."

"You picked me because of who I am, didn't you? Because you knew I wouldn't walk away from a problem. No, I don't like him very much, but I'd have a hard time just leaving him here."

"We picked you because of why I said. In a very limited pool, you were the best choice. As it turned out, a lucky one for us— and for him—but a damned unlucky one for you. Straight truth, Molly: it begins to look very much like somebody wants this defection to fail. On top of that, somebody's afraid of what our friend might have said, or else what he represents. The taxi driver who took you to the Rafetna Palais is dead; Tom Little is missing. Or at least it seems—''

"Oh no, oh God, no! But you don't think—you think they're connected?''

He nodded solemnly.

"That's why you asked Yuri if he'd been alone with Tom Little!''

"That's why." He didn't say more; he could tell by her eyes that she understood the implications. She looked toward Yuri, and then back at O'Neal.

"Then why did you ask if I would walk away and leave him?" she asked softly. "They would kill me either way."

"You never know. Maybe I'm reading more into this than I should. Maybe Tom will turn up."

"But you don't think so."

"I ask myself why the KGB would let Yuri out of Bodamwe, given what he knows and what his pictures might show. I keep coming back to the same thing. Somebody in Rafetna needs protection."

"What about his pictures? When they get developed, won't—"

"What about the pictures?" O'Neal said harshly. "If they're killing people over this, do you think that film is going to get back to Langley? It was probably destroyed before we even left Bodamwe."

"What are you going to do?"

"I have to get some answers."

"They'll kill you, too."

"If I'm guessing right, they'll kill all of us if they get a chance."

"Then why haven't they done it? We've been out in the open since we got to Rome."

O'Neal looked around. An Italian with his arm slung loosely around the shoulders of an overweight American girl ambled down the path. Two businessmen lost in conversation strolled toward the couple. Three somber Japanese stood pointing cameras at the cypresses in the distance. "You're right, and it could be anybody. Unless we lost them." But both Hartley and Jones had known the hotel, or could have found out. "Sammy's death was made to look like a robbery, and Tom's body—if he's dead—hasn't even been found yet. Whoever it is doesn't want what he's doing to be obvious. So I don't think it would be done openly. Whatever they do, it'll be something subtle."

"How do you kill three people and make it look subtle?" Even in the sun she was shivering.

"I've been thinking about that. A terrorist bomb would be a good way."

"That's subtle?"

"The reason is. Anyone would take it for an act of terrorism, not for what it really is."

"I can't believe I'm standing here talking about how I'm going to be killed," Molly said. Yuri was no longer staring at them. He was looking down at the ground.

O'Neal took her arm and began walking slowly back toward Yuri. "We need to split up," he said. "I have things to do, and I can't be dragging you two along. And anyway," he added, talking more slowly, "it'll make it a hell of a lot harder on whoever it is."

"What are you going to do?"

"Find out."

"And where do we go in the meantime?"

"Someplace safe. And you don't know Rome. Is there any place you do know?"

"Yes—"

"Don't tell me," he interrupted. "Go somewhere you will be safe. Don't even tell me where it is; on this one, don't trust even me. Molly"—he stopped walking and pulled her around to look straight at her—"it's your life and his. And whatever it is that he is or has or knows. Are you going to be able to handle that?"

"Do I have a choice?"

"At least let me say I'm sorry I got you into it." He reached into his pocket and brought out a wallet. "One thing you can say about the Company, they can fund you well if they want." He pulled out several large American bills and handed them to her. "And in cash," he added, "no traceable records. I'll create a diversion, and you take him to a place you know well. Stay there with him until you get the all-clear from me. Make it a safe place, Molly, make it a place where you can both hide."

"And not the States."

"For obvious reasons. Keep it in Europe if you can."

"What will the signal be?"

He thought for a few moments. "ABC. America, Britain, Canada. That's simple enough—the good ones are always simple. Look in the classifieds of the *International Herald Tribune*. You ought to be able to get that wherever you are."

She nodded.

" *'Lassie, Come Home,'* the message will say. And it will be signed with two of those letters. The first one stands for an embassy; the second one stands for the country. 'A B' means the American Embassy in Britain; get it?"

She nodded again.

"Just a single letter means that embassy anywhere in the world. So you'll hope that it is just signed *A*, which'll mean any American embassy you can get to. That clear?"

"I think so.

"And if I never see an ad?"

He sighed. "Let's hope you see one." She looked at him for a long moment before he finally reached into a pocket and brought out a pad of paper and a pen. "Whatever you do, don't contact anyone you know—no friends and no relatives. They're not going to understand this, and if you need help, you're going to need more than they can give. I'm also giving you a number to call. Use this one only in case of emergency, or in case the money runs out and you haven't heard. Ask for Cathleen. No matter who answers or what they say, ask for Cathleen. I'm not going to write the name down, only the number. You'll have to remember the name. And remember this, Molly: if something happens, if you have a real emergency, this is going to be the only place you can trust."

She took the paper and folded it carefully.

"And one more thing," he added. "I have to do this; you don't. If it comes down to your life or his, if it comes to that . . . dump him."

She caught her breath but said nothing.

"You understand?"

She nodded.

"You're mighty quiet all of a sudden."

"I'm scared stiff."

"Good girl. Keep it that way. It may be what saves you. He could use a good dose of that himself."

She laughed halfheartedly and he felt relieved. At least she could still recognize humor; she was going to be okay. "I think we'd better get back to him," O'Neal said, "before he begins thinking we're plotting against him."

Yuri stood as they approached. "Let's go," O'Neal said, "we'll work it out as we walk." He bent to pick up his bag and Yuri lifted his own and Molly's. O'Neal shot a glance at her and she grinned; he nodded at her. This guy might make it after all, he was thinking.

"We're going to split up," O'Neal said to Yuri. "I've got work to do and Molly's going to take you to a safe place. We'll walk out of here, get into a cab, and then you two follow my lead. If anybody is tailing us, we're going to lose him. Molly, you go to a train station or the airport or wherever you have to go. Right?"

She nodded.

"Yuri, you follow her. Do what she says. She knows when to contact me, and how." O'Neal took a deep breath and walked a little faster. "If you want to keep yourself safe, you'll do that."

At the street, O'Neal flagged down a cab and opened the passenger side of the front. Yuri and Molly got into the back with their bags. "Colosseum," O'Neal said, and settled back while the driver wove his way through traffic. It's going to work out, he thought. If I can get these two taken care of, I can find out who it is—and why—and then we can put an end to it. He might have felt smug over the way he'd handled her, letting her think she was choosing the place when he knew damn well what she would choose. But there was nothing to feel smug about; he'd gotten himself into a hole, and them, too. And maybe . . . He closed his eyes and tried not to think it was wrong to have given Molly the phone number. And the name.

At busy times, traffic courses around the Roman Colosseum half a dozen vehicles abreast, their speed and proximity defying all but the bravest pedestrians. As their car entered this maelstrom, O'Neal turned to Molly. "When I say so, get out of this cab, grab the nearest empty one and tell him to take you to the Spanish Steps. He'll probably take you to the bottom of them, unlucky for you. When he gets you there, run up the steps— you're young—and grab another cab from the piazza at the top. At this time of day there should be quite a crowd there and you should be able to lose anyone who might have managed to follow you that far. Get out of there fast and go wherever you're going." He paused. "You'll hear from me," he added finally and handed her a wad of Italian lire. Then he turned around and looked out the passenger window, watching for another cab. When he saw an empty one pull up in the traffic alongside, he nodded toward it without even turning around. He called through the open window to the other driver and the driver nodded in return. *"Basta,"* he said to the driver beside him. The man looked at him in surprise. *"Lento,"* O'Neal said, and the driver muttered something, but the taxi slowed down. "Now!" O'Neal said.

Without a word of good-bye, Molly opened her door and stepped out of the cab, reaching for the door of the other taxi. From behind came the irritated blasts of a dozen car horns. She slid over in the seat to make room for Yuri and the bags, and said to the driver, "Spanish Steps, please." The driver nodded without turning around and Molly settled back. "Maybe it'll work," she said to Yuri. He nodded, but his face was turned away as he looked out the back window.

The driver let them out amongst a horde of other vehicles at the Piazza di Spagna. Molly paid him and grabbed her bag from Yuri, but he resisted.

"It's going to be a hard enough climb with one bag," she said. "I'll manage it." She pushed past umbrella-shaded flower stalls and through the crowd without even looking to make sure he was keeping up. They ran up the first flight, then walked the next. Getting a second wind, they pushed their way, running again, up the last flight and she waved to a taxi. Stepping into the cab, she said, "Airport."

"Fiumicino?" the driver asked.

She nodded, still catching her breath.

"Where are we going?" Yuri asked.

She shook her head and he understood. Neither of them spoke again all the way to the airport, each looking out the window, each lost in thought.

At the airport she paid the driver and got out. Yuri followed her through the glass doors. Once inside, she turned to him.

"Athens," she said.

8

IN RAFETNA, AS IN MOST SOVIET EMBASSIES THROUGH-
out the world, the *referentura* was a room within a room,
with heavy sound insulation between the two. Viktor Evchenko pressed the button hidden behind the light fixture outside the unmarked outer door. Within a few moments a buzzer
sounded and the door, which had been tightly locked, opened
to Evchenko's push. He was now in a tiny room similar to a
vestibule with shelves. No papers or briefcases were allowed
into the *referentura*—no notes could be taken of materials
within. Evchenko stood before the peephole of the steel door
that led to the inner, sound-proofed chamber. An armed guard
opened it and Evchenko nodded at him as he passed through.
Now Evchenko stood before a third door; the bottom half
was solid steel and the top half was a heavy metal grille.
Evchenko asked the duty clerk for the morning cables and
the clerk shoved two ledger books toward him under the grille.
One contained the general cables to the Embassy; the other,
slimmer, contained messages to be seen only by members of
the KGB.

Evchenko signed for both ledgers and moved to a cubicle
with just room for a small metal table and a stiff-backed
wooden chair. He eased his bulky frame onto the chair and
lit a cigarette. Then he opened the slimmer ledger first and
read the latest entry. He leaned forward, staring at the bare
wall in front of him. He was thinking of Cherpinsky last
night. Evchenko had returned immediately to the Embassy
residence after meeting with the American. The duty sergeant
had looked mildly surprised when he'd come into the building, as if he hadn't expected anyone back so soon. Evchenko
was almost positive the sergeant had been drinking, but he'd

not said anything. The man had acted sober and that, as any sane man knew, was as much as one could expect. With only a passing nod at the sergeant, he'd taken the stairs two at a time. A dozen strides had brought him to the door of Klebanoff's room and he didn't even hesitate in opening the door. Had he been that certain that the information was correct? Perhaps. In fact, almost certainly yes, although he had not consciously thought of it at the time. He had simply done what any good operations officer would have done in his place: check the contents of the bag before paying the price. He had, of course, found the room empty.

Cherpinsky had been livid and had darted around like an angry badger, trying to place blame, and Gregor Danielovich Bunin's head was on the line. Evchenko had almost felt sorry for Bunin, if indeed anyone could pity such a poor excuse for a man. He would have liked to have seen Bunin squirm for a while, but necessity required that Evchenko lead Cherpinsky off to another room and tell him the truth—or at least the part of the truth Evchenko chose to reveal. That Evchenko had known beforehand that Klebanoff was defecting; that he had had to keep his own counsel on this because someone in Rafetna needed protection. It was obvious that Cherpinsky had been surprised. He'd wanted to ask who it was, but Evchenko didn't give him the opportunity, nor would he have told Cherpinsky if he'd been presumptuous enough to ask. Cherpinsky had run a finger across his thin mustache, but said nothing, and he'd even come perilously close to forgiving Bunin.

The Americans did indeed have Klebanoff and they had taken him to Rome on the three o'clock plane. That part had been just the way the American had said it would be, but that was just the beginning. Evchenko had spent the remainder of the night checking the rest of the contents of the bag. He was no fool.

In Rome, Fiumicino was not the cinch it had once been, and that was where the trouble had started. They should have known that the American agent O'Neal would not be stupid; in fact his own countryman should have know that. For those reasons it had not been as easy as it might have been. He looked again now at the message in the ledger: *Arrived Rome. Lost them in transit. Not at usual American safe house. Using all contacts. Further information would be useful.*

Using all contacts. He almost smiled. Was there someone

in the American Embassy in Rome as well? He had not come up empty-handed in his overnight investigation. We have common interests, the American had said, and he had not been bluffing. Evchenko had heard rumors before, but this was the most solid hint that had ever reached him. The group didn't even have a name that he was aware of, though some of the whisperers referred to it as Phase II. An innocuous enough name. The American would, of course, deny the contact if it came to that. There was little risk on his part, but Evchenko's career could ride on what happened in the next day or so. It was for security's sake, and Evchenko realized the importance of that as well as anyone, but all communications between embassies, even between KGB *rezidents*, had to travel through Moscow. The Americans could communicate directly. It gave a great advantage to them in cases such as this, not only because it took so much less time, but also because denial was so much easier, in case things didn't work out.

In this instance, it was not merely a matter of letting Klebanoff escape, though that was certainly bad enough, but if Phase II, or whatever they were called, were involved, then he had his backside to cover as well. There was no telling who was included, and that was half the power of it. No, there was no getting around it: now that Moscow was aware of the events, he would have to accommodate the American. At least it was not as if he were going against his country's best interests. The fact was, Klebanoff could be a very powerful propaganda weapon in American hands; he wondered if the Americans even realized what they had. Defecting ballerinas and chess champions were one thing—one could expect them to be self-centered. But a defection from the ranks of the *nomenklatura*, who had everything anyone could aspire to, including the best educations and special treatment in all phases of their lives—special stores to shop in, special schools, special travel accommodations, special hospitals and doctors—who had, in short, everything that every Soviet citizen aspired to, was a recognition of a terrible failure. A *shum*. A scandal.

No, he had no choice, and if that happened to serve the purpose of Phase II—well, he would not be concerned about that. One can hardly be held responsible for the actions of organizations that may indeed exist only in the minds of the gossipmongers.

The only bad thing was: he was going to have to talk with the American again. He brushed cigarette ashes off the table and left.

President Wole Akinya was speaking from a platform situated just where the Twenty-fourth of July Street opened onto Independence Square. His imposing six-foot frame was visible to fewer than one-third of the nearly two hundred thousand people gathered at the square, but the loudspeakers ensured that even those who could not see him would be able to hear. He had been a wrestler in his youth and he had retained that proud bearing that marked local wrestling champions; his only concession to age was a pair of wire-rimmed glasses. If he was aware that he was standing less than fifty yards from where a man had been found murdered only hours before, he gave no sign of it, just as he gave no sign at this Independence Day celebration that the fighting in the eastern provinces might endanger the republic. He had been urged by his advisers to wear the traditional robes, both as a reminder of his familial links to tribal leadership and because those robes would further accentuate his size. It was, they told him, not only good politics, but also a kind of intimidation. But instead, he wore a tailored black suit and dark tie. He was the only man on the platform not in traditional garb and the only one in black. Above his head fluttered the fringe of a red-and-yellow-striped awning—the colors of the Bodamwean flag—sheltering Akinya and the other dignitaries from the early afternoon sun. Amidst all the color and pageanty, speaking in the gentle voice that, his people had learned, belied a will of iron, this ramrod figure dressed in black was, unwittingly or not, awesomely intimidating.

Four blocks from the Square an American walked slowly by a shop window. The store was closed for the holiday, but he paused in front to look at the books displayed there. He saw in the glass the reflection of another man, another European as the Bodamweans would say, approaching. He did not look up or in any other way acknowledge the approach of the other man.

"You were telling the truth," the other man said. He lit a cigarette and stared at the books in the store window.

The American didn't even bother to respond.

"However, one cannot raid Fiumicino as one once could. They were very clever—"

The American looked at the other's reflection in the glass. "You lost them," he said, and the anger in his voice was clear.

"We will find them again. We have contacts, of course. But if you know anything that could help find them sooner . . ."

"I can give you the name of the hotel."

"They are not there; it has already been checked."

The American did not ask how they knew. He paused for only a moment. "I'll work on it," he added curtly.

The other man nodded and walked off. The entire exchange had taken less than a minute. There was still no one in sight.

"This country would be a hell of a lot easier," the American grumbled to himself, "if there were public phones."

Edwin Lopes II, called Sonny by everyone who knew him, stepped out of the Embassy, nodded to the Marine guard, shook each leg the way runners do before starting a race, and set off for home. He'd looked at his watch before leaving and it was just after seven. One might have thought that the heat would be diminished by now, but in summer Rome soaked up the sun all day and radiated it into the night. After five years, Sonny Lopes told himself, one ought to have gotten used to it. "Run in the morning," Sheila always said with unassailable logic. But Sonny was not a morning person; he could not function bodily before at least five cups of coffee, a situation that made both morning sex and the morning run beyond the realm of possibility. Besides, it was an excellent way to leave the office behind. His colleagues who drove back and forth to work arrived home more frazzled after negotiating Roman traffic than they had been when they left the office. On the other hand, after a five-mile run, Sonny reached home ready for a quiet walk around the garden, a quick shower, and a smooth drink.

He'd been taking this same route home since the beginning. It never occurred to him to vary it, and he would have resisted the idea if it had been suggested. He knew all the shopkeepers, all the little old grandmothers, even all the stray cats and dogs, after having done the route so long. He was a fixture in their lives as much as they were in his: during the weeks, two years ago, when he'd had to give up running for a while to nurse a badly sprained ankle, his acquaintances along the way worried so much about him that they finally contacted the Embassy. The result had been seven enormous bouquets of flowers.

He was somewhat later than usual this evening, but as he

rounded the second corner he saw Signora Blue sitting in her usual spot in the middle of the sidewalk. That was not her real name, of course; it was the name he had given her because on her traditional widow's black dress she always wore a ceramic pin of cerulean blue. It was as if she were telling the world: I may be a widow and that may in this country relegate me to the background, but I am still an individual. He admired her for that, though he'd never said more than "good evening" to her.

He nodded and smiled as he passed her and she put down her crocheting as she always did and followed him up the street with her eyes until she could no longer see him. "Good evening," she repeated, and smiled to herself. They were the only English words she knew.

As Sonny ran past a narrow doorway in his third mile, a man stepped out as if to jog beside him. Surprised, Sonny turned to look, then stopped in utter astonishment. "Dennis? My God, Dennis." He cleared his throat and spat into the gutter. "You scared the hell out of me!"

"Let's keep going," O'Neal said, walking briskly.

Sonny grabbed his arm, still breathing deeply from the run. "Dennis, what the hell is it?"

"I have to talk to you, Sonny, and it has to be now."

"You can come home with me—My God, it can't be that important. Sheila can throw on a couple more chops."

O'Neal was already shaking his head. "No, nobody can know you talked with me, not even Sheila. Something major is going wrong, Sonny, and I wouldn't have met with you if I could have thought of another way. I need your help. Nobody is going to suspect you—we weren't that close as friends, and anyway nobody will guess I'd turn to the Social Security Attaché. Nobody thinks guys like you know anything."

"You are, aren't you."

It was not a question and O'Neal knew what it meant. He also knew that Sonny didn't actually expect an answer.

"You're wrong, you know," Sonny went on. "It's just because it would be such good deep cover that half the Embassy thinks I am one of you guys. It's only those of you who really are who know for sure that I'm not." He wiped his forehead with the back of his hand, but ignored the rivulets of sweat running down the side of his face. "Look, I've got everything, including practically unlimited travel on Uncle Sam, and no one questions it. It would be perfect. No, the fact is, people do think I am, instead of suspecting the obvious ones, like you. So, what can I do for you?''

"In the first place, I repeat: don't let anybody know you talked to me. That's to keep you alive, Sonny, and I'm not kidding. Remember those old TV movies about some guy getting the plague and anybody who comes in contact with him dies? Well, I've come in contact with someone and they're dropping like flies around him and now I'm bringing you into it. And if the wrong people ever find out that you spoke to me, your life won't be worth shit either.''

"You'd better slow down, Dennis, you've lost me already.''

"Is there somewhere we can talk that's not as public as this?''

Of course. It was almost three years since Dennis had been working in Rome, Lopes thought. And he had never known this neighborhood that well. After running through it for five years, Lopes knew where they could go, and it was only a few blocks away. Strangely, he did not feel frightened. He'd known Dennis only casually back then, though their wives had been better friends. In those days he had only vaguely suspected that Dennis might be CIA, because it was indeed a favorite Embassy game— trying to guess who the spooks were. He'd always thought Dennis was a pretty level-headed guy; if he was running scared now, there must be something very major that was breaking.

9

VLADISLAV BORDOVID SAT MOROSELY ON A STRAIGHT-
backed wooden chair in an anteroom to the second-floor
Kremlin office of the General Secretary of the Communist
Party of the Soviet Union. He was now alone, although six
other men had been sitting in identical chairs at ten-thirty in
the morning. From time to time, one of the guards within the
meeting room had opened one of the tall wooden doors and
announced a name or two and those persons had risen and
entered the meeting room. Sometime later, each had left. It
was now nearly four o'clock in the afternoon, and Bordovid
was the only one remaining. A guard had announced the
lunch break sometime between one and two, but Bordovid
had decided to stay, not daring to take lunch in case they
resumed the meeting early and he would be absent. Now he
was sorry. He hadn't had anything to eat since eight this
morning, and then only a glass of mineral water and a biscuit
left over from yesterday. He had worked through the night,
not even taking time for his usual breakfast at the Center's
basement restaurant.

He looked at his watch and shuffled the folder of papers in
his hand. He should have taken the time to shop yesterday. Except that there had been no time—not for shopping nor for anything else, including eating. It was no wonder that his stomach
was growling. By the time he got out of here, the stores would be
packed and he couldn't even guess how long it would take to find
a doll that drinks and wets its diaper. He knew perfectly well what
Vera was trying to do. She could have gotten the doll for Lina
herself, probably a lot easier than he. And he wouldn't be surprised if she had. But this was her way of rubbing things in. She
would never let him forget his failure, even now that she had a

new husband and her cherished posting in the West. And Lina. What reason had Vera to rub his nose in it, except to win one more victory. As if the victory she had already won weren't the only one that counted.

Galina. She would be four on Monday, and he hadn't seen her in thirteen months. It was hopeless. He'd had one afternoon with her then, playing with her in Gorky Park, treating her to ice cream, and that was all Vera had allowed him. The next day she and her big-shot husband had taken the train to Odessa for the rest of their vacation. And this year she wasn't even coming back, using her pregnancy as an excuse not to travel. He scuffed his foot against the parquet floor. She probably wasn't even pregnant; she probably just needed a reason not to come back this year.

For seven years they had been married, and for seven years he'd heard the same refrain: "Why can't you get posted to the West? Everyone else comes back with such wonderful things, and all we manage to bring back are a few stupid-looking African masks and some silver that is so badly done it could have been made in Tashkent, and I can never find anybody who will pay decent money for such things." Was it his fault he'd been assigned to the KGB's Tenth Department? Because he was fluent in French he'd thought he would be assured of continued assignments in the Fifth Department of the First Chief Directorate, which would mean Western Europe—France, preferably. But no, they'd transferred him to the Tenth—French-speaking Africa. How could he be blamed for that? One might as well ask if it was his fault that his great-grandfather had been an officer in the White Russian Army—a fact that had come to the attention of one of his superiors six years ago and may very well have had to do with his transfer two months later from the Fifth Department to the Tenth. Western Europe might not be the United States, but there were plenty of resalable consumer goods available there.

He'd known when he'd married Vera that his position and his prospects had something to do with her interest in him. That was assumed; one did everything one could to move up or at least to maintain one's position. He'd done exactly the same— she was attractive, educated, her father an officer in the army; everyone had thought they were a good match. Both sets of parents had encouraged the marriage. It was expected that one traded on those things as best one could, but he'd assumed there was also something personal that had attracted her. However, once they were married, things changed: what had looked to her, from the outside, as unimagined privilege now turned to dross as she began to see his limits as compared with the possibilities farther up the ladder.

When Sergei Krivitsky, his superior at his posting to Conakry, in Guinea, had made a play for Vera, Bordovid had been angry but had controlled his rage. After all, one had to be careful about accusing one's superiors. And anyway, Krivitsky's tour in Conakry was almost over. Six months later, as Bordovid had expected, Krivitsky returned to Moscow. Four months after that, Vera received a letter from him; he had been transferred to the Eighth Department and was going to Athens. Within a week, Vera had gone, taking the baby with her. At that time, Galina had been eighteen months old, a blond and pink miracle that still filled Bordovid with awe.

For appearance' sake, Vera remained in Moscow until the divorce went through, a procedure that was complicated not only by the system's reluctance to grant divorces but also by security considerations surrounding the divorce of a KGB officer. Bordovid fully expected to be recalled to Moscow, and he hoped desperately that eventually the true reason for Vera's actions would come to light and his superiors would realize that a change in Bordovid's own posting could save the marriage. But he had never reckoned on Krivitsky, who merely stepped in and announced his intention to marry Vera once the divorce was complete. All obstacles suddenly vanished.

And now his little Lina was to be four, and it was anyone's guess when he would see her next, and what she wanted most in the world was a doll that drank and wet its diaper. Even in the KGB Store Bordovid had never seen such a toy. If he could shop at the Central Committee Store, perhaps there he could find one. If he had access to stores in the West, almost certainly he could find one. He sighed and looked down at his feet and listened to his stomach rumble.

The guard opened the door and nodded at Bordovid, who stood and nervously smoothed his jacket. He ran thin fingers through his pale hair and wondered if he looked as nervous as he felt. Then he walked into the General Secretary's conference room.

It was larger than he had expected, high-ceilinged, carpeted and paneled in wood, and in its center was a long table, polished until it shone. Facing the door, looking sternly down on all the proceedings in this room, was a large oil painting of Lenin. The

General Secretary sat at the head of the table, facing Bordovid as he entered. Valery Sazanov, Bordovid's immediate superior, sat in the middle of the table, to the General Secretary's left. Bordovid stole a glance at Sazanov. Sazanov's left eyelid drooped, a sure sign that he was tired, or frustrated, or—it occurred to Bordovid—afraid. With rising apprehension, Bordovid looked at the other men at the table.

Lieutenant-General Nikolai Demin, Sazanov's superior and Chief of the Tenth Department, also sat on the left-hand side, but closer to General Secretary Kalishev. Bordovid had seen Demin on many occasions, and the man always intimidated him. For one thing, Demin was huge, with hands the size of hams and vast eyebrows that hovered over threatening black eyes. At six feet six, Lieutenant-General Nikolai Demin towered over nearly everyone, and his voice, aggravated from years of shouting, was as rough as a graveled road. In an organization designed for intimidation, Nikolai Demin was master of the art.

The fourth person at the table, sitting to General Secretary Kalishev's immediate right, was General Leonid Morov, Chairman of the KGB. The men, and their order of seating, were not lost on Vladislav Bordovid as he took in the scene. The General Secretary, the Chairman of the KGB, the Chief of the Tenth Department, Sazanov, and Bordovid. The Party, the KGB, and a clear line pointing directly at Bordovid's responsibilities. Even to the most ignorant, it would have been obvious that something was amiss.

Bordovid's eyes returned to Sazanov, who now clearly looked stricken. He decided against looking again at any of the others, in case they should take it for insolence. He was going to have to walk a very careful line, the more so because, as usual, there was too much he didn't yet know.

A chair had been placed for him at Sazanov's left, slightly back from the table, and he took it, careful not to change its position. He opened the file to show he was ready, and glanced down at it as if to make sure it was really there.

"Vladislav Vasilyevich," Demin began, his ragged voice unusually quiet. "Tell us exactly what contact there has been with the station in Rafetna."

"Since . . ." Bordovid began, unsure how much they were asking.

"Since two days ago," Demin said brusquely.

"There has been considerable cable traffic, due to the Independence Day celebration in Rafetna yesterday, for the last several weeks. As you may know—"

Demin cut him off. "We're not interested in that. On the Klebanoff affair is what I meant."

Bordovid cleared his throat. "At five A.M. Moscow time, yesterday, we received a cable from the *Rezident* in Rafetna. It was our first indication of a problem. He—the *Rezident*—had been told by an American counterpart of a possible defection of Yuri Klebanoff. For obvious reasons he took time to confirm that the defection was real—the first indication seemed to verify this. The American made an unusual suggestion . . ." Bordovid paused and glanced around the table. He had no way of knowing what these men had already been told, or what conclusions they had already drawn. "Our representative—"

"Evchenko," Demin said.

"Just so, Viktor Evchenko. It was obviously a time for caution. The American seemed to be insinuating that there was a connection between the services that Evchenko should be aware of." Bordovid paused, mentally reviewing what he had just said, and then went on, convinced he was still straddling the line. "As you know, it takes a certain amount of time for the cable traffic to be coded and sent and decoded at this end—even highest-priority items. Evchenko, knowing this, and also knowing that time was important, went himself to the airport, with backup, of course, to check out the information he had received. Having been warned that arrest in Rafetna would prove disastrous, he stopped short of intercepting the defector, but he did verify the information that he had received." Bordovid cleared his throat. "If I may make comment here . . ."

The men on both sides of the table turned to the General Secretary, who nodded. Bordovid continued. "We all know that one always treats a contact with one's opposite number in a very cautious way. Although the providing of sensitive information to such a person is a way of proving one's good intention, at this point there was no way for Evchenko to know what the American counterpart had in mind, but as you can imagine, there were some very interesting possibilities." Bordovid cleared his throat again, and eyed the bottle of mineral water that stood beside Sazanov's place. He wondered if it would be considered impertinent to ask for a drink.

"That is one of the reasons," he went on, "that Evchenko did no more than verify the information he had been given. After verifying that Klebanoff left, he returned to the *referentura* and sent a further message. This one confirmed the flight, gave the flight number and the scheduled time of arrival in Rome. At that time, he assumed that his role in the operation was finished. The defector had left Rafetna and he had passed all pertinent information on to us." He brought himself up short. *Shit*, he thought. It had been good right up until the end. He took a deep breath, hoping that no one had caught what he had said.

But it was a short-lived hope. With narrowed eyes, Demin asked, "All pertinent information? He made a report on the girl that accompanied Klebanoff?"

"Yes," Bordovid said.

"And?"

"She is an employee of an American so-called aid organization. We always assume those people are CIA," he said off-handedly.

"Background?"

"We've run a check on her. She was also in the Peace Corps. Another CIA front."

"Where?"

"Central African Republic, two years ago."

Lieutenant General Demin's eyes bored into Vladislav Bordovid's. "But the plane went to Rome. Does she have connections in Rome?"

"Not that we have been able to determine."

"But she dropped out of sight in Rome."

"Yes . . ." It would be better to volunteer it than to have it dragged out of him. No matter how much he'd like to mess Krivitsky up, it would be foolhardy to stall further if it was to be at his own expense. Perhaps he had delayed enough already so that Krivitsky would find it impossible to trace them. A black mark against Vera's husband. He restrained himself from smiling. "It seems likely in a case like this that a person, especially a trained agent, will go to ground."

"That's just the point, isn't it?" Demin asked impatiently. "If she can't get back to the States, then what will she do?"

"That is what I was trying to tell you," Bordovid said, still not smiling, but pleased with himself that he had made it look as if Demin were impeding his report. "We recently received the information that she spent some years of her youth abroad, in Greece. We suspect that she may have gone to Athens."

"How long have you known that?" Demin demanded.

"Just since this morning. It is fresh information." It had come to him yesterday, through a friend who owed him a favor. They would not know how to trace it, and would therefore have to take his word on how long he'd known.

"Athens," Demin said. "If you will excuse me a moment," he said to the General Secretary.

Kalishev nodded, and then spoke for the first time since Bordovid had entered the room. "Is there more to your report, Vladislav Vasilyevich?"

"No, Comrade General Secretary," Bordovid said.

"Then thank you very much."

Bordovid rose and left the room, preceded by Lieutenant-General Demin, who hurried off down the long hall. Bordovid walked more slowly, replaying the scene in his head. It occurred to him that Chairman Morov had said nothing during the whole time. Even Kalishev had spoken, but not Morov. He wondered what that meant. But as far as his own performance was concerned, he was satisfied. He had presented everything in the best light possible. It was not his fault that the people in Rome hadn't been able to handle the rest. And then he smiled to himself. Sergei Bogdanovich Krivitsky, he said to himself, go fuck yourself. I don't care if you never find them. Serve you right.

But he couldn't help wondering why it seemed that there was more than met the eye here. The Party never liked it when one of its own defected, especially one of the children of the New Class, who ought to be more grateful. But he'd seen defections before, if not as intimately, and there was something else going on this time. Two of the other men who'd been waiting outside the conference room were GRU, he knew that. He wondered what "the Neighbors," as the KGB and the GRU politely if distantly called each other, had to do with this. His own superior, Valery Ivanovich Sazanov, had mentioned Phase II and it was not the first time Bordovid had heard that term, though he'd never put much stock in its existence. But from what he'd heard, Phase II, if it did exist, had connections in the military, which might explain why GRU men had been brought in for questioning. And it might also explain why his superior had looked so stricken. Bordovid caught his breath. If there really was such an organization, and if this defection had anything to do with it, they could all be dragged down by it.

He walked on determinedly. He would not think of that. He would leave right now and go back to the Center, to the KGB Club in Building 12, and perhaps among all the other imported things there he would find the doll. In the meantime, Vera's second husband was about to be pulled in the stew. And if it really was the Army, if the crocodile really had slipped its chain, then God help them all.

Colonel Boris Nikolayevich Travkin returned to his desk, checking his watch. It had been almost three hours since he'd left the Secretary General's meeting room. He had returned immediately to his office, completely satisfied with himself. He had looked Kalishev directly in the face and said that he had no knowledge of what the American CIA person could have been talking about. There were no joint operations between the GRU and the CIA in Africa—or anywhere else—at the moment. He would certainly know, if there had been. Among all the questions, there had been no reference, not even an oblique one, to Phase II. In this meeting, the one with Baklanov whom he had just left, it had been the same. Though rumors had come to Travkin's ears, he ignored them. There were always rumors, he held. That was one thing that had not changed since the Revolution. He never said that openly, but anyone who had half a brain knew it. In any bureaucracy there were bound to be rumors. One did not give them currency by repeating them. He had always taken that stand, and been respected for it. In return, he had learned more than his share of secrets. People trusted him because they thought he never repeated a confidence.

It was nearly five now. He could put in another hour or so at his desk and then leave. As principal aide to Colonel General Baklanov, Chief of the Fourth—African—Directorate of the GRU, he had plenty of work to do. Baklanov was nearly seventy and maintained the position mostly for the prestige it gave him, but he did little real work. Everything that went to or came from Baklanov's office moved across Travkin's desk. It was an ideal situation.

Travkin pulled his chair out and sat down, noticing that an additional stack of papers had been placed in the center of the desk. Then he noticed something else. At the near right-hand corner of his desk, placed as if left there after perusal of a report, was a single rubber band. Travkin picked it up, rolled it between his thumb and middle finger for a moment, and then deposited it in the desk's middle drawer. Then he rose and shoved the chair back close to the desk, without even having glanced at the new stack of papers. The rubber band, lying there as if innocently placed, was a signal more agitating than either of the meetings had been.

Travkin rode the elevator to the main floor of the nine-story building that he and his colleagues called the Aquarium, passed through the electronic inspection equipment, submitted to the same hand search that everyone, including the GRU's chief, underwent on entering or leaving the building, and walked out into the pale sunlight. He nodded to the old men sitting on scattered benches as he always did. These pensioners would notice nothing different, would have nothing to report. He walked along the narrow lane beside the Institute of Cosmic Biology, and out, finally, at the edge of the Khodina Airfield. Another five minutes and he hailed a taxi, giving an address on Kitayskiy Proyezd. Once there, however, he didn't enter the building. Instead, he walked toward the river and into the park.

He bought an ice cream from a sidewalk vendor and walked slowly along, careful not to let the ice cream drip on his dark-blue suit. Ahead of him, two little girls in pale summer dresses skipped along the walk, holding hands. The fluffy white bows at the crowns of their heads bobbed in unison as they skipped. He smiled in spite of himself. An ice-cream treat, a reminder of childish happiness—what else could a man ask? He knew the answer to that: maintaining things the way they were. One did not step off into the abyss if one didn't have to. Life had been good to him and he wanted the same for his children and grandchildren. It was the best of reasons—to leave to one's grandchildren all the good things in life that one cherished.

He walked for almost half an hour, had doubled back twice and was satisfied that he was not being tailed. He turned a corner and went a few blocks, then turned another corner and walked to the end of the block. He glanced up as he neared the corner and saw the detergent box placed in the second-story window. He nodded to himself: it was so innocent. An old man could be forgiven his eccentricities. If he misplaced his box of detergent, leaving it in the window occasionally instead of putting it back in the closet where it belonged, who was to complain?

Travkin mounted the flight of stairs two at a time and knocked at the door to the left. He waited but heard nothing from within and raised his hand to knock again, but just then the door opened a few inches. Kozlov peered out, his eyeglasses sliding down the length of his bulbous nose. Seeing Travkin, he grunted approval and opened the door further. A record player in the sitting room was playing Tchaikovsky, loudly.

"You took long enough," Kozlov complained when he had closed the door. He was dressed in pajamas, and through an open door Travkin could see a rumpled bed. He wondered if Kozlov was sick again.

"I was in a meeting with Baklanov. The dogs have howled at last. Kalishev is calling in everybody who has anything to do with Bodamwe, or even with Africa. I was with them for an hour. Then, of course, Baklanov had to know what the meeting was about."

"How much does Kalishev know?"

"From me—nothing. From his questions I would gather that he still knows very little. Maybe he's heard rumors, but he knows nothing for certain. Even the rumors never have had any names attached."

"You're sure of that?"

"As sure as one can be. I make it my business to hear most of the rumors."

Kozlov shook his head. "I have never understood why there are any rumors at all. Who is talking?"

"It could be the Americans, you know."

"No, it comes from within our group. It has to."

"People talk. People have always talked; it's the Russian essence to bare one's soul. With a few drinks under the belt, who knows?"

Kozlov turned away in disgust. He walked to the small kitchen table and sat down. A knife lay on the table, amid crumbs of bread and cheese. "Don't waste my time with that line; that's the one you give other people."

Travkin sat on the other side of the table, unbuttoning his jacket. The room was stifling, and still Kozlov kept the windows shut tight. "It works beautifully. You know perfectly well there are always rumors. No one places any more credence in this one than in any of the others. How many times in the last months have you heard that Kalishev was almost out? Or that he was ill, because someone hadn't seen him for a day or two? If one hides one's rumor behind all the others, no one pays it any attention."

"They will pay attention if that Klebanoff upstart gets into the wrong hands."

"He already *is* into the wrong hands."

Kozlov nodded, as if his point were proven.

"He is still seen by the Americans as only a defector. Maybe he doesn't even realize what he has."

"What are you doing about it?" Kozlov asked.

"My job. Burying our group so well no one knows it exists. It's not up to me to dispose of Klebanoff as well, is it?"

Kozlov shook his head. He picked at the crumbs of bread, wetting his index finger and dabbing them up, placing them on his tongue. "That is being taken care of."

"By our people?"

"By whoever can."

"You're going to depend on the Neighbors for this?" The question sounded more like an accusation than Travkin intended.

"Your friends in the KGB have reason to be embarrassed. It was their fault he got away. They may not know what damage he can do, but they still have that responsibility and they don't take it lightly. They are going all out for him. I hear they think he's gone to Athens."

Travkin would have liked to know where he had heard that—Travkin hadn't known it. For a man who apparently hadn't left his rooms all day, Kozlov stayed on top of things. "We have men in Athens."

Kozlov nodded. "And so does the American contingent. We are not lacking for manpower."

"Then you are satisfied that he will be found and disposed of."

With fat thumb and forefinger Kozlov placed a crumb of cheese on his tongue. "He will be disposed of; you can count on that. And further, you can be assured that by the time General Secretary Kalishev decides what to do about it, it will be too late. We will do whatever is required." He seemed to be sitting straighter in the chair and his voice was as firm as ever. It was suddenly easy for Travkin to remember that this overweight man in pajamas, picking at crumbs of bread and cheese, had once been a general of the Soviet Army and was still very much in control. "What I want you to tell me is exactly what Kalishev asked you and what you told him in response," Kozlov said.

Travkin nodded and proceeded to recount in detail the transactions of the meeting with the General Secretary.

Viktor Evchenko stood at the window, gazing out over the darkening city. The gold of the setting sun had turned to a purple haze and that color now warmed the white and gray limestone of the city in response. It would be quite beautiful here, he thought, if it weren't so damned hot. Back home in Leningrad the sailors used to say that a red sunset meant fair weather for the day to come, but here that old saying meant nothing. It would rain tomorrow as surely as it would be hot; and then the sun would come out and steam the city until it seemed that the Christian myth of hell might indeed be a reality. The Africans would go about their business, ignoring the weather, but the whites would suffocate one more day, and tick off one more numeral on the calendar of the assignment to Rafetna.

And somewhere, he thought, bringing himself back from his reverie, this woman Molly Davison and the defector Yuri Klebanoff are hiding and someone is going to find them. It was not his worry now, thank the Fates. Let the people in Moscow worry about it. He tapped his cigarette lightly against the window to knock off the ash. He could imagine that in Moscow the tangled threads had only begun to be unknotted.

It had already occurred to him that the American could have bungled. *We have interests in common,* he'd said, as if Evchenko should have known. And it had struck Evchenko like a hot iron across the chest: perhaps he should have known. Or perhaps it was the American who was wrong, a more likely mistake. From the start, the Organs of Internal Security had been given publicity. Their role was to prevent the collapse of the Soviet Union from within, and the mere public knowledge of their existence was a powerful deterrent. Military intelligence, on the other hand—the GRU—remained shadowy. Its responsibility was to prevent collapse of the Soviet Union from without, and because of its extremely secretive nature, many of its accomplishments were credited to the more well-known KGB. Though each group called the other "the Neighbors," each one steered a wide path around the other. Each group hated the other. Nevertheless, the chief of the GRU was always a KGB general. It was the only way that the Party and the KGB could maintain control over the Army, the third and strongest element of the troika that ran the Soviet government, the group that the other two called "the crocodile," and whom they had, out of self-defense, to keep tightly chained.

It would have been so like the Americans to have confused them, so like them to think that a hint dropped to one was as good as a hint dropped to the other. As if the two groups that even the few clean Embassy personnel lumped together as "the Vikings" or "the savages" were not entirely separate, as if they ever communicated with one another or shared intelligence. It was a way of keeping things under control, because neither group ever knew what the other was reporting—separate organizations, separate codes, separate reporting channels, even separate communications hardware. The separate reports came together only at the highest levels. It was one more way of maintaining iron control, although Evchenko had always suspected that men who were truly bent on circumventing the system would find a way to do so. On the other hand, a system like that, designed to deter renegade activity, also made it just as difficult to assess blame, because there was so rarely the opportunity to take independent action.

And therefore, whatever the American's actions meant, at least he, Viktor Ivanovich Evchenko, was not to blame. He had done the right thing from the start. Klebanoff may have been his responsibility, but he could justify his actions on the basis of what the American had told him. A good operations officer would pass the information back to Moscow, as he had done. If the rumors were true, there would be demands and explanations and recriminations going all the way up to the Politburo. The Army's leash would be tightened; heads would roll in the GRU. And Klebanoff was a dead man, no matter how well-connected he might be. He could not be allowed to defect with impunity; even bringing him back for trial would be unacceptable.

He wondered how the Americans would handle their own. As usual, American politics were an enigma. Americans didn't seem to care about what their government did, as long as it could be justified by their own peculiar moral code. Or as long as the public could pretend that its government was doing nothing at all. Americans lived in a world of plastic and dreams. They knew nothing of the real world and they cared for nothing beyond the fad of the moment. *Nekulturnye*, Evchenko suspected. All they cared about was making money and watching television. He'd seen American television once, and it was definitely *nekulturnye*.

In the meantime, Evchenko had positioned himself. He'd passed everything on; let the men in Moscow sort it all out. That was their job, after all. When he was a child, during the siege of Leningrad, his mother used to gather roots and nettles, leaves and scrapings of bark; once she even cut up a shoe she'd found somewhere and thrown it in. He'd stand on a chair and watch the pot boil, wondering what the stew would taste like this time. Intelligence was like that, he knew. It was nothing more than putting together everything that could be found and then seeing what it tasted like, or smelled like. Or felt like. And, in the end, it was easier being one of the ones who provided the nettles than one of the ones who decided what kind of stew it was.

* * *

In McLean, Virginia, Cathy O'Neal opened the door to the basement stairs and called down into the semidarkness, "Two minutes!"

A disinterested voice floated up from below. "Yeah."

"I mean it, Jason."

"I said I'm comin', Ma. Jeez!"

She smiled and shook her head. Who could blame him? Who wouldn't rather mess around with a computer on a rainy summer day than go to the orthodontist?

She walked toward the kitchen to get her purse, but paused in the hall as the doorbell rang. Don't let it be one of the kids, she thought, it's hard enough to get him to go the way it is.

She opened the door and was surprised to see Glenn Pastrella standing there, and another man she didn't recognize. Dennis had worked with Glenn in Rome . . . Then she realized and stepped back, her hand going to her mouth in horror. "Oh, God, no," she whispered.

Jason O'Neal came stomping up the stairs, grumbling about having to go to the dentist. As he rounded the corner, he stopped in his tracks. Mr. Pastrella and another man he didn't recognize were standing in the foyer, and Mr. Pastrella had his arms around Jason's mother. And she was crying.

10

YURI KLEBANOFF SAT ON ONE OF THE TWIN BEDS
with his legs outstretched and tried to read the book Molly
had lent him, though he thought it was stupid. It only confirmed what he'd suspected all along: that Americans were
less cultured than most Russians thought. If a well-educated
person like Molly could waste her time on a book like this,
a book about some crazy plot to blow up the Parthenon, when
any thinking person could just look out the window and see
quite well that the Parthenon had not been blown up in recent
times, then obviously the culture level in America was not as
high as he had thought. And that, somehow, gave him a per-
verse sort of pleasure. He supposed, to give the Americans
their due, that there were people in the Soviet Union who
read foolish things, too, but certainly everyone he knew read
books that made one think, or at least elevated the mind. He
failed to see how the mind could be elevated by this kind of
drivel.

He looked at his watch and wondered how much longer
Molly would be. She had the idea that it was not safe for him
on the streets of Athens, as if there might be posters mounted
everywhere with his picture on them. He knew perfectly well
that this was not the case, but he supposed she was wise to
be cautious. The first thing she had done on arriving in Greece
was to buy a pair of scissors and cut her shoulder-length
wheat-colored hair until it was as short as a boy's. He had to
admit that it made her look very different. One noticed her
eyes more—wide and blue, the color of the summer sky. His
own hair was still that strange red color that had been washed
into it at the American Embassy in Rafetna.

Because of her caution, he sat cooped up in this hotel room

and she went out once or twice a day to purchase food and English-language newspapers. She spoke Greek—not much, she insisted, but well enough to get by—which was more than he did. So it did make sense that she should be the one to go out, though he was getting very tired of this room. And it was hot. But at least the heat was dry here, much like in Dioula, and therefore bearable.

He closed his eyes. The city noises filtered in through the half-opened balcony door. That the room should have a balcony was a pleasant surprise. It at least allowed him a chance to step out and look up at blue sky . . .

There was a noise, not a street noise, but like something in the room. He opened his eyes and looked to his left. The doorknob was turning slowly. Automatically he hitched himself up straighter on the bed. He didn't need to look at his watch again to know that it was not the right time of day for the maid. His eyes flicked to the chain lock, and he realized that he had forgotten to attach it again when Molly went out. She always reminded him and he always did it. Except this time. The door was locked, but not chained. If whoever was outside was good enough, they would be able to get in without difficulty. Even if the chain were fastened they would still be able to do it; they would just make more noise in the process. He'd heard the whisperings when he lived in Moscow. When he was a student, an economics professor, a Jew, had been in the habit of criticizing the government quite brazenly in class. Eventually someone had come in the night and pounded on his door and led the man away, his frightened wife cowering and crying in a corner of the apartment. A good friend of Yuri's had lived across the hall and had recounted the story the next day over tea. It had been foolish of the professor to have been so outspoken, everyone agreed. Yuri had wondered if more would have been said if he hadn't been there. There had often been times when he had wondered what would have been said if he hadn't been present. Everyone knew of someone, or even more than one, who had heard that awful pounding on the door in the night. Yuri had always supposed that if such things happened in the West, they would be a little more subtle. They would probably force the door, he imagined, without the pounding.

He eased his legs over the side of the bed, hoping the old springs would not broadcast his movement. His back to the wall, he moved sideways toward the open balcony door. The

knob had stopped moving and there was a curious, soft clicking sound. He rounded the corner of the door and slid outside. The balcony was narrow and perhaps two meters long.
He stood against the wall of the building and tried to assess
his options. The edge of the next balcony was almost two
meters away; he doubted that he would be able to jump that
far. And even if he did, there was no way of knowing that
the door of that room would be unlocked.

From inside the room he could hear a gentle creak and at
first nothing, then a whispered voice. He flattened himself
against the wall, then realized how foolish that was; surely
they would look out here. He eyed the next balcony again,
and the one below, which was even farther away, but a drop
down instead of a leap across. But the balcony below was
littered with chairs, and he would have little chance of jumping down there without being heard. He had no choice; he
had to try going across.

Quickly he climbed the railing, perched precariously on it
for a moment judging the distance, and then he leapt. His
foot caught the very edge of the balcony and glanced off. His
outstretched hands grabbed the metal railing and clung to it,
his body hanging below. The railing shuddered with his
weight, but held. His whole weight on his arms, he pulled
himself up and over the railing. He had made it.

He looked back. They had not come onto the balcony yet—
of course, he realized now, they would check the bathroom
first. In one quick movement he reached for the door, but it
was locked. There was no time now; they would be looking
out at any moment. He stepped to the far side of the balcony
and climbed over the railing, working his hands down the
metal bars until he was clinging to the surface of the floor of
the balcony, his hands hidden by a flowerpot. If he had
guessed right, from their angle of vision on the next balcony
they would not be able to see him hanging here. If only he
could hang on until they had gone. Even as he thought that,
he heard the voices more clearly, and he knew they must have
stepped onto the balcony next door.

"Where are they, then?" one of the voices said. The man
was speaking in Russian.

"Obviously not here," said the other.

"Sightseeing?" the first one said, his voice muffled, as if
he had turned away. "Would they do that? Maybe they have
gone to her embassy. Wouldn't that be convenient?"

"Their luggage is in the room. It is clear that they will return," the other said.

"Then we will wait for them."

Yuri heard the sound of scuffling feet and the balcony door was closed and latched. His hands were going numb and he did not know if his arms had the strength to pull his body back up to the balcony. He looked down at the balcony below, and this one was empty of chairs. He gauged the angle and swung his body forward as he let go so that he would land on the balcony and not on the railing. He tried the door and found it latched, but now he was not so worried about the noise and he forced the door open, walked through the darkened and empty room and almost out into the hall before it occurred to him to stop and think. He was on the floor below their room; it was possible that there were others somewhere in the hotel. One of the men had said "Where are they?" *They.* The men were looking for Molly as well as for him. And that meant they must not have found or followed her. He was going to have to find her before she walked into this trap. But how could he do that? He didn't even know where she had gone, and to stay around the hotel would only advertise his presence in case there were lookouts posted at the entrance. But he would have to get out of this room before its occupants returned. Slowly he opened the door and peered out. There was no one in sight.

Molly shifted the string bag to her other hand and pressed the fourth-floor button on the elevator board. She could not blame Yuri for his frustation at having to stay in the room all the time, yet she couldn't quite bring herself to let him come out. Alone, she could blend in, but the two of them would be a different matter. It was definitely too risky. He had been angry at her insistence that he stay in the hotel, this morning particularly; perhaps it wouldn't pose too great a danger for him to go out at night, when it was dark. She'd think about that; she'd think about taking him out tonight. He certainly deserved it. He'd been stuck in the room for almost three days now. It couldn't be very enjoyable, especially in this heat.

He had not been as difficult as she had feared. He seemed to enjoy teasing her, and she gave him wide latitude with that. There was definitely an edge in his taunts, but she suspected that in the same situation she'd also be feeling frustrated and unsure. Other than that, he communicated very little. Whatever was going on in his mind he was keeping to himself. Yes, he deserved to get out; and it might loosen him up.

The elevator stopped and she stepped out. No one in the hall—good. She walked to the door and knocked twice. She heard the springs on the bed creak as he got up, and she felt the vibrations of his feet on the old floor. He unlocked the door and stepped aside as he opened it and she entered. She was in the room and the door was closed behind her before she realized that someone else was there. And then she turned to Yuri and her face fell. It was not Yuri at all; he was nowhere in sight.

"Where is he?" asked the man who was still seated.

"Who?"

"You know who I mean. Where?"

She looked from one man to the other. Where *was* he? "I don't know who you're talking about," she said, trying to make her voice sound unconcerned.

"Don't play games. You are registered as two. Molly Davison and Thomas Little. They have seen your passports downstairs. Where is this 'Thomas Little'?"

They had not found him. Surely they had searched the place. Where, then, had he gone? "He went to the American Embassy."

The man who had opened the door smiled. He had already locked the door behind her. "That much I doubt," he said.

They both spoke English with accents—Russians, she guessed.

"Doubt it if you like," she said archly, "but that's where he went."

"In that case," the seated man said, "we shall know soon enough. You might as well sit down, Miss Davison," he added, letting her see the handgun that he pulled from his jacket pocket, "because we shall just have to wait for him." There was a silencer on the gun.

She looked distractedly around, lowered the bag to the floor, and sat down as far from the two men as she could manage. Yuri must have gone out, against all her orders. She wondered how soon he would come back. Then, panic still rising, she wondered what they would do with her if he didn't come back.

Yuri looked at his watch. Something was wrong. She had not returned, and it was long past time. Unless . . . unless he had missed her. Unless, for example, she had been on her way up the elevator as he sneaked down the stairs. He had been afraid to take the elevator, afraid of who else might be there when the doors opened. The stairs had been a better gamble; he could see who was coming up or down. He could turn and run if he had to. In an elevator, he could be caught like a fox in a trap.

He was standing now in a shop across the street from the hotel. He had noticed it on his third time past. At first he'd walked slowly down the street and then back, watching for her, always watching for her. On his first pass, he'd seen a little group of tables sitting under an awning and it had made him think of Rome. He had just about decided that he could probably manage to order a coffee—surely if he spoke English slowly and clearly they would understand him—but then he realized that he had no money to pay with. She had the money; he had seen O'Neal give her a whole wad of American bills and she had changed some to Greek at the airport, but it had not occurred to either of them that he should have any. He almost certainly had some Bodamwean currency in his pocket, but that was not going to do him any good. He didn't even know where one could go to change money—a bank probably. Would he recognize a bank if he saw one? He didn't know the word for bank in Greek, nor any other words in Greek for that matter, and anyway, the small amount of Bodamwean currency he had would be of little use. He wondered how many rubles he had, and he wondered if anyone would be suspicious if he tried to change them.

This shop was apparently something for tourists. It made him think of the hard-currency shops in Moscow, which, because of his father and grandfather, he'd been able to patronize. The difference was that here everything was for tourists; in the hard-currency shops, only some things were. This shop made a good place to wait, however, because he could look at these things indefinitely and not be bothered. It was curious, however; he had never been in a store where the customers were allowed to handle the merchandise as much as they could here, except the most modern of food stores in Moscow. He wondered how they could control theft. There were a lot of things he was going to have to learn about the West. But, of course, America would be different. Everyone knew what terrible crime rates they had there. In American stores the customers wouldn't be able to touch the merchandise until they purchased it, just like in Soviet stores. That was, after all, the more logical way of doing things. It just went to show how backward a country Greece must be. Still, there was much here to impress him—the number of cars on the street, for example.

He looked at his watch again. Something was definitely wrong. It was more than two hours since she had left the hotel, almost an hour since he had gotten away. She had never been gone half this long before. Something must have happened to her on the street. Or else she had gotten back to the room without his having intercepted her. If that was the case, they had her and they would be waiting for him. He was going to have to find out.

He closed his eyes and tried to think. He couldn't go back, and he knew no one else to send. But he could phone. If he had money, he could phone. Would they answer the telephone? If she was not there, almost certainly not. But if she was there . . . if she was there they would make her answer, if only to make everything seem normal. And if she did answer, they would be listening to every word. He looked at the hotel across the street. Their room was on the back side. He had no money in a strange city where he didn't know the language or the customs or whom he could ask for help. He was going to have to try something.

His eye caught on a blouse hanging from the ceiling, white cotton with blue embroidery. It was the sort of thing that a member of the Moiseyev might wear for a performance. He had even seen an occasional university student dressed in a similar blouse, as if trying to look like a peasant, though why anyone would want to look like a peasant was beyond his understanding. He reached up and took down the blouse, hanger and all, and looked at it more closely. The plan was still forming in his mind. *You make a very believable American,* she had said, and he hoped now that she hadn't just been trying to make him feel at ease. He had believed it then, because he hadn't known her. Now he realized that it might not have been the truth.

Nearby, three girls, almost certainly Americans, were trying to choose woven shoulder bags. They laughed and teased among themselves as each tried one and then another bag. This was going to have to be good, he thought, this was going to have to be very good.

"Excuse me," he said, holding the blouse and walking toward the girls, "do you like?"

They looked at him in surprise for a moment before the tallest of them spoke. "It's very nice." She tossed her long blond hair back and he knew somehow that she was meant to notice how pretty it was. And it was pretty.

"It is for my sister," he said to the blonde. "She is about your size. Would this fit, do you think?" He held it up again.

"For your sister?" the blonde asked.

"Yes."

"Sure," one of the others said. She was smaller, very attractive in the face, more attractive than the blonde, who, besides her hair, was not all that good-looking, he had decided.

"I want to buy present," he said, still holding the blouse uncertainly.

"It's very nice, very pretty," the third girl said. She had short dark hair, cut much like Molly's was now. "You're not an American, are you?"

"Yes, I am."

"No." The small one was shaking her head. "You can't be."

"But I am." Had Molly been lying then, to make him feel better? Did he really look so much like a foreigner?

"But your accent . . ."

He laughed, relieved. "Oh, certainly. I was not born in United States, if that is what you mean. But I am citizen now."

"Then where were you born?" the blonde asked, tilting her head. Her hair fell in waves over her shoulders. "I love the accent."

He smiled slyly. "Guess."

"Not French," the blonde said.

"No," the short-haired one said, "it's eastern European, isn't it? Czech? Polish? It's not Russian?"

He smiled broadly. "You are correct. I am Polish."

"Really?" asked the pretty one. "Are you really?"

"Why are you surprised?" he asked. "Have you never met Pole before?"

The blond one shook her head. "Not one that was born there. How did you get out of Poland?"

"Oh," he said, smiling more broadly, "that is story for telling over long dinner and much wine. It is not story for hot place like this."

"Where are you staying?" the blond one asked.

"In hotel. With my brother. And you?" He smiled at her and she tossed her head again.

"At the Hilton. Where is your brother now?"

"He waits for me back at hotel. He is one year younger, but better looking. Do you have plans? Perhaps we could all do something and he could join us."

The blonde smiled proprietarily. "Sounds great to me. Too bad you have only one brother."

He chuckled. "You do not know Polish men or you would

not say such a thing. Believe me, you will not need anyone else.'' He would play to her, he had decided; she was clearly the one used to getting her way. ''If there is telephone I can call my brother. He can meet us at your hotel.''

''Will you buy the blouse first?'' the short-haired one asked.

''Oh,'' he said, looking down and sounding sheepish. ''I cannot. I haven't any money. I am—I forgot word—I spend money too much. My brother does not let me carry money with me. It is foolish, I know; but I would have bought everything in store by now if I had money.''

''And I suppose you don't have plastic either,'' the blonde said.

Plastic? He forced the grin to stay on his face and hoped his voice wouldn't betray him. ''I'm sorry . . . I haven't.'' *Plastic?*

''But, you see,'' he added quickly, ''I love to give gifts away. I like to buy clothes and things for my sister, or for . . . '' His voice trailed off. He would let them, especially the blonde, draw their own conclusions, and perhaps by now they had forgotten about this plastic. He smiled what he hoped was a disarming smile and reached up to put the blouse back in place. ''Another time I will bring my brother and we will buy this. For now, we will forget about Elizabet and have good time together. My sister—I did not tell you this—is . . . What is word? She cannot walk.''

''Crippled?'' the blond girl asked.

''Yes. She was in automobile accident. Her fiancé, man she was going to marry, was killed. She is very unhappy person now. I feel sorry for her and so I buy her things. You understand?''

All three nodded sympathetically.

''But she will feel better someday,'' he added. ''She is beautiful woman, blond hair, like yours.'' He nodded at the blonde. ''Other man will come into her life. We will not be saddened by thinking of her now; she has long happy life before her, I am sure.'' He smiled broadly again. ''And we have long happy evening before us. Shall I tell my brother to come to your hotel? What good thing can I tell him to convince him to join me and three pretty ladies?''

''I don't know about the rest of you,'' the small pretty one said, ''but I was planning to go for a swim when I get back. It's so damned hot.''

''Good. A swim. I will tell him to bring our swimming things. Where is it we will go for swim?''

The blonde smiled indulgently. "At the hotel pool," she said. "Doesn't your hotel have one?"

"No," he said uncertainly. A pool at a hotel? But the sea was only a few miles away. "Do you know where there is telephone? I am sorry, but we only arrive in Athenae this morning. I know nothing."

"Never mind," the blonde said, taking his arm. "We'll help you. There must be a telephone at one of those little kiosks on the street. And I'm sure one of us has one of those token things to use with it."

The shopping momentarily forgotten, the other two girls followed the blonde and Yuri out of the shop. He hoped that none of them would notice that the hotel he was going to call was right across the street.

The sound of the telephone was shrill in the little room. Molly jumped at the noise, then looked quickly to the man in the chair next to the balcony door. He was the one with the gun, at least the gun she had seen. He looked at her for a moment, as if weighing his options. "Answer it," he said finally. He lifted his gun again in warning and the other man moved with her toward the telephone stand.

When she picked up the receiver, the taller man took it from her hand and leaned close so that he could hear both sides of the conversation. "Hello?" she said.

"You returned." It was Yuri.

"Yes—"

He interrupted her. "Is someone there?"

She hesitated just a moment and he began speaking again, this time in Russian.

"I know you are there," he said. "Don't try to pretend you are not. You want me, not the girl. If you are interested in making a trade—the girl for me—say something."

The Russian shot a quick glance at the man across the room. Then he pulled the phone away from Molly and said one word, *"Da."*

"Listen carefully. You will bring the girl, and her bag, to the Acropolis. We will make the exchange there, in that public place. You will not dare to shoot her there—"

"Wait," the Russian interrupted him. He held out the phone to the other one. "You'd better listen to this," he said. "He's offering an exchange."

The shorter Russian stood and walked slowly to the telephone. "An exchange," he repeated slowly, but there was no expression in his voice and his companion did not know if he was surprised, or even if he would agree to such a thing. "Yes," he said, taking the telephone, "speak."

"Listen carefully," Yuri repeated. "You will bring the girl, and her bag, to the Acropolis. We will make the exchange there."

"No, it is too public."

"I am not a fool, you know. You will shoot us both if I do not allow her some protection. You cannot have me for nothing. Her life is the price you will pay. I have plenty of American money and can disappear as easily as I can blink my eyes. Make up your mind. Do you want the dove in the bush, or do you want the eagle?"

"All right," the Russian said slowly. "Where will you be?"

"You will see me."

There was silence while the Russian thought about that.

"Well?" Yuri asked impatiently.

"I do not like the Acropolis. There are guards."

"They are not policemen," Yuri said firmly. He was trying to think of the book; it did not seem as if the guards in the book had been policemen.

"Below the Acropolis then. Before you make the climb. You will allow me that precaution."

"Yes. All right. Below." Yuri paused, as if thinking. "In one hour. And do not bring any surprises. If you do, you will never see me again. I have an American passport and plenty of money. I can buy tickets to anywhere, new passports, whatever I need."

"Then why do you do this?"

Yuri sighed. "Because I am not like you. If I were, I would not have had to leave. I will not take my freedom at the expense of the girl's life. Perhaps even you could understand something like that. Besides, we both know who my grandfather is. In the end, he will not allow a little mistake to taint the family name. He still has power."

"Perhaps you are right," the Russian said, and hung up. "But you may not live to know it, and certainly the girl won't," he added, still speaking in Russian. He looked at his companion, who was standing next to the girl, and then he looked at her. Neither had moved. "Does he have money?" he asked her in English.

"Yes," she lied. She would not help them. If it mattered that he had money, she would let them think he did.

"Pyotr," he said softly, "how long from here to the Acropolis by car?"

"Fifteen minutes."

"Good. Then we have forty-five minutes to arrange things."

Yuri looked at his watch. "How long from here to the Acropolis?" he asked the girls.

"Walking or by taxi?" the pretty one said.

"Taxi."

She shrugged. "Fifteen minutes, maybe. I thought we were going back for a swim."

Fifteen minutes, Yuri thought. Then he would have forty-five minutes to arrange things.

11

YURI GLANCED AT HIS WATCH. ANY TIME NOW. HE looked across the street at the blonde, Cindy, who stood at the store window. She had listened to his story, and she had stayed. He had allowed himself the vanity of thinking that she had been disappointed to hear his explanation, but she had still stayed. As had the one with the short dark hair, Laurel. She seemed more intelligent than the others. And that was good. He would need her. The pretty one had refused; she'd gone back to the hotel. Well—he shrugged—he didn't need them all anyway. He would not permit himself to wonder if this would work. It would work; he would make it work. He looked down at the cigarette in his hand and back to the doorway. He'd had his eyes glued to that doorway for more than five minutes. Come on, he thought, come now, give yourselves enough time. Across the street, a ten-year-old boy lounged against the side of the building. He was dressed in a ragged shirt and dirty pants. He looked very good.

A gray car drew up to the front door of the hotel. Yuri stiffened slightly and put the cigarette into his mouth. A tall square-shouldered man in a dark suit opened the door of the hotel and stepped out. He looked up and down the street. It was one o'clock in the afternoon and the streets were filled with shopkeepers and secretaries leaving work and going home for dinner and the siesta. Yuri struck a match and lit his cigarette. The girl stepped out of the shop two doors from the hotel and began sauntering toward it. The little boy, his eyes on Yuri, stood straighter. The man at the hotel door stepped toward the car and opened the back door; then he walked hurriedly toward the hotel again. Yuri took the cigarette out of his mouth. The boy began walking briskly.

* * *

The shorter man had his hand firmly on Molly's arm, and his other hand was in his coat pocket. It was not particularly subtle, but no one seemed to notice. They had ridden down the elevator alone—the taller man having gone ahead to run interference. Now, as they walked across the lobby, no one paid any attention. Scream, yell, kick, she thought. *If it comes to your life or his,* O'Neal had said, *dump him.* A trade, they had said. They had told her that much. They needed her now. Until they had him in view, they needed her, and they had a silencer on the gun. They would not take their chances on letting her go. If it was a choice between the two of them, they would take Yuri, but until they had Yuri in view they would kill her if they had to. Her best chance, if there was going to be any chance at all, would be after they made contact with him. Then their attention would be focused on him. She wondered what Yuri had in mind, if he was really offering a trade. *Dump him.* She wondered if she had the nerve to do that. She wondered what she would have the nerve to do.

The other man was holding the door for them, and beyond the door and the sidewalk was a gray automobile. It would be only a short walk, not much of a chance. Now? she wondered. Now, or later? The gun pressed into her ribs. She stepped out into the bright sunlight.

A blonde was coming from her right and Molly saw the movement before the blonde felt it: a child grabbed the girl's shoulder purse and began running. He plowed into the Russian who held Molly's arm, then dodged on impact and darted around him. The girl reacted immediately, screaming at the top of her lungs and chasing after the urchin, her arms waving, yelling for help in English. At the same moment, Molly felt the grip on her arm loosen. She turned quickly and saw the Russian beside her begin to fall. Simultaneously, the Russian holding the door sagged to the ground. Without even looking around, she began running, and suddenly there was someone running beside her and a dark-haired girl grabbed her hand and darted through the gathering crowd with her. She looked in astonishment at the girl but the girl nodded and kept on running. Half the rush-hour crowd was chasing after the little boy and the other half was gathering around the screaming blond, who had planted herself next to the two Russians. As Molly glanced back, she could only see a confusion of bodies, and then she realized that the two Russians would see the same—and maybe two women darting through the crowd—and she knew that even they would not dare to shoot now.

At the first corner they turned left and ran halfway down the block, then crossed the street despite the traffic and the honking horns and continued running to the next corner. As they rounded the corner Molly was brought up short by the grinning face of the little boy. With a look of triumph, he held aloft the purse he had stolen.

"You're Molly," the girl said, leaning against the side of a building to catch her breath. "Tom'll be here in a minute. The others'll take a little longer."

"Who are you?" Molly asked, still panting. "What others?"

"My name is Laurel, and I'm—" She paused at the sound of running feet and looked in the opposite direction from which they had come. Yuri was running toward them, grinning broadly.

"How did you like that?" he called to them as he came closer. "We did it!" He had stopped running and was walking briskly. "You did it, I should say," he added as he approached, looking from the boy to Laurel. "But what do you think about me?" he bragged to Molly. "I made it up."

She stared at him openmouthed in surprise. The delight on his face was like a child's at Christmas. "Very good," she said, nodding her approval.

"And you have your bag," he said, taking it from her. "And your money, I hope. We need it. I promised." He looked at the boy, and the boy handed the purse to Laurel.

"Who is everybody?" Molly asked.

"It is Laurel," Yuri said matter-of-factly, "and Ghorghis. That is good Ru . . . Polish name; I guess good Greek name as well. And Ghorghis' big brother, and his friend. And Cindy. We go now?" he asked the child.

The boy nodded and led them back in the direction from which Yuri had just come. "My new friends," Yuri said. "Americans and Greeks. We did well, don't you think?"

The boy led them down a long block and then into a narrow side street, bringing them at last through an open door and into a coffeeshop. Small tables were scattered at random in the large room and at this time of day only a few of them were occupied. At the rear, two men dressed in black leaned over a *tavli* board, oblivious to the rest of the world. The men closer to the front stared in open curiosity at the four, particularly the two women. There were no other women in sight, and Molly knew the men were not used to seeing females here. The boy led them through the large room to the back, where a cooler and a high counter divided off a small kitchen area in which the coffee and tea were brewed. They walked right past the mustachioed cook and went out the door at the back to an alley between the buildings. There the boy paused, looked around, and leaned against the building. "We wait," he said.

A few minutes later a husky Greek stepped through the door from the coffeehouse, saw them all standing there and nodded in approval.

"It went well?" Yuri asked anxiously.

"Of course. The girl is just behind."

As he spoke, Cindy came through the door, followed by another Greek. She was smiling at him and talking rapidly, though it was clear from the look on his face that he understood little of what she said. She caught sight of Laurel and interrupted her monologue. "Wait until Denise hears! She'll be green with envy!" She paused and looked at Molly appraisingly. Then she tossed her blond hair and smiled at Yuri. "Worked like a charm didn't it?" she asked him.

The Greek held up a bag. "Yours?" he asked.

Yuri took the bag. "They brought it?"

"They wouldn't have wanted to leave it in the hotel," Molly explained. "They wouldn't have wanted that trace of you there. I knew they were discussing it, even though they spoke in Russian. They decided to bring it. I think they were especially concerned about leaving your camera. It's inside the bag."

"It worked very well then," Yuri said; then added quietly to her, "I promised them money."

"How much?" She reached into her purse.

"I didn't know how much to say. They asked for a hundred dollars apiece. But finally they said fifty."

"You bargained with them?"

He shrugged.

"All of them? The same amount?"

He shook his head. "No. Only the men. They will give the boy something. And for the girls, fifty dollars for both them together."

Molly took the bills from her purse. The taller Greek reached into a back pocket and pulled out a passport. Without a word, he handed it to Yuri.

"You gave him your passport?" Molly asked.

Yuri shrugged.

She gave the money to the men. *"Efharisto poli."*

They nodded and one put his hand to his head, as if touching an invisible hat. The boy grinned. "We did good job!" he said.

"Very good indeed." Molly smiled at him. Then she turned to the girls. "And I have you to thank as well. You can't know how much."

"Never mind about the money," Laurel said. "It was worth every minute. The most exciting thing that's happened since we left home."

But Cindy held out her hand for the bills. "It was worth it," she admitted. She smiled at Yuri and tossed her hair again. "Can we go for that swim now?"

"I am afraid not," he said, "but perhaps these men . . . " He looked toward the Greeks.

Her face fell for the briefest of moments. Then she turned to the taller of the Greeks and smiled warmly.

"One more thing," Yuri said, "for your own safety, do not tell what happened today. Do not tell anyone." The blonde frowned and he saw that. "At least," he said, "if you must tell, wait until you are far from here. Wait long enough. It is for your own sake." Then he turned to Molly. "We shall get out of here. Ghorghis says he knows special way."

The boy nodded solemnly and led them through a maze of alleys until he brought them at last to a small square bordered on one side by a subway station.

"You bargained with them," Molly said.

Yuri was gazing out the window of the subway train and he didn't turn to speak. "I did not know how much to say. But I thought—one never knows—they might lower their price. And they did."

"And what if they hadn't?"

He shrugged. "I would have agreed."

The woman in the seat across from them, large-breasted and dressed in black, coughed vigorously and held a crumpled handkerchief to her mouth, then dabbed at her damp face. She looked weary, and Molly wondered vaguely if the woman understood English.

"I suppose we should mail money to the hotel for our room."

Yuri nodded wordlessly.

"You did very well for someone who doesn't know his way around," she said lightly. "And thank you," she added, serious now.

He said nothing.

"How did you find them?"

"The girls were in tourist store. They were easy. We had to go looking for men. But that girl, that blond one, she was good bait."

"She had her eye on you, you know."

"I know."

Molly looked at him curiously, but he stared straight ahead.

"How did you get them to—"

"We will talk later," he interrupted.

The incline of the subway tracks was so gradual as to be imperceptible, but slowly light filtered into the tunnel, then glimpses of the street were seen, and finally the tracks were running at ground level. Yuri, sitting by the window, stared out. The rush hour was over now, and the streets were nearly empty. A solitary man swung a cane jauntily. A barefoot boy in shorts ran around the corner of a building. A black-and-white cat slept in the shade under an automobile. The train tracks ran down the center of the street, and the buildings began to change now— houses instead of stores, their windows shuttered against the heat of midday. The woman across from them got out at one of the stops and the car was nearly empty. "How much longer?" Yuri asked.

"Not much," she answered. His earlier ebullience was gone. He had seemed almost like a child then; now he was guarded again. What was it? Why did he close up? She remembered what O'Neal had said and she wondered if he was sorry he'd asked for asylum. And yet he certainly had had his chance to go back. She'd thanked him for that, and he'd said nothing. She remembered her own thoughts—of dumping him, as O'Neal would say—and she felt a sudden stab of guilt. Well, maybe she wouldn't have done it anyway. She would never know now. O'Neal. She wondered what he was doing in Rome. When we get to Piraeus, she thought, I'll look for a *Herald Tribune*. He'd said to watch the classifieds. *Lassie come home.* She could not imagine the world he must live in. She'd made a point of buying a paper each day since they'd left Rome, but the one she'd bought today was still lying unread in the hotel room with the food she'd brought back.

"Why do you think islands will be safer than Athens was?" he asked quietly.

"We have to go somewhere until O'Neal lets us know it's safe. Maybe they won't think of the islands. At least they won't know which one." After a moment she asked the question that had been on her mind. "How did they find us?"

He shrugged. He was looking out the window. They were almost out of the city now, but he could see factories and the mud flats of the bay. "The subway in Moscow is much nicer than this one," he said. "It is cleaner, and I think the trains are faster. They are newer, not at all like this one. Soviet people take better care of things, I think."

"You know that the subway in Moscow was built by American engineers."

"I believe the one in New York is even worse than this."

She laughed ruefully. "Are you hungry?" They hadn't eaten since the rice pudding and bread they'd had for breakfast.

"I can wait."

"We'll pick something up in Piraeus."

He nodded absently and she wondered what he was thinking. It was not a good sign that he was talking so fondly of home, at least that was what O'Neal had said. In Piraeus, she promised herself, or on the boat, she would try to get him to open up.

By the time the train reached Piraeus, only a few stragglers were left. Yuri followed Molly through the station, took her bag as she changed more dollars for drachmas; waited patiently while she pored over the boat schedules and bought tickets; then trailed after her as she made her way out of the station, picking up a *Herald Tribune* at a newsstand, and headed for a side street where she bought apricots from a sidewalk vendor, bread at a bakery so small that the baker—still dusty with flour—sold his bread to passersby through a window on the street, and cheese from a shop even tinier than the bakery.

The boats were lined up at the docks on the other side of the street, all painted white, their names emblazoned in black or blue or gilt. They were larger than Yuri had expected, and he saw some with open bays into which cars and trucks were driving. Sea gulls, crying mawkishly, circled overhead, while on the ground passengers hurried toward the boats, carrying baggage and boxes and string bags of packages wrapped in newsprint.

An occasional wide-eyed child clung to a parent's skirt or pant leg. There seemed no order to him, no organization, no way of knowing where to go or what to do. It was the same as when he had left the hotel. It was as if he were playing a game in which everyone except him knew the rules. How did everyone know where to go? He would not even have known where to buy the tickets. "Where do we go?" he asked.

She was checking the tickets. "We're looking for the boat named *Alonysos*. We're going to Paros," she added lightly. "You'll like it. You can swim there."

He thought of the girl Denise, who had gone back to the Hilton so that she could swim, rather than stay and be part of his plan. "Is the swimming so nice?"

She looked at him, squinting in the bright sun. "I think it is. Do you have to be critical about everything?"

He stared at her. "Is that what you think, that I am critical about everything?"

"Sometimes it seems that way."

"I saved your life."

"I thanked you for that. You didn't even say 'You're welcome.' "

"You did not need to thank me. You know I would have been lost in Athens without you. I had no money and I would not have known how—"

"You did very well, you know. Incredibly well. But I may never forgive you for bargaining over me!"

He blinked his eyes and looked away. The moment was past; she'd realized that as soon as she'd spoken, teasing him about the bargaining.

"How long will we be on boat?" he asked, his voice stiff and cold.

"Four or five hours." She shifted the bread to the other hand, put the newspaper under her arm, and tried to take her bag from him. But he clung to it wordlessly. Damn you, she thought, why do you close up? And damn me, she added, because she had not had the sense to keep her mouth shut.

They found the *Alonysos* near the far end of the docks, newly painted, its name in bold black lettering across its wide stern. An officer smartly dressed in summer whites looked at their tickets and waved them up the gangplank. The ship was nearly ready to sail, its outer decks and chairs already filled to overflowing with Greeks and Europeans and Americans. Some had spread sleeping bags or foam mattresses, as if planning to sleep through the journey. They picked their way through this throng, entered the cabin on the second deck and found, miraculously, two seats together by a window. Molly set her packages down, claiming territoriality. "This look good?" she asked.

Without even looking around, he nodded. "It is fine."

"Yuri . . ." she began. He handed over her bag and she stowed it beneath the seat.

"Maybe you should make it Tom."

She sat down by the window and he sat next to her. The seats were more like airplane seats than she had remembered, same long-wearing, easy-care fabric that was meant to resemble good upholstery, same vague and unobtrusive pattern in blue and green and brown, same line-up of seats all facing the same direction, unlike the subway seats that had faced each other. That was one thing: at least they would have more privacy. Outside the broad, dingy window that was more like a train window than what one usually finds on boats, she could see the deck and the railing, and, beyond, the sea, green-black here in the harbor from oil, she supposed, and who knew what else. The window ledge was shiny, as if freshly varnished, and the floor beneath their feet was cleaner than she would have expected. Defensively, she felt better about that; one thing Yuri would not be able to criticize. Except for the window, the boat was in very good condition. She supposed it would be pretty hard to keep the windows of a boat clean, what with sea spray and all.

"How about some lunch?" she asked, unwrapping the cheese and handing it to him. He broke off a piece and handed it back. Across the aisle, toward the center of the boat, an elderly man was maneuvering his way through a monstrous grilled cheese and tomato sandwich.

Yuri took the bread from her lap, broke off a piece, and handed it to her. "Thank you," she said absently.

"You are welcome." His voice was firm, the words precise.

She glanced up, and he was looking at her. In the silence that passed between them she could feel the rumble of the ship's engine as the boat pulled away from the dock.

"It was not for you to thank me, you know, for—for what I did," he said quietly. "It would be nice if I did it out of bravery or friendship or something, but I had to do it. Without you, I would not have known what to do, or where to go. I would not have known whom to trust. I had no money. No, I had no choice."

"You could have called the police. You could have called the Embassy. You did not have to do it yourself."

He shook his head. "I am not a fool. I do not know all that O'Neal told you in that park in Rome, but I can understand some things. This business has gone very wrong. O'Neal does not know whom he can trust. You are in as much danger as I. No, I could not have risked doing anything else."

She glanced about. The boat was steaming out of the harbor. Outside the window, on the outer deck, the railing was crowded with people watching as Piraeus faded from view in its own haze. Another time she would have been at the railing herself, but not now. This time she was going to handle it better. "I still have a right to thank you. You saved my life."

"Someday perhaps you will have occasion to thank me, but not for this. It is I who should apologize for bringing you into it. You would be safe in Rafetna if it were not for me."

"You didn't bring me into it; O'Neal did."

"It was for me that he got you. If it had not been for me you would not have been needed."

"It wasn't your fault. It was my choice."

"It was not your choice. They made you do it."

"No, they didn't. I chose to." Well, sort of.

"I thought they made you do it. I thought they forced you. Then why were you so angry?"

"What makes you think I was?"

"I could see it. You didn't like me at all when we met. It was as if—as if I were some weight that you had been forced to carry. You were not happy to be doing it."

"Was it that obvious?"

"I could see it."

"But it wasn't you. I wasn't angry at you. I was angry at O'Neal, because he had tricked me into it. No, tricked is not the word—he used me; he used an argument that I could not refuse. He probably knew . . ."

He turned away and stared straight ahead. A little girl dressed in red toddled by in the aisle, but he didn't seem to notice. "Do you believe in God?" he asked finally, still not looking at her.

"Yes. Why?"

"Then, do this: when you pray to your God, pray that you will never find yourself alone in a place where you do not know how things are done, where you have no power and no friends and, worse, no understanding, where all you can do is put yourself in the hands of strangers and hope that what they do for you is for your own good, and not just for theirs.''

You might find him a bit arrogant, O'Neal had said, and she had indeed thought that. Had, in fact, still thought it until a moment ago. She reached out and laid her hand lightly on his arm.

He turned and looked at her hand. ''That is why it is not for you to thank me,'' he said at last.

Suddenly she felt as if she knew more about him than she had a right to know. And also less. She looked down at the bread lying in her lap and the crumbs there and on the edges of her seat. Slowly she brushed the crumbs to the floor. ''Are you sorry you left?'' she asked.

She felt, rather than saw, him stiffen slightly. ''No,'' he said quickly. ''Yes,'' he added more slowly, ''perhaps in some ways. It is not easy thing. Even if things work out well, it is not easy thing.''

''Why did you do it?''

He turned to her again, his face composed, serious. ''We will talk about it, but not now. I promise you we will talk about it.'' He smiled softly. ''Have you ever been to Greek islands before?''

''Yes, many times.''

''Then you cannot know how it is for me to be on my way to this place. We hear things; I have seen pictures. It seems as if Greek islands are paradise. Are they really so beautiful? Is sea really so clear? Is sky so blue?''

She laughed gently. ''You will love it, I promise you.''

''Will we be able to find hotel? We will not arrive until evening, is that not true?''

''Yes, but early in the evening, and the evenings are long. If we are lucky, we will find a home to stay in. People meet the boats and offer room in their homes.''

''In real houses? Wouldn't that be nice? And will we share room again?'' He looked at her slyly.

''A room, yes,'' she said, ''but, like at the hotel in Athens, not a bed.''

''I thought American girls . . .''

But she saw the grin beginning. ''You have a lot to learn,'' she said, grinning back.

She opened her eyes. The sound came again, more clearly now that she was concentrating. Someone in the seat ahead of them was throwing up. Two middle-aged women had been in those seats. She wondered vaguely if they were still there. Seasick. Thank God that was one thing she didn't have to worry about—perhaps, she thought ruefully, the only thing. Beside her, Yuri still breathed deeply. Let him sleep, she thought. While she had been dozing, her head had fallen lightly against his shoulder. It was still there; she had not moved it, fearful that the movement would wake him. He deserves the rest, she thought. She closed her eyes again. We both do. She did not fall asleep again, but it was comforting sitting like that with her eyes closed, the noise of the engines, the chatter of the people surrounding them, safe in the cocoon of this boat. No one could have followed them. No one could know they were there. And that brought back the question she'd been wrestling with since this morning, since she'd walked into the hotel room and seen, not Yuri as she had expected, but the other two men . . . How did they know? Even O'Neal hadn't known where she was going. How could they have been followed? When she'd asked Yuri that, he'd only shrugged, as if it should have been expected. Is that the world he comes from? she wondered. Is that what he is used to? She thought about the airlines. Could someone have gotten a passenger list? Could they have been traced in that way?

She felt Yuri stir beside her; his breathing changed. She lifted her head and saw him open his eyes. "Did you sleep?"

"I must have," he answered. "And you?"

She nodded. "Are you hungry?" She reached into the bag for an apricot.

He shook his head. "Didn't I see that you bought newspaper? Is it *Herald Tribune* again?"

She'd introduced him to the *Herald Tribune* their first day in Athens. He'd been intrigued with it, both because he'd had little experience with Western papers, and because it amused him that a company in Paris would publish an American-style newspaper for an expatriate readership.

She had forgotten about the paper, which she'd stuffed down beside the seat. She retrieved it and handed it to him. When he was finished with it she could check the classifieds.

He glanced at the front page, scanning the headlines. He found the newspaper a curiosity. In looks it was much like a Russian paper, but there was something about the tone . . . He looked at the picture on the front page with a practiced eye. American police officers carrying away demonstrators in Washington. Not bad. He would have photographed it a little differently, but not bad. And anyway, *Pravda* probably would not have printed a picture of such an activity in Moscow even if he had taken one. He opened the paper. He looked at the pictures on the second page, and on the third . . . "Molly." He said it so softly it was only a whisper. He was not sure she even heard him. His throat felt suddenly constricted. "Molly," he said again.

He felt her turn in her seat, felt the warmth of her as she leaned closer, heard the breath catch in her throat as she read the words under the picture, then scanned the article that ran alongside it. Four people killed in a Roman café: one French woman, one Italian man, and two Americans. The picture showed the sidewalk café in disarray, tables turned over, chairs upended, a flowerpot broken, bodies strewn around like broken dolls. Four killed . . . seven wounded . . . witnesses claimed two, or maybe three, gunmen with ski masks (ski masks? he wondered) had fired automatic weapons from a passing car . . . terrorists, the police speculated . . . two previously unheard-of groups had claimed responsibility . . . the dead were named: the French woman, the Italian man, the two Americans: Edwin Lopes II, the Social Security Attaché at the American Embassy in Rome, and Dennis O'Neal . . . He stared at the name, as if looking at it would change it into something else, into some other person's name.

12

"WOULD YOUR . . . HAVING GONE TO THE WEST . . .
emasculate, once and for all, your grandfather's faction?
Would they be trying to stop you for that reason?"

They were walking along the quay at the far end of the
town. Fishing boats in bright crayon colors, their weathered
lines tied to iron rings in the cement of the quay, rocked
gently in the early morning sun. A barefoot fisherman, khaki
pants rolled to his knees, sat in a yellow boat mending his
nets, his bare toes catching the webbing of the net to hold it
taut as his fingers worked the bobbin. He did not look up as
Molly stopped to watch him work. The water, deep green,
reflected a thin rainbow of oil floating on its surface. Above,
the sky was cloudless blue, as blue as the Greek flag that
hung limp outside the police station at the other side of the
quay. Already the air was warm.

"They might try to stop me, but they would not be doing
this other killing. Why would they kill O'Neal? Why would
they kill the ones in Rafetna?"

Molly took her eyes from the fisherman and moved on,
Yuri walking beside her wordlessly. They had not spoken of
O'Neal since last night, avoiding the subject as if not speak-
ing of it would somehow make the report of his death a lie.

They'd debarked at Paros amid a hubbub of other tourists,
both Greeks and foreigners. Even so, Molly had managed to
locate a shy ten-year-old at the edge of the crowd who'd been
sent by her mother to meet the boat from Athens and bring
home visitors for the empty room on the second floor of their
tiny house. There were two single iron beds in the room,
with a small table between them and a sink against the wall
at the foot of the beds. The toilet and shower were crammed

together in a three-foot-square stall on the street level, down a circular metal outside staircase.

Yuri had grinned, amused, as Molly bargained for the price of the room. "You see," he'd whispered, watching the child's mother maneuver her bulk down the winding staircase after the deal had been struck. "I was right to bargain for you. Things are done that way, are they not?"

It was then that she had turned back into the room and sat on the edge of a bed. "Do you want to tell me about it now?" she had asked.

And he had sat on the other bed, his knees almost touching hers, and told her how he had done it. It seemed almost a faraway dream now—how he'd gotten the girls to help him by telling them part—but only part, he insisted—of the truth. He'd said Molly was his sister, though he thought neither of the girls really believed it. In fact, maybe they didn't believe any of it, since he'd already told them a completely different story. But that was to get them to help make the telephone call. He'd explained that to them carefully. He still let them think he was Polish, that he and his brother and sister had escaped to Greece from a vacation in Yugoslavia, but that his brother had disappeared while they were in Athens. He'd let them think about that for a while. He'd been afraid they might decide it was too dangerous, and in fact that may have been what caused the pretty one to leave. But by then the blonde was too interested in him personally (he was not too proud to point that out), and the other one was intrigued by the politics of it all. So the two had agreed to help and then they all had set out to find the boy who would play the role of thief and the two men to attack the Russians from behind in order to give Molly a chance to escape. The men were each only to deliver one hard blow to the base of the neck . . . no more—and then escape. It would not do, Yuri had warned them, to be caught by the police. And they were very good, he bragged again, didn't Molly think? Had she even noticed the one in the hotel lobby, the one who had followed her and the Russian to the door and struck him at just the right moment? No, she admitted, she had not noticed; nor, for that matter, had she seen the one on the street who attacked the Russian holding the door. But what had given him the idea for it all?

He had leaned back then, resting his shoulders against the wall of the little room, grinning. A lesson from their own books, he had said. When the KGB comes to take you, he went on, serious now, they always come in the night. Why was that, did she think? He didn't even give her time to respond. For one thing, he explained, they come at night because it is when people are at home. Not just the ones they come after, for of course they could come to the workplace just as easily. But they also come then because others will hear the commotion, will know what is happening, will whisper about it for days after. And why would they do that? She sat up straighter at the question, and again he went on without giving her a chance to answer. To strike fear into the others, of course, to terrorize not only those who are taken, but their neighbors and friends as well. It is part of the instrument of fear by which the people are governed. He'd laced his hands behind his head then, leaning against the wall, and let her think about that for a while.

Then he sat up again. But there was another reason, he told her. And that is that in the night, awakened by the pounding at the door, one is at one's most vulnerable. Then is the time to strike; then is the time that the victim is least likely to think clearly, and can therefore be taken more easily. He grinned, and the look of superiority that had irked her in Rafetna was back on his face. And that is what I did to them, he said triumphantly. I told them we would make the trade at the Acropolis, and so they were prepared to be cautious there. They assumed getting you into a car would be easy, that you would not struggle, thinking you would be released—or could escape—when they made the trade. And they assumed that you would have no help, because I was supposed to be at the Acropolis. I did to them what they would do: I caught them when they were most vulnerable. He said it with satisfaction and, folding his arms, leaned back again.

And your passport? she had asked. You gave those Greek men your passport? For security, he responded. Do you think they would have trusted me, whom they had never seen before? I promised them each fifty dollars, but they had a right to demand a deposit of some sort. The passport was for that. And the girls, she had asked, what did you give them? He shrugged. Only my word, he said, grinning broadly. But they were not in such danger; they did not have to come into actual contact with those men. But the boy took the purse; it could have been a plot to steal the purse—you could all have been in on it. Were the girls really that foolish? An empty purse, he laughed. The girl had already taken everything out of it. They were not so stupid! Nor, he added as an afterthought, was I. I managed it. And she had conceded him his point: he had indeed managed it. And that was how they had left it. Tomorrow . . . she had thought then; we will worry about the rest of it tomorrow. And yet when tomorrow came, nothing had changed. O'Neal was dead; they were on their own. And it was only a matter of time before they would have to make a move.

The water of the bay glistened now in the summer sun and the barren hills on the other side wore shades of brown and dusty green. A flock of gulls noisily trailed a late fishing boat toward the dock. An elderly woman in a gray cotton dress waited, hands on hips, for the boat as it neared the quay.

"One would think that the most important problem is what kind of fish to have for dinner," Molly said.

Yuri nodded.

"Is it as nice as you imagined?" she asked, turning to him.

His eyes took in the sweep of the bay. They had already walked past the beach, empty now in the early morning. Ahead, a grove of cedars sheltered another, smaller beach, and amongst the trees a red tent could be seen. "It's very quiet early in the morning, isn't it?"

"Do you prefer crowds?" she asked. "Wait a couple of hours."

"No," he said. "This is very nice. I am not crazy about crowds. But it is not for us to enjoy, is it? We must be thinking about what we are to do now that we no longer have O'Neal."

"Yes," she answered. She had spent most of the night thinking about exactly that.

She turned and they headed back toward town. A policeman had come out of the station ahead and leaned against the doorway, drinking a glass of tea. Molly quickened her step, and beside her Yuri kept pace. "What are we going to do?" he asked again.

"We'll buy swimming suits and then we'll rent ourselves a couple of mopeds and ride out to the other side of the island, to a beach that won't be so crowded. And then we will talk."

"About how we will get back?"

"Eventually. But first, about who you are and what you are. And exactly what there is about you that is making someone kill off anyone you may have talked to." And then, she thought, when I know where we stand, I'll call the number O'Neal gave me.

The beach itself was small and sandy, not more than a hundred feet across, the sand stretching perhaps twenty yards back from the water's edge. Beyond that were buff-colored rocks, the same shade as the sand, which rimmed the beach and stretched along both arms of the inlet. Against the rocks, the sky was deep blue, the color of blue Yuri had come to expect in Greece. The water was green-blue and clearer than any water he'd ever seen. As they walked out from shore, the sand at the bottom stirred into clouds that refracted the sunlight. He turned around. Behind them, the clouds of sand slowly settled back to the bottom again. Molly dived into the water and he turned to watch. Ahead of him, her legs scissors-kicked the water, her green suit almost invisible against the hue of the sea. When her head broke the water again she was laughing and she gave her head a quick sharp twist to shake the water from her eyes and the hair from her face.

"C'mon," she called, and plunged in again. He dived in after her. She was a much better swimmer than he.

Fifty yards from shore she stopped swimming and turned to wait for him, treading water. He swam awkwardly, like someone who knew the proper movements, but had never used them. As he came nearer, he held his head out of the water, watching her.

"How deep is it here?" he asked.

"Over your head, for sure."

Treading water beside her, he looked back toward the shore. They had bought a red canvas bag in town and filled it with bread and cheese, fruit and beer. He could make out the bag from here, leaning in the shade of a rock at the side of the beach. "Beautiful, isn't it!" he exulted.

"Isn't it?" she agreed. But she was watching him, enjoying his pleasure.

He looked up at the sky. The sun was high; it was, perhaps, as late as eleven o'clock. "Are you hungry?" he asked.

Without answering, she dived straight down. He watched her legs grow fainter and fainter below him, then she was coming back up, face up toward the surface, in exactly the same spot she had left. She shook her head free of water again. "It must be twenty-five or thirty feet deep," she said.

"You are showing off."

She blinked the water from her eyelashes. "Yes," she admitted. "But you have to agree, it's a wonderful place to swim."

"Have you been here before?"

"Yes." She turned and started for shore. He followed after her. She was swimming slowly, he knew, so that he could keep up.

They sat facing the water, their backs against the rocks. He had a pickle in one hand and a torn-off piece of bread in the other. "My grandmother used to say that if you swam without an undershirt on you would catch pneumonia. I never went into the water without an undershirt when I was a child."

"Did your grandmother live with you?"

He looked at her sideways. "I lived with her."

She broke off a piece of cheese and held it out to him. He nodded, and she laid it atop the bread he held. "You didn't live with your parents?"

He shook his head. "They have both always worked. My grandmother lived in my grandfather's dacha—in Volnov, outside of Moscow. Of course, he has lived in Moscow since long before I was born." He took another bite of the pickle. "When my parents were married, my grandmother moved out into country. There was no longer reason for her to live in big city, and she had always been country person—she grew up on farm in Georgia. That was where she met my grandfather; he was there to collectivize farms and in those days she agreed with that."

Molly frowned. "In those days?"

"Her family had no land of its own. If they had, she would have felt differently." He shook his head. "She would have been kulak then, sent away by Stalin and probably murdered. But of course they didn't know about those things then; that came out later. They believed what they were told in those days. That is probably why she was afraid of pneumonia from swimming. What did she know about swimming, growing up working some landowner's land for barely enough bread and gruel to keep from starving?" He put the rest of the pickle in his mouth. "She was very pretty in those days. She insisted on proper wedding before she would go off with my grandfather. He was so taken with her that he would have agreed to anything. But she never got used to Moscow, and in later years she only lived there because she had to. By then, his life was politics, and she counted for almost nothing. But she raised their daughter—my mother—to be proper daughter of official.

"My grandfather's dacha was small at first, but that would not have mattered to my grandmother. Over time some rooms were added to it. My grandfather came occasionally—he always brought friends or associates when he came. I do not think he and my grandmother were ever alone together in same room since before my mother was married."

"But they didn't get divorced?"

He looked at her in surprise. "No, of course not. We are much too prudish people for that. No, he could not have risen like he did if he had been divorced. And Babushka would not have divorced him. I am sure he had mistresses. It would have been kept very quiet, however. For all I know, he still does. She stayed in Moscow as long as she did for my mother's sake, but that is all. She would have done anything for my mother. After my mother's marriage, there was no reason. When my sister was born, my mother took leave of absence from Institute for short time; then talked my grandmother into coming back to Moscow to stay with Tasha while my mother went back to work. My grandmother did that, but for less than year. Then she moved back to dacha, taking Tasha with her. Later, when I was born, my mother didn't even take leave, just went back to work as soon as she could. Grandmother took me to dacha, too, and raised us both. It was when Tasha was visiting in Moscow that she was killed. That was car accident. Someone ran into side of car; he was almost certainly drunk and it was late at night. Tasha had been to ballet—she loved ballet. Can you imagine? Killing granddaughter of Soviet Premier? I wonder if he is out of prison yet." He took a bite of bread and cheese. "He probably is not."

"Your grandfather must be quite old."

"He is—but still vigorous. It is not usual, as you may know, for former premier to retain very much power in Soviet Union, but my grandfather has. Dimitri Kalishev is General Secretary now, but my grandfather still controls old faction, those who went through Revolution, and under him they still have some power. Especially in Army. Kalishev has not yet managed to wrest that from him." He turned to the canvas bag and broke off another piece of cheese and selected one of the tomatoes from a paper bag. "My grandmother is much younger than he is. She was fourteen when they met."

"What will she think when she learns you have defected?"

He didn't respond.

"Didn't you say that she was—"

"In mental institution. Yes. It is one of the things they do."

She broke off another piece of bread. "Meaning?"

"She has old ways still. Even after living in Moscow; even after raising perfectly good modern Communist woman like my mother and having been married to my grandfather, she still is . . . who she is. She does what she wants and says what she wants, and of course my grandfather's position has always protected her to some degree. He did not like it, but what could he do? One could argue that for her to be like that in Soviet Union she must indeed be crazy. It finally seemed easiest way: let her do as she pleases in mental institution where no one will pay attention."

"But that's awful!"

"One could say she had choice. She could have gone along and kept quiet but she would not. She used to say 'I will not change history of my life just to suit some young *durak*.' " He laughed fondly at the memory. "She is very strong person. She raised me much more strictly than my mother would have."

"It can't have come as any surprise, then, when you defected."

He looked down at the sand and dug with his toe into it until his foot was half covered. "You know I do not like use of that word."

"Why? Isn't it the truth?"

He drew a deep breath; his eyes squinted toward the horizon. "There is no word like that—defect—in Russian. 'Traitor' is word that is used. I do not think I am a traitor." He turned and looked at her. "Do you not love your country?"

"Of course, but—"

"No but. A person's country is like his mother. It may treat you badly, but still . . . she is your mother. You may grow up and leave home, you may have very different life from what your mother had, but she is still your mother. A man matures and finds a woman and marries her and goes to live in their own home, away from his mother. Do you think that means he no longer cares for his mother? Do you think he has forgotten his mother? The way her hair shone when sun was on it, the way her face broke into a wide smile when he pleased her, look of pride on her face when he took first in a race. No, one may come to love another country, just as one may come to love wife or stepmother, but that does not mean that first mother is forgotten. Even if she has been difficult to live with, even when he has left her because he must do it to survive . . . still, she is his mother. To leave country because one must, that is not anything to be ashamed of, but to be traitor—no, that is not same thing at all. You know, if things changed in Soviet Union, if I could be kind of person I was raised to be, I would go back. I have not turned my back on her, or betrayed her. It is more that she has refused me than that I have betrayed her.''

The water washed gently against the sand in tireless rhythm. A sea gull circled slowly overhead. Yuri brushed his hands together and leaned back on one elbow. ''You know, when I listened to you talking at airport in Rafetna, it was like hearing about life in entirely other world. It would not be difficult to see why you would have trouble to understand this.''

''I don't—I didn't know you were listening to all that. I thought you were ignoring me. Good God, you must have been bored to death.''

''Not at all. It was fascinating. To think you were growing up in way you did, and at exact same time I was living with my grandmother in Volnov. Can you imagine two such different lives?''

She looked at him as he sat beside her, half-turned toward her, and once again she felt the same frustration. ''You amaze me, Yuri. Just when I think I have you figured out, just when I think I understand you, you throw me a curve.''

''Curve?''

''You say something—or do something—that makes me think I haven't understood you at all.''

With his fingers he drew a circle and then an X in the sand. ''What is to understand?'' he asked. When he looked up again his face had closed like a door, his eyes were as blank as any shuttered window.

She lay back in the sand, covering her eyes with a forearm. she would stay here as long as she could stand the midday heat, and she would listen to his voice only and not look at him, not be distracted by that closed face, by those unrevealing eyes. "What was it like, growing up in that kind of world?" she asked.

It took him so long to respond that it was an effort of will not to look at him just to make sure he was still there.

"One cannot think of Volnov without thinking of birch trees. The dacha was in forest of birch. In winter it was world of almost complete white surrounding us; in summer, breeze drifted through forest, and leaves . . . shimmered . . . green on one side, and almost silver on other side. Do you know birch trees?"

She nodded and he must have been watching her because he continued. "In autumn it was white-and-yellow forest, yellow leaves fluttering in sun. I loved those trees. Do they have birch trees in America?"

"Yes."

"My grandmother had strawberries in little square plot in the sun, and we picked strawberries in summer. She made them into jam and in winter we sweetened our tea with it. A special treat. It was only place I ever ate strawberries. And there were raspberries growing wild, and blueberries. I went to little school in village part of time, and part of time my grandmother taught me, though it was soon that I could read better than she and do better mathematics. But there were many books to read; she was always buying books for me. I think she did not ever go to school when she was child, but she is smart lady and taught herself many things. She can make vegetables grow from rocks." He chuckled.

Molly moved her arm enough to catch a glimpse of him. He was lying on his stomach, propped up by his elbows, and he was smiling to himself. She closed her eyes.

"My grandmother was friend to anyone. In village she took me to carpenter, and he gave me scraps of wood. And nails. I carried them home like precious gifts. She found a hammer and I built things. Boats mostly. There was little pond near dacha. I sailed them. There was time when I was going to be naval architect. 'You will design boats for us both and we will see the world,' she used to say. And I used to dream of doing it."

He was silent for a long time, but she said nothing and at last he spoke again. "When I was eleven years old it was as if my parents suddenly discovered they had a son. My father came one day with new clothes for me. In a Zil automobile. He took me back to Moscow, to the apartment they had. My

parents got me into best schools, because they wanted me to
go into foreign service—that is where the best opportunities
are. There were things the other students knew that I didn't,
because I had only gone to village school up to that time, but
many things I knew that they didn't. Some of books that my
grandmother had gotten for me were books not allowed to
the public to read. I hadn't known that before I went to Moscow. I never knew if she did, either.''

She heard him rummaging in the bag, the crinkle of paper,
and then a chuckle. "She had not exactly prepared me for
life of Soviet citizen. They say, 'A spoonful of tar will ruin
a barrel of honey.' Until I learned to keep my mouth shut, I
was like that tar. Who I was saved me until I learned that
. . . has always saved me, I guess. And one learns—even I.
To vote at meetings, to applaud at right times, to ask correct
questions and to have correct width of trousers and length of
hair—all those things that show one's willingness to fit in.
Desire, even. Because worst thing in the world is to be different, to not fit, to let one's nighttime conscience be one's
daytime conscience as well. That, after all, is my grandmother's crime.''

"Did you go to visit her after they—''

He didn't answer the question. "When I was fourteen my
father gave me a camera. I loved it immediately. Taking photographs—it was like being an artist. To see something and
to make art of it—I had never known that before. After that,
I forgot about being naval architect. I never wanted to be
anything else but photographer. My parents still talked about
foreign service, but I only wanted to be photographer.''

There was a long silence. She moved her arm and opened
her eyes, but she could not read his face.

"If you could go back to being that little boy in the birch
forest, would you?'' she asked.

He turned to her. "If you could still be that little girl rol-
lerskating on smoothest sidewalk in town, would you?''

She smiled, embarrassed. "You really were paying attention to all that.''

"Of course I was. You are all I have now.'' He rolled over
and sat up, his back to her.

His back glinted with stray grains of sand. She brushed
them away, and he turned and looked at her over his shoulder,
and his eyes seemed a darker color than they had been before,
as if she were seeing them now, really, for the first time.

"Who is there for you?" he asked. "Who cares about Molly Davison?"

She smiled at the question and looked away from him. "My father," she said. Who thinks I'm in Rafetna, she thought. Who will miss my weekly letter, but will just assume that I've been too busy to write. And who's better off thinking that than knowing the truth.

"Who else?"

She shrugged. "I told you my mother's dead. And I don't have any sibs—brothers and sisters. Lots of friends. I guess everybody has friends."

"Boyfriends?"

She grinned and shrugged again. "Nobody serious."

"Why not? You're certainly a very pretty woman."

"Sheboygan, Wisconsin, is a very nice town. And a girl who goes into the Peace Corps may be admired there, but when she comes home, she sees the world in a different way. Different things seem important to her than they do to other people." She looked away from him for a moment. "It becomes harder and harder to find someone who thinks the same way."

He was silent for a long time. "For both of us," he said finally, "we cannot go back to the way things were before. Who are we running from? Do you know that?"

"You mentioned Americans in the Dioula. How do you know what they were?"

He shook his head. "In spite of different upbringings, we are not so different, you know. People are same all over world. Rebel camps were full of rumors. It was supposed to be secret, of course, but one cannot deny what one sees. I saw Americans. Believe me, I can tell difference between Americans and Soviets."

"They could have been Western Europeans."

"No. They were Americans."

"And you took pictures of them."

"Yes, but I don't remember if there were any on the film I brought with me."

"A fat lot of good that does us, anyway. O'Neal said the film's probably been destroyed by now."

"I am not a fool, Molly."

"What is that supposed to mean?"

"In Soviet Union I would not trust KGB. Why do you think in America I would put all my trust in CIA? When I dressed to leave Soviet Embassy, I put my film for Tass—two rolls—in my right-hand pocket. I put my other film—also two rolls, but pictures I had taken for myself—in my left pocket. When O'Neal asked me for my film, I gave him what I had in my left pocket.''

Molly stared at him in astonishment. ''You didn't! But where's the other film now?''

''Here, in this bag. Under loaf of bread. I keep it in my pocket usually, but of course when we are swimming, I cannot take it into the water.''

''Why didn't you tell me before? Why didn't you tell O'Neal?''

He gazed away from her, his face serious. ''I don't know whether that film is important or not, but as long as I have it, no one else knows, either. It is my only protection. Do you wonder that I have become cautious about it?''

''Why do you tell me about it now, then?''

''Because now it is your protection, too.''

''And you don't even know if it shows Americans with the rebels.''

''No. I wish I did.''

''Why would there be Americans in the Dioula? Mercenaries, do you think?''

''You should know better than I. America is land of free enterprise, is it not?''

She glanced at him, but couldn't tell whether or not a smile glimmered at the corners of his mouth. He was not looking at her; his eyes followed a sailboat near the horizon.

''Why did they kill O'Neal?'' he asked after a while.

She sat up beside him. ''Or the others? For God's sake, why kill a taxi driver? It doesn't make any sense.''

''Maybe they didn't. Maybe it was someone else—just co-incidence.''

She drew an apricot slowly out of the bag, its furred skin warm from the sun. ''O'Neal didn't think so.''

''What good would it have done to kill taxi driver?''

''He didn't even see you. I've turned that over and over in my mind—he didn't even turn around and take a look at you.'' It was at the edges of her mind, teasing her because she couldn't quite grasp the thought that stayed hidden there. O'Neal had apologized to her. O'Neal had told her to get out, had said *Go somewhere you will be safe. Don't even tell me where it is*, as if he knew . . . What was it that O'Neal knew, or suspected? Someone in the Embassy, almost certainly, but something else, something that teased because it stayed just out of her mind. The taxi driver. Her mind kept coming back to that. Why would the taxi driver have been killed when he hadn't even seen . . . hadn't even seen . . . "I think it is not who you are," she said slowly. "And it may not be the photographs, either. It is not who you are that would have gotten the taxi driver killed. There is only one thing that could have done that—something you know. Something you might have said that he could have heard. Someone in the Embassy is afraid of what you might have said."

"That is why O'Neal asked me if I was ever alone with Tom Little, was it not? Because someone thought I might have said something to him. And O'Neal was killed because I was with him. And you would be killed if they had a chance—but they had a chance. And they didn't do it."

"Because they needed me to lead them to you."

"That didn't save O'Neal."

"Maybe they already knew that we had left the country by then."

"But it was Soviets who came after us in Athens."

"Two groups? *Two groups?*" she asked incredulously.

"That," he said, looking at her, "or the Soviets and the Americans working together to kill us."

"Something they both want to hide." She understood now. "Russians and Americans in the Dioula, working together. Not American mercenaries, not at all. Americans sent there— by whom? Who is being protected? Who doesn't want that known?"

He didn't respond.

"Why would Soviets and Americans be helping each other when we're supposed to be enemies?" she asked.

"Molly," he said, "is there anywhere we can go? Is there anyone we can trust?"

"Maybe. O'Neal gave me a phone number. He said we could trust the person who answers the phone."

"Who is it?"

"I don't know."

"You trust someone when you do not even know who they are?"

"O'Neal said we could."

"O'Neal is dead."

"All the more reason. It proves he was on our side."

He shook his head. "I would not trust something like this."

"What would you trust? Do you have something better? No, Yuri, this is all we have. But we'll give it one more day. We're safe here and we have enough money to last for a while. If it still seems right tomorrow, we make the call."

"Will we go back to same place tomorrow?" he asked.

She smiled, "You liked it, didn't you?"

"It is beautiful. Don't you think so?"

"There are other beautiful places on this island," she teased.

"No," he said. "I want to go back to that one."

They were sitting at a small table on a terrace overlooking a pine-draped beach. A busy waiter walked by, paused, and lifted the bottle of wine from the table. "More?" he asked. Molly nodded and he poured the last of the wine into her glass. "And for the gentleman?" he asked.

Yuri covered his wineglass with a hand. "No, thank you," he said. "I have had enough."

The waiter walked off, carrying the empty bottle back to the kitchen.

"What is name of fish again?" Yuri asked.

"*Barbunia*. Red mullet."

"It is very good."

"Isn't it." She looked to her left. Through the trees she could see the sun, sitting just above the horizon. "Well, if you don't want to try another beach, there's no reason we couldn't go back to that one."

"We can rent mopeds again. We will have one more good day." He could not keep the excitement out of his voice and his smile stretched across his face. This time he was not hiding it. We deserve it, she told herself. We deserve at least one more day.

"Shall we have dessert?"

He shook his head. "Not for me. I could not eat another thing. Do you want?"

"Not now. Maybe later."

He signaled the waiter for the check. She smiled. He was learning.

They walked back toward the town in silence. The street was filled with Greeks just strolling, enjoying the evening, and with tourists, hurrying to or from a restaurant or a hotel or just now leaving the beach. "I'm glad it was you that

O'Neal got," he said finally. "But I should not be," he added, his voice serious now. "It has made danger for you, and I do not like that I did that to you."

"You didn't know."

"I do not know what I am doing. That is whole problem."

She saw that his eyes were on the couple ahead, the man's arm around the woman's waist.

"You are only person I have now, Molly. Sometimes—sometimes I am afraid to trust even you. Other times I am frightened at what I have done to you. They will kill you like they killed O'Neal if they have chance. Sometimes I think I should leave you in this beautiful place and let them find me without you."

She slipped her arm through his. "No, Yuri. Look at O'Neal. Our leaving him didn't help him any."

"If I thought it would save you, I would do it."

They sat on a pile of rocks that served as a seawall and watched the sun sink into the sea amid a sky of vivid pink. "At least let me say that I am sorry you were brought into this," he said.

"No point in being sorry now. It's done."

"Yes, but still . . ."

"It'll be okay," she said. "We'll work it out somehow."

He took her hand and held it silently and they both watched the fading sky in the west. *You are all I have now,* he'd said. And he'd asked her whom she had. It was not going to be easy, none of it, and she was not at all ready for any of it. She stood and smoothed her skirt. "Would you like some *loukoumathes*?"

"Louk—?"

"Like a doughnut. Do you know what that is?"

They walked across the street and bought two trays of *loukoumathes* and carried them back to the rocks. "My grandmother used to make something like this—*khvorost*. It means 'twigs,' because that is what they look like."

"You miss her, don't you?"

He looked away. "I did not see her very much in last few years."

"Because she was in the hospital?"

"Because I could not bear to. It would not have mattered if she was in hospital or not. I think she almost likes it, in fact. She can be herself there. And she has all those people to look after. She is very good at that. She should have been nurse. Or teacher. And she just takes care of them all there, as if she were nurse instead of patient. No, it is not for that reason. It is because I think she might have been disappointed in me.''

She said nothing, watching the sky grow darker over the water.

''She did all correct things with me. I was member of Young Pioneers, and, later, Komsomol, everything. She did her best with me—she seemed to think I would grow to be like my mother.''

''But you were not like your mother.''

''No. My grandmother wanted me to be, and for long time I pretended I was. She knew that was only way to success and she wanted that for me. No matter what she was herself, she wanted that for me. But despite everything, in the end I guess I disappointed her.''

''It couldn't have been much of a surprise.''

''One always wants for one's children what is best for them, even if it is to be quite different from one's own self.''

''But in this case . . .''

''No.'' He shook his head. ''She loves Russia. She would not have wanted me to leave.''

''But she brought you up to be someone who almost had to leave.''

He looked at her in the half-dark. ''Even so,'' he said softly, ''she stayed. She would have expected me to stay, too.''

13

ALVIN JONES HAD ACCOMPANIED THE BODY BACK
to the States. As soon as he'd heard the news in Rafetna he'd
flown to Rome, where he'd bullied the authorities into hurrying their investigation enough to release the bodies early—no
small feat in Italy—and then he'd ridden the comman-
deered Air Force plane back to Andrews. Two foreign service
personnel killed by terrorists. It was the least the government
could do. Edwin Lopes' widow had insisted on accompanying
his body, as well. She was a frail-looking blonde, her eyes still
teary, her nose red, her cheeks pale. She had sent the two children back early to their grandparents, but she had insisted on
staying and coming back with the body. A mistake, Al Jones
thought, but it was not worth the hassle to argue over it. In the
end, he supposed the woman had a right. And anyway, Lopes'
body was not his concern.

Cathy O'Neal had been at Andrews when the plane landed,
accompanied by Glenn Pastrella and another man whose name
Jones didn't catch. He'd never met Cathy before, but he understood immediately why Dennis had seemed to think so highly
of her. She was tall, almost as tall as Dennis had been, he'd
guess, with short hair that framed her face in auburn waves. She
had hazel eyes and a fair complexion; she looked ten years
younger than she must really have been. She smiled graciously
when he introduced himself and she shook his hand in a firm
grasp. Whatever grief she experienced had been dealt with pri-
vately. There were no tears and she was completely composed.

In silence, she watched the casket being lowered from the
plane and carried to the waiting hearse.

"Would you like to ride back in the hearse?" he asked her.

"Yes."

Jones turned to Pastrella, who was making small talk with the other man. "Glenn, can you follow us?"

"Sure," Pastrella said.

"Father Jack—"

"Never mind, Cathy, I'll be right behind with Mr. Pastrella. I can understand that you would want to be with him." He put his arm gently around her waist; he was a good three inches shorter than she. He's a priest, Jones thought as he opened the door for her.

The driver pulled slowly off the tarmac, following the other hearse, the one carrying Lopes' body. Jones watched the vehicle ahead in silence until they had cleared the gate and then he turned to her. She sat between him and the driver, her hands folded in her lap. "I'm sorry to have met you under these circumstances," he said.

"Yes."

"It can't have been the kind of homecoming you were expecting."

He was watching her face; the surprise seemed genuine. "Expecting?"

"You knew he was on his way home, didn't you?"

"He had another four months . . ."

"But he must have contacted you and told you."

She was shaking her head. "Told me what?"

"That he was coming back. I'll have to admit it came up in a hurry, but it was my understanding that he was going to call you."

"He never called." She spoke slowly, quietly.

He wondered if she knew he'd be able to check the phone records. She seemed sharp enough; he guessed she would know that. "I'm quite surprised," he said. "The story we gave out in Rafetna was that you were having trouble with one of the kids and he had to come home to help straighten it out. It was my understanding that he was going to call you to coordinate your stories." If she was as smart as she seemed, she would know better than to ask anything else.

She shook her head again. "Well, he didn't."

"Even so," he said, "I recognize it must be a terrible blow. If there's anything I can do, be sure to let me know. I'll be around, and I'll stay in contact. It's not going to be easy. He was one of the best people I ever worked with."

"I appreciate it," she said simply.

* * *

Al Jones gazed into the water of the Reflecting Pool. Even Washington's July weather was preferable to Rafetna's. "He didn't call her," he said.

Henry Draper stood next to him, half a head taller and completely bald. "Are you sure of that?"

"As sure as I can be, but we should check it. Can we keep an eye on her mail?"

"That's tougher, you know. Why would he have written her?"

"If he got suspicious he might have. He could have thought of a telephone tap; he might have thought a letter would get through, that the mail wouldn't be checked."

"But he would have gotten home before a letter would have."

"If he became suspicious, he could have realized he might not make it home at all."

"Then why would he bring her into it? If he was suspicious, he wouldn't have wanted to do that, would he?"

Jones shrugged. "You never know."

"The mail thing is not that easy to pull off these days, Al. Are you sure it's worth it? We could raise some uncomfortable questions."

"It could raise a hell of a lot more questions if we leave any holes. And we'll tap her phone, too."

Draper began walking again. He liked to keep moving, Jones knew. For the same reasons, he preferred meeting outside, even in the muggy heat of summer in Washington. "What's the point in tapping her phone now? He's dead."

"Just in case. You never know who she might be trying to call. What can it hurt?"

Draper looked at him. "You really don't trust her, do you?"

Jones took a last long drag on his cigarette and flipped it toward the water. "He was a sharp guy and he thought the world of her. If we're going to keep a lid on this thing, we've got to keep it on. We check her mail; we tap her phone. You're right, I don't trust anybody."

"What about the film the Soviet guy gave you?"

"Exactly. Case in point. I suppose those were his so-called artistic pictures. Landscapes. Women pounding millet. They sure as hell weren't what Tass sent him down there for."

"He outsmarted you."

"That time. It won't happen again."

"You think he still has film?"

"He may. Or maybe he knew all along they were nothing. He put up a fight about giving them up. He probably thought the undeveloped film would buy his freedom. The developed pictures sure as hell wouldn't've.''

"Is there anyone else we should keep an eye on?"

"Half a dozen."

"Same thing?"

Jones nodded.

"How do you figure the Lopes thing?"

Jones shrugged. "O'Neal thought Lopes was a safe bet. And he ought to have been, except we figured it that way. In the end, we knew he'd have to go to someone. Even an O'Neal can make a mistake. After all, he was only an analyst. It might have been different if he'd been trained for covert action.''

"You act pretty calm when the real fish is still out there."

Jones flashed a confident smile. "Don't worry about them. Two amateurs—and one's a woman. And the other one's not worth much either. I've met him; he's spoiled and he's arrogant. He's part of their ruling class and that means you can almost certainly count on a few things: he's never had to find a job, never traveled on his own, never even bought anything from an ordinary store, or, probably, eaten at a restaurant that was open to the public. He'll drag her down, every step of the way.''

"They can still do a hell of a lot of damage."

"But to do it they have to surface, and we've got the surface covered.''

Molly sat on the sand and watched Yuri clambering on the rocks at the edge of the beach. They'd bought film last evening and he'd been taking pictures half the morning, including several of her. She'd tried to avoid that, but he'd insisted. It seemed harmless enough, and the use of the camera had brought a vitality to him that she hadn't seen before. And a volubility.

"Are there really millions of homeless people in America, wandering the streets?" he'd asked. "How can a country that claims to be richest in whole world allow such things?" Without even giving her time to answer, he went on. "You are like us, I think. We too have our privileged classes—well, I am part of it. Was, at least.''

She'd stared at him. "Then why did you leave?"

"Why did you go to Africa?"

"But aren't things getting better? Aren't things becoming more . . . free, more open . . . for people than before?"

"Is that you what think?" he'd asked. "You have read about *perestroika*—how do you think it will work? That everything will suddenly be like capitalism? Let me tell you. Men in power can talk all they want. Do they give up their dachas? Do their wives give up their fur coats, their designer clothes, their opportunities to shop in West? And if they do not, why should lesser people give up anything? If a man's position as factory manager allows him to take some profit on the side, or allows him to have more privileges than someone else—perhaps larger apartment or shopping privileges at restricted stores, or membership in restricted organizations, or opportunities to vacation at restricted resorts—do you think he will give it up? Do you think he will easily give up any power he has over others? Do you or anyone else think that KGB will give up what it has? Do you think that people will now be free to say whatever they wish—even criticize KGB—and nothing will happen? Is that what you think this new openness is about?''

She'd shaken her head. ''But Kalishev keeps saying—''

''*Glasnost.* You don't know Russian language, do you? That word means giving publicity to something that is already well known. It is as if before we pretended that the walls weren't there. Now we admit that they are there, but the fact doesn't make them any lower. Oh yes, Kalishev keeps saying things and already there are some changes, but so far they are only surface things. Men like my grandfather and his friends are not only ones who resist. Anyone who will lose power, anyone who will lose privileges, even anyone who will lose rank will resist them.''

''But surely the ordinary people—''

''The ordinary people! The ordinary people know nothing. Do you know why Khrushchev lost power? Because he tried to limit terms of office for high officials. Simply that, though it was made to look like other things. One reaches high ranks of power in Soviet Union and one finds there are all those privileges that common people know nothing about. High salaries, good apartments, dachas, government cars with chauffeurs, special railway cars, special treatment at airports, special resorts and hospitals that ordinary people cannot use, special schools for children, special stores where there are no lines and quality goods are available—even things from the West—at reduced prices. And all that power. And none of those people—they are called *nomenklatura*—were willing to give up all that. They wanted life-long careers, as they had expected, not to have to return to ordinary life, and not only for themselves, but for their children as well. Once, only very promising students went to Moscow State Institute of Foreign Relations. Now the school has become the private preserve of the families of men in highest power. So men in power turned against Khrushchev. It was not hard, of course, because there were many things about him that dismayed them, but they would not have thrown him out if he had not threatened their position in life. So, he failed to alter Soviet system. And after him Kosygin tried and also failed. If Kalishev succeeds this time, it will be miracle. And, let me tell you, Soviet people no longer believe in miracles. Yes, a man may now sell ice cream from his own stand on the street, a farmer may be encouraged to grow as much as he can on his own plot, but men at the top will not change.''

"It will begin at the bottom," she'd suggested. "It will begin at the bottom and be so successful that things will have to change at the top as well.''

He'd burst out laughing. "You are dreamer! Listen, Soviet Union is very large country. One cannot just snap one's fingers and say, 'Now you are all free to do and say whatever you want; now you are all suddenly responsible to make your factories turn out a profit and fire those people who stand in the way of such goals.' Did you know that it has always been taken for granted that people would not be considered too drunk to be at work as long as they could remain standing? How many people do you imagine spend their workdays leaning against walls, because as long as they are upright, they are not sent home? In past, such people's jobs were protected. In truth, it was very difficult for anyone to be fired—except for political reasons, of course. What will those people do now? Do you think they will suddenly all give up alcohol and become model workers? Even sober, a worker's job, his apartment, his medical care when he is sick— his whole life is only possible with the help of the State. We learn that from childhood, all of us. It is why I had to learn to keep my mouth shut, even me. You notice, I learned; I liked those Zil automobiles and those big apartments as well as any-one else. We see and do not see; we think and do not think.''

He'd grinned slyly at her, raising one eyebrow. "Do you know how factories work? Regional First Party Secretary is most pow-erful person in any area. He can make factory managers in his area successful by making sure they get raw products they need. That is not easy task—getting materials when you need them. In turn, factory managers pay money, or goods from the facto-ries, for that kind of help. Do you think Regional First Party Secretaries all over Soviet Union will suddenly give that up? Do you think factory managers will suddenly find raw goods flowing to them without the help of what you would call bribes? What do you think will become of a society that is turned upside down like that? I will tell you. It will not allow such a thing. It cannot. Too many people would not know how to survive. Maybe it can happen slowly, but it will not happen quickly. No, it will not.'' He shook his head.

"In the West, we believe people want to be responsible for themselves—that they would jump at the chance.''

He'd nodded. "Because you are used to it. In Soviet Union, such a thought is frightening. *Perestroika* you have heard of, but there is another word that is too firmly ingrained to be thrown away lightly. *Perestrakhovka*. Have you heard that one? You can say it means collective responsibility, that I will not accuse my co-worker and he will not accuse me. That everything is decided by committee, so if things turn out badly there is no one to blame. Lives have always been circumscribed in Soviet system; one has very little responsibility. Even men at very top decide everything in committee, and do you know that no official record is kept of Politburo meetings? Who says what, who favors what or opposes what? I have not been to such meetings, of course, but I grew up overhearing what my grandfather and his colleagues said. I think that there is even very little discussion at those meetings, at least very little dissension. Somewhere in background decisions are made, and at meetings proposals are put, and no arguments are expected and none are forthcoming. It is all decided. Nothing is anyone's fault. Decisions are made and then justifications are found. But responsibility? There is no such thing. And I am also frightened by it. How will I succeed in West? How well will I do? In society where my father does not have important job, am I good enough photographer to keep job? I never had to worry about that. In West, I will.''

She watched him move away, focusing the camera on a curve of rock, and she wondered about him. "But you were a child of privilege, and you chose to turn your back on it,'' she'd said.

"I chose to leave,'' he'd answered, "but it would have taken more courage to stay.''

She'd wondered if, in his position, she would have had the courage to leave.

He came toward her now. "I'm hot!'' he called. "Let's swim!''

* * *

Yuri reached for the towel, shook the sand from it, and held it against his face. Then he rubbed his hair with it. "What is phone number he gave you?" he asked.

"I don't know." She was pulling a pair of shorts over her swimsuit. He'd teased her about that; half the beach in town was covered with bare-breasted women. Her concerns with propriety had seemed to him curiously out of place. "Let them dress the way they want," she'd responded, "and I'm going to dress the way I want."

"How do you know it is someone you can trust?"

"Because O'Neal said it would be."

"And O'Neal is so expert? Then why is he dead?"

She bent to put the lunch things back into the bag. He wasn't as bad as she'd once thought, but he could still be annoying. "Look, we call whoever it is. We find out. Then we make up our minds. We haven't committed ourselves. If we don't like it, we drop out of sight again."

"Can they trace phone calls? If you call, can they find out where we are?"

"We've already dropped out of sight in Athens. It'll take them about two days to realize we've gone to the islands. We'd have to cut out of here anyway."

"We have enough money to stay for a long time, though."

"Sure, but not here. No, Yuri, we make the first move today. Then if we have to keep running, we still have plenty of money."

He looked back at the water. Small waves rolled gently into the beach. The sun, in the west now, cast purple-hued shadows against the rock and sand. "I hate to leave."

She followed his gaze, pleased that he had enjoyed it so much. At least, she thought, he'd had his paradise for two days. "Shall we have *barbunia* again for dinner?"

He grinned. "And *loukoumathes* after?"

"Why not?"

He snapped the towel in the air, then folded it and stuffed it into the side pocket of the red bag. She bent to take her watch from the opposite pocket and as she did, his hand brushed her cheek. When she straightened, he was watching her. "I hate to leave, too," she said.

For a moment she thought he was going to kiss her. But then he turned away and reached for his camera. "One last shot," he said.

She looked at her watch, crowding the other thoughts out of her mind. By the time they returned to town, showered, and got to the telephone office, it would be close to seven. The office closed at eight.

"We'd better get going," she said, standing.

He picked up the red bag and walked beside her toward the mopeds.

The OTE office was in a small separate building in the center of town, with the telephones ranged along one wall and the cashier's counter opposite. The wide doors on both the remaining walls stayed open during hours of business to let the sea breeze blow through. The floor was always sandy, and at busy times it was strewn with tourists waiting for an available phone in order to call home for more money, or the next island for a hotel, or the mainland to change airline reservations. Now, with most tourists on their way to dinner, it was almost deserted. A woman, bare feet shod in dilapidated blue plastic sandals, shouted in Greek into one of the phones, her right hand gesturing wildly, strands of hair flopping about her head as she continued her diatribe.

Molly took a token from the cashier and walked to an open phone. She looked at her watch again: five minutes to seven. On the East Coast it would be five minutes to one; in the West it would be almost ten in the morning. She was not sure of the area code, but wherever it was, she hoped someone was there at this time of day.

A cable television installation truck stood parked in a residential area of McLean, Virginia. A workman, his belt dangling screwdrivers, wirecutters, lengths of cable, and electronic testers, reached into the truck, then slammed the back doors shut and ambled back across the grass of a large home. Inside the truck, another man sat before an electronic board, his right hand holding one earpiece of a set of headphones against his ear. A bored look was on his face as he adjusted a dial on the board in front of him. A third man tipped back precariously on a three-legged stool in a corner of the truck and read the sports section of *USA Today*. It was hot in the truck. The man with the newspaper leaned down and picked up a thermos. Unscrewing the cap, he took a long draft of iced tea. "Hot as hell," he said.

The man with the headphones heard the phone ringing and automatically glanced at a digital readout. Twelve fifty-six. He made a penciled notation on the pad in front of him.

"Hello?" That was the O'Neal woman.

"Is this Cathleen?" It was another woman's voice. Probably another sympathy call.

There was a moment's hesitation on the O'Neal woman's end. Perhaps she didn't recognize the voice. "Yes," she said quietly. There was a hint of anticipation in her voice.

"I was told to call you. I'm—"

"Don't tell me!" the O'Neal woman interrupted.

The man quickly swiveled the headset and jammed both earpieces against his ears. "Frank," he said quietly, flipping a switch. The hollow sound of an open speaker filled the truck.

The O'Neal woman had paused. Now she was talking again, and her voice, sounding calm and firm, filled the truck. "Can you make another phone call right away?" she asked. The man at the electronic board turned the dial down slightly.

"Yes," the other woman said tentatively.

"Then I'm going to give you another number. Call it in five minutes. Not sooner. Tell the person who answers everything you can. She'll tell you what to do. Trust her. Do you have a pencil?"

"Just a minute."

"Quickly."

"Okay."

The Jones woman spoke a number. The man at the electronic board wrote it down as she gave it. Area code 213. Southern California, he thought. "Call her. Trust her," the O'Neal woman repeated. Then the phone clicked. A moment later, the other phone clicked too, ending the connection.

The two men looked at each other across the truck. "Bingo," said the one with the newspaper. Then both men turned to the electronic board again as the sound of a phone being dialed came through the speaker. Above the digital clock was another LED display, and both men watched the numbers appear on it. It was not the same number the O'Neal woman had just given out.

She could hear the phone ringing. Holding her hand over the receiver, she called, "Charlie!"

From upstairs the answer came. "Yo!" She could tell by the sound of it that his door was shut.

"Down here on the double!"

She could hear the door open upstairs and Charlie bounded down the steps. "Go over to Westons'," she said before he even reached the bottom, her hand still over the receiver. "Get Jason and take him to Father Jack's immediately—"

"Hello." It was a woman's voice on the phone.

Cathy held up her hand to indicate she wasn't finished. "I'm calling for Alvin Jones," she said into the phone. "Is he in?"

"Just a minute, please."

"—take him to Father Jack's," she went on, her hand over the receiver again. "Don't tell Mrs. Weston or anybody else where you're going. Leave him there and go get Scott at baseball practice. Take him there, too—"

"This is Al Jones," the voice said in her ear.

"Mr. Jones, it's Cathy O'Neal. I'm sorry to bother you."

"No problem. Anything I can do?" he said, but she had her hand over the receiver and was mouthing the rest to Charlie. *Go out the back*, she was telling him.

"Mom—"

"Well, it might not be anything at all . . ." *I'll call you at Father Jack's*, she mouthed to Charlie. *It's important; do it. Your father—*

"You never know, Cathy," Al Jones was saying. "It's always better to be cautious. What is it?"

"I got this phone call . . ." She grabbed Charlie's shirt as he went by. *I'll call*, she mouthed again. "Just a minute, Mr. Jones, I think there's someone at the door. I'll be right back." She could hear the back door shut behind Charlie as she set the receiver down. She went out the back door too, closing it quietly behind her, leaving the receiver still on the telephone stand in the front hall.

She knew Marge was home; she'd seen her a few minutes ago out in the garden. She was still there, trimming her roses. "Marge," she called, pushing through the hedge that divided the yards. "Can I use your phone? Something seems to be wrong with ours."

"Sure. You know where it is."

"Yeah. I'll let myself in. The roses are gorgeous."

Marge turned back to the roses and Cathy ran into the house. Inside, she dialed the kitchen phone. While it rang, she looked at her watch. Cutting it too close, she thought. The phone kept ringing. Come on, she thought, I've burned my bridges, you've got to be there.

On the seventh ring a groggy voice answered. "Hello?"

"It's Cathy," she answered. "Are you awake?"

"God. What time is it?"

"Come on. Are you awake?"

"Oh my God, Cathy," the voice moaned, "do you know what time it is?"

"Dammit!" Cathy said harshly. "Are you awake?"

She could hear the exasperated sound of a breath being exhaled. "I am now."

"Listen. This is important. The most important thing you've ever done in your life. Someone is going to call you in less that two minutes. Find out everything you can. Give her the number of the place with the scarecrow family and tell her to call there tomorrow. You know the place I mean."

"Cathy—"

"You know."

"Yes."

"Give her the number and then get out. Get out as fast as you can. Don't go to work; don't do anything. I mean this, Gloria; it's important. Go stay with someone you can trust. I'll be at the place by tonight. Have her call me there tomorrow—anytime. And you call me there tomorrow, too."

"Cathy, this is crazy."

"Just do it."

"I can't. I've got—"

"I don't care what you've got. You have to."

"You can't just call up like this. You don't know what I—"

"Gloria. Please. I'll explain it. Just do it. Get out of there as fast as you can after the phone call."

There was a moment of silence. Gloria was sharp. Surely there must have been times when she had wondered. Cathy was counting on that now. "Okay," Gloria said finally.

"Thanks," Cathy said, but the phone was already clicking in her ear. She looked at her watch. Less than a minute to spare.

She ran out of the house, through the yard without even saying anything to Marge, and back into her own house. She lifted the receiver from the table. "Mr. Jones? Are you still there?"

"Yes." His voice sounded testy.

"Oh, listen, I'm really sorry." She was watching the dial of her watch. "You know, if it's not one thing it's another. I guess with Dennis gone, you know, things just seem to be piling up. Sorry if I sound out of breath. I was calling you from upstairs and I had to run down to answer the door and then back up—"

"You were saying something about a phone call."

"Yes, I got one just before you called, and it seemed a little strange . . ." The time was up. She'd like to give it another minute, at least another half. "You know, Dennis always told me that if I got strange phone calls, I should assume they were for him, but in this case, I didn't know what I should do. I think I know who it might have been. In any case, I told them to call a contact Dennis has, it's a number I've heard him use. I don't know if that was the right thing to do or not—"

The man with the earphones looked across at the other one. "Is she screwing us?" he asked.

In response, the other looked at the digital clock.

"Hell," the one with the earphones said, "she is, isn't she."

"I'll jam it," the other one said, reaching for a receiver and punching in the number from the pad of paper. Simultaneously, the one with the earphones pressed two buttons and the conversation with Jones was cut off. They stared at each other as the sound of the other number ringing busy filled the truck.

"What's the number?" Al Jones asked.

"Ah, just a minute, it's right here." She reached for the phone book and flipped it open to the Yellow Pages. Coventry Florist. She read him the number. She looked at her watch again. "I hope that was all right," she said. She was watching out the window now.

"Sure," he said. "Next time, though, maybe you shouldn't give out numbers when you don't know who's at the other end. Maybe you should just refer them to me."

"Frankly," she said, still looking out the window, "I hope there isn't a next time. Good-bye, Mr. Jones." She hung up without waiting for him to say good-bye. Nothing yet. She ran into the kitchen, grabbed her purse, paused just long enough to make sure her wallet was in it, and slipped out the back door. A minute later, two men strode up the front walk and rang the doorbell.

Cathy O'Neal ran through the backyards of her neighbors and out, finally, to another street. There she slowed to a walk, her mind still working at full speed. The boys taken care of, that's good. She had her purse; she needed to get to a bank. She needed transportation. She paused, thinking, then turned left, hurrying along the road. She kept going until she came to a blue Dutch Colonial. Seeing a car in the drive, she walked briskly up to the door and rang the bell. "Come on, Sylvia," she said out loud, tapping her finger against the doorjamb of the house. When the door opened, she smiled, wondering how disheveled she looked.

"Syl," she said.

"Cathy! Come in."

"Oh, I can't. Listen, my car stalled out over on Balcom Road, and I've got a million things to do today. Everything's just been piling up; I'm trying to get the boys ready to send them off to my sister in California and it's all just going crazy. And Charlie, you know, just got his driver's license. He's off somewhere or other with . . . with Dennis' car. Any possibility I can borrow yours?"

"Sure. No problem."

"Syl, I don't want to put you out—"

"Cathy, listen, it's the least I can do. Keep it for as long as you want. Do you need to call a service truck?"

"No, I did that already. They offered me a ride home, but it was really close enough to walk. But I got this far and thought, well, maybe if you weren't using your car for the rest of the afternoon, I could still get some things done. Charlie or I can bring it back before supper, if that's okay with you."

Sylvia Morris took both of Cathy's hands in hers. "Cathy, really, Fred and I thought the world of Dennis, think the world of you as well. If there's anything we can do, anything . . . Lending a car is nothing. Take it. Keep it as long as your other one is in the shop. Really. Let us do that for you." She turned and pulled a set of keys from a hook near the door. "Take the Dodge; it's in the drive. I can't guarantee how clean—"

"Thanks a million," Cathy said, taking the keys. "I'll get it back as soon as I can."

"Don't worry about it. Really." Sylvia gently pulled Cathy closer and kissed her cheek, then put a hand on Cathy's shoulder. "Take care of yourself. It's good that the boys are going away. Indulge yourself. Cry your eyes out, buy yourself a five-pound box of chocolates and a big book and lose yourself, take that stupid backpack of yours out of the attic and go camping. Go up to Maine. Do something that makes you feel good."

"I will."

"Promise? I'm going to be checking up on you."

Cathy stepped back. "I will; I promise. And thanks." She turned and walked toward the car. She took one deep breath and turned at the car and waved to Syl, who was still standing in the doorway. *Buy a five-pound box of chocolates and a big book and lose yourself.*

She looked at her watch. She would stop at a branch bank out toward Leesburg Pike and withdraw everything she could. She started the engine and backed out of the drive. Then she'd turn around and head for Chevy Chase, where she'd pick up the Metro and take it all the way to Washington National. She'd call Syl from a booth and tell her where the car was—she'd leave the keys under the seat and lock the car when she got out. At the airport she'd buy a ticket and pay for it with a credit card. They'd probably be able to trace the card, but she needed to make the money last as long as it had to. And somewhere she'd also have to make a call to Father Jack. She pressed her back against the car seat and tried not to think too much of Dennis. Good God, she thought, what is it? Why did you give her the name? What really happened in Rome?

Molly and Yuri watched the sun finally slide completely beyond the horizon. They had not spoken for half an hour.

"Five o'clock is going to come early," he said.

"I know," she said, but she didn't move.

"You said yourself that they could not possibly come until morning. First thing in morning, we will be gone."

"It would have been better if we could have gone tonight."

"I don't blame him. I would not want to go that far at night, either."

"But these people are fishermen. They go out at night all the time."

"Around their own islands. Not as far as this." He took her hand and gently pulled her up from the seawall. "If you don't feel like sleeping, we can go back to our room and you can teach me how to act American."

"It isn't going to work, Yuri. There's no way we can do it all."

"Of course it will. It worked this far, did it not?" He kept her hand in his.

"How can we end it? Who can we trust?"

"You must decide that," he said.

She kicked a pebble in the street and then heard it skitter away, although it was too dark to see where it had gone.

"In Soviet Union," he said, "one is cautious about trusting. For sake of self-preservation, one must always be suspicious of another's motives. I was suspicious of you at first." He saw her quick glance. "Yes, I was. Why would you help me escape? You must be CIA, I was sure of that. Why should I trust you; perhaps you would report everything I thought and did to the authorities. Then, when you struck out at O'Neal in Rome, I was confused. You were angry that he was CIA. That ought to mean that you were not one of them, but then why were you doing this? Because he had forced you? Because they had something against you, some . . . blackmail or something? If not that, then why? Why would you put yourself at risk for someone you did not even know? I could not imagine any reason. Unless, of course, it was all a sham. Unless you really were CIA and just pretended not to be. How could I know the truth? In Soviet Union there would be only two reasons for someone to help KGB—maybe three. Because they were also KGB, or because they wanted to curry favor with KGB—for future considerations—or because KGB forced them to. There would be no other reason. Now I know"—he laughed—"I think—that it was just because of the kind of person you are."

"Anyone would have done it."

"Not anyone, I think. Not even any American, no matter what you say. You will have to decide for us. You talked with Cathleen and the other. You will have to decide if we can trust them."

"His wife. Good heavens, Yuri, it was his wife. Now she's in danger, too, I suppose. It must have been why she made me call the other number. They were probably tapping her phone."

"You will feel better after we leave. You will feel safer then."

I will not, she thought. We will run and run and run, and there will never be a time or a place when we can stop. It was a mistake to have made the calls; it had only brought the other two into it. Better to have just stayed here; better to have stayed here a few more days and enjoyed it and then let them come. In the end, she thought dejectedly, they are going to find us anyway.

General William R. French fastened his gray eyes on Stephen White. "A royal fuck-up," he said quietly.

White said nothing.

"A goddamn royal fuck-up. Civilians, for God's sake! Goddamn civilians."

"We do have it covered. We're doing the best we can."

"Covered? Goddamn it, *covered*? I don't want the best you can. I want to know where they are! What the hell do you mean by covered, anyway? You let the O'Neal woman get away, didn't you? You let them call her and she snookered you and now you don't have her or them!''

''We're working on it—''

''I don't want to hear 'working on it.' I want to hear that you know where she is. How the hell can someone like her wipe the floor with your people?''

''We've listened to the tape over and over again and there's nothing. There's nothing to indicate who was calling. You heard the tape yourself.''

''There has to be something. There always is. And she was on to it like a flash. She knew. How the hell did she know?''

''We've checked the Long Beach number.''

''And?''

''It's her sister, we've gotten that far. But she must have cut out right away. She's an actress; does mostly TV stuff, although she's in a play down there at the moment. Nobody you ever heard of. She's bound to be in contact with her agent.''

French stood and shoved his chair against the desk. ''Don't count on it. Are you tracing the calls?''

''We know they came from Greece but we could have figured that already. I told you about the Russians in Athens.''

French nodded. ''We're going to be up to our ears in shit if we don't get this thing covered. For real.'' He turned his back and gazed out the window.

I'm going to be in the shit, White thought; you guys have got your asses covered too well to have to worry. ''They think they're in the islands. The phone traces will pinpoint it for them.''

''If they haven't already moved on,'' French said.

White had already thought about that. ''They still have to get back to the States.''

''They don't. All they have to do is get to a newspaper. One fucking newspaper.''

''There's nobody they can trust over there. They must have figured that out. That's why they called the O'Neal woman. They're trying to get back. They're not going to feel safe until they do. And they're right. That story is nothing without Klebanoff to back it up. We kill him, we kill the story.''

''You have to find him first.''

''We have every airport covered. Every customs agent is looking for him. The Russians supplied us with pictures.''

''Nice of them, considering,'' French said sarcastically.

''The key is still the O'Neal woman. They contacted her; they had to have gotten her number from O'Neal. We find her, we find them.''

French turned to face him again. His form was outlined against the window by the pale light of dusk. The lights in the room were off. "And how are you going to find her?''

"We're turning her life upside down. She contacted her sister. That's got to mean something. Of all the people in the world that she might have contacted, why her sister? Both of them are civilians; one of them is bound to have made a mistake. We're combing both places for traces of them. We already know the O'Neal woman took a borrowed car as far as Chevy Chase. She left it a mile from a Metro line; we assume she took the Metro into town. We're covering the cabs right now.''

"I can tell you where she went without all that. Try National Airport.''

"We are. We're going counter to counter with her picture.''

"When you've found her,'' General French said into the semi-darkness, "let me know.''

Valentin Yevseyevich Kozlov, retired general of the Soviet Army, was in full uniform, with a mass of service ribbons and medals attached to his chest. He rarely wore the uniform these days, preferring to putter about his apartment in his pajamas. On the occasions when he had to meet a contact in a park or at a cinema, he dressed in the dark, drab clothes of a pensioner. No one ever looked at him twice. No one ever realized that he had once come near to leading the entire Soviet Army. No one ever thought that this obscure-looking man was engineering the biggest coup in the history of the Soviet Union. Now, he leaned forward so that he could hear better, and accidentally knocked over a bottle of vodka. Paying little attention, assuming one of the waiters would hurry over to clean it up, he spoke to the man on the opposite side of the table. "No. You know I have been ill recently and I have heard very little.''

His companion clicked his tongue. "Then are you unaware. Valentin Yevseyevich, that the esteemed General Secretary of the Party has been running in a whirlwind?''

"No. What is the cause of it?''

The man across the table leaned closer, though there was no one within hearing distance. On a raised platform at the front of the large dining room, a young and pretty singer from the Bolshoi was singing something from Moussorgsky. Kozlov would, under other circumstances, have been interested in hearing how she did, but these dinners were never places to appreciate music, no matter how good it was. Hardly anyone paid attention—they were always too busy stuffing their mouths and congratulating themselves and each other on having been invited. At the head table, General Secretary Kalishev seemed deep in conversation with an aide."

"One always hears rumors," the man said to Kozlov. "His health appears to be excellent."

"Were the rumors about his health, then?" Kozlov asked ingenuously.

"Not his physical health." The statement was accompanied by a raising of eyebrows.

"Then what?"

"That is what everyone else would like to know."

Kozlov turned away in disgust. This one knew next to nothing. He glanced about the room. There were plenty of others, some of whom were bound to know how far Kalishev had moved. But Kozlov could already make a good guess. From the outside, people thought the Central Committee was quick to spring to action, but he knew they were wrong. In reality, it moved with the speed of a turtle, which was to be expected under the circumstances. No one wanted to make mistakes. Until Kalishev had sorted it all out, he would do little. On the other hand, military men were trained to act decisively, and that was what would give Phase II the upper hand. By the time Kalishev had considered all his options and their ramifications, Yuri Andreyevich Klebanoff would be dead and the project would have been saved.

14

MOLLY STOOD AT THE BACK OF THE CAÏQUE, TRY-
ing to keep from shivering. Though the early morning sun
shone fully on her now, a southwest wind still blew cold
across the water. Beside her, Yuri leaned over the side of the
boat, his eyes closed, his face pale; she was afraid he was
going to be sick. The fisherman stood in the center of the
boat, a weather-hardened hand casually on the wheel, his
bare feet splayed on the worn wooden deck. His name, he
had said, was Marko Lefkos. Closer to the bow, Marko's ten-
year-old son faced into the wind, a grin of excitement lighting
his face. Molly wondered if he had ever been to Ikaria before.
Even now, after more than two hours at sea, the caïque's
engine coughed spasmodically as if in complaint over this
unexpected trip. But Marko merely nodded and looked at the
plume of black diesel smoke that escaped the exhaust pipe
above his head—visible proof, he seemed to think, that there
was nothing to worry about.

"Papa! Papa!" The boy's voice could not be heard above
the engine noise, but they could see his mouth forming the
words as he pointed off in the distance. Marko smiled indulgently. Molly squinted but could see nothing. Marko pointed
toward the horizon, but still she saw nothing. She concen-
trated where Marko had pointed and finally she saw it, too:
the faint shape of a large boat in the far distance.

She look questioningly at Marko and he spoke Greek words
that she did not understand over the chugging engine. He
leaned toward her and this time she caught the shouted words:

"Plio . . . aftokinito."

"Apo?" she asked.

"Patmos."

She nodded. It would be on its way back to Athens—no problem. Yuri had turned a questioning face toward her. "It's only a car ferry from Patmos," she said. They watched the ferry as it steamed across the horizon, going in the opposite direction. There was no reason to be concerned. The ferry could only barely be seen; their caïque, much smaller, would not even be visible from the other boat.

The boy's cries could be heard again now, even over the engine. He was clinging to the mast, jumping up and down in excitement, and pointing. The three at the back of the boat followed the direction with their eyes and saw a pair of dolphins leaping amid sun-glittered waves. Yuri grinned in delight. "The Greeks think they bring good fortune," Molly said to him. "With luck, they'll stay with us all the way to Ikaria."

It was late in the afternoon when the caïque chugged into the harbor at Aghios Kirikos. The town clung to the side of the hills, as if in fear of tumbling into the sea, and the pale buildings looked even paler against the dark-green trees that covered the mountainsides. A few townspeople stood on the quay, curious about the unfamiliar boat, watching as Marko brought it closer.

The child—Molly had learned his name was Costas—had lost his earlier boyishness and was now all manly business. He had looped the line carefully and was holding it, standing at the gunwale, ready to leap to shore as soon as his father brought the caïque close enough.

The main part of Aghios Kirikos, like most island harbor towns, was strung along one street that ran the length of the harbor. Molly could see the tables of a *kafeneion* spread outside its doors, with men in dark-colored shirts and baggy pants gathered in groups of local gossip. It was not the best of circumstances, she knew; not enough tourists came to Ikaria, and certainly few of them came in chartered caïques. The inhabitants of Aghios Kirikos would remember—and gossip about—the man and woman who had come this way. She wondered where she could find a public telephone.

Cathy O'Neal sat in a lawn chair just outside the cottage door, close enough to hear the telephone when it rang. She tried to concentrate on the book in her hands, but her mind kept wandering, going over the last twenty-four hours, wondering what she might have forgotten. She'd flown to Boston

and rented a car and driven straight through, getting to Jones-
port, Maine, just before two in the morning. Within ten minutes Gloria had called; she'd been calling every half hour
since 8 P.M. Pacific time. She was worried about Molly, about
Cathy, and, probably, about herself. She'd told Cathy what
Molly had said, the words spilling out almost faster than she
could speak them: the defection, the killings, Dennis' suspicions. Cathy had stood in the silence of the cottage, the receiver pressed against her ear, her eyes closed, listening, and
without realizing, nodding. Since Dennis' death she'd known
without knowing; now, hearing the story, it was almost as if
she had already heard it before.

When Gloria had finished, she'd stood silent, her mind still
confirming what she'd suspected all along. "Cathy?" Gloria
had said. "Are you still there?"

"I'm thinking," she'd answered. And she was thinking—
thinking about everything she'd done, and wondering if it had
been right. "You've talked with her, too," she'd said finally.

"Don't you think I know that?" Gloria's voice had been
surprisingly calm; she knew how volatile Gloria could be.
"And you, too," Gloria had added. "She contacted you, too.
They can't know what she told either one of us."

The floor lamp cast a circle of gold on the pine floor. Outside, the fog had closed in, and she could not even see the
lights of the Wilson house, twenty yards away. "I know that,"
she said. "I'll have to stay here until she calls. You told her
to call, didn't you?"

"I told her, but what if she doesn't?"

"Gloria, if you're scared, think how scared she must be.
She'll call. If she called me in the first place, it's because
there's nowhere else for her to turn. Gloria, you can get to
the airport, can't you?"

"Yes . . ."

"Good. Get a flight out as soon as you can. Fly to Pittsburgh. Make whatever connections you have to. When you
get there, rent a car and drive to Albany. I know you don't
like driving, but you'll have to do it. Anybody who doesn't
like driving shouldn't live in Los Angeles, by the way."

"You've told me that before."

"Leave the car at the car-rental place at the Albany airport.
I'll pick you up there at six o'clock in the evening day after
tomorrow. That's tomorrow my time; the day after on your
time."

"Not until then?"

"You figure it. I have to wait here for her to call. I have to have time to drive there myself."

"What're we going to do then?"

"We'll talk about it. Gloria, be calm. Don't panic. We can work it out."

"You didn't talk to her, Cathy; I did. And what if she doesn't call?"

"She will." She paused. "I have to wait here until she does. If I don't make it by six-thirty, come the next day at the same time. Keep coming until I show up."

"And what am I supposed to do for money until then?"

"Use plastic. We'll worry about how we pay for it later. If you do need to get money out of your bank account, go to an electronic teller and take it out that way. Don't walk into a bank."

"But can't they trace me through the credit cards?"

"Probably. But they can also trace us a half dozen other ways as well, so I'm not sure it matters. But we may need the cash later."

"God, Cathy, I had no idea you and Dennis lived like this."

"Is that what you think? Gloria, this isn't TV; this is the real world. I've never done anything like this before in my life."

They'd hung up then, but she'd been unable to sleep.

It was almost noon now, a warm day for the Maine coast, but still she was bundled in jeans and a sweatshirt that she'd found in a closet. She'd almost certainly left them there the last time they'd been up. She tried not to think of that. She was trying not to think of anything that involved Dennis, especially Dennis and this Molly person. She was ashamed to feel that way, but she knew she was not going to feel differently until she had met Molly—and perhaps not even then. Was it really worth his life? she kept asking herself. And the other question kept coming back: why had he given her the name?

A gull wheeled high in the air above her head, and she watched it play the air currents. Against a clear blue sky it plunged and then hung as if suspended for a moment, then it flapped its wings twice and caught another current and rode it, skimming to a landing on the water. It sat there for a while, bobbing on the waves. A blue-and-white lobster boat

chugged by, coming in from a morning of checking the traps,
a stack of extra traps balanced in a pile at the back of the
boat, a plume of smoke rising from the diesel exhaust pipe.
The lobsterman stood at the wheel of his boat, rubberized
boots up to his knees, a cigarette dangling from his mouth.

Inside the house, the phone rang. She jumped up, paused
to take a deep breath, and walked inside.

"Hello?" she said into the receiver.

"Is . . . this Cathleen?" The voice was faint, the line full
of static.

"Yes, this is Cathleen, but you're going to have to speak
up. I can barely hear you. Where are you calling from?"

There was a pause. Then the voice came through again,
this time slightly louder. "Greece. An island."

"My sister told me what you said. There are two of you?"

"Yes."

"You want to get back to the States?"

"I want to get somewhere . . . safe."

"Do you know who it is?"

"No. Your husband . . . told me not to try to guess, not
to trust anyone except you."

She closed her eyes. Dennis . . . "Do you have money?"
she asked. "Do you have passports? Can you get to an airport?"

"Yes. To all of those."

"How much money?"

"A lot. Enough."

"How long would it take you to get to an airport?"

For a moment there was only static on the line. Then she
heard the voice again. "I don't know. I don't know where the
nearest one is. Maybe two days."

"Not sooner?"

"Maybe. But I wouldn't count on it."

"It could take you another day, then, at least, to get over
here."

"I know."

Cathy stared into the receiver, thinking. "Take the first
flight you can get to Montreal," she said finally. "You may
have to switch planes in Paris or London. Maybe both. After
you land in Montreal, go to the information booth in the
airport and ask for messages for Cathleen. Cathleen Booth.
That's Cathleen for me and Booth as in 'information booth.'
Got that?"

"Yes. Cathleen Booth."

"I'll expect you there in about three days."

"If we don't run into any problems."

"Are you going to be all right? Can you make that?"

"Yes. The message will tell me where to meet you?"

"Yes."

"Cathleen . . . I'm sorry about your husband."

"Thank you." Then she added, "Take care."

"You too. Good-bye."

The telephone clicked in Cathy's ear. Molly, whoever she was, had sounded younger than she'd expected. She looked at her watch. It was the better part of the day's drive to Albany; she could start out now and stop overnight along the way, or she could try to get some sleep tonight and leave early tomorrow morning.

"Well?" Yuri asked.

"I spoke with her finally. Cathleen . . ."

"What will we do next?"

"We hire another boat for tomorrow. I wonder where we can find a map. Turkey . . ." she said, more to herself than to him. "We need to aim for Turkey, unless there's an airport closer."

The Athenian leaned casually against the doorjamb. His eyes, behind dark glasses, could barely be seen. Christina Lefkos did not like that; she felt uncomfortable talking with people whose eyes she couldn't see. One never knew what such people were thinking. To show her disapproval, she didn't let the man see her own eyes; instead, she stared beyond him, shading her eyes from the sun.

"I asked at the *plateia* where a man could hire a boat. They told me your Marko will do that. I am wondering if it is true," the man said.

"If they told you that at the *plateia*, then you already know it is true," she answered. She was not overly anxious to help such a man. On the other hand, it was always possible he was from the police. One never knew what obscure law one might be breaking these days. But in her whole life on Paros, she had never known it to be against the law for a simple fisherman to make a few extra drachmas by hiring out his boat.

"They say he has the best boat, the one most equipped for a long distance."

"It was his father's before him," she explained defensively. "Marko and his father have always taken good care of the boat."

"A caïque, is that correct?"

"Yes."

The man nodded his approval. "Caïques are indeed indestructible. Even in a *meltemi*, a caïque would be safe."

"My husband would not be foolish enough to go out in the *meltemi*, even in that boat," she responded indignantly.

"I was not suggesting that he would be, only that in the worst of storms, if one had to be out in a boat, one would be fortunate if the boat were one that could survive. They told me also that your husband has gone somewhere. I was hoping to hire him before nightfall. When do you expect him back?"

"Not before tomorrow."

"Has he hired out to someone else, then?"

"Yes."

"They told me that he was gone this morning when they came back with their catch, that he did not go out last evening as usual. He must have left very early this morning. Then it must really be true that his boat can go long distances."

"Long enough."

"Long enough so that he will not be back until tomorrow. Does he often go so far?"

"I am sorry. I must get back to my work." She turned to walk back into the house.

"One more moment, Kyria Lefkos." The man pulled some bills from his pocket and held two out toward her. "I would like to leave a deposit for chartering his boat. He can reach me at the Xenia. You say he will not return until tomorrow evening?"

She took the money cautiously. Two hundred drachmas. She nodded her head once, firmly. "Tomorrow," she said.

"There is a storm coming from the south," he said. "Perhaps a *meltemi*. I hope he has not gone in that direction."

"No," she answered. "He went to Ikaria."

"Ikaria? I would have though he had hired out to tourists. I would have thought they would have gone to Thíra, or perhaps to Mykonos. It must not have been Americans, then."

"Oh yes," she said smugly. "It was two Americans, a man and a woman."

* * *

From the Lefkos home, the Athenian walked to the OTE building. There were no empty telephones available and he would have to wait. He looked with vague disinterest at the others in the place. Mostly tourists. Everywhere they went, they seemed to be camping out—on the beach, at the tavernas, here in the OTE. Bags strewn on the floor, barefoot and dirty, they were truly a disgusting lot. Though it was not bright inside the building, he kept his sunglasses on. He liked wearing them because they made him feel distanced from the people he had to work among. He was one generation removed from a mountain village in the Peloponnese, and he returned every Easter to his father's village. Though even today there was no running water in the village, the people there kept cleaner than most of the tourists he saw these days. There was a sobriety and an industry that even many of his father's fellow villagers had lost since they had moved to the city. Not so with him; he knew the true values of life. He knew also how to deal with those who still lived in the villages.

When his turn came for a telephone, he stepped close to it, shielding the instrument with his body while he dialed. He was so used to such precautions that he performed them without even thinking. When the telephone was answered, he spoke his name, then gave the information he had gathered. "They are only one day ahead of us," he reported. "They have gone to Ikaria."

"Can you get there today?"

"Of course not. I will have to charter a boat, and no one would leave for there now; it is too far. They will insist on waiting until tomorrow."

"All right. Leave tomorrow, then."

"There is only one thing," he said, proud that he had thought of it. "It is always possible that they could have changed their minds at the last moment and not gone to Ikaria. If I wait one more day, I can speak to the man who took them there. He can verify their actual destination. In the end, it could save valuable time."

There was a moment of silence. "That is very true. Wait another day, then. Speak to him. Make sure of where they have gone. You're sure it was to be Ikaria?"

"That is what the fisherman's wife said."

"Speak to him. Make sure."

"And then go?"
"And then go."

In Athens, John Schlatter set down the telephone and leaned
back in his chair, looking at the map of Greece on the opposite
wall. Ikaria. Moving east. It would probably be a good idea to
contact Ankara.

He stood and walked closer to the map. In its lower left corner, bordered by an orange square, was a small inset, labeled
"Map of Communications in Greece." Black lines showed rail-
ways; white lines showed shipping routes; orange lines showed
domestic air routes. He stared at the orange lines for a few
moments, then looked for the island of Ikaria. There was no air
transportation from Ikaria; the closest flights were out of Samos,
three-quarters of an inch to the east on this small map; the next
closest from Mykonos, an inch closer to Athens. He stared at
the map for a while, his eyes following all the routes, all leading
to Athens. His eyes found Paros, closer to Mykonos than the
airport at Samos was to Ikaria. If they had wanted to take a
plane, it would have been much easier to charter a boat to Mykonos in the first place. Unless, of course, they had never intended to go to Ikaria; unless that was just the cover.

He stared at the map for a few moments longer. Then he
turned back toward his desk. He would call Ankara. And he
would send someone out to Hellenikon Airport, also, just in
case.

Molly handed a fifty-dollar bill to the fisherman. He stood at
the harbor beside his green-and-red boat and took the money
without looking at her face. She knew he thought it odd that she
should be transacting this business instead of Yuri. "At five
o'clock, then," she repeated in Greek.

He nodded wordlessly.

"How long will it take us to get to Samos?"

He looked above her shoulder. "Five hours, perhaps," he
said. "Maybe less."

Probably more, she thought. He would underestimate the time
as a matter of policy. "We will see you in the morning," she
said, holding out her hand.

He took it reluctantly and shook it once, then let it go. He did
not look at Yuri at all.

"*A theo,*" she said and picked up her bag. "He does not

approve," she said to Yuri after they had walked a few paces. "He thinks you should have handled it."

"But he will take us?"

"For the price he asks, he can't afford not to."

"Why didn't we have Marko take us all the way? He seemed much nicer."

"He is nicer," she agreed. "Unfortunately, he is not familiar with the passage from here to Samos. There's a lot of sea between here and there, you know."

"From here to Samos, and then from Samos to Chios," he said, saying the names that were only words to him.

"Or to Rhodes. Or to Athens if we can get a plane from Samos in good time."

Cathy O'Neal drove along the road that dipped and curved among the blueberry barrens. The early morning sun skimmed the gentle rises and shone more fully on the east-facing slopes. The hollows were still in shadow. The berries showed pale blue now; harvest was another few weeks away, but already the barrens looked more blue than green. A single house, its cedar-shake siding weathered to gray, stood on a hill to her left. Beyond, a saltwater flat showed low tide. Sea gulls circled over the water. More gulls strutted across the wet sand. She looked at her watch: 6 A.M. She would be in Albany in plenty of time. She wished she had more money.

Alvin Jones walked slowly by the panda exhibit. The pair, sent to America during the Nixon thaw with China, were not in sight. Beside him, taking two strides for every three of Jones', was Henry Draper. Draper's bald head shone with perspiration.

"The two women are sisters," Draper said. "Originally from western Pennsylvania, but there's little family left there anymore. Both their parents are dead."

"Other siblings?" Jones asked.

"Only the Wallace woman. She seems to have dropped out of sight, but we're getting a line on her. We have checks at the airport and we're making the rounds of her friends. Cathy O'Neal flew from National to Boston, where she rented a car. The family has a summer home in Maine. It's been in the family for a couple of generations. O'Neal and his wife used it regularly. As far as we know, the sister in Long Beach seldom came—you could understand why. It would make a great rendezvous point—coast of Maine and all. They could even bring them in by boat. We've got someone going up there, but you know, we're bound to run short on manpower. You can only go so far with the secret-project business, and then you run into someone who has a right to know.''

They walked in silence as a pair of Japanese men with cameras stood back to focus on the sign for the panda exhibit.

''For this, no one has a need to know.''

''This is beginning to look like one hell of an operation.''

''It is.''

''Is the DDO handling it?''

Jones walked along in silence before answering. ''It goes higher than that.''

Draper shook his head. ''I didn't think the Director handled anything anymore.''

''It goes higher than that,'' Jones said with a slight smile.

Draper stopped in his tracks. ''Hell, there isn't anything higher than the Director himself.''

''Yes, there is,'' Jones said.

15

THEY SMELLED SAMOS ALMOST BEFORE THEY SAW
it—the sharp scent of pine drifting across the Aegean—because
the island, more than any other in Greece, was still heavily
covered with pine forests. And what they saw first of Samos was
the great mountain Cerceteus, its bald head rising from the surrounding forest.

Molly leaned against the gunwale and looked at her watch. It
was five hours already, and it would be at least another hour
until they got to the port. "You didn't get sick this time," she
said to Yuri.

"I did not get sick before."

"You did. You were as white as a sheet."

"That is not same as being sick."

"Yuri, you were!"

He turned away, looking again at the blue-black sea. "My
grandmother used to say that men were not made for sea, that
sea is proper domain of fish, and land is proper domain of man."
He shrugged. "Of course, she never saw sea in her whole life,
nor even very large lake, I suppose."

"You'll miss her, won't you?"

He looked at her, her short hair blowing in the wind. "There
is great deal I will miss."

"Are you sorry you did it?"

His eyes fell to his hands, resting on the gunwale. "I am sorry
for things that have happened—O'Neal being killed. And," he
added without looking at her, "I am sorry that you are also in
danger."

She nodded silently and he looked at her then, at her hair
blowing wildly around her face, at her cheeks turned rosy by
the wind and the sun, at her eyes squinting against the sun

187

on the water. "If going back to them would end it, I would," he said. "It is not right for anyone else to die because of me."

"It doesn't matter now," she answered, turning toward him so that her voice could be heard over the wind and the boat's clattering engine. "O'Neal thought so, and it seems logical. They're afraid of what you know, and now I know it, too, so it wouldn't do any good for you to go back."

"I would still do it," he said, pulling away a curl of green paint.

"No, Yuri, you couldn't. If you went back, O'Neal's death would mean nothing. If what you know is that important, bring it out with you."

"Maybe it is only what is on my film."

"It's not that and you know it. The film hasn't even been developed yet."

"They do not know that."

"They could figure it out. When would we have had time? Besides, Sammy was killed without getting a chance to see any film."

Yuri looked out across the water, his eyes narrowed. "How many dic? What is it worth?"

"It seems to be worth a great deal to someone."

"Then how do we make sure we get it back? What do we do when we get to America?"

"Cathleen will help us decide. We need to get it to someone who knows what to do with it—a newspaper, perhaps. What you know, and maybe the photographs to back it up, have got to be really important. Sammy and Tom in Rafetna. O'Neal in Rome. Those Russians coming after us in Athens—"

"They are part of it, you think?"

"They have to be."

"Soviets and Americans working together—it still does not make sense," he said.

"But you saw it yourself in the Dioula, and that's why it's important for us to get back safely as fast as we can. We're going to need all the help we can get." She looked toward Samos, close enough now to make out white houses against the trees. "If we can get a plane from here, we'll take it."

"Even if it takes us back to Athens?"

She paused for a long moment. "We'll see what kind of connections we can make," she said finally.

The green caïque docked at a little town that was barely worthy of the name. There was one taverna on the beach at the side of the quay. The caïque's captain had not spoken a dozen words on the whole trip. "This can't be the main city on the island?" Molly asked him.

"This is Koumeika," he answered.

"Where is the main city? What is its name?" she asked.

"Vathí," he answered, waving his hand vaguely to the right. "Over the mountains."

"But why didn't you take us there?"

"You said to Samos. This is Samos. You did not say which town."

"I don't know the names of the towns on Samos. I thought you would take us to the main port."

"This is good enough," he responded with a shrug. "You can take autobus from here."

"No, it's not good enough. I want you to take us there."

"That is too far." He picked up her bag and deposited it over the edge of the boat onto the quay with an air of finality. "To Samos, you said. This is Samos." As if to emphasize the point, he revved up his engine. "I go back to Ikaria now. You take autobus."

"How much can I pay you to take us to Vathí?" she asked, pulling out several bills.

He barely glanced at the bills. "Nothing. I am not going to Vathí. I am going back now to Ikaria."

"I will pay you whatever you ask."

He puffed on the stub of a cigarette without looking at her. "To Koumeika and back is one day. If I go to Vathí, I cannot get back home in one day. I do not want to go to Vathí."

"But I will pay you as much as you want."

"To sleep in my own bed at night. That is what I want." His eyes, surrounded by a web of lines in a weathered face, looked back toward Ikaria.

Molly motioned to Yuri with a resigned sigh. "Come on," she said. "We might as well get off. He's not going to take us any farther."

At the taverna, she asked about buses and found that one would leave for Vathí at five o'clock. She also learned that a plane for Athens left every morning from the airport at Vathí. They ordered souvlakia and beer and then sat down at one of the outside tables and tried to decide whether it would be more risky to change planes in Athens or to push on toward Turkey.

* * *

John Schlatter covered his eyes with his hand and listened to the voice over the telephone. As often was the case, the connection to the islands was difficult. "They definitely went to Ikaria," the Greek was telling him. "I spoke to the fisherman who took them there himself. And—a bonus—he had to spend the night there because of the distance between Paros and Ikaria, and so he knows that they hired another boat to take them Samos today. They were to leave early this morning, so they should have gotten there by noon."

"Is there any chance that they could have changed the destination at the last minute? To some other island?"

There was a pause as the Greek considered that. "No, I think not. Marko, the fisherman, told me that the caïque they hired to Samos is owned by an old bastard. He will hold them to the agreement. If he agreed to Samos, that is where he will take them."

"Even if they offer him a great deal of money to go elsewhere?"

There was another pause. "Of course," the voice finally came over the line, "for a great deal of money it is hard to know what a man will do."

The American nodded silently. O'Neal had left Bodamwe with plenty of American money, almost none of which had been found on his body in Rome. Which probably meant that the Davison woman had more than enough to buy whatever she wanted. In the case of a trained agent one could make an educated guess, but in the case of an amateur . . . He looked across the room at the wall map. Athens to Paros to Ikaria to Samos. Continuously east. And Samos is only a stone's throw from Turkey. He couldn't blame her for being reluctant to come back toward Athens. They had almost been caught in Athens—she had indeed been caught. They would be very hesitant about coming back. Almost certainly they would push on to Turkey. He actually hoped that was what they would do. The Turks were a great deal easier to deal with; the Greeks had dug in their heels ever since the overthrow of the colonels and made the Americans pay dearly for every ounce of cooperation they received.

He heaved a sigh and said, "Thank you," and then cut the connection with his finger. Then he dialed Bill Metzger. Maybe . . . with some help . . .

"Hello," Metzger's voice came over the phone.

"Bill, it's John Schlatter. I've got a problem. Do you have a couple of minutes?"

"Right now? Sure. I was just cleaning up some things. You going to the Marine thing tonight?"

"I'd like to, but this'll come first. You want me to come over there?"

"Whatever. No one's around here. Helen's already gone."

"I'll be right there." Schlatter got up and walked around his desk. He paused at the map. Paros . . . Ikaria . . . Samos . . . And then where? If anybody could turn the screws on the Greeks it would be Metzger, the air attaché, who'd just worked out a deal for repair of Greek air force planes using U.S. military mechanics and American-made parts at cut-rate prices.

Alvin Jones leaned back in his chair and pressed a button on the cassette player. Once more the squeals and squeaks of the rewinding tape punctuated the silence of the room; then there was only the sound of the empty tape passing through the machine. He pressed the STOP button and then pressed PLAY. He closed his eyes to concentrate and heard the taped burr of a telephone ring. There had to be something, he kept thinking . . . something.

"Hello?" The voice on the tape had become familiar; he could repeat the short conversation now by heart. He mouthed the next words with the tape. "Is this Cathleen?" Then a heart-beat of silence, then, "Yes." That pause. He rewound the tape once more and started it again from the beginning. "Hello?" Then: "Is this Cathleen?" And then he grinned. Very good, he thought. Simple. The best ones are always simple. He rewound the tape, farther back this time, to make sure. There had been other calls; he could make sure he was right. But there was almost no need. He was certain already.

The car pulled forward slowly to the customs booth and the uniformed officer leaned down to look in the window on the driver's side. "Citizens of what country?" he asked.

"United States," said the woman behind the wheel. Her hazel eyes swept over him with a kind of vague interest that he'd gotten used to after four years at the border.

He bent down farther to see the woman on the passenger side. "And you?"

She nodded. "United States."

"Where are you going?"

"Montreal," the first woman said.

"For how long?"

She smiled. "Depends on how long it takes us to spend our money. A week, maybe."

"What are you bringing into Canada—anything other than personal items? Any firearms?"

"No."

"Have a nice visit."

"Thank you."

The woman accelerated slowly and, in the rearview mirror, she could see the customs agent bending over to the next car. "It's just about as easy going back the other way. We should be able to do it, shouldn't we?"

Gloria Wallace stretched her legs out in front of her as much as the Escort would allow. "There's an awful lot you haven't told me."

"There's an awful lot I don't know," her sister countered.

"You must have known your phone was tapped. How did you know that?"

"I guessed."

Gloria swiveled in her seat to face her sister. "Level with me, Cathy; you owe me that much. I came clear across the country. I gave up a really good spot that might have led to a continuing role on a daytime series. My agent is probably blowing a gasket." She rubbed her finger across the scar on her left hand, but she willed herself not to look at it. Cathy knew perfectly well why she had come; she did not need to remind her.

Cathy O'Neal caught the speed-limit sign as she passed it— 80 km per hour—and let up on the gas without even glancing down at the speedometer. "Dennis was with the CIA; I suppose you guessed that. He did various things from time to time. In Bodamwe he was collecting information, I guess. That's what he did most of the time—not the kind of things you read about in spy novels. He had some local assets—that's what they call the local people who do the footwork. I never knew too much about it, of course. I do know that most of the time he sat in an office—or met someone somewhere and listened to what they had picked up. Then he put it all together, a piece here, a piece there, until it made some kind of pattern that made sense. That was his job, really, putting bits and pieces together to make sense of them."

She pulled into the right lane suddenly and just as unexpectedly turned off onto an exit ramp. She turned right at the crossroad and drove for a quarter of a mile before turning onto a gravel side road and stopping. "Let's get out and walk for a while."

She opened her door and stepped out, surprised at the heat after the air-conditioned car. Gloria, without speaking, got out on the passenger side. On both sides of the gravel road the grass was almost knee-high, waving gently in the evening breeze. The two women came together near the front of the car and began walking, the gravel scrunching beneath their feet.

"I guess we have a lot of talking to do in the next few days," Gloria ventured.

"I'm sorry. I had to get out of that damned car. I've been cooped up in it too long." Cathy looked at the ground as she walked. Their feet threw up small puffs of white dust with each step. "He was supposed to be in Bodamwe; he was killed in Rome."

"I thought they said it was terrorists."

"They did. It makes a pretty good story, doesn't it? That was the first piece. What was he doing in Rome? Well, I suppose it could have been explained, but why was he with Sonny Lopes? Sonny was definitely not with the Agency and they weren't particularly good friends when we lived there, so why would they have been together at that café? I wondered about it at the time, but there was no one I could ask." She stopped and turned around. The sun, low in the west, threw the shadow of the car halfway across the road. Without explanation, she began walking back toward the car. "Someone from the Embassy in Rafetna flew back with the body. I thought that seemed a little unusual. I met the plane at the airport and we rode back together, and he pumped me all the way back. He was very good at it; I shouldn't have noticed what he was doing. I suppose I had my antennas out. I seem to do that when I'm in an emotional state sometimes. He wanted to know if Dennis had been in touch with me."

"Wanted to know if he'd told you whatever it is this defector knows?"

"That's what he was looking for, I'm sure, but of course he wasn't that crude about it. They know how to do those things. But it was clear to me: he wanted to know if I'd had any communication from Dennis."

"You couldn't have been just imagining it?"

They were back at the car and Cathy leaned against the fender, still not ready to get back in. "No. He was after one thing. Had Dennis called me; had he written me. I told him he hadn't, which was the truth . . . That was another piece." She shaded her eyes and looked across the field. She breathed deeply of air sweet with the scent of ripening timothy. "I haven't smelled that for a long time," she mused. In the distance a dog barked. "Two days later Charlie added a piece. He just got his driver's license this summer and he's been using every excuse he could think of to drive the car. He'd been on some errand or other and came back with the news that a cable TV truck had been parked all day just around the corner. It wouldn't have been anything remarkable except that the neighborhood was just rewired this spring. There was something wrong with the way they had done it in the first place, so everything had to be redone. In the spring they warned us; you know, people around McLean can get pretty paranoid over something like that, given the types of jobs some of them have. Including Dennis, of course. But there was no warning this time, so Charlie commented about it. Nothing major; I wouldn't even have thought about it if it hadn't been for the other things. So, another piece."

She walked over to the side of the road and pulled a blade of grass, putting the tender pale-green stem end into her mouth and pulling it between her teeth. "Then Molly called, and I knew." She bent down and pulled up a handful of grass and spread the blades out in her open palm. Without looking up she went on. "Long ago, when Dennis first got into this—when he first realized what being in a job like that might mean—he made a couple of deals with me. One was that we would have as normal a family life as we could have, given the situation. He would not bring his work life into his private life. I thought at the time it was a big concession, but I came to know that nearly all of them try to do that. Some are more successful at it than others . . . The other was something else: a code, a way of letting me know that something was wrong, a way of warning me to be on guard. At the time I couldn't imagine why I would ever need such a thing, and when I asked him he couldn't even give me an example that made any sense. But still it seemed important to him that there be something. So we settled on something, something that would be very subtle, something that he could say to me—or write to me—that would not mean anything to anyone else but would be a warning." She let the grasses fall, one by one, from her hand. Then she brushed her hands together and looked up.

"Cathleen," Gloria said.

"Yes, exactly. He would call me Cathleen."

"It's what she called you when I talked with her. I wondered why she would call you that. No one ever has, have they? He must have told her to."

"I think she doesn't even know it's a code. She thinks it's really my name."

The grasses rustled in the breeze.

"Why did he give it to her?" Gloria asked.

Cathy walked around to the other side of the car before answering. "Because he must have known that there was no one he could trust, no one she could trust either."

"But Cathy," Gloria said across the top of the car, "why bring you into it? If he knew that, he surely knew how dangerous it would be for you."

"It must be really important."

Gloria stared at her across the top of the car without speaking.

"Maybe it was desperation," Cathy said softly. "The one person he knew he could trust. I brought you into it, didn't I?"

16

MOLLY STOOD AT THE CLOSED FRENCH DOORS, looking out. It was early; morning was still only a broad, pale rose band in the eastern sky. The wind had come up in the night, whipping the waves against the seawall, tossing spray halfway across the street toward the hotel, rattling the shutters against the wall. She could see from the window that a small boat had come loose from its moorings, the waves pounding it against the seawall, its barefoot owner ignoring the salt spray in a desperate attempt to salvage what he could of his boat.

Last night everything had seemed so easy. The plane would leave this morning at seven-thirty for Athens, less than an hour's trip. They would have just under an hour layover before the Olympic flight to Montreal. They could book the flights under different names—nobody checks the passports against the passenger manifest, do they?—and slip through Athens unnoticed.

It had made sense then. Now she wondered if Samos had lulled them into a false sense of security. Yesterday they had taken the bus through the forest-covered mountains; then the road had turned away, toward sweeping views of neatly tilled fields, with cows and donkeys placidly grazing at the side of the road. They had passed an old woman, the lower part of her face covered Turkish-style, who was bouncing along atop a pile of twigs and branches on the back of a donkey. She looked up as the bus went by, and waved. Beyond the fields the sea had shone almost purple in the late afternoon sun.

Later, at a restaurant next to the hotel, they had sat outside and ordered fish shish kebab and *horiatiki salata* and watched evening come, darkening the sky and the sea beyond the seawall. The water had ben calm then, and the reflections of the lights on the far side of the bay slid across the water's surface. Above, in Apano Vathí, the lights of houses followed the ridges of the hills overlooking the harbor. Samos had seemed a safe place then: Greek, where she knew the language, where she understood how things were done, where she could manage quite well; and insulated, surrounded by the placid sea. It had been easy to think that the familiar was preferable to the unknown. *A place you know*, O'Neal had said.

She had only been to Turkey once and she didn't know the language. They had learned in the afternoon that one could rent a caïque and be on the Turkish mainland in two or three hours, but what then? Where was the nearest airport? Izmir? How would they get there? She had looked out over the calm, protecting sea and known that they could pass through Athens by mid-morning, and by noon Eastern time they would be landing in Montreal. It seemed much more comfortable than starting out once again in yet another boat, this time for a country about which she knew so little.

Now she was having second thoughts. Perhaps they had never guessed that she and Yuri had gone to the islands. Perhaps they were still looking for them in Athens. *They*. Whoever they were. If that was the case, then surely the Athens airport would be scrutinized. It would not be possible to slip through, even with assumed names.

She opened the French doors and stepped out, leaning over the edge of the balcony to see far to the west. There were no clouds, only the wind—a *meltemi*, the ferocious summer windstorm of the Aegean. She shivered and stepped back inside, closing the door behind her. If they chose Athens it would be quicker, and they would be on more familiar ground; if they chose Turkey it would take longer and they would be more uncertain, but, perhaps, in the end, safer.

The rattling of the wind at the windows and shutters obliterated the sound of Yuri's footsteps until he was quite close to her, still looking muzzy from sleep.

He looked out the window. "It is stormy. Do we still go to Athens this morning?"

"It's only wind. There won't be any rain."

"Do we still go?"

"It's what we decided last night, isn't it?"

"Last night . . . in some way things seemed different then," he said slowly. "Safer perhaps."

"In just over twelve hours we can be in Montreal."

"If nothing happens in Athens." He turned to look out again. "I thought you might have wakened early for the same reason as I—because you have second thought. Because like me you are afraid of going to Athens again."

Without a word she walked over to stand beside him. They both looked down at the crashing sea on the other side of the road. The barefoot man still struggled with his damaged boat, but he was being helped now by two others. "I am afraid about going to Athens," she said finally. "But I'm also afraid about going on to Turkey."

"We could stay here," he said softly, still watching the men fighting the storm.

She took a deep breath. She could feel the warmth of him beside her. Without thinking, she put her hand gently on his back. He turned to her, his face serious, his eyes searching hers. He kissed her once on the mouth, and again on the cheek.

Her arms went around him, her face warm against his chest.

"Mollinka," he said softly, brushing her hair back with his hand. *"Mollush.* Maybe we should stay right here."

"I wish we could," she answered, looking up at him.

He kissed her again, and she responded, her mouth against his, her arms holding him tight. His hands held her face, then slid down to her shoulders, her back, caressing her gently. In that moment, she wanted nothing more than to shut the world out and hide in his arms.

"John." The voice was quiet behind him.

Schlatter turned abruptly and saw Bill Metzger two paces behind. Schlatter was coming back from the code room, the overnight messages in his hands. "Any luck?"

Metzger allowed a wry smile to flit across his lips. "The Lord spoke and the Red Sea parted."

Schlatter frowned slightly.

"Your office, this time, I think," Metzger said, and fell into step beside him.

"Well?" Schlatter asked, closing the door behind them.

"They were very cool last night when I called them. Very noncommittal. I tried going around to turn the screws on them a little, but General Demirgis was out of the office for the day. So they said. I thought I'd struck out. Then this morning, when I got in at seven-fifteen, there was a message waiting for me. Demirgis' office had called and said that it was all arranged. All we have to do is go down to the airport and run through the ID routine." He grinned and spread his hands.

Schlatter recognized the gesture. "You want to make any guesses?"

"I don't know, buddy. It's your ball game." He put his hands in his pockets. "If I had to make a guess, I'd say that somehow they think it's in their interest."

"Yeah," Schlatter responded, "and it took them overnight to realize it."

"As I say, it's your ball game."

Schlatter nodded and turned back to his desk. He wondered who had put the pressure on. Whoever it was, overnight would have been plenty of time. "Thanks, Bill. I appreciate it."

"That's it, then?"

"If they're going to cooperate at the airport, I guess it is. I'll let you know if I run into any roadblocks."

"You don't trust them."

"Would you?"

Metzger grinned. "Hell, no." He turned and walked out of the office, closing the door again behind him.

John Schlatter walked over to the wall map. Okay, he thought, come this way now. He buttoned his top shirt button and tightened the tie that, until now, had hung loose around his neck. He grabbed his suit jacket from the rack. He was going to have to look as official as possible, just in case they were having second thoughts. And in the meantime, something sat wrong at the pit of his stomach. We're not supposed to be on the same side, he thought. But then he brushed the thought back. The orders had come direct from Langley. He'd seen stranger things in his life. He looked at his watch. Seven thirty-five. It was rush hour, of course, but most of the traffic would be coming into the city. He could be at the airport by eight or soon after. Then it would be anybody's guess how long it would take to go through the designated channels. We'll see, he thought, we'll see how much they really want to help us.

The plane was scheduled to leave Vathí at seven forty-five, arriving in Athens at eight-thirty. The flight for Montreal left Athens at nine-twenty. Cutting it close, Molly had thought, but better that than to hang around the airport too long. As it was, they were going to be late—the plane didn't leave Vathí until almost eight. She tried to relax, but her hands gripped the arms of her seat. It's the best we can do, she kept telling herself. But she just wanted to close her eyes and have it all be over.

Beside her, Yuri turned and looked closely at her. "You're frightened," he said softly.

"Aren't you?'

"Yes." He took a deep breath and let it out. "Do you think the false names will fool them?''

"If all they look at is the passenger manifest, yes. If they've got people posted where we have to go through customs—where we have to show our passports—that'll be a different story.'' He put his hand over hers on the arm of the seat and leaned back and closed his eyes.

John Schlatter sat hunched forward, his elbows on his knees, and stared at the floor. Surreptitiously he slid his left arm against his leg, using the friction of the fabric of his sleeve against the fabric of his pants to pull his sleeve back and expose his watch. He would not let the Director's secretary see that he was concerned about the time. It was Schlatter's conviction that bureaucratic imperative demanded supplicants be kept waiting. The less sure the bureaucrat was of his position, the longer he kept people waiting. Schlatter had been sitting for almost twenty minutes. It was also Schlatter's policy not to let the bureaucrat know how annoyed he was by the wait. There were better ways to make a point—or to get even. And it was no time to annoy a man whose help he might need.

The door was opened by a small, slight man with a narrow, precise mustache. "Mr. Schlatter," he said.

Schlatter stood and walked forward quickly. "John Schlatter," he said, extending his right hand.

The man stepped back, opening the door wider, making room for Schlatter to pass him and proceed into the office. Then he closed the door and only then did he put out his hand to shake Schlatter's. "Ioannis Petrides. We seem to have the same first name." His English was very good, with a British accent over the Greek, and he spoke with clipped precision. "What can I do for you?''

"Has General Demirgis spoken with you?" Schlatter asked.

"Not with me directly." Petrides walked back behind his desk and sat down, motioning Schlatter to a chair on the supplicant's side of the desk. "Perhaps you can explain more fully." He reached for a silver cigarette box, opened it, and extended it to Schlatter. Schlatter shook his head. Petrides replaced the box, then pulled a pack of Marlboros from his jacket pocket and shook out a cigarette. He tapped one end against the box in an almost reflexive action, then put the cigarette in his mouth and lighted it with a Bic lighter.

None of this was lost on Schlatter, who wondered idly what brand of cigarettes was in the silver cigarette box. Probably, he thought, consciously chauvinistic, Greek ones.

Petrides leaned back in his chair and blew a long cloud of blue smoke into the air, watching as it dissipated in the shaft of sunlight from the window behind him. His arm was outstretched, leaning on the arm of the chair, the cigarette held daintily between his index and middle fingers in what Schlatter took to be a pose of sophistication.

"We are very interested in two people—a man and a woman—traveling with American passports." He had waited until Petrides had settled himself, under the assumption that until then Petrides was more interested in the effect he was making than in anything Schlatter had to say. "We have reason to believe they have been in the islands. We also have reason to believe that they will be heading back for the States as soon as possible. Possibly via Athens, although not necessarily. They have been in the eastern Aegean as far as Samos. They may have gone on to Turkey."

Petrides nodded and exhaled another cloud of smoke, which drifted malevolently over his desk. "Of course this is a very busy season. The busiest, in fact. Thousands of tourists will pass through the airport today, and every day this month and next. And that does not count the domestic flights. As you can imagine, my men have their hands full."

"I appreciate that. Perhaps you have heard from General Demirgis—"

"I assume you want these people arrested."

"No. We only want to locate them. It would be enough to know which flight they are taking back to the States."

"And how much manpower can you commit to this project, Mr. Schlatter?"

Schlatter cleared his throat. "We had hoped that your men might be able to handle it."

Petrides extended both arms, palms held upward in a gesture of helplessness. "As I have told you, my men already have their hands full."

"They would only have to watch for them. Two people, a man and a woman. I would provide the names on their passports."

Petrides cocked his head to one side. "They could have gotten false passports."

"Not likely."

"Your people could go over the passenger manifests," Petrides suggested.

"It is possible to buy a ticket in a false name," Schlatter said.

"Only if one pays in cash, Mr. Schlatter."

"But it is still possible."

"But when they check in for an international flight, they'll have to show their passports."

"And if their connecting flight begins on one of your islands, are the people there always so diligent?"

Petrides took a long draw on his cigarette and, lifting his head toward the ceiling, exhaled slowly. "If you want to locate these people through their passports," he said at last, "you will have to speak to the Director of Customs."

Schlatter willed himself not to look at his watch. "It was my understanding that the customs people had already agreed to this."

"I would not know about that," Petrides said. "The Director of Customs would have to tell you about that."

"Are there planes every day from the islands? From Samos, for example?"

"From some islands every day. From others only certain days of the week. From Samos . . ." Petrides paused and opened a drawer. He withdrew a stapled sheaf of papers and leafed through the pages. "From Samos," he repeated without looking up, "every day, of course. The plane arrives in Athens at eight-thirty." He looked at his watch. "That means it would have come in just ten minutes ago."

Schlatter stood. "If it was on time."

Petrides gazed at Schlatter but said nothing. His look told Schlatter that he did not accept the proposition that a plane might not be on time.

"Can you tell me when the next plane leaves for the United States?"

Petrides gazed for a moment at Schlatter before turning his attention back to the stack of papers. He leafed through them, slowly, and Schlatter surreptitiously looked at his watch again. "That would be at nine-thirty," Petrides said finally. "A TWA flight."

"How likely is it that the flight would already have been booked?"

Petrides frowned. "Booked?"

"Sold out."

Petrides took another long drag on his cigarette, then tamped it out carefully into a silver ashtray. "Who knows?" he said, shrugging. "As we have said, it is the height of the tourist season. I would not want to try to find air tickets in or out of Athens at this time of year."

"With luck . . ." Schlatter began, knowing how often luck could play a part in something like this. "Would you be kind enough to direct me to the office of the Director of Customs?" he asked.

"Of course." Petrides rose and came out from behind his desk, extending his hand. "Perhaps we will have dealings again in the near future, Mr. Schlatter."

"Perhaps indeed," Schlatter responded. But not if I can avoid it, he thought.

"Robust" would have been an appropriate description of Constantino Maroulis in all respects. He was quite tall for a Greek—nearly six two—with broad shoulders, a barrel chest, and hands large enough to carry four ouzo bottles each—by their bottoms. His face was broad and permanently flushed under an unruly mass of coarse black hair. He wore a luxuriant mustache behind which the corners of his mouth disappeared when he smiled.

He was smiling from behind his desk as the secretary let Schlatter into the room. He'd only kept Schlatter waiting seven minutes.

"Please excuse that I keep you waiting," Maroulis said, standing, waving a broad hand toward a chair. "I was speaking on telephone. It was," he grinned, "Mr. Petrides, warning me of you coming. You look for two Americans."

"Yes, and it is very possible that they have arrived this morning from Samos."

"From Samos. And going to?"

"The United States, I should think."

"Ah! And so you come to me, for customs inspection, because you think they will be leaving Greece. You wish them—ah—detained, I think."

"No, not at all. I merely wish to know what flight they are proceeding on. If your men have their names and their pictures, it should not be difficult to identify them."

Maroulis smiled broadly. "Not difficult at all. But you do not wish more than that?"

"Mr. Maroulis, if your men can do that, they will have done us a service. I am sure General Demirgis—"

Maroulis burst into laughter. "Army is not so powerful as once was, Mr. Schlatter. I do not answer to General Demirgis."

"I'm sorry, I did not mean to imply—"

"What I want to know is, what did you do to anger Ioannis Petrides?"

"Was he angry?"

"Another word, perhaps. I think it is 'offend.' "

Schlatter shook his head. "I have no idea."

Maroulis stood and walked from behind his desk. His limp was apparent and Schlatter's eyes instinctively went to the Greek's legs. The left leg, kept still as the man walked, was noticeably shorter than the right. Maroulis saw Schlatter's look and clapped him on the back. "Old war wound," he said. "I was a child only, but you see what shrapnel can do."

"I'm sorry."

"It is nothing. I have lived more than forty years with it. And do not worry about offending Ioannis Petrides. He is only bureaucrat. While I," he added, his eyes dancing wickedly, "I am *large* bureaucrat!" And he burst into laughter.

The two men walked together toward the door, but Maroulis paused, his hand on the knob, before opening it. "You are sure you do not want them detained? It would not be difficult."

"Yes, I am sure." His orders had been clear. Nothing was to happen at the Athens airport, or anywhere else where Greek officialdom would be involved. Whatever was going to happen, was going to happen once they got back. He glanced at his watch. It was just after nine o'clock. The TWA plane left in less than half an hour.

The plane had landed fifteen minutes late at the Olympic Terminal, at the far end of the tarmac from the International

Terminal. Buses waited to ferry the passengers to the other terminal, but when everyone had boarded, the buses still sat on the tarmac. Agitated, Molly looked at her watch. It was eight forty-five; they had just thirty-five minutes to make their plane. She rose from her seat and made her way through the crowd in the aisle to the front of the bus.

"Why aren't we leaving?" she asked.

"We wait for one more airplane," the driver responded.

"We can't do that. We'll miss our flight out of Athens."

"Not long. It has already landed, see." He pointed to a plane taxiing slowly along the runway.

"We'll miss our flight!" she repeated.

"No, they will hold it for you."

"But, look," she exclaimed, growing desperate and not believing for a moment that the flight would be held, "there's no room in this bus anyway. People are already standing in the aisles."

"Don't worry. They will move back. There will be room."

"But can't another bus—"

"All buses full. Never mind. The airplane will wait for you. And if not, you will have one day in Athínai, free hotel for you. Not so bad, I think." He turned away.

"We *have* to make our plane," she said firmly.

He turned in time to see her pulling her wallet from her purse. "I wait," he said pointedly.

She sighed and turned, pushing her way back to the seat Yuri had been holding for her. "No go," she said, collapsing back into the seat. Though it was still fairly early in the morning, the crowded bus was like an oven. She wiped her damp forehead with the back of her hand.

Yuri caught her hand in its motion and held it in both of his. "I have been thinking," he said softly, so that, even in the crowd, only she could hear. "If something happens—you know what I mean—I will make some kind of disturbance. Even if I think something is almost to happen. They will be after me particularly; you are only young woman and they will think you will be easy. No," he said quickly, seeing the look come into her eyes, "listen to me. It is true. Men always think women can do nothing. It will save you. I will make disturbance; you will run."

"It won't matter, Yuri. You know as well as I do that they will still be after me. Look at O'Neal and the others."

"Yes, of course, they will. But let us not allow them to do

it so easily. Let us not allow them to catch two at one time. Maybe you could still escape.''

"I don't think . . .'' She tried to pull her hand away, but he held it fast.

"You do it, if that happens. It will be easier, one instead of two. You will do it.'' He withdrew one of his hands from hers and reached into his pants pocket. He had to half-straighten in his seat to pull out the two canisters of film. "You will keep these,'' he said, putting them into her hand on his lap. "You will have them.''

"There's no need for that.'' She tried to give the canisters back, but he refused to take them.

"If we both get back, we will have them. If not, you will still have them.''

"And if just you—''

"No,'' he interrupted. "There is no way I could be the one. I know nothing about how to do things in the West. How to travel, how to buy tickets, how to find place to stay. It will be you or neither of us. I remember,'' he added, smiling slowly, "how you struck out at O'Neal in that hotel room in Rome, how you accused him of lying to you about being CIA. I remember how you got us to Athens and to the islands. You are a resourceful woman, Molly. You will know how to do it, if it comes to that.''

He was right, of course. He would, truly, have difficulty knowing what to do in a world where permits were not required for movement from place to place, where families of party officials were not given special treatment, where one was constantly confronted with choices and decisions of the sort that he had never had to make. And yet, "No,'' she answered, "we'll stay together.''

He put his hand to her lips to silence her. "You do it,'' he said, "for O'Neal and me and the others. If it comes to that, you do it.''

Those last words, spoken quietly, were not even audible over the commotion that had begun at the front of the bus. "Move back! Move back!'' someone shouted in English. "There's more of us to get on!''

"*Allons! Allons!*'' another voice shouted.

"What the hell—look at the time!'' came a voice behind them.

"Let's go! Let's go!''

"*Vamos!*''

"Ach, du lieber—"

The bus engine roared, and those who were standing clung to the aluminum bar overhead or to seat backs or to each other to keep from losing their balance as the bus driver sped toward the International Terminal. Molly drew a long breath and looked at Yuri. He smiled slowly and squeezed her hand and then let it go. She put the canisters into her purse.

Five minutes later they were at the International Terminal, and five minutes after that they had been rushed through customs, along with nearly a hundred others trying to make morning flights out of Athens. Molly grinned at Yuri and he smiled back as they walked away from customs. Their plane was already being called for the first boarding. Nothing had happened. They had made it.

17

ALVIN JONES SAT ON THE LONG SIDE OF THE BURIED-
ash conference table, near one end. His blue-and-white striped
seersucker jacket hung open. It was another hot day in Washington, but when one came to a meeting in the Executive
Office Building, next door to the White House, one dressed
for it. He was the first to arrive. Before him, on the table,
lay a clean pad of legal paper and a pen. He had not brought
notes to the meeting and he did not actually expect to take
any away, but he knew propriety. The walls of the small conference room were covered with maps: across from him hung
a map of the continental United States and Canada. He mused
once again that any good United States map that included
Alaska would perforce show Canada. On the other hand, he
thought, it indicated the thinking of some of the men who
used this room. The wall to his right was completely covered
by a map of Europe; behind him was a huge world map; to
his left a map of South America. Above the South American
map was a metal brace that held additional roll-down maps.
It amused him that there was nothing in this room that would
make a curious visitor think there was any particular interest
in Africa.

"Mr. Jones." Lieutenant Colonel Stephen White walked
into the room and nodded briskly at Jones. He seated himself
on the same side of the table, but near the opposite end. He
carried a briefcase which he set, unopened, on the floor. He
was followed almost immediately by General William R.
French.

Jones rose when the general walked into the room and
leaned across the table to shake his hand. He had met French
just once; all other contact with him had been by telephone

208

or cable. French was tall and lean with fine features and silver hair that belied his age; he was not yet sixty. His eyebrows, thick patches of black on a perpetually tan face, were startling in their incongruity, and he used them as punctuation marks to his words. One read French's eyebrows the way one read other men's eyes. They were at rest now, lying heavily above gray eyes, as if ready for action.

French had been the President's National Security Adviser for three years, and if any man had ever been Cabinet material on the strength of his looks alone, it was William French.

He had graduated in the top third of his class at West Point, and had held commands in both Korea and Vietnam. Between wars, he had filled positions stateside as well as in NATO. He was a tough commander on the battlefield, and a tougher officer behind a desk. When angry, his eyes became the color of steel and his will turned to iron. His subordinates had always, behind his back, called him "The Ram," with a mixture of affection and awe. William R. French always got what he wanted. There were those who thought he would not be satisfied until he became President.

One minute after French entered the room, August Lansdale appeared in the doorway. He paused a moment. "This it?" he asked French.

"Yes," Stephen White answered.

Lansdale walked in, closing the door behind him. "Alvin," he said, leaning over the table to shake hands with Jones. He shook White's hand and nodded at French in the kind of greeting one gives a person one has very recently spent much time with. He sat down on the opposite side of the table from Jones. Stephen White cleared his throat and all eyes turned toward him.

"Director Thompson could not be here," White began. "He affirms that Alvin Jones can speak for the Agency and knows as much as anyone."

Lansdale shot a glance at French, and French's eyebrows remained immobile.

"Therefore," White continued, "those of us in this room know as much about the situation with Harbinger as anyone." "The situation" was what it had come to be known as among the few who were even aware. They rarely even used the project name, Harbinger. "We've activated a moving search system. That means any time their names go into a computer we'll pick it up—credit cards, plane reservations, whatever. That's in addition to the regular grit work. The initial reports are in. Mrs. O'Neal rented a car in Boston and was at the family's summer home in Maine, but just briefly. She left it, still driving the rental car, yesterday morning, just before our people arrived. We have not been able to pick up on her. Her sister, Gloria Wallace, flew from Los Angeles to Pittsburgh day before yesterday, and rented a car. The car was returned at the Albany, New York, airport last night. We do not have any reports of her taking any flights out of Albany, but of course she could have used another name and bought the ticket with cash.'' He glanced up.

Jones was sitting with his eyes closed, a habit he'd learned early in his career. It intensified his concentration.

''The two women are originally from a small town in west central Pennsylvania,'' White concluded. ''There has been no sign of them there. We are assuming there was a rendezvous, perhaps at Albany, but as yet there's no confirmation.''

Jones opened his eyes and looked at the map facing him. Boston and Maine. Pittsburgh and Albany. What the hell would she do? If she was smart, something deliberately . . . The cars were rented at Pittsburgh and Boston. The hometown, and the summer cottage. His eyes ranged the map. Hell, he thought, if I were running from the U.S. government, what would I do? And then he grinned. Canada.

White's voice went on. ''We have a positive trace on the other two as far as Samos, Greece. We have a possible on a flight back to Athens this morning. Our man in Athens was at the airport getting the run-around when the flight from Samos arrived. By the time he had Greek customs in line, two morning flights had already taken off—one for Paris and one for Montreal. There was a possible ID by an airport shuttle-bus driver of the girl. He's not positive and he didn't see the defector at all. If it was she, she took one of those two flights—or else she's still in Athens—because Greek customs affirms that she didn't take any of the later flights. Given the previous events in Athens, one might think she would want to get out of there as fast as she could.''

''Does the Athens man know about those?'' Lansdale asked.

''Not fully. That was a Soviet operation,'' White said. ''And if it turns out that the bus driver was mistaken and she was not the one at the Athens airport, then the best guess is that they're going through Turkey. Between us and the Soviets, we've got Ankara and Istanbul covered. Any international flight she can take will go through one of those.''

Jones's eyes were still on the map. Straight north from Albany; it couldn't be more than two hundred miles. ''What time does the flight to Montreal get in?'' he asked.

French raised his eyebrows.

''Twelve-thirty local time,'' White said. ''We'll have a man there—''

''Do the Canadians know?''

''We'd just as soon keep the Canadians out of it,'' White said. Jones nodded, understanding.

''What's the scenario?'' Lansdale asked.

''He'll follow them. It's likely they'll make contact with the O'Neal woman and her sister. We'll scope it out before we move in on the targets.''

''Were you planning to wait until they get back to the States?'' Jones asked.

''He has latitude. Disposing of targets would be easier if they came back here, but they might not do that immediately. If he has an opportunity, he'll take it, wherever it is.''

Lansdale shook his head, disagreeing. ''He should take them out immediately, wherever he is. The first thing they'll do is call the press.''

''We don't know that,'' French said. ''The Canadians are acting pretty touchy right now. We don't want to have to take targets out on their territory if we don't have to.''

''We can't afford to take a chance, Will,'' Lansdale countered, his voice rising just slightly.

French's eyebrows pursed, but he said nothing. This is not the first time they've argued this, Jones thought. If he were in Lansdale's shoes, he'd be nervous, too. Retired from the Army, Lansdale wouldn't be able to hide behind government secrecy, as the others could. As an independent consultant, he'd be hanging in the wind if things went wrong.

''How many have you got up there?'' Jones asked. ''Just one?''

''Yes,'' White said.

''Running it pretty thin, aren't you?''

''It's *Need to Know*, Al, you ought to be aware of that,'' French said. ''It has to be a tight organization.''

''Then you'll have two of us,'' Jones said abruptly. ''I'm going to try to make it.''

French glanced at his watch. "It's too late."

"How much more is there?" Jones asked, pushing his chair back.

"What's the point?" Lansdale asked.

"She knows me. She's likely to trust me. In fact, I know three of them. I'm the only one in the whole damn operation that can say that." He put his hands, palms down, on the table and looked at each of the others in turn as he spoke. "And I think I've figured out the signal between them. If I'm right about that, they'll trust me."

"And if you're wrong?" Lansdale asked.

Jones narrowed his eyes and looked straight at him. "Isn't it a little late to be asking that question? You didn't want them taken out in Rafetna; we couldn't find them in Rome; it didn't work in Athens. They're going to be awfully tired of running. The O'Neal woman is pretty sharp, but we've got a handle on her now. The best way to control it is from the inside. We're going to have four targets up there; if they split up, we're dead. Did you think about that? We need someone to move in on them and control them from the inside." He turned abruptly to White. "What do you know about the O'Neal woman and her sister? Does either of them have any press contacts?" He grinned. "An advantage to us, their being in Canada. It gives the line-listeners over in NSA a clear field to listen in on the calls. How soon could you add to the watch list over there?"

White nodded. "We can make it priority."

"If there's not much more," Jones said, "I can be there in less than two hours."

Jones glanced at French and French was nodding slowly. "How much more is there?" French asked White.

"That's it."

"Are we contacting the Soviets in Canada?" Jones asked.

French's eyes drilled Jones in his chair. "*We* are not contacting the Soviets anywhere. This has got to be completely deniable, you know that. Any contacting that's done will be done by Augie Lansdale—no one else. Keep the government out of it. Understood?"

Jones understood. French had hit the ceiling when he'd heard that Jones had contacted a KGB man in Rafetna. But then, Jones knew, French hadn't been trying to plug the dike in Rafetna. It was always easier to quarterback from five thousand miles away. One thing about French, he dressed you down good and solid, but he didn't carry grudges.

"He's the number-one target," French said to Jones. "Without him, it's only hearsay."

"No," Lansdale said, looking across the table at White. "The photographs, if he has any more. Without them, even his story is questionable."

"The photographs and the Russian," French said.

Just about halfway between Washington and Baltimore, in the rolling Maryland countryside, on a vast tract of land, lay Fort George G. Meade. And within the boundaries of Fort Meade, protected by its own series of Cyclone and barbed-wire and electrical fences, scanned by closed-circuit television cameras and occasionally patrolled by armed guards with attack dogs, was a complex of buildings occupying the most secure piece of real estate in the United States. The buildings within the complex were surrounded by parking lots that stretched almost as far as the eye could see, and yet few if any of the thousands who worked there would readily tell outsiders the name of the agency for which they worked, and they certainly would never tell in any detail what it was that they did.

In casual conversations, Linda Allsberg always told people she worked for the State Department. If they asked what she did, she told them she was a translator, but she made her job sound so uninteresting that they rarely probed further. Those were not complete fabrications: she was a translator, and some of the work she did certainly benefited the State Department, as well as the military and the CIA and the FBI, and certain selected friendly governments. What Linda really did, however, was listen to tapes—tapes made of conversations on certain specific bugged telephones, tapes of conversations in particular rooms in which recording devices had been hidden or which could be targeted by outside listening devices. There even were tapes made of conversations that took place in certain targeted automobiles.

Linda's language expertise was Russian; her subject area was the Soviet military. Somewhere in the vast complex of buildings that comprised the National Security Agency the tapes were gathered and separated according to subject matter and then distributed to linguists who prepared transcriptions of the tapes. Because a linguist worked as part of a team, each team member might hear only occasional references to a problem or an event and might not comprehend its full importance. It was not the responsibility of the linguists to evaluate what they heard; that was the job of the analysts to whom the transcriptions were passed. But occasionally, when outside attention was given to an event, such as the Chernobyl accident, the linguists understood only too well the implications of the conversations they heard and translated.

On this day, Linda Allsberg arrived late, and in a bad mood. The parking problem at the facility had gone beyond horrendous and into impossible. This morning she'd left her Columbia apartment in plenty of time, had arrived at six-fifteen, hoping to get a decent spot for once, and still had been forced to park in one of the satellite lots. In addition to that, the shuttle bus had been late in its rounds of the satellite lots, and the temperature, even so early in the morning, had risen above eighty degrees. It was going to be another scorcher. And now here she was, sweaty already, and the room was, as usual, a chill sixty degrees.

She grabbed the sweater off the back of her chair and pulled it on. Elaine Test, who occupied the cubicle to the left, leaned around the fabric-covered divider. "Parking problems again?"

"Don't even mention it," Linda said. She slid the tape she'd taken from the input bin into the player and picked up her earphones.

"Hey," Elaine said, "give yourself time to calm down. Take a look at the newest on E-mail. Somebody up in analysis has written the most scathing—"

"Just what I don't need. Reading about somebody else's hassle. As if I don't have enough problems of my own."

Elaine raised her eyebrows. "This go beyond the usual?"

Linda let out a long breath and forced a smile. "No. It's just so frustrating to get here before dawn practically and you still can't find a place within two miles of the place to park. And then when you come in—"

"Yeah, I know. All those empty executive places. Well, you know they're working on it."

"Give me a break, Elaine. Those guys aren't going to give up their perks. People like you and me are pretty far down on the totem pole."

"Well, you know what they say. If you can't beat 'em, join 'em."

Linda turned in her chair. "You know, it wouldn't be all that bad. Even if you ended up with an assigned spot in the back forty, at least you'd know where it was. You wouldn't have to spend a half hour every day just looking for a place."

"I'd rather take my chances on finding something closer."

"Not me." She put on the earphones and punched a button. As she listened, she began keying a translation of the tape into the computer in front of her. Then she punched FAST REVERSE before pushing the PLAY button again. She listened to the conversation once more and pressed the STOP button. She leaned on her elbows, her hands clasped, her chin against her thumbs. Again. She'd heard it first almost a year ago. For a long time the references had been so rare as to be almost meaningless. But very recently they'd begun to crop up more often and she'd pointed them out to her team chief. He'd taken her transcriptions and read them through quickly, expressionless. "I'll pass it on," he'd said. "It certainly looks interesting, doesn't it?"

The next day he'd come by her desk. "Forget about that Phase II business," he'd said offhandedly. "Turns out it's nothing. And I guess they already know all about it anyway."

But she'd had a hard time forgetting about it, because whatever it was seemed to be agitating the Soviets, and she couldn't understand why nobody on this side seemed interested. Since then, she'd made it a point to try to get the tapes from that particular source—she knew it was somewhere in Moscow, but that was all she knew.

That had been a week or so ago, when the talk had mostly been about "the man" and, later, about "the targets." After the second time, the conversations were about "them," and she had no clue as to who "they" might be, except that within a day "they" became "the man and the woman," and then, just "they" again. Whoever *they* were, they had been in Rome, and then Athens, where they were apparently almost intercepted by the GRU. And that was interesting, she'd thought, though she'd passed the transcriptions on and no one else took particular notice. The first interest had definitely been KGB. It was rare for an interest to be passed from one service to the other—territoriality was of utmost importance to the Soviets.

And now here it was again, and once more in a way that aroused curiosity. *The Americans are taking care of it,* one voice had assured the other, and for the first time she had heard the word *Harbinger.* She'd jotted it down and looked at it. Harbinger. *The Americans are taking care if it; they call it Harbinger.* There was a cynical chuckle from one of the voices. *Can we trust them?* the other had asked. *They want it as much as we do,* the first had said. *You never can tell, can you?* the other had responded.

She finished the translation and held it in her hand for a moment, as if weighing the papers. If she went back to her team chief and showed him the new translations, maybe this time he'd think it was something. On the other hand, she'd been passing everything on all along, and no one had picked up on it. No one else seemed to think it was important. *Can we trust them? They want it as much as we do.* What? What did the Americans want as much as the Soviets?

Almost exactly twenty miles, as the crow flies, to the southwest of Fort Meade, in Landover, Maryland, Glenn Pastrella carefully laid the papers out on his desk in order and skimmed each of them again, one by one. The codes on their upper corners indicated their origins: National Security Agency telecommunications intercepts, taped conversations from a telephone line the Soviets thought was secure, a report from a Central Intelligence Agency field operative. As information went, it was a good deal more than scant, but it was still not as much as he'd like.

There were two more reports, which he still held in his hand. He didn't bother to reread one of them; he knew it now almost by heart. Two men killed at a sidewalk café in Rome: a Social Security Agency representative named Edwin Lopes II and an Agency man, Dennis O'Neal. Presumed perpetrators: terrorists. Dennis O'Neal. Dennis. The back of his neck felt cold.

He glanced at the other report. It had come from a friend at the State Department, in response to a casually worded request. The body of Thomas Little, a State Department employee in the field for just over a month, had been found washed up on a beach near the city of Rafetna. There had been multiple abrasions to the body, some caused before death and some caused after, consistent with the fact that the beach where Little had apparently been swimming was strewn with boulders. Immediate cause of death: drowning. His friend at State had told him the Department was satisfied with the autopsy report; there was no reason to suspect foul play and the beach was known by the locals for its dangerous undertow. Little, who was new in Rafetna, probably had not realized how hazardous it could be.

Pastrella had been with the Agency almost twenty years. He was a senior intelligence analyst and, even if he did say so himself, a damned good one. As a professional, he'd long ago learned to shove his personal feelings aside—there was no place for them in the kind of work he did. But this one was not all that easy. This one was Dennis. And he'd begun to wonder if the way he felt about Dennis had anything to do with what he was thinking.

He'd been with Dennis in Cyprus, trained under him there. In the early seventies, in Cyprus, it had been easy to watch the Greek Cypriots' patriotism and think nothing could stand in their way. It was Dennis who had prepared the reports warning that the Turks would not sit by and let the Greeks take over the island. In those days Dennis had been like a voice in the wilderness. No one else was saying those things; no one else believed Dennis. But when the outbreak came and the Turks rolled over the Greeks, only Dennis was not surprised. The Agency had taken a licking on that one. He'd never forgotten the way Dennis looked at things, the way he took nothing for granted, the way he believed nothing that he could not independently prove.

And he had to smile now as he remembered the late-night arguments over glasses of milk-colored ouzo (though Dennis always called it *raki*). No matter what they began talking about, the subject always came around to the same thing: Dennis, who could be clear-headed about anything else, who would take no one else's word for anything, was a firm believer in God, and a staunch Catholic. As the son of two lapsed Catholic Italian immigrants, Pastrella had never even set foot inside a church, and he was unable to comprehend what he saw as Dennis' single blind spot.

He'd never known a man he'd admired more than Dennis, nor anyone who had taught him as much. He tapped the papers softly on the desk. He'd never known a man whose loss had devastated him more.

"Are you sleeping?" Yuri whispered.

She opened her eyes. The cabin was bathed in indirect sunlight. All the shades had been pulled down on the windows at the left side of the cabin. They sat in the middle section, lucky to have gotten any seats at all. On the other side of Molly was an elderly Greek woman, dressed in black, her head thrown back, her mouth open, snoring. "Are you kidding?" she replied. "Do you really think I'd be able to sleep?"

He put his hand on her arm. "Frightened?"

She took a deep breath. "Yes. Aren't you?"

He grinned and nodded. "A little."

His hair was still reddish from the dye they had put on it in Rafetna, though now dulled considerably. His skin, already slightly tan from the African sun, had turned a deeper brown in the islands. His eyes, green-gray, smiled at her now. In the last few days she'd come to read those eyes, to recognize hesitation, laughter, amusement, and even fear in them. They were no longer guarded, as she had first seen them. She knew the look in them now as well: he trusted her. She looked away and wished for the thousandth time that it were all over.

"Molly Davison has eaten grilled worms and pigeon heads in the Central African Republic," he said. "She has . . . fended off . . . the advances of married men who should know better—"

In spite of herself she began to laugh. "What are you doing? Don't tell me you remember every single thing I ever said—"

"She has talked back to the CIA and dealt with Greek men who think a woman's place is to be silent and to walk three paces behind her husband." His eyes were merry. "What possible things to fear can Canada hold for you?"

"No Greek man on earth expects his wife to be silent."

"Well, the three paces, at least, then."

His eyes held hers, and her mind was flooded with the things she knew about him: the little boy making toy boats by the pond; the grandmother with the wonderful stories and a folk remedy for every ailment; the parents, distant even when they were in the same room; the student, listening to the whispers, knowing that even his closest friends were guarded because of who his grandfather was. She knew what he was doing now. "Yuri . . ." she whispered, but he put a finger to her lips to silence her.

Then he wrapped his arm around her and held her close and spoke against her ear. "It should probably be Tom Little until we are safe." Still holding her, he kissed her once. "In these past days, you have become my best friend. I never thought that would happen."

She leaned back so that she could see his face. "Neither did I." How long had she known him? A few days—a few days in the islands, a few days of running and hiding and having no one else to trust. Best friends. They had come to trust each other with their lives. They could tease and laugh at each other, and at themselves. What else was there? She wondered how she would have felt about him if she had met him under normal circumstances. *You might find him arrogant*, O'Neal had said, and, at first, she had.

He pulled her close against his shoulder. "When I was at the university," he whispered, "there were always those we suspected as being informers. You know, to the police, to the KGB."

He was silent for a while, but she said nothing.

"We used to call them 'Pavliks.' " He sighed. "That's a long story I'll tell you someday—Pavlik Morozov is supposed to be a hero to young people. He told the authorities that his father had been helping the kulaks, and so his father was executed. Well, if there was someone that one of us suspected of being an informer, we'd start talking about Pavlik something-or-other— Pavlik Ivanov, or Pavlik Smirnov, or . . . whatever. It was a signal." He chuckled. "Sometimes they'd start to talk about Pavlik when I joined them. I can't blame them, but at the time I hated it. I knew what they were doing. I think the informers always knew, but there was nothing they could do. We need to have a signal like that."

"Canada will be safe," she said.

"Just in case."

Just in case. She closed her eyes. She had thought that once they got to Rome it would be over. She had thought that they would be safe in Athens. In the islands. *Just in case.* It will never end, she thought. Not until they kill us. Even in Montreal, somehow they will know. "You think it's a mistake, going to see Cathleen?"

"It's too late. We already are going there. But if something happens that makes one of us suspicious . . . you could say, 'I think you are going to like America,' or I could say, 'I think I am going to like America' . . . That could be a signal. No one else would guess. It sounds like normal conversation. What do you think?"

She didn't want to think. She was tired of having to worry about what would happen in the next place, around the next corner. "I think it's fine," she said.

"And if it happens, and if you get the chance, you will run."

"No."

"You will."

There was no point in arguing with him, she'd learned that. "Was Pavlik . . . what was his name?—ever a hero to you?"

"Morozov. Pavlik Morozov. His picture was in every elementary school when I was a child. Before we knew better, he was a hero to us all."

"I wonder if he ever came to regret what he did."

"You can be assured of that. His grandfather killed him for it."

She looked at him in surprise, but he wasn't smiling now.

"There is a world that you know, Molly, and there is a world that I know," he said.

Going through customs with only carry-on luggage was comparatively easy. Even so, the Canadian officials were thorough and correct. They opened each bag; they asked about contraband. *Almost home*, Molly kept thinking through it all, *almost home*. The customs officer looked at Yuri's passport, then at Yuri. Molly had wondered if there would be a problem with the obvious discrepancy between Yuri's name and supposed nationality and his accent. But he'd managed to answer all the questions with single syllables, and his accent was barely noticeable. To the native French-speaker questioning him, perhaps it was not noticeable at all.

Once out of customs, they joined the throng headed toward the exits. Molly glanced around, but saw no one she recognized, nor did she see anyone who appeared to be watching them. With Yuri at her side, she walked rapidly until she caught up with a porter pushing a cart loaded with baggage. "Where does one get messages?" she asked.

"Information touristique," he answered, pointing to the escalator, but without slowing his pace. "Upstairs."

She led the way up the escalator, then looked around the vast hall that confronted her. There, down toward one end, was the red-and-white dual-language sign. *Information touristique*. Tourist information. Let there be a message, she thought, let us get out of here safely.

"Is this where one gets messages?" she asked.

The woman turned and pointed to a compartmented box at the corner of the booth. "You may leave one there," she said.

"No, I am receiving one," Molly said.

"Your name, please."

"Cathleen Booth."

"Un moment . . ." The woman stepped to the box and lifted one slip of paper from the second compartment. "Yes, for Cathleen Booth."

Molly took the folded slip and opened it. The writing was large and filled the small sheet of paper: "Cathleen, meet me at the St. Jean Hotel—room 312. You can take a taxi—C.O."

She turned back to Yuri. "Okay, we're—"

It was a face she had hoped never to see again. He was coming toward them now, beaming a broad smile, his hand held out in greeting. "Molly!" he exclaimed, grabbing her hand in both of his and pumping it enthusiastically. "You remember me, of course—Alvin Jones. And Tom!" He turned his attention to Yuri, but still held Molly's hand. "It's still Tom, isn't it?" he asked in a lowered voice. "A lot's happened since I last saw the two of you. I guess you know some of it, but I'll bet you don't know all of it. Are you expecting to meet Cathleen? I have an updated message from her. Here, let me take your bag." He took Molly's bag from her hand before she could react. "Let's get out of here." He moved on, his hand lightly on Molly's back, as if to guide her.

Molly's mind was racing. *Cathleen? He knew about Cathleen?* "What's the message?" she asked.

"Trouble at home, unfortunately. She sent me to stand in."

"I had not expected to see you again," Yuri said.

"Nor I you, as a matter of fact. Which just goes to show how things sometimes work out." He was hurrying them toward an exit, but Yuri slowed deliberately and turned toward Jones. Molly, between them, looked from one to the other.

"It is quite nice that you come to meet us at airport," Yuri said. He extended his hand and Jones shifted Molly's bag to his left hand and shook Yuri's hand with his right. "I have said to Molly before," Yuri went on, "but I say it again from bottom of my heart: I think I will like America very much. With officials like you . . ." but he was no longer looking at Jones. His eyes were on Molly and his face was pale and serious, and a wall had come down behind his eyes. Jones' right hand was still tightly clasped in his.

She took a breath. Yuri was talking again, and looking at Jones now, but she no longer heard the words. For a moment she heard nothing but the sound of the blood rushing in her ears and she could think of nothing but Yuri's eyes.

Then she looked around and saw a cluster of people standing near the doors. "Jim! Jim!" she called, lifting her hand as if to wave. And then she was running, toward the crowd, barreling her way into its center, snaking and weaving around the astonished people, until she was beyond them, and she kept on running toward the exits, clinging to the shoulder strap of her purse, not stopping until she was outside and had come to a line of taxis.

Behind her, Yuri had dropped his bag and was holding Jones with both hands.

But Alvin Jones remained calm and merely smiled at him. "This place is loaded with police," he said. "Do you want me to call for their help? I can prove who I am; what proof do you have?"

Yuri relaxed his grip.

"I also have a gun in my pocket," Jones added. "You would be very foolish to try to escape. We can let her go. You're the one we want."

Hearing the words, Yuri felt a chill creeping over him. He did not look in the direction in which Molly had disappeared. He stared at Jones and he knew that his eyes showed nothing.

He had not noticed the man who had darted around them and raced after Molly.

18

"HOTEL ST. JEAN," MOLLY SAID, SLAMMING THE TAXI door.

The cab merged slowly into traffic, but she was looking out the back window. A man had run out behind her and was just now getting into a taxi. A chill ran through her. Jones had met them. How had he known? *Cathleen asked me to come*, he'd said, as if he'd known that Cathleen was to meet them. *The only one you can trust* . . . O'Neal had told her not to trust anyone from Rafetna. But Cathleen must have trusted him, or else how would Jones have known? She'd felt fear when she saw him, and it was clear Yuri hadn't trusted him either. And now she was being followed? She closed her eyes tightly, trying to will her heart to stop racing. She was just getting paranoid. No, she told herself, after running halfway around the world, she had a right to be paranoid. She glanced back; the taxi was still there. So close to home—they should have been safe by now.

The taxi turned onto the expressway, heading toward the city. The expanse of gray road and concrete apartment buildings took her by surprise after the blue sky and sea of the Greek islands. The road signs were in French and English, and even though she'd been able to read most of the Greek, somehow the English and French made things seem more comfortable, almost like home. She looked back and the taxi was still following them. I'm definitely being paranoid, she told herself impatiently; why shouldn't another taxi be heading toward town?

"Do they follow us?" the taxi driver asked.

"I don't know. Surely not," she added, shaking her head. "Most of the traffic is going this way, isn't it?"

He looked into the rearview mirror at the cars behind and then at her. Without explanation, he let up slightly on the accelerator and pulled into the right-hand lane. As he watched in the mirror, a gray Mercedes pulled past them on the left, then a green van. She turned in her seat to look back, but she could no longer see the taxi.

"He is two cars behind us," the driver said. As he spoke, a white Taurus slipped from behind them into the lane to the left and sped up to pass. But the taxi—she could see it now immediately behind the car following them—was maintaining the same speed.

"Not the Hotel St. Jean," she said with quick decision. She would have to lose them. Whoever it was. "Take me to . . . to . . . Is there a Hilton Hotel?"

"Yes."

"Take me there, please." She closed her eyes and tried to think. Yuri. They have Yuri. She had to find Cathleen without leading whoever it was to her as well. How had Jones known they were going to meet Cathleen? Maybe he really was on their side? Or maybe Cathleen didn't know? Was it a trap at the St. Jean Hotel? No, that couldn't be. If Jones had known Cathleen was there, he wouldn't have had to meet them at the airport . . . Then how did he know about Cathleen? *The only one you can trust*, O'Neal had said. His wife. His own wife. And then she remembered the phone calls: Cathleen hurriedly giving her another number, and then that person giving her yet another number where Cathleen could be reached—a safer number. She'd wondered at the time—and fully understood now—Cathleen's phone must have been tapped. Jones knew about Cathleen because he'd heard that first conversation. But how did he know about Montreal?

"They still follow," the driver said. He had pulled into the middle lane again and, looking back, she saw that the taxi was still behind them.

"How far to the Hilton?" she asked.

"It is in the center of the city. Not so far."

She rummaged in her purse until she found a pad of paper and she ripped out a page. She took a pen from her purse and clicked it open. She would have to be careful. She would have to do it just right.

She barely noticed when the city began taking over in earnest, or when the driver turned east onto Sherbrooke and wound his way through the city streets. She didn't even see the hotel until the cab pulled up right in front of it.

"Are they still there?" she asked, willing herself not to turn around.

"Yes."

She'd not had a chance to change money, but she knew American dollars were good in Canadian cities—they were easy to change and worth more. She palmed him the fare, and a ten-dollar tip. "Get out when I do," she said, "and stop the man as he gets out. Give him this note." She slipped the folded piece of paper into the driver's outstretched hand. "Are you ready?"

He looked at his hand, and back at her. In disgust, she slapped another ten into his hand. "Now?" she asked.

He smiled contentedly. "Of course."

"Let's go, then." She emerged from the taxi and, looking straight ahead, dashed up the steps and into the hotel. Once inside, she slowed and turned to look back, but the view was obscured. She ran around a corner to a window that overlooked the half-circle drive. The cabbie had handed the note to a man in a gray summer-weight suit. He read it, must have read it over two or three times, spoke briefly with the cabdriver, then reached into his pocket and handed the driver a couple of bills. Molly smiled wryly. Not a bad way to make a living. The man in the gray suit looked at the hotel then and she stepped back out of sight. She turned around. There was no lobby in view, only a long arcade with brightly lit shop windows. The time to get away was now, while he was still occupied outside.

"Is there another exit?" she asked a bellhop who was carrying two suitcases toward the door.

He motioned vaguely toward her left and kept going. She started down the arcade, walking fast, then broke into a run. If he came in, he would surely see her. There was a dress shop on her left, circular racks of blouses spaced randomly. A dress shop—dressing rooms. He wouldn't dare. She ran inside, and saw a curtained arch to her right. The dressing rooms would be beyond. She could hide. She could also be cornered. She realized now that the back of the shop opened to another arcade and she ran straight through, finding herself at last in a vast open mall. She glanced around. More shops on one side, exits to the street on the other. She paused, trying to orient herself. She had entered what she had thought was the hotel, but had run straight ahead through the arcade, then turned left. The exits, then, must lead to the street that ran alongside the hotel. What had happened to the man in the gray suit? And what had happened to the hotel—was it on the floors above? She walked quickly now, trying not to attract attention, moving farther through the mall, farther back from the front side of the hotel. Finally, when she judged she had gone far enough, she walked through an exit and into the sunlight. She had no idea where she was or where the Hotel St. Jean could be. It took her less than two minutes to flag down a taxi.

The phone rang in a tiny apartment in a working-class neighborhood of Montreal-Ouest and Alvin Jones answered it.

"I followed her to the Bonaventure Hilton Hotel downtown," Hamilton said. "She knew she was being followed and she had the driver give me a note. You want to hear it?"

"You bet."

"It says: *'By now you know the film Yuri gave you was worthless. He kept the film of the rebel camps and I have it. I'm willing to make a trade—Yuri Klebanoff for the film. I will leave a message for Alvin Jones tomorrow at the airport. If you don't want the pictures plastered all over America's front pages, you'll do exactly as I say.'* She didn't sign it. And she's not registered at the Hilton."

"Hunh," Jones grunted.

"There's more. For an extra twenty bucks, I got her taxi driver to tell me that before she realized she was being followed she asked him to take her to the Hotel St. Jean. Then when she discovered I was following her, she switched to the Hilton. I told him she was my fiancée and we'd just had a fight. You know how these Frogs are—they get soft in the head over romance. The money didn't hurt, either."

"Cut the crap and go to the St. Jean, then."

"I'm on my way." The phone clicked and Jones replaced the receiver.

He walked into the other room, where Klebanoff, his hands tied behind his back, was sitting on the edge of a bed. In a chair that just fit into the tiny room, another man ate a croissant sandwich with ham and cheese. "It looks like he wasn't lying to us," Jones said to the man in the chair. "She does have the film." Then he turned to Klebanoff. "She's won you a reprieve—at least for a day or two until we see what her terms are. She wants you back." He lifted his eyebrows. "You two must have had a real good time in Greece."

Klebanoff said nothing.

"This is when you'd expect me to slap you around," Jones said. "Your side would do it for sure." He leaned against the doorjamb and folded his arms. "You know, it's nothing against you. It was just not your good luck to have defected with what you happen to know."

"What do I know?"

Jones let out a long breath. "That's just the question, isn't it? What do you know? And who would believe it? And what do the pictures show? I don't suppose you've had a chance to develop them yet, have you? Of course not, because she's talking about film, not pictures."

He turned and walked out of the room. If he could get the film away from her, he could dispose of the Russian without any hassle. Let the Soviets take care of their own. After all, if they hadn't let him get away from them in the first place, none of this would have happened. He stood at a dirty window that overlooked a vacant, weed-strewn lot. It had been years since he'd killed a man with his own hands. Even longer since he'd been party to having one of his own taken out to protect an operation. He didn't especially like the feel of it.

He leaned his forehead against the cool glass. He was getting old. He wished it were all over. He'd gone beyond wishing that none of it had happened in the first place. That was the kind of thoughts the green ones had. It *had* happened, and he was enough of a professional to know that once it begins, the only thing left is to see it through. What he thought of Harbinger, or any of the rest, no longer mattered. He'd long ago learned that things were never black and white; that kind of thinking was for politicians. And the military brass. The ones who did their work for them knew better.

Molly paid the fare and stepped out of the taxi. The St. Jean was on a quiet street off Sherbrooke, only a few blocks east of the university. It seemed like a good choice. Fleetingly, she thought once more about Cathleen. She was going to have to trust Cathleen implicitly. Could she? O'Neal had thought so. *If you have a real emergency, she's going to be the only one you can trust.* God, his own wife.

She pushed open the door and walked into a cool, dim lobby. It was a small, old-fashioned hotel, unlike the Hilton, lined in burnished mahogany and walnut. She paused a moment to acclimate herself, and a bored-looking bellman in a green uniform with faded gold braid gazed absently at her. Beyond him were the elevators. She pressed the UP button and the elevator doors creaked open; she stepped inside and punched 3. The doors closed and the elevator moved slowly upward. *The only one you can trust.* Her mind kept coming back to Jones at the airport. How had he known? And had the man following her been with Jones? She'd counted on that, to get the message back to Jones. But if he wasn't . . . She'd seen the cabbie deliver the message. He was; he had to be. The elevator door creaked open and for a moment she remained in the elevator, her stomach feeling as if it had been left back on the first floor. *The only one you can trust.* Not even the cabbie. She recalled the brief conversation and the money passed. No, not even the cabbie.

The woman who opened the door had titian hair and meticulous makeup. She did not look at all the way Molly would have expected O'Neal's wife to look. "Cathleen?"

In response, the woman opened the door farther and stepped back.

"You must be Molly." A second woman had risen from a chair and stepped forward, her hand outstretched. Molly recognized her voice. She was taller than the other, her hair shorter and darker, and she wore almost no makeup at all.

"I'm sorry about your husband," Molly said, walking into the room.

Cathleen took Molly's hand in both of hers. "At last," she said, smiling. "But where's . . . Yuri?"

"They met us at the airport—"

"They?"

"Alvin Jones. He was in Rafetna with your husband."

"What's he doing here in Montreal? How could he have known?"

Molly shook her head. "He said you told him. Anyway, he has Yuri, but I got away." She looked around quickly. "I think you should check out of here."

"Did they follow you?" the other woman asked, her voice rising in panic. "God, Cathy—"

"They tried," Molly interrupted. "I think I lost them, but I can't be sure. The taxi driver could have—"

"Yes," Cathleen said, turning abruptly. "We'd better." She opened a closet door and began quickly pulling clothes off hangers. The other woman bent down with a sigh and yanked a suitcase out from under the bed. "What about this Yuri?" Cathleen asked as she put things into the suitcase.

"I'll tell you all about it," Molly said. "But we'd better get out of here first. Is there anything I can do?"

The other woman had moved into the bathroom. Cathleen piled the last of her clothes into the suitcase and met her in the doorway. The woman was still shoving things into a makeup case. She handed items to Cathleen, who tossed them into the suitcase and closed it.

"That's it, I think," Cathleen said. "I was travelling pretty light. We had the adjoining room for you . . ."

"I've still got money. I can pay for it."

"Let's get out of here." The other woman's voice was urgent.

Molly turned and hurried out of the room. She punched the elevator button and looked at her watch. How long had it been? She wasn't even sure. She heard the elevator pulleys clanking. *Come on*, she thought. Beside her, Cathleen shifted from one foot to the other. The door opened finally and it wasn't until Molly saw the elevator empty that it occurred to her that she ought to have worried that it might not be. They stepped inside and the door closed behind them. She hadn't been up there more than five minutes.

At the lobby, the elevator door opened and Molly started out, then stepped right back in.

"What—"

"I think it might be him," Molly whispered. "The guy at the desk."

Cathleen peered cautiously out and saw a man, perhaps thirty-five years old, talking with the concierge. Molly looked around her shoulder and took another look. "Same suit. I think it's him."

"Watch it, Cathy," the other woman said. She reached around Molly and pressed the 6 button, and the doors closed noisily. Molly looked in surprise at the woman, who still held her finger on the button. "I'm Gloria," she said. "I guess we haven't been introduced, but we talked on the phone." She turned to Cathleen. "What do we do now?"

"We could take the suitcase back and not check out," Cathleen said slowly. "We could probably slip out somehow."

"Then neither of us would have any clothes." Gloria looked at Molly for a moment and half-laughed ruefully. "None of us, I guess."

"Will he recognize you?" Cathleen asked Molly.

"Probably."

"But not us. At least, almost for certain, not you," Cathleen mused to Gloria.

"Cathy—"

"Even if we tried to put the suitcase back in the room, he could get there before we got away," Cathleen said.

The elevator shuddered to a stop and the door opened at the sixth floor. A cleaning lady with a cartful of dirty linens blocked the door. *"Excusez . . ."* she said, and moved back to let them out. Then she shoved the cart into the elevator and the door closed behind her.

"What do we do now?" Gloria asked.

"I have money. We can buy clothes," Molly said.

Cathleen looked at Gloria. "Anything in there you can't part with?"

Gloria shrugged. "I guess not."

Cathleen walked to the nearest room. Its door stood open; the beds inside were stripped but not yet remade. "If we're lucky, they'll hold on to it for us," Cathleen said, putting the suitcase down.

"But I'm keeping my makeup case," Gloria said, clinging to the bag that hung over her shoulder like an outsized purse.

"It's a deal."

Molly was watching the lights above the elevators. The cleaning woman was on her way down to the basement, and the elevator had stopped at 4 and at the lobby on the way. The other elevator had come up from the lobby and was just now stopping at 3. "How much you want to bet that's him?" Molly said.

"Or he might be taking the stairs," Cathleen said.

"Either way, now's our chance." Gloria pressed the button. They all watched the lights as the elevator which had been at the third floor now made its way back up.

"What happens if it stops on its way back down and he gets back on?" Molly asked.

Gloria shot her a glance. "If you're going to worry about something, worry about what happens when this door opens in a couple of seconds and he's standing there."

"He couldn't be; he got off at three," Molly said. But Cathleen had already taken her arm and was pulling her toward the open room.

"It's your game, Gloria," Cathleen called back to her sister. She shoved Molly into the room and closed the door behind them.

Gloria Wallace touseled her hair and unbuttoned another button of her blouse as the elevator door creaked open. The man paused when he saw her, and she looked at him with a broad, lazy smile. He was over six feet tall, with dark-brown hair cut short—nice-looking if not handsome in a medium-gray suit.

"Going down?" she asked. He hadn't stepped out of the elevator.

"Did you see a woman in a blue-and-white dress up here?" he asked. "Maybe with one or two other women?"

Gloria laughed, a throaty musical sound, and looked both ways down the empty hall before stepping into the elevator with him. "I don't see anybody," she said, looking straight into his eyes. "I would have thought it was a little early in the day for that kind of thing." She drew a compact from her bag and opened it to inspect her lipstick. "I suppose," she said, still looking in the mirror, "you could always just go down hallways and knock on doors." She snapped the compact shut and looked sidelong at him. "But in the meantime, are you getting out or are you going back down?"

He looked at her and smiled and stepped out of the elevator. She pushed the LOBBY button, then immediately pushed the OPEN DOOR button. The door stopped closing halfway and began to creak open again. Gloria leaned out from the elevator and called to his retreating back: "*My* room number is 620 and I'll be back in an hour or two." He didn't answer or turn around and she watched until he came to the exit stairs and pushed his way through the door. Then she darted across the hall and knocked once on the closed door. "Cathy!" she whispered and the door opened. All three dashed across the hall and into the elevator before the door had a chance to close again.

"Now," Gloria said triumphantly, "you will see how those of us who have to scramble for jobs keep others from beating us to it. The easy, all-purpose way of making an elevator into an express." She jammed a scarlet-nailed finger against the LOBBY button and kept it there all the way down.

There was a young family in the lobby, with two toddlers climbing over the luggage as the husband paid at the desk. To the side, an elderly couple pored over a map of Montreal.

The concierge looked up in surprise at a childish shriek and saw the women hurrying out. "Madame," he called, "there was someone asking for you. Did he find you?"

"Oh, yes," Cathleen called back over her shoulder. "We met him in the hall. Thank you very much."

The concierge turned back to the business at hand and the

three women stepped out into the afternoon sun. Gloria raised her hand for a taxi and a driver pulled up slowly beside them. "So civilized," she said, getting in. "So unlike anything in the U.S." Molly and Cathleen got in beside her. "So unlike anything else that's going on, in fact," Gloria added.

"Ville-Marie, please," Cathleen said to the cabbie. She leaned back in the seat. "Do you want to tell us about it?" she asked Gloria.

"I did my Evangeline Mercer act."

Cathleen turned to Molly. "Gloria was in the soaps. She's an actress on TV."

"He wasn't too bad-looking, actually," Gloria went on, buttoning her blouse. "But I think Molly has a lot to tell us."

"As soon as we get out of the cab," Molly said.

Cathy O'Neal took a long slow sip of coffee and replaced the porcelain cup in its saucer. "We need to get another hotel."

"We need to get some clothes," Gloria said.

Molly said nothing. They'd listened to her story, had asked questions, had added what they knew. She'd looked from one to the other, intrigued by their similarities and their differences. They were both long-legged and slim, though Cathy—she knew now that the name Cathleen had been only a code—was a good three inches taller than her sister. Her hair was dark auburn, cut short so that its gentle waves formed a halo around her face. She had a habit of running her fingers through her hair when she was thinking. Her makeup was hardly detectable and it was difficult to guess her age. Her face was lean and square-jawed, with wide, intent hazel eyes. Composed and informal, she was a handsome woman.

Gloria was dramatic from the top of her head to the tips of her scarlet-painted toenails. Her titian hair, half a dozen shades lighter than her sister's (and, Molly guessed, a color Mother Nature had never created unassisted), fell just to her shoulders in luxuriant, gleaming curls. She had startling green eyes surrounded by lashes so thick they could not possibly be real. Though she had inherited the same rose-colored complexion as her sister, she enhanced it with the skill of an artist. She sat now with her long legs stretched out under the table, and she moved her saucer back with a straight-fingered motion of a woman who is used to protecting a manicure.

"I'd like to get the film developed," Molly said finally. "I'd like to know what we really have."

"You're not actually going to make a trade," Gloria said. It wasn't even a question.

"I have to."

"You don't bargain with the Agency," Cathy said gently.

Molly turned to her. "I have to try."

"Give up the film for him?" Gloria asked. "If it shows anything incriminating to anybody, there's no way you can give it up, no matter what. My God, Dennis died for it. And if it turns out that it doesn't show anything, they won't make the trade anyway."

"They won't know what the pictures show. Only we'll know that. If we could find a quickie developing place, we could know right away what we have to bargain with."

Cathy smoothed back her hair. "We might be able to find one of those places to develop film while you wait. It could be worth knowing."

"Cathy . . ." Gloria began, but the look from her sister silenced her.

"Are we ready to go?" Cathy looked at the half-eaten sandwich on Molly's plate.

"I guess I wasn't very hungry," Molly said, standing.

Cathy put a hand lightly on Molly's back as they walked slowly toward the front of the café. "It's possible to feel pretty close to someone when it's just the two of you against the world."

"I know."

"But that's not real life. At a time like that, everything's magnified. On the one hand, annoyance can feel like hatred. On the other, liking can feel like loving. You were with him how many days?"

"Ten." Ten days.

"If you met him under normal circumstances, you might not even especially like him."

In fact, she hadn't liked him at all when she'd met him, but she wasn't about to tell them that. "You don't understand. He saved my life. In Athens he literally saved my life. And here, this afternoon"—her voice almost caught and then she recovered—"he gave me the chance to get away. I owe it to him. I have to try."

"You owe him nothing," Gloria said harshly. "He's the defector; you were brought along for his cover. He owes you."

They paid their bill and the cashier directed them to a photography shop she thought did quick developing. It was underground, in the vast network of shops and underground passages that lay beneath the center of the city. They had entered from the foot of McGill Street, and walked quickly past the shops until the passage opened into a full-fledged underground mall. They paused just for a moment to get their bearings, then moved quickly on until Molly saw the sign ahead: PHOTO GILBERT.

The young man behind the counter was dressed in gray pinstripe pants and a paler gray shirt. His fingernails were perfectly manicured, and his hair, short on top and longer on the sides, was slicked back behind his ears. He barely moved his mouth as he talked, as if afraid to show his teeth. Without even asking, Molly spoke to him in French. When she handed over the film, she did it with hesitation. Even though she was anxious to see the pictures, she was suddenly afraid that they would be worthless. They were her last link to Yuri—they were her only bargaining chip for him.

They waited in a quiet corner of the mall, just a few steps from the photo shop. Molly felt more comfortable with the place still in sight, the photo-finishing machine in clear view as it rotated slowly. Gloria's eyes strayed to a nearby dress shop, but she said nothing.

"We'll see what's in the pictures," Cathy said. "They may turn out to be nothing."

Molly nodded, afraid she would be right. Even Yuri had not been sure what was on the film.

"If the pictures are nothing, then it's pretty thin," Cathy went on. "Only Molly's word for what Yuri said he saw, and no way to identify who the Americans might be. Who would believe that?"

"But someone is awfully worried about what he saw, and maybe about the pictures," Molly said. "It's something we have to bargain—"

"Molly," Cathy interrupted, "you don't bargain with the Agency. If they have something you want and you have something they want, they'll get what they want without giving anything up. Even if those pictures showed the President of the United States rolling over and playing dead for the Soviet Premier, we wouldn't be able to use them to buy Yuri back. The best thing we can hope for is that they might make it so that you—we—can stop running."

Molly looked away. She knew Cathy was right, but knowing it didn't help. *If it comes to your life or his . . . dump him.* "If they show something—"

"If they show something," Cathy said briskly, "we call the press. The only way they're going to back off is if they no longer have anything to hide. And the only way they're not going to have anything to hide is if it's all out in the open anyway. Then they'll be so busy covering their own tails they won't worry about the three of us."

"And if they don't show anything?" Gloria asked.

"Then we've got the CIA and God knows who else after us," Cathy said.

"Unless we can make a trade for Yuri," Molly said.

"You still don't believe it, do you? You think you can deal with those guys."

" 'Those guys' are guys just like your husband, Cathy. Alvin Jones worked with him, for God's sake. And in the end, even that didn't matter, did it?" Cathy was looking at her open-mouthed, but she didn't care. "If those pictures don't show anything, then there's only one thing that'll hold them back, and that's for Yuri to talk to the press. *He saw* Americans in the Dioula. No matter what the pictures show, he knows what he saw. Maybe he would even recognize *who* he saw. Maybe the Agency doesn't usually make deals, but if that turns out to be the case, we're going to have to figure out a way to get them to *want* to make a deal."

"Either way, we're going to need the press," Gloria said.

"Any suggestions?" her sister asked her.

Gloria shook her head slowly. "The *Washington Post* is always doing exposés; don't you know anybody on the *Post*?"

"That's not the sort of social contact an Agency man and his wife like to make," Cathy said. "Molly?"

Molly shook her head. "Does it have to be someone we know?"

"I guess it doesn't. But we're coming out of the blue with a pretty wild story. It would help if somebody already knew we weren't loony tunes to begin with."

"I do know someone," Gloria said slowly, "but I don't know him very well. And it's the *Los Angeles Times*. It would be better if it were an East Coast paper."

"Why?" Molly asked.

"Because we're here, and because the story is a Washington story. No paper's going to want to go with only what we have to tell them, no matter how great the pictures are. They're going to have to investigate it, and that means Washington."

"Any major paper has a Washington Bureau," Molly reminded her.

"But the guy I know works out of LA. I don't know how they do those things."

"It's not up to us to worry about that; the newspaper can work that out," Molly responded.

"Is there any reason why you wouldn't want to contact him?" Cathy asked.

"No."

"Then let's hope we've got something to show," Cathy said.

In the time that was left, Gloria wandered off to the dress shop. Twenty-five minutes later she came back, carrying two shopping bags. "Okay," she said, "I'm set for another few days. Now all we need is to buy a piece of luggage to carry our stuff. And for you to buy yourselves something. I'm going to get pretty bored looking at you dressed in the same clothes all the time. To say nothing of how you'll smell after a while!"

"Mademoiselle!" A teenager came to the doorway and called to Molly. He was still putting the prints into two envelopes.

"Combien?" Molly asked him.

He rang it up and she paid. Then she scooped up the envelopes.

As if by silent consensus, the three walked away from the shop, Molly already opening the first envelope. Cathy and Gloria looked over her shoulders as she thumbed through the prints. There were plenty of photographs of the Bodamwean rebels, toting automatic rifles, hunkered down in makeshift pillboxes, marching in loose formation down a dirt path, on a break drinking what Molly recognized as bottles of *diamshee*, the potent Bodamwean beer. Occasionally one or more white faces appeared in the prints. Each time, Molly paused and the three stared at the faces, caught at a moment of instruction or walking alongside the rebel troops. Each time they concluded that the clothes and the haircuts almost certainly identified the men as Russians.

She came to the end of the pile with an empty feeling. There had been none of Americans. She looked at the pile in her hand, suddenly realizing that these were the first of Yuri's photographs she had ever seen. She started to thumb through the pictures once more when Gloria's voice at her ear startled her.

"The other set?"

Molly shoved the prints back into the envelope and took out the others. She began looking through these in the same way—

more black faces. On the fourth print she stopped. It was a distance shot, and there was no way anyone could recognize the face. The man was wearing what looked like khaki fatigues and an Australian bush hat. He was not—definitely not—a Russian.

She shuffled through the prints faster now, looking for more white faces, looking for the bush hat again. Five prints later she stopped again. Two white faces this time, and one was the bush hat. The other man was hatless and he appeared to be younger. This had been taken from much closer, though the angle and the foreground indicated that it was probably shot from the seat of a passing vehicle. The two had probably not even realized they'd been photographed.

Cathy reached out and gently pulled the print from Molly's hand. She examined it closely. "I've seen this man," she said finally.

"Who is he?" Molly asked.

"I have no idea, but he definitely looks familiar." She tapped a fingernail against the picture. "I don't think I know him. Maybe I've only seen his picture. But I've seen him somewhere before."

Without waiting for the print Cathy held, Molly continued through the pile. She was rewarded with two more distance shots of the man with the bush hat, and, finally, another close-up of the younger man. Cathy took that one from her and stared at it. "Yes, definitely," she said, "I've seen him or his picture somewhere before."

Molly looked at the two standing beside her. "What do we do now?"

"We call the press," Cathy said. "We've got something. We've definitely got something."

Molly felt the backs of her arms grow cold with a sudden chill. She knew there was no way anyone in her right mind would trade these pictures for a Russian defector, and it was no consolation at all that she knew Yuri would not want her to.

want to open, he could always threaten to close off
through the blackmail it still was to her.

19

ALVIN JONES SPAT COFFEE INTO THE SINK. IT WAS
cold. He set the mug down on the counter without rinsing it.
Hamilton hadn't been able to find them at the Hotel St. Jean,
which meant that the women were running. Or that the cabbie
had lied. Or that Molly had been sharp enough to tell him
the wrong hotel in the first place. That one wasn't likely. He
looked at his watch. Three-fifteen. He shouldn't be so hard
on himself. He'd only been in Montreal just over three hours
and he already had half of what he'd come for. And Molly
was offering to help him get the other half. In the end, it
didn't much matter whether they found her today or not. She
wanted to make a trade, and that meant one of two things:
either she already knew the film was worthless without the
Russian, or else she was so desperate to get him back she'd
give up anything.

He shook his head on that one. She was young; they'd been
together a week and a half with no one else to depend on. It
would make sense. The O'Neal woman would know better,
or at least she ought to. He had to be careful with this; to
make a wrong assumption would be devastating. He knew
what logic told him: if the message that Molly promised for
tomorrow still mentioned a trade, then the film couldn't be
worth much and they needed the Russian. But if she didn't
offer a trade tomorrow, it meant that the Russian was irrelevant. That's what logic said, but whoever said women were
logical?

The best thing for him would be if she still wanted to trade.
There was no way he could lose on that one. It would probably mean that the film was nothing, but he'd still end up
with all three—the Russian, Molly, and the film. If she didn't

238

want to trade, then he could worry. That would mean she thought the film alone could save her.

William A. Ellery leaned back and looked at the ceiling, his massive body tipping the chair precariously. He pressed a forefinger on the edge of his desk as if for balance. Though it was halfway through summer and the rest of LA was tan, "Big Bill" Ellery made a religion of keeping out of the sun. His broad face was as smooth as a baby's bottom, and as pink. Tufts of gray hair, wiry as an Airedale's, showed in front of his ears and circled the lower part of the back of his head; otherwise he was bald.

"How well do you know this person?" he asked, still staring at the ceiling.

"Pretty well," Ted Richter responded.

"Pretty well as in you've been at the same party a couple of times, or pretty well as in you grew up with her?"

"Pretty well as in I almost married her."

Ellery's chair lurched forward and he grinned at Richter. "I didn't think you were the marrying kind."

"I'm not, but I would have married her."

"Why didn't you?"

"Because she found me in bed with her best friend."

Ellery snorted. "What makes you think she isn't trying to screw you? She makes up a story, you write it, we print it, and it turns out to be another *Washington Post* junior-drug-addict piece of shit and you end up with egg on your face."

"She isn't that kind of person. Besides, that was a long time ago. She's had plenty of chances since then."

"Why does she call you? You're out here, she's back there. Why doesn't she call an East Coast paper?"

"You know damned well. A stranger calls with that kind of story, how much do you think anyone's going to believe it? They had to call someone they knew."

"Hell, a stranger called me out of the blue with what sounded like a cockamamie story about an army lieutenant named Calley being in the brig for wiping out a whole Vietnamese village of civilians. I knew it couldn't be true, because there was no way the army could have kept that quiet, and besides, who would have believed that American boys would have done such a barbarous thing? I almost let it go, until I realized how little he was asking for it. Hell, I figured I'd tell him I'd buy it and then if it turned out to be nothing

I'd just forget about paying him. Whether they believe it or not, a paper's always going to listen. A paper's always going to investigate—''

"Sure. And the first part of the investigation is going to be the source. They haven't got that kind of time. They needed to call someone who would hit the ground moving.''

"There's one thing you haven't told me.''

Richter straightened and raised an eyebrow, but said nothing.

"How much do they want for it?''

"Nothing.''

"I don't believe in gift horses.''

"Actually they do want something. Their lives. They're running scared. They think the only thing that'll save them is to get the information out.''

Ellery pressed his palms together in front of his face. Ted Richter was a good journeyman reporter, nothing more than that. Steady and a hard worker, but he'd never shown the flashes of creativity and the depth of insight that the greats have. He knew Richter was tired of the LSD stories—larceny, sex, and drugs—that were the mainstay, along with suburban politics, of the metro desk, but he had no way of knowing if Richter was ready for something like this. Even if it turned out to be true. On the other hand, it *was* Richter's story. He knew what it was like to want to move on, and if this thing turned out to be true it would be for Richter the chance that every reporter dreams of. And there was something else that nudged. The supposed defector was a journalist, too. A photographer, but still a *news* photographer. It shouldn't have made a difference, but it did.

"Okay,'' he said finally, "we'll go for it, but we're going to do it this way. You go to Montreal and talk to them—see what they've got, including the alleged incriminating pictures. And the negs. The pictures are nothing without the negatives. Pictures can be doctored, remember. I'll call the Washington Bureau and tell them to start putting out feelers. And we're going to have to contact Moscow and see what we can get on this supposed defector. You have his name in writing?'' He took Richter's proffered notes and copied from them. "You realize,'' he said, still writing, not looking at Richter, "what you're going to look like if this thing evaporates?''

"I'm going to look like a reporter who knows a story when it comes up and bites him in the leg.''

Ellery chuckled. "Then let me ask you this. Have you thought about what kind of firestorm you could be in the middle of if it turns out to be true?"

"Is that supposed to scare me off?"

"It's supposed to make you walk into the head and look in the mirror and ask yourself if you really want to step into this shit. Even Woodward and Bernstein had their moments, you know, and there were two of them."

Ted Richter leaned his hands on the desk and met Ellery's eyes. "It's my story and I want it."

"Then go do it. But I want it clean and I want good attribution." Ellery watched him turn on his heel and walk out of the office. The determination was there; maybe this one was a sleeper.

Y.P. Vagnerian buttoned his jacket. Even for a Moscow summer it was cold. He shoved his hands into his pants pockets and sauntered toward the monument. A woman hurrying toward him was carrying tissue-paper-covered flowers. He guessed that they were carnations. She was in her thirties, with hair that strange metallic-yellow color Slavic women get when they try to dye their hair blond. She shouldn't have bothered, he thought. She was not bad-looking for a Russian, and the hair only detracted from what would otherwise have been an almost classic face. He smiled at her but she ignored him. It didn't matter. In a couple of days he'd be back in Stockholm, where the blondes were real. Assuming everything went well.

Approaching the monument now, he could see Treacher coming from the opposite direction. He knew Treacher had seen him, though neither acknowledged the other. He paused at the back side of the monument and looked up, then slowly made his way around to the front. Treacher was standing there, gazing at the heroic Mikhuna sculpture, *The Worker and the Collective Farm Woman*, symbolically raising the hammer and sickle.

"They're masters at it, aren't they?"

"Among other things." The fact that he answered at all meant Treacher didn't think he'd been followed. It was a hell of a way to run a newspaper, as they say.

"I had a message from your boss," Vagnerian said, still looking at the monument.

"I gathered."

"You know of a Yuri Andreyevich Klebanoff?"

"I know of an Andrei Klebanoff. Would this be his son?"

Vagnerian didn't react. "If he's the editor in chief of *Pravda*, it would."

"He is."

"And that makes our friend the grandson of . . ."

"Yes, it does. Former Premier Butakov."

"Let's walk," Vagnerian said.

They turned to their right and strolled along Prospekt Mira.

"It's no wonder they didn't trust the phones or the cables on this one," Vagnerian mused. "The guy defected."

Treacher kept on walking. "It'd be damaging to the Butakov faction, but not necessarily fatal. The army is pretty solidly with them."

"The guy is a photographer for Tass. At least all this is what he says. He's been in Bodamwe; ever heard of the place?"

"West Africa, isn't it? Oh, yes, that's where the fighting is, isn't it? I've seen pictures in the Soviet press—"

"Klebanoff's, no doubt. He's been photographing the fighting for Tass. He defected in Bodamwe, and he brought pictures with him, along with some interesting stories. It seems that not only do the rebels have Soviet advisers back there in the bush, they've also got American ones."

Treacher stopped for a moment and looked straight at Vagnerian.

"Yes," Vagnerian went on, "Americans and Russians working together. He's got pictures of that. Your editor hasn't seen them yet, and neither has anyone else except the people who brought him out. The CIA is scrambling, which means there's some kind of government involvement, official or otherwise. Does this sound like here-we-go-again time?"

"What, exactly, do they want from me?"

"Confirmation of Klebanoff's identity, for starters. Any rumors would be helpful as well."

Treacher nodded. "In other words, they want to know whether or not they can believe this guy. I don't blame 'em. Have you got a picture of him?"

"No. They haven't even got Klebanoff anymore. Your friendly neighborhood CIA has him."

"What have they got, then?"

"Someone he told this to. And the pictures."

"What if they turn out to be nothing?"

"They supposedly definitely show Americans. And they're recognizable. How long would it take you?"

"I should have something in twenty-four hours. Maybe a lot sooner if I'm lucky. How does that sound?"

"They can live with it. Be careful with this one, Judd. It's both sides; keep that in mind. They wouldn't have asked you if they didn't think it was essential to verify—"

"Hell," Treacher said, smiling slightly, "this is going to be an interesting one."

"There's already been at least two people killed on this one, maybe more. And it looks like the CIA was fingering 'em. Keep a low profile; don't ask questions in the wrong places. Use only the sources you can absolutely trust. That comes straight from Big Bill."

Treacher ran his tongue across his lips. "Is that it?"

"Get what you can as fast as you can, but watch your backside."

"I'll meet you here tomorrow. Same time." Treacher began walking faster, and he was grinning now. The adrenaline was flowing.

Vagnerian slowed and turned to his left. As long as he was here, he'd take a look at the zoo.

It was raining, a gentle summer morning rain that barely disturbed the spikes of blue delphinium that bloomed just beneath the window. Raindrops slid down the window, but the sound of water Molly heard was not the rain; it was the shower running in the bathroom behind her. She looked at her watch and shook her head. Gloria had been in the shower for almost forty minutes; it was a wonder she didn't turn into a prune. Cathy had been gone for longer than that. She had finally decided to call and check on her boys. She hadn't done that before, but she reasoned now it was no longer any secret that she was somewhere in Montreal, so she might as well call. Molly hadn't worried about that; Cathy was smart enough not to call from the immediate neighborhood. That was why they'd chosen this hotel—it was only a short walk to the Honoré-Beaugrand metro station. From there they could be in the center of the city in only a matter of minutes. No taxis, and little likelihood that anyone would be able to trace them to this tiny tourist hotel on the far northeast side of Montreal.

Molly watched a single drop roll down the window and lose itself in a little puddle of water at the bottom of the pane. Cathy had lost a husband, but at least she still had the three boys. And Gloria had Cathy, and whatever it was that she had with that reporter, Ted Richter. Molly's mind strayed to that one for a moment. It was obvious that there was something between those two, something uncomfortable. No one had said anything, though, and Molly wondered if Cathy had felt it, too. Both of them had someone.

Molly thought of her father, going about his day in Sheboygan—he'd probably been up for hours already, even though it would be an hour earlier there, even though he was officially retired. He would be thinking, if he thought of her at all this morning, that Molly was in Rafetna. He'd worried about her going to Africa again, and that seemed incredibly ironic now. She had never been in this much danger in Africa. She understood now why O'Neal had told her not to contact any family or friends. It would have been the first place they would look for her. Her father's phone was probably tapped. She smiled to herself, wondering who was listening in on his conversations and what that person would think of the early morning phone calls, whether they'd be bored by the endless discussions of water temperature and wave height and appropriate fishing lures. Maybe they'd think it was some sort of elaborate code. Serve them right.

In the bathroom, the shower had stopped. It was not true that she had no one. She had called Cathy and Cathy had been there for her. And Cathy had called Gloria. And Gloria had call Ted. But Yuri . . . she put a forefinger on the pane, against a drop on the opposite side, and slowly followed it down the window . . . Yuri had no one.

The bathroom door opened and Gloria stepped out wrapped in a towel, another towel draped loosely around her hair. She was better-looking than Cathy, Molly had decided, though without makeup her complexion was not nearly as fine as Cathy's. She'd learned that the startling green of Gloria's eyes came from a set of contact lenses.

"Feeling down?" Gloria asked her, bending over and gently toweling her hair.

"No."

Gloria straightened and held the towel to her head. "It's not that easy to lie to an actress. Other people listen to the words; actors look at the body. The set of your shoulders is telling me something your mouth isn't. You want to talk about it?"

"Cathy is helping me because, in a sense, her husband asked

her to. But you came all the way out here from California. Why?"

Gloria plopped into a chintz-covered chair, turned to hook both tanned legs over an arm, and resumed slowly toweling her hair. "She's my sister."

"You could be killed."

Gloria didn't respond.

"Wouldn't it have been easier to have gone to a friend in Washington and asked for help, rather than have her sister fly all the way from Los Angeles?"

Gloria stopped rubbing her hair and looked up at Molly. The thick dark lashes, at least, were real. "She's my sister," she repeated.

"You barely see each other. The last time you were together was—"

Gloria didn't say anything for a moment, and Molly saw that she was rubbing her right thumb against the soft flesh between thumb and forefinger on her left hand. When she finally spoke, her voice was slow and measured. "Cathy's seven years older than I am. We grew up in a little town in western Pennsylvania, but we always summered in Maine." She looked up. "That was the place you called when you talked with her for the first time. That's the place I spent every summer of my life until I went to California."

Molly nodded.

"We had a little sailboat that we played around with—just a skiff, really, with a single sail and a centerboard. It was a fairly protected cove, and our folks let us go out by ourselves. Cathy was thirteen that summer, and I was six. It was probably the first summer they let us go out alone." She held the towel against her hair, sitting as if she, too, were listening. "It was after supper, and somehow we got out of the cove. Our parents hadn't even realized we'd gone, or they would have called us in before things got out of hand. A storm came up and the waves were pretty good-sized for a couple of kids in a boat like that. And it got dark faster than we expected. And, frankly, we got scared and disoriented—neither of us had been out there after dark before and things look different the farther one gets from shore. Cathy tried to take us in, but we were beating against the wind, and the next thing we knew . . . the boat capsized. Luckily we both came up on the same side of the boat, but I was terrified. I was only six, remember. I'd cut my hand pretty bad on something going overboard and it hurt like hell, and we were both freezing—have you ever tried swimming off the Maine coast? It took me about one minute and I was hysterical.''

She toweled her head again, slowly. ''She was probably as scared as I was, maybe more so because she was old enough to know more things to be scared about. But she shoved me up on the hull as far as she could push me, to get me as much out of the water as she could, and she held me there with her own body. And she kicked, trying to force our way toward shore. And she sang. All the songs she could thing of . . . 'John Jacob Jingleheimerschmidt.' 'Ninety-nine bottles of beer.' 'Daisy, Daisy . . . ' '' Gloria smiled and shook her head at the recollection. ''It would have been a hell of a lot easier for her if she hadn't done that, if she'd just tried to get us to shore. But she knew I was scared and she made me sing with her, so that I'd forget about being scared.'' She began singing softly. *''I've got rings on my fingers, bells on my toes, elephants to ride upon, my little Irish rose . . . ''* Her voice was thin and childlike. ''God knows how long it was. Finally we got close enough to shore that we could hear people calling for us, and she yelled across the water to them.

''We heard an engine start up then and Phinney—he was a lobsterman and as big as a barn—came out toward us, shining a light, sweeping it across the water until he caught us in it. Dad was with him and they reached over and pulled us aboard. Phinney took off his shirt and wrapped it around me. It smelled like fish and sweat and diesel oil. And then he put a slicker over that, but I was still shivering so hard I thought my bones would break. Dad put his arms around both of us and held us close, and cried. The only time I think I ever saw him cry. Not saw, I guess, because it was dark, but heard.''

She dropped the towel on the floor and fluffed her hair with her fingers. ''We didn't go out in the boat again for the rest of the summer, even on the warmest days. Our parents never said we couldn't, but we didn't go. No one ever said much of anything and I never spoke of it again. It was ten years before I could think of that time and not shiver with cold and terror.'' She looked at Molly, squinting nearsightedly because her contacts weren't in. ''Neither of us has ever discussed it, but I know damn well—I always have—that she saved my life.''

''And is there something that Ted Richter owes you?''

''Not really.'' Gloria stood and walked toward the closet.

''But there's something between you,'' Molly persisted.

''Well,'' Gloria said, opening the door and staring into the closet as if she had a dozen dresses to choose between, "maybe he owes me an apology."

By the time Cathy returned, Gloria was dressed. Cathy was in an ebullient mood—the boys were fine, Father Jack was managing okay, no one had been around. She'd taken that to mean that either no one had figured out what she'd done with the boys, or else nobody cared about bothering them. Either way, she was relieved. Gloria mouthed something to Cathy that Molly couldn't see, but she did see Gloria tilt her head in Molly's direction.

"Something wrong?" Cathy asked, walking toward her.

"I'm glad the boys are okay."

"Molly?"

Molly took a deep breath. "I have to try to get him back."

Cathy shook her head. "They won't trade."

"I have to try. If they won't trade, then what *can* I make them do?"

"Nothing. I know that's not a very satisfactory answer, but it's an honest one. I don't know a lot about the Agency, but I know enough not to try to outsmart them."

"You called your sister because you knew she'd help you—because she owes you." Cathy shot a quick glance at Gloria, but Molly went on talking. "And she called this Ted guy because he owes her . . . for something. Maybe he is the only newspaper person any of us knows, but he still owes her. And—let's face it—I called you only partly because your husband said you were the only one I could trust. I also did it because by then I figured he owed me something. We each called someone else in, even though we knew it would be dangerous for that person, for the simple reason that we knew that person wouldn't say no. That person owed us. I owe him. I'm the only one who can help him and I owe him. I have to try."

"No. No. And no," Cathy said.

"Cathy," Gloria said softly.

Cathy turned to her sister and a look passed between them. Cathy walked over to Molly and put an arm across her shoulders. "What will you trade them?" she asked gently. "Yourself? Ted is already in Washington with the pictures. You're not going to get them back now. The damage is done as far as they're concerned."

"We can get more prints made. Ted can have it done down there."

"You'd offer to trade prints for him when they'd have no guarantee that you haven't already gotten another set made? And you don't have the negatives. They aren't going to buy a pig in a poke like that."

"We could pretend that we never got the film processed. We could buy some film and shoot it and give it to them and let them think it's the film Yuri shot."

Cathy shook her head. "They won't buy it. They'll look at it before they give him up."

"There has to be a way out," Molly said desperately. "I told him I'd leave a message for him today. I have to do it; I have to give Yuri a chance to get away."

"You don't even have a plan!"

"I don't have to have a plan. All I have to do is make an offer. We can figure out a plan later."

"Oh, sure," Gloria said. "Simplest thing in the world. Just tell them where to rendezvous with us, and then we figure out the plan."

"Well, why not?" Molly demanded, her voice rising with desperation. "Is that any crazier than coming all the way across the country just because your sister asks you to, with no explanation or anything?"

There was silence in the room. Molly stared defiantly at Gloria. Gloria looked at Cathy. And Cathy, her arm still loosely laid on Molly's shoulders, stared out the window. Finally Cathy spoke. "Sunday. Tell him Sunday. Tell him to bring Yuri and you will bring the developed pictures and the negatives. Tell him that he can see one of the pictures first to make sure it's worth the trade, but to be ready to trade then. It'll be then or never. He'll just have to trust that you're not keeping back an extra set of the prints. Once he sees the one picture, he'll know that he has no choice but to accept your terms. One chance only, Molly, we'll give him no more than that. You'll have to convince him. You will meet him next Sunday at noon—exactly at noon—at the Cathedral downtown. It's called Mary Queen of the World Cathedral. On the right-hand side as you face the altar, near the front, is a statue of Saint Anthony. It's an open chapel—there are candles in front of the statue and people pray there. Saint Anthony is the one with the Christ Child in one arm and a lily stalk in the other hand. There. In front of that statue. At noon."

"How do you know all this?" Gloria asked.

"I stopped in after I called Father Jack."

"I thought we agreed that we wouldn't stay out in public unnecessarily," Molly said.

Cathy took her arm from Molly's shoulder. "I was out anyway, and I felt I needed to. And it looks like it's a good thing I did.''

Gloria was counting on her fingers. "We've got four days to figure out a plan," she said.

"And when is Ted coming back?" Cathy asked. "They've got five days to get their story put together."

Delany Morris leaned over the desk, smiling to himself and nodding his appreciation. It was more than he had expected, though God knew what he was going to do with it. The prints covered the entire desktop, laid out in approximate subject-related groupings. The largest, covering the top two-thirds of the desk, was the group showing only the rebels. The smallest, composed of five prints, was the most carefully displayed. Three good close-ups; one mid-range; and one distance shot. He was pretty sure who the one guy was, but he hadn't a clue about the other. He was waiting for Redmond. He knew that Ted Richter was standing anxiously behind him, but he hadn't yet said much to him. He was slightly jealous, since Richter was somebody off the metro desk, but his better sense told him that it was preferable to be in on a group effort than not to be in on it at all.

The door opened behind him and Delany straightened and turned. "These them?" Redmond asked, walking directly to the desk. He hadn't even acknowledged Richter's presence.

Delany nodded and pointed at the five prints in the lower center of the desktop. Redmond picked up one close-up and then another, and Delany wished for the millionth time that Redmond weren't such a good poker player. Redmond shoved his glasses farther up on his nose and drew the third close-up off the desk, giving it a good once-over, as if to make sure he hadn't been mistaken. Then he turned to Richter. "You're Ted Richter."

"Yeah."

"I saw the piece you did on teenage shootings in Watts. Good piece of work. You know what you have here?"

"That's why I brought them. So that you guys could tell me."

"First off," Redmond said, "you've got lots of rebels. That's good. The arm bands place them. So does the *diamshee*. Only a Bodamwean stomach can handle that stuff." He turned back to the desk. "And the armored trucks are definitely Russian. This one," Redmond said, pointing, "the guy with the hat, is the tough one. August Lansdale. U.S. Army retired. 'Augie' to his friends. Works as a sometime consultant to the Pentagon. Rumored also to be on the payroll of Defense Systems, Inc. Ever heard of them?''

Richter nodded.

''Thought you would have. Just about the nation's largest defense contractor. Augie Lansdale—about as wound up in Eisenhower's infamous military-industrial complex as a man can be.''

''And the other one?'' Richter asked.

''Hell, you didn't need to bring me in to identify the other one, did you?'' Redmond asked Morris.

''No,'' Morris conceded. ''But I didn't tell him who it is.''

''Lieutenant Colonel Stephen White,'' Redmond said to Richter. ''He's an aide to General William R. French. Yeah,'' he said, seeing Richter's reaction, ''you got it: the President's National Security Adviser.''

20

ALVIN JONES NODDED AT THE WOMAN BEHIND THE tourist information desk and folded the paper. He turned away, smiling. Molly was still offering a trade. And she'd had the film developed and she claimed . . . His mind backed up and went over it again. She'd *said* she'd had the film developed, and she'd *said* there were damaging photos. But she'd also demanded that he bring Yuri along with him. No further chances. See what you're buying and then buy it on the spot or back out. It was almost too transparent, of course. The pictures were nothing, just the bait to get him to bring Yuri along. Whatever they had in mind depended on that, obviously. And also depended on not giving him time. It was pretty clear, then. The pictures were nothing; only a ruse to get him to bring Yuri.

Molly and the O'Neal woman and her sister. That's all he knew for sure. He wondered if there were others. Surely they had to have others to think it would work. Surely the O'Neal woman would know better than that. Unless, of course, it was Molly alone. He had no proof that they'd ever gotten together. It was possible that his mention of Cathleen at the airport had scared her away from the O'Neal woman. It would be an outside chance, but he couldn't help smiling. Molly alone would be a cinch. Even the three of them ought to be a piece of cake. Three and a half days. Hell, in three and a half days, he could have half of Washington up here. No need to bring in the Canadians. They'd only ask questions, and in three and half days he could manage anything he needed by himself. *A trade*. It doesn't work quite like that, Molly, he thought, smiling. The O'Neal woman should have known that. She'd seemed pretty sharp.

He walked briskly toward the exit doors. He'd go straight to the church and take a good look before he worked out a plan. He reminded himself not to think of it as a cinch. From the beginning, nothing had worked according to plan. That was what happened when amateurs got involved. You couldn't count on them for anything—not to act dumb, not to act like professionals. Even O'Neal had screwed him. Hell, Dennis, he thought, if you'd just gone along with a naval evac, none of this would have happened. A quiet pickup at sea by a chopper. It would have been dark. Dennis wouldn't even have seen the markings until it was all over. And there were Cubans within long helo range. It could have been done so easily, so quietly. He smiled to himself. If he had a nickel for every plan he'd ever made, and another for every one that hadn't worked out, he could retire.

Now that was one hell of a negative way to think. What made the difference between the amateurs and the professionals was the up-front knowledge that the plan might not work, and the ability to adapt to whatever came down. Contingency plans, sometimes made on the fly, had saved more operations than he'd care to count.

He pushed his way through the exits. It was still raining, had been since early morning. Almost like a mist, really. He waved to a taxi. And it was cold, or at least cold by Rafetna standards. Cold and damp and rainy, which was a hell of a lot better than hot and humid. *"Cathédrale"* he said, stepping into the cab. "Marie Reine du Monde."

The cabbie nodded. "Marie Reine du Monde," he repeated.

Jones sat back in the seat. Molly was still a factor. He would not be able to take her out in the church, which was, of course, why she had chosen it. The cathedral at noon on Sunday morning. Even the most experienced hit man would balk at that. But she had to come out. Even from a church, eventually you had to come out.

This time Y.P. Vagnerian wasn't so rushed, so he rode only as far as the Shcherbakovskaya Metro Station. Coming out of the station, he crossed Mira and turned onto Zvyozdny. He didn't need to look at his watch; he knew he'd given himself plenty of time. Besides, he'd gotten used to summer in these latitudes, and he could guess, from the pale light of the sky, that it was between nine-thirty and ten in the evening. It was a good time for a rendezvous. Muscovites were themselves still strolling the streets. An early showing at the Kosmos Cinema was letting out. He felt more comfortable in crowds and he mingled with them as some strolled leisurely toward the grounds of the Exhibition of National Economic Achievement.

Instead of turning left into the park at the main entrance, however, he continued toward the large Exhibition Pavilion—the one that had been used at Expo-67. In Montreal, as a matter of fact, he thought with a wry sense of irony. Coming from the Pavilion, he approached the sculpture from behind. The lowering sun tinted its chrome-nickel steel rose, and that, somehow, softened the effect enough that Vagnerian almost liked it. In another hour or so it would only be a silhouette against the sky, and Vagnerian would like it even better.

He walked slowly around the twenty-five-meter sculpture and noted casually that Treacher wasn't in sight yet. Three scrawny bouquets—two of red carnations and one of white— leaned against the base of the sculpture. From their looks, they had been there most of the day. Perhaps they were the leavings of bridal parties. God. Only in a Marxist state would bridal couples leave bouquets at monuments to the labor force.

He strolled away from the monument down another crosspath until he found himself almost directly behind the VDNKh Metro Station. Then he turned up Mira and again walked toward the monument.

He wandered thus for an hour and a half, never taking the same path twice within forty minutes' time, never looking at his watch, never, in short, giving the appearance of waiting for someone. By then it was virtually dark, the monument only a massive shape against the lights of the city. He walked along Mira as far as the Shcherbakovskaya Station and took the next subway train toward the Ring. He would switch trains twice before going to his hotel, just in case. He was beginning to feel uneasy. There were a lot of reasons why Treacher might not have made it tonight, but it still wasn't like him. And Vagnerian had hoped to be on his way back to Stockholm by tomorrow morning.

The man across the table from Delany Morris stubbed out a cigarette and immediately lit another. Morris tried not to wince noticeably. It was a losing battle, anyway. If he weren't so stubborn—and so convinced of the dangers—he'd have thrown his hands up in surrender and begun smoking again himself.

"The Department knows nothing about it, nothing," the man said quietly, the cigarette barely clinging to his bottom lip.

Delany, leaning forward so that he could hear, tried not to breathe in the smoke as he looked at the man's eyes. He was usually a good source, although clearly nervous about this face-to-face meeting. He preferred the illusion of anonymity that telephone contact fostered. Morris was cautious about phone calls on this one. In the next booth, Morris could hear a southern male voice trying to seduce some female who was clearly trying to keep the relationship platonic. He resisted the urge to stand up and tell the guy off.

"That's a pretty inclusive statement, when you think of how many people work at State," Delany said casually.

"I'm talking about official knowledge. I'm talking about what the Secretary knows. I guess you'd agree that if the Secretary knew about it, I'd know, too."

Morris nodded, granting that.

"Of course I'm not talking about individuals. How the hell can anyone be certain of that?" He took a long drag on the cigarette and then tapped the ash against the side of the ashtray. Morris knew the sign, and he waited. The man took another long drag, blowing the smoke down toward the table, from where it could diffuse itself against his clothes, or gently waft back up into Morris' face. Then he rolled the ash against the astray. "I mentioned your name in a couple of contexts—"

"I'm not comfortable with that," Morris said, leaning closer.

"Not your name personally, the paper's name. That you were wondering about the terrorist attack in Rome. That maybe your paper was doing some four-parter on the new terrorists. Something that would get someone's attention if they knew anything." He leaned back in the booth and Morris knew that signal as well.

"You'll let me know if you hear anything else?" Morris asked.

"You bet." He placed his palms on the edge of the table. "I'll go out first. Give me a good few minutes." Then he rose, pulling with him the briefcase that had been sitting on the seat beside him, and walked back toward the front door.

Morris took a last sip of the watery Scotch and thought about minor government officials who liked to talk to the press. A feeling of power when they were quoted—*A State Department source, asking not to be identified, said* . . . ? An effort to manipulate the real power brokers? An attempt to rectify perceived wrongs? He reached into his pants pocket for his wallet. All those things, probably, and more. Hell, half the time it was the way the government got its own information out. He shrugged. He'd go back to his office and make some more calls, but he had decided to proceed with caution. There was something about this that he didn't like the smell of.

When Morris walked into the office, Marge handed him a call slip. He didn't recognize the full number, or the name, but the exchange number intrigued him. He knew that number and he grinned to himself. Maybe.

At his own desk, he dialed the number. When a voice answered, he said, "This is Del—"

"Yeah, Del," an overly friendly voice broke in. "How are ya, old buddy? I was thinking the other day: we haven't played squash in so long I can't even remember back that far."

He didn't recognize the voice, and he knew how long it had been since he'd played squash—since he was in high school. "Yeah," he said, "maybe we should get together."

"You busy this afternoon?"

"I could arrange it. Where did you have in mind?"

"Well . . . hell, for old time's sake, how about Century Squash and Racquet? They still take nonmembers, I think."

"Four o'clock too early?"

"Make it four-fifteen. Remember, I have to come farther than you do."

Yeah, Morris thought, cradling the receiver, all the way in from Langley.

He was still sitting at his desk, staring into space and wondering what that was all about, when his phone rang again. "Morris," he said, holding the receiver with his left hand and reaching for a pencil with his right.

"Got a minute?" It was Redmond.

"Yeah."

"I'll be right there."

When Redmond arrived, he was holding a sheet of paper and he sat down on the edge of Morris' desk. "Telex from Moscow," he said, his voice husky. "Judd Treacher was struck by a car as he crossed Gorky Street at four o'clock this afternoon, Moscow time. Drunk driver."

Morris rose. "How is he?"

"Dead."

Morris blinked twice. "Who else knows?"

"About Treacher or about the other thing?"

"Either one."

"Just the two of us, on both counts. I wanted to tell you first. I'll post the telex."

"When did you get that?"

"Twenty minutes ago."

"Shit. Four o'clock Moscow time. Took 'em long enough."

"There's only one rationale for that. Somebody was holding it up."

"Looks like the big guy wasn't being paranoid after all. Christ. Treacher. Whatever the hell this is, we're not playing in the same league we've played before."

"Do we have anything on this end yet?"

Morris looked down at his desk. "A phone number." He handed it to Redmond and watched the reaction. "Yeah. Interesting, isn't it. I'm meeting him this afternoon."

"You still want to?"

"More than ever. Hell, he answered the phone. Whoever he is, he's not hiding behind any covers. It must be his real number. You got a gym bag I could borrow?"

Morris walked into the Century at four-fourteen, wondering how he was going to recognize the guy. He scanned the lobby, but didn't see anyone who looked likely. The girl behind the desk, appearing young enough to be still in high school and tan enough in her white shorts to have spent the last six years in Florida, smiled broadly at him. "Can I help you?"

"I'm waiting for someone."

She nodded and her smile turned wider yet. He knew he wasn't that good-looking.

"Is your name Morris, by any chance?" she asked.

"Yes."

"There's a message for you." His hopes fell as she fumbled through some papers covering the desk. The guy had gotten cold feet. "Here it is." She handed him a piece of paper, folded and sealed with a strip of tape.

He opened it, ripping the paper in the process—whoever the guy was, he wasn't taking any chances—and he read the terse note: *Shannon Bar. Right away.* "Thanks," he said to the girl, stuffing the note into his pocket. Now he wished he hadn't brought the gym bag.

The Shannon Bar was three streets over, a place frequented by construction workers. Not the kind of bar where he'd be likely to see anyone he knew; and probably not the kind of place the other guy would either. It was a noisy place with green-painted fiberboard walls and cardboard cloverleafs encircling the clouded mirror behind the bar. He scanned the half dozen men and couple of women standing at the bar and decided that none of them was a likely candidate. He walked along the row of booths toward the back, but it wasn't until he reached the second to the last booth that a man looked at him, caught his eyes on the gym bag, and said, "Morris?"

Morris slid into the booth and took in the man sitting opposite him. Unlike most of the patrons, he was dressed in a suit. Morris would have put him around forty, with close-cropped hair beginning to show gray and dark-brown eyes. "And you are?"

"I'd rather not say."

"I'm sorry, but it doesn't work that way. I don't have to print it, but I have to satisfy myself."

"The name won't mean anything to you, anyway."

"But the position will? I like to keep things clean. I like a name."

The man wet his lips. "Glenn Pastrella." His voice was so low that Morris could barely hear it. "This has got to be on background."

Morris tilted his head. "My editor doesn't like stories without attribution."

"You guys do it all the time."

"What do you want me to say: 'A CIA source says—' "

"No!" Pastrella whispered. "Nothing like that." He leaned back. "Maybe this was a mistake."

Morris leaned forward. "Okay," he said. "We'll do it on deep background. What is it?"

Pastrella took a long breath, an obvious attempt at relaxation. "A friend of mine at State told me your paper was looking for information."

"Yeah."

"Would it by any chance have anything to do with anything going on in a certain West African country?"

"If your friend at State told you anything, you already know that."

Pastrella nodded. Morris winced. This guy was going to have to be led along. It was obviously the first time he'd done anything like this, and he didn't seem too sure he wanted to be doing it now.

"I'm surprised you knew to contact me," Morris said. "I didn't think my name was attached to anything. If you know anything about this, you might know why I'd like to keep a low profile for a while."

"Your name wasn't. My contact had to do a little pushing. And, yes, I can understand why. Dennis O'Neal was a good friend." Pastrella began turning the ashtray slowly.

Morris said nothing. Over the years, he'd learned the value of silence to a reporter. Most people were uncomfortable with silence. Most people would do almost anything to fill a void.

"I've had to be very cautious," Pastrella said finally. "It's one of the most important things Dennis taught me. Dennis was in Bodamwe to nail down links between the rebels and the Soviets. What was he doing in Rome? What was he doing with Lopes in Rome? Why did he just happen to be at the café when those terrorists opened fire? Dennis didn't believe in coincidence, and neither do I."

"Are you looking to me for answers? Reporters are more used to asking the questions."

Pastrella shook his head. "There's some kind of an interest in Bodamwe. I can't quite get a handle on it; it's some kind of 'black' operation."

"Funded with 'black' funds? Is it a CIA operation?"

"I don't know. I don't even know about the funding. I think that the Center for Strategic Information might be involved."

Morris looked intently at Pastrella. "Does the CIA ever run 'black' funding through there?"

"Not that I know of," Pastrella said, "but I've never been involved in a 'black' project. I don't know how the funds are handled."

"What makes you think the Center is involved?"

"Robert Jacobsen. His name has been mentioned."

"Who's doing the mentioning?" Morris asked.

"You're sure this is off the record?"

" 'Off the record' means I can't even print the information, unless I can get it from another source. It's just meant to push me in the right direction, that's all. When we started this conversation, you said you wanted it on background. 'On background' means I can print the information, but I can't say who I got it from. 'On deep background' means I can't even say it came from someone at the CIA. Let's get it straight: what are we doing here?''

"I don't want it known that someone at the Agency gave out any information," Pastrella said, his hand moving to encircle his glass.

"But you didn't mind giving me your office phone number."

"Yeah. Let's say I thought I might need to establish some credibility. What do you know, anyway? Why are you asking questions?''

Morris straightened. "Mr. Pastrella, at four o'clock this afternoon, Moscow time, one of our men in the Moscow Bureau was killed by a drunken driver. I don't believe in coincidences, either, and he was trying to get answers to the same kind of questions I am. I don't believe I want to be in the business of telling an Agency man what I know, or why. I'm not interested in being the next victim. If you want to tell me what you know, that's fine. My company is in the business of printing the news. We try to stick to the truth, as best we know how. Frankly, I'm not always so sure of what your Company is trying to do.''

Pastrella licked his lips and then took a slow swallow of the drink in front of him. "Have you ever heard of an organization called Harbinger?''

"No.''

"It's one of those vague things you hear about from time to time, and nobody—with the obvious exceptions of the people who are supposedly involved—knows whether it's an apocryphal organization or whether it's real. Dennis O'Neal was killed in Rome. A young State Department employee was found drowned in a supposed swimming accident off the coast of Bodamwe. Within twenty-four hours of Dennis. A local that sometimes worked for the Embassy was supposedly killed by a robber on the same day the drowning victim disappeared. No, there are extremely few coincidences in the real world.''

"Hey!'' the barman called out to Morris. "You want something to drink or what?''

"Yeah,'' Morris answered. "Bring me a beer. Whatever's on tap.'' He turned back to Pastrella. "And Harbinger?''

"It's a secret organization. I've seen references from time to time. My guess is that it's heavily weighted with people like Jacobsen, either retired military types or some who aren't yet retired. And, one would assume, probably some from the defense industry as well.''

"It's pretty hard to draw the line that separates those guys.

As I remember, Jacobsen's first job in retirement from the Air Force was as chairman of the board of Defense Systems, Inc., wasn't he?''

"For three years, and then he moved on to CSI," Pastrella said.

"And what does Harbinger do?''

"Nobody seems to know. A lobbying group, maybe; a conduit between the defense contractors and the military, maybe; maybe only an organized version of the old-boy network."

"Or maybe a group who likes to keep the Cold War hot, so to speak?''

Pastrella shrugged.

"Retired army colonel August Lansdale—might he be one of them?'' Morris asked.

"It's possible; the name has come up. Another, almost for certain, would be Admiral Jonathan Westlake, retired from the Navy. He replaced Jacobsen at Defense Systems."

"What about Lieutenant Colonel Stephen White?''

Pastrella frowned. "Stephen White?''

"Aide to General William French."

He nodded. "National Security Council. Why do you ask about him?''

"What do your friends at State say Dennis O'Neal was doing in Rome?''

"They don't. That's one reason I came to you."

"And why have you linked Harbinger to this?'' Morris asked.

"Because the name has come up in communications I've seen recently. There seems to be a link between Harbinger and West Africa.''

"Why would a group of American military types be interested in West Africa?''

"If I knew the answers to all the questions I have, I wouldn't have come to you."

"Why did you come to me?'' Morris asked. "The CIA isn't usually in the habit of getting its information from the press. How do I know you're not on a fishing expedition from them? How do I know you haven't been charged with finding out how much the press knows about Harbinger? How do I know that Harbinger isn't one of the Agency's own 'black' projects?''

"You have my word on it, and Dennis O'Neal was one of my best friends. I came to you because I've gone as far as I can go without raising suspicions."

Morris shook his head. "I still don't understand what makes you link Harbinger with this.''

"By all rights, Dennis had the expertise to be station chief in Rafetna, but Alvin Jones was sent over for that. Why? Alvin Jones had been in Washington for the last fifteen years or more. The last time he was overseas was in Bangkok, heading a clandestine operation. And he was working under Jacobsen."

"Are you trying to link your own Agency with this?"

Pastrella sipped his beer, then set the glass down slowly. "I don't know."

"What is Alvin Jones doing in Montreal? Do you know that?"

"No."

"I suggest you find out." Morris rubbed his thumb against the cracked linoleum that covered the table.

"That's what I came to you for, for you to find out."

Morris shook his head. "The CIA doesn't ask the press for help in intelligence matters."

"I'm not working for the Agency, I'm doing this on my own, can't you get that straight?"

"You don't strike me as a cowboy."

"What makes you think—"

"Listen, Pastrella," Morris said, leaning forward again. "What do you make of it: your Harbinger—American military types—working in cahoots with the Russians. Why would they be doing that?"

"I have no idea."

"Why don't you try finding out."

"I told you: I want you to pursue it."

"You've already hit pay dirt on it, haven't you?" Morris asked. "You didn't mention the Russians to me, but you weren't surprised when I mentioned them. You already know more than you've told me. If you want me to pursue it, you'd better tell me what you know."

Pastrella looked at his beer again and it was so long before he spoke again that Morris thought he'd pushed too far this time. "I think you're right," he said finally. "Americans working with the Russians, and Harbinger is the link. I have no idea whether it's official or not; God, I hope it's not. But when you have men at the level that there is involved here, it almost doesn't matter. They can execute whatever they want, as long as it's kept under wraps. Dennis must have known something. They're scurrying like hell in Harbinger."

"They have a right to be. Dennis was bringing out a defector from the Soviets who had proof—I've seen the pictures, Pastrella."

"But why?"

"This is Washington, Pastrella. The name of the game is politics, and the point of politics is power. Don't tell me you sit over there in Langley and think it's just a game between the skins and the shirts. You're not that naive." He looked up as the barman stepped around the end of the bar and brought his beer.

"We don't usually serve the booths," the barman said. "You gotta come up to the bar and get it yourself."

"Sorry. It's my first time in here."

The barman nodded and set down the beer. "One buck," he said.

Morris extracted a crumpled bill from his pocket and handed it to the barman. He looked back at Pastrella and the man was sitting with his hands clasped in front of his face. Morris could only see the top half of Pastrella's face. "If you were to open up Harbinger," Morris said slowly, "what would you expect to find?"

Pastrella shook his head. "These men already have power."

"Power and money, Pastrella, power and money. In simple terms, they're not interested in better U.S. relations with the Soviets. What they want comes with the bristle of armaments."

"Hell, we're not that friendly."

"And if these guys have their way, we never will be. Those rebels in Bodamwe? Everybody wonders if they've got Soviet backing. Hell, that's what O'Neal supposedly was there for, wasn't he? Well, if the Soviets wanted to keep their backing so secret, how come they had a photographer from Tass there to record the whole thing? I'll tell you why. Because there is not just one group, called Harbinger, there are two groups. One here and one over there, and both have the same aim in mind: to raise temperatures between the two countries. That's where the power is for those guys, and that's how they hope to topple the Kalishev regime and bring the hard-liners back."

Pastrella stared at him.

"Correction," Morris said. "Bring the hard-liners back on both sides. A Soviet victory in West Africa would do that."

"And Dennis got in their way."

"Dennis, and a few more."

"Then what is Jones doing in Montreal?"

"You find out, Pastrella. You find out, but watch your ass. If he's there on Company business, it means he axed his own man in Rome."

The sound of Pastrella's quick intake of breath could be heard even over the noise of the bar.

"Yeah, Pastrella, that's some Company you work for."

"I don't believe it was an Agency operation."

"You find out, Pastrella; you find that out."

21

"NO," TED RICHTER SAID. "NO WAY."

"We're going to do it whether you help us or not," Molly said. "But we could sure use your help."

"Reporters report the news; they don't make it. And anyway, it's a cockeyed scheme. You think with this much notice the CIA isn't going to be crawling all over that church?"

"It'll be twelve noon on Sunday, in the Cathedral in downtown Montreal. It'll be crawling with tourists—that's what it'll be crawling with."

"No," he repeated.

"You have to understand about Ted, Molly," Gloria said. She was sitting sideways in the chair, her long legs hanging over the arm. She didn't look at either one of them; she was examining her fingernails. "He has to be in control. He doesn't believe in making himself vulnerable. He's not going to help us because he knows damn well there's no way he could control that. Besides, he only knows about looking out for himself; he doesn't care about other people."

"That's not fair, Glo."

She looked up at him. "Isn't it?"

Ignoring Molly, he stepped closer to Gloria. "They killed a goddamn reporter in Moscow."

"That's not all they killed," Molly said. "They also—"

"And they can get you, too. There's nothing sacrosanct about you just because you're women."

"I guess we already know that, don't we, Ted," Gloria said quietly.

He took another step closer to her. "I told my boss that this was on the level, that you weren't just trying to get back

264

at me, that that was a long time ago and you weren't the vindictive type.''

She stared at him for a long moment. ''Is that what you guys do in the city room all day? Talk about your conquests, talk about the women you've—''

''Shut up, Gloria.''

She stood and faced him. ''I guess we don't really want anyone like you, anyway. You'd probably only get in the way.''

''Gloria, a reporter doesn't get involved in the story. You know that.''

Her eyebrows arched. ''Don't they? What about that woman who went undercover to do the story on the mental hospital? What about the guy who got a job at the zoo so he could report on whether or not they mistreat the animals?''

''Where's your sister?'' he asked. ''She's got more sense than to go along with a scheme like this, I'll bet.''

''It's my sister's 'scheme,' as you so cleverly call it,'' Gloria snapped. ''She's the one who chose the church. And right now she's out shopping for our lunch. We try not to make a habit of displaying ourselves in every downtown bistro that we can think of.''

He turned to Molly. ''This is a hell of a risk.''

''Not for you. We're not even asking you to go inside the church,'' she responded.

He threw up his hands. ''Okay. Okay.'' He turned back to Gloria. ''Okay.''

''The most frequently driven car in Montreal is a gray Honda,'' Gloria said. ''I sat at a sidewalk café long enough to make a survey. And the most frequently delivered line is 'Mademoiselle, could I bother you for the time?' One would think in a city like this men could be a little more creative.''

Alvin Jones drove down the long, curved, narrow lane. He could not yet see the house. He'd moved Yuri Klebanoff there the second day, when it had become evident that he would have to hold the Russian for a while until he could figure out a way to unload him. He liked the place—west of Mirabel Airport, off the road to Lachute—it was convenient to both Mirabel and Laval airports, though admittedly not so convenient to the city. But he'd let Hamilton worry about the city for now. In the meantime, he had the Russian in a safer place, a place from which he would not be able to escape. He'd used the house once before, a long time ago. Its location had always been one of its assets; its structure was another. Though it looked from the outside very much like any of the other farmhouses in the vicinity, certain aspects had been changed to make it what it was today—one of the finest safe houses the Company owned. The building was made of gray stucco-covered concrete block, its doors were reinforced steel with double locks that required two sets of keys, its windows—set with reinforced steel mullions—were kept locked at all times. Electronic alarms were set into every window jamb.

He could see the house up ahead now. There were no cars in the drive; he had expected none. Hamilton was still in the city. Anders would be here alone with the Russian. A house like this made it possible to keep someone like the Russian with minimal escort.

He pulled the car up close to the side door. As he stepped out, he surveyed the house with admiration in the light of early evening. The Company held it through a dummy corporation. As far as any of the neighbors were concerned, it was used mostly for retreats, conferences, occasional hunting, or cross-country ski outings—perks for spoiled American executives. Around the house were open fields. Good for hunting, good for cross-country skiing, good for security. The trees along the drive were almost the only trees in sight. They masked the cars driving in and out from any possible curious neighbors. They also masked three electronic beams at twenty-foot intervals that gave warning in the house against anyone approaching on the gravel drive.

He drew a set of keys from his pocket and unlocked the upper lock, then the lower one. As soon as he shoved the door open he could hear the sound of the television in the front of the house. He stepped into the kitchen and locked the door behind him with care. When he turned around, Anders was standing in the doorway to the dining room.

"Find them yet?" Anders asked.

"We found where they were day before yesterday. They seem to be staying one night at each place and then moving on. This time it was small hotel on the northeast side of town. They're smart—moving around makes them harder to find. You can't cross off anything; they might move back there the next day."

"You could leave flyers, in case they show up somewhere you've already been."

"We'd have to bring in the Canadians if we did that."

"And you still don't want to call them in?"

"Washington says no." He pocketed the keys and, looking down, his eye caught a spider scurrying across the black-and-white tile floor. He moved his foot to block the spider's path. It paused just a moment, then changed direction. Jones watched until he could no longer make out the spider against the black tiles. "Of course they aren't trying to find this needle in the haystack. How's our guy?"

"Same. Won't say a word."

Jones walked past Anders, through the unlit dining room with its stiff-backed mahogany chairs and its table still draped in sheeting, and into the living room. Yuri Klebanoff sat in a brown plush chair of indeterminate style, his right ankle resting on his left knee and his handcuffed hands lying on his right leg. The evening news was on TV, but Klebanoff didn't seem to be watching. He had told Jones that he didn't understand French, but Jones didn't necessarily believe it. Klebanoff had, after all, spent the last several months in Bodamwe, and it was a good bet that he didn't speak Wolof.

"Everything okay?" Jones asked.

Klebanoff looked at him but didn't respond.

"I got those films you were carrying developed. Nice pictures. Nice beaches you were at. Molly looks good in a swimming suit, doesn't she?"

Klebanoff still didn't say anything. Jones sat on the arm of a chair just a few feet away. "I guess you were both telling the truth; she does have the pictures. Which means we have to take her seriously about making a trade for you." He was watching the Russian, but Klebanoff didn't react. It was the first time he'd mentioned the trade to him since the day they'd taken him. Jones tapped out a cigarette and offered it to Klebanoff. The Russian shook his head, and Jones put the cigarette into his mouth. "I suppose you thought we'd torture you or something. No, we'll leave that kind of thing to the KGB, or the GRU, or whoever would be most interested in you." He lit the cigarette and inhaled shallowly. "I'm trying to quit, but it's not that easy." He blew out the smoke, his eyes squinting. "Yeah, she wants to make a trade, the pictures for you—she's serious, I guess. She says she's seen the pictures, and they'd be something we would want. Which tells me something. Either they're not anything we'd be interested in at all, or else she wants you back mighty bad. You sleep with her while you were in Greece?'' He took another drag on the cigarette and Klebanoff stared at the floor.

"Hell, I would have," Jones grinned. "She's not a bad-looking piece of ass, is she?"

Klebanoff looked up from the floor. "We have better in Soviet Union. I have had much better myself. Your American women are too—what do you call it—skinny. And too neurotic.''

"You guys like 'em good and round, don't you? All those potatoes you people eat. You sleep with a lot of women in Russia?'' Jones reached over and tapped the cigarette into an ashtray. "I guess you get plenty of chances, with the apartment shortage and all. Probably someone like you gets a fairly nice apartment, but even so, I wouldn't have thought you'd be all that experienced in American women.''

"I have seen movies.''

Jones nodded. He stood and walked over to the television and turned it off. "You watching that?" he asked. He stood in front of the set and folded his arms over his wide stomach. "What's in the pictures?''

"I told you before, I don't remember individual rolls.''

"Why would she want to trade them for you?''

"I don't know.''

"Something going on between the two of you?''

Klebanoff stared at him for a long moment. "I do not understand,'' he said at last.

"Did you sleep with her? Is she in love with you?''

Klebanoff's face broke into a slow, wide grin and his eyebrows arched conspiratorially. "What do you think?'' he asked.

Jones stared back at him and then at Anders, who was standing in the doorway. Then Jones walked out of the room, through the dining room and into the kitchen. He'd been there when Molly had first met Klebanoff and he'd seen her reaction. She hadn't thought much of him then, and it was no wonder. He was an arrogant son of a bitch. If she wanted to make a trade, there was one thing for sure: it was not because she was so anxious to get him back. And that told him what he needed to know about the pictures.

He opened a kitchen drawer and pulled out a telephone directory for Ottawa. Despite what French had said, it was still the cleanest way to get rid of Klebanoff.

* * *

"I never had any desire to be a blonde," Gloria said, fluffing the wig's platinum curls. She screwed up her face as she looked at her reflection in the mirror. "Nope. I am definitely not a blonde." She pulled the wig off and reached for the other one, a brown wig with long straight hair. "Now this one has real possibilities." She pulled it on and contemplated herself in the mirror, tucking an errant strand of hair back under the wig. "What do you think?"

Sitting at the counter beside her, Molly nodded. "Not bad. Definitely better than the blonde."

Gloria wound the brown hair around her hand and held it at the back of her head. "Horn-rimmed glasses."

"Take out your contacts," Molly said.

Gloria nodded.

"Different makeup. No fingernail polish."

"File my nails down." Gloria grinned in delight at Molly's reflection in the mirror. "This is the most fun I've had since we got here!" She pulled the wig off and unpinned her own hair, letting it fall once again around her shoulders. She frowned at her image in the mirror. "Wigs make your hair look like hell." She pulled a brush from her bag and stroked it through her hair. "On the other hand," she said, "you're not too bad as a platinum blonde."

Molly looked doubtfully at her own reflection. "But the style is ridiculous."

"Sure," Gloria said, nodding. "They always think women who want to be blondes are trying to look like Zsa Zsa Gabor. Never mind. We can do something with it."

Molly frowned.

"You scared?" Gloria asked.

"Not yet."

Gloria put her hand on Molly's arm. "Good girl." Then she slipped the brush back in her bag and stood. "I can't wait to meet this guy."

"I hope you get the chance."

Gloria slung the bag over her shoulder. "What do you think? Denim skirts?"

"Sounds good."

"I think so, too. After all, we have to assume they won't know the first thing about women's fashions. They ought to be able to get denim right."

"Loose-fitting blouses," Molly said.

"Plaid. Goes good with the denim."

"No, a solid color. Let's keep it easy for them."

"And a blazer for me."

Molly looked at her in surprise.

"Yeah," Gloria said, hitching the bag strap higher on her shoulder. "Maybe off-white."

Cathy O'Neal sat in the passenger seat of a gray Honda and watched the automobile showroom across the road. Next to her Ted Richter drank coffee from a Styrofoam cup. Inside the showroom a salesman was talking with a young couple. The wife held a baby in her arms, jiggling it to keep it quiet while the salesman talked. Her husband finally noticed and took the baby from her. The salesman, as if on cue, nodded, walked half a dozen paces to the wall behind a counter and pulled a set of keys from a rack and another object from underneath the counter. The couple followed him out of the showroom. The two in the Honda had an almost unobstructed view of the new car lot.

The salesman unlocked the door on the driver's side and reached in to unlock the back door. The woman got into the back and her husband handed her the baby. Then he closed the door and got into the front, behind the wheel. Meanwhile, the salesman walked around the back of the car, slapped a magnetized license plate onto the rear license holder, and continued around the car and unlocked the passenger side. After getting in, he handed the keys to the young man behind the wheel.

Cathy looked at Ted, and he was still watching the car as it pulled slowly out of the lot. "You're sure you can do it?"

"You bring it to me. Duct tape and I will take care of the rest."

"Then this one's a good as any," she said.

He nodded and turned the key in the ignition. He drove down the street in the same direction that the other car had gone. After two blocks, he turned to the right. Then, three streets later, he turned left into a residential area. At the next corner he spotted a high hedge that blocked the house behind it from the street. "What do you think?" he asked.

Cathy looked it over. The neighborhood was quiet. Even on a summer Saturday morning, there was no one in sight. The houses were quite widely separated. She liked that. "Looks good," she said.

He pulled into a driveway and turned around. "You'll remember how to get here?"

She looked at him without saying anything, and suddenly he felt like a fifteen-year-old who's just insulted his mother.

Without another word, he drove back to the auto dealer and pulled into the parking lot, far enough away from the showroom that they could not be seen. "Give me fifteen minutes," she said, getting out of the car.

He nodded, but decided to wait until she came out again with a salesman.

Cathy O'Neal walked up to a salesman. "I'm interested in an Audi 90," she said.

"*Mademoiselle, un moment* . . . one moment." The salesman had a stricken look on his face as he hurried off toward the offices.

Moments later a tall slim salesman appeared from the same direction. "May I help you?" he asked in English.

"I'm interested in an Audi 90," she repeated.

The salesman stepped over to a car and opened the door on the driver's side. "A very nice car, indeed. Does Madame have a preference in color?"

"Not particularly. Well, perhaps gray, or dark blue. May I test-drive one?"

"But of course. We have only one or two on the lot at the moment, and I do think we have a gray one. Just one moment, please." He stepped over to the counter, pulled a key off the key board, and reached around under the counter for a license plate. "If Madame will follow me . . ."

He led the way out into the lot and opened the car door for Cathy. "You'll notice the fine solid sound as I close the door," he said. He closed the door then and walked around the back of the car, bending to slap the license plate onto the back. Then he got into the passenger seat beside her and handed her the keys. "Please, drive it just as you would your own."

She pulled slowly into the traffic. Ahead of her by almost a block, the gray Honda was in the right lane. She drove two blocks and then turned to the right, then three blocks more and turned to the left into a residential area. Ahead, almost at the corner, a gray Honda was parked. She drove slowly, reaching for the air-conditioner switch as she drove. It came on, and she smiled at the salesman. "We often go to Florida, you know, and air-conditioning is just about essential down there.''

"You're from the U.S.," he commented.

She smiled at him, then looked back at the street as she made a slow right turn. "How did you know that?"

"Your 'outs' and 'abouts' betray you. I suppose you would say that ours betray us."

She had slowed the car to a stop. "Doesn't it seem to you that it's awfully cold on our feet? Is there a way to change the air flow?"

He bent down to look under the dashboard, and she saw, in the rearview mirror, a man dart out from behind the parked Honda. She leaned forward and turned a switch. "Perhaps this . . ." and the car was flooded with sudden sound. "Oh, I guess not," she said apologetically. "I'm afraid I'm not very mechanical."

The salesman turned the radio down. "It is a very fine radio," he said. "AM and FM dual speakers front and back. Very fine tone, don't you think?"

"Yes, indeed."

"And this must be the vent control," he said, pushing a lever. The cool air did in fact cease flowing from the lower vents.

"As I say," Cathy said, "we do go down to Florida for the winter, and I'm sure you know that it can be quite warm and humid down there, even in the winter. My parents live in Florida." She checked the rearview mirror, as if to make sure there was no car coming behind her, and she saw the man opening the door of the Honda parked at the curb. "You're right," she added, pressing lightly on the accelerator again, "I am from the U.S. But my husband is Canadian. We've been living in Pittsburgh, but he was just recently transferred back to Montreal. It hasn't been any problem for him." She had picked up speed and was heading back toward the main street. "His French is quite excellent, but I still have a long way to go. I'm delighted you speak English so well. He asked me, you see, to take a look at an Audi 90. He has become quite enamored of them, and he'll buy one if I like it. What's your name? I'll have to be sure to tell him to ask for you when he comes into make the purchase."

The salesman reached in to his pocket and handed her his card. "William deJust," he said. "It has been a pleasure."

She parked the car in the lot, handed him the keys, and

shook his hand. "I'll be sure to give my husband your card. You couldn't have been kinder to me. And I certainly am impressed with this car. I do like the color. Will you be working on Monday?"

"I plan to."

"Good. I'll tell him to ask for you then." She looked at her watch. "Oh, goodness! Look at the time! I'll be late for my hair appointment. Thanks again!" She dashed off toward the customer parking area, just as a gray Honda drove into it.

The salesman tossed the keys up in the air and smiled to himself. He was still new enough to be believe that he had an almost certain sale for Monday. He walked around to the back of the car to retrieve the license plate, and stopped. It wasn't there. He stood at the back of the car for a moment, frowning. He was almost certain that he'd not forgotten to put a plate on before they went for a test drive.

The gray Honda drove out of the customer lot.

Some five hundred miles south, in Columbia, Maryland, Linda Allsberg savagely thrust a vacuum cleaner across the living-room carpet. Carolyn Fritz, with whom she shared the apartment, appeared in the doorway, barefoot in shorts and a T-shirt.

"It's my week to clean," Carolyn shouted over the noise of the vacuum.

"I know."

"You invite someone over or something?"

"No."

"Turn the stupid thing off, Lin; I can't even hear you. What's the matter, anyway?"

The vacuum shut off briefly. "I know it's not my turn. I just feel like doing it, okay? I just feel like vacuuming, okay? Is it such a big deal?"

"It is when you act like you're about to bite my head off. Which you've been doing for the last couple of days, I might add."

"Sorry." Linda turned away and the vacuum roared once again. It hadn't even been a real apology and she knew it. This wasn't the way things were supposed to be. She really liked Carolyn. She really liked her job. She'd wanted to work in D.C. since she was a kid growing up in Tempe. And even working for the National Security Agency hadn't bothered her, until the last week. She believed in it. She believed that strong security agencies were the first and last lines of defense. But something wasn't working right.

With an undergraduate major in Russian and East European Studies and a master's in linguistics, she had indeed found a job in D.C. Though some might have found the work routine after a few years, she still thought it fascinating. She knew the sources of some of the tapes, and had some guesses about some of the others. The story had been given out that the Soviets had finally caught on to the fact that the NSA had cracked the electronic codes that protected the conversations party officials held over their car telephones. But she'd heard enough tapes to know that those conversations were still being recorded. She also had a strong suspicion that the *Vertushka*, the closed Kremlin telephone system that is installed, maintained, and monitored by the KGB, was also being monitored by the NSA.

And that was only a small part. Virtually all telephone conversations, all telecommunications, in fact, were vulnerable to NSA listening stations and satellites. And even that didn't include the countless recording devices hidden in Embassy walls, in office heating ducts, behind lavatory mirrors. Only telephone and telecommunications within the borders of the United States were supposed to be inviolate. Supposed to be. But she had also heard enough to suspect that there was, in reality, no such thing as inviolability. The other side of that paradox was that some of the most obvious things sometimes passed through. One could never tell; but one ought to be able to assume that if an NSA staffer herself called attention to an anomaly, someone ought to pay attention to it. On the other hand, she had realized some time ago that it was not a matter of lack of information—the intelligence services were drowning in raw information—it was more usually a lack of good analysis or evaluation, sometimes even a matter of timing. In a bureaucracy that big, there were bound to be mistakes.

She knew that the tapes were run through computers and tagged for specific watchwords that appeared on them. Words to be placed on the watch lists were nominated by the NSA itself, or the CIA, or the FBI, or State, or heaven knew who else. It was not unheard of for a translator even to suggest a word, if it appeared in a suspicious or unusual context.

What nagged now was that she had been hearing things on the tapes that seemed important to her, but nobody else appeared to care. It was almost as if she were being stone-walled, and that not only annoyed her, it scared her. It was one thing to miss a crucial piece of intelligence; it was quite another to bury it.

There had been more this week and she could no longer ignore it. It was definitely bothering her. Phase II, whatever it was, had become a major concern of the Kalishev faction. Three ministers had discussed it openly in a meeting. And new elements had come into play. An American was doing something in Montreal. Messages had come into the Soviet Embassy in Washington concerning Phase II, and another had been picked up going into the Soviet Embassy in Ottawa. There had not been this much agitation across the board in the Soviet Union since Chernobyl.

On the other hand, it was true that someone had picked up on Phase II at last. The expression had joined the watch list, but belatedly, and there was no telling how much had been missed. And because of what she'd heard previously, she'd also suggested that Harbinger be added to the list. But no one had followed up on that, and that was what had finally made her wonder who the hell was passing on the lists and why they didn't seem to believe what she reported. Or maybe it was that they didn't want to believe it.

She slammed the vacuum into the leg of a chair and swore at herself when she pulled it back and saw the pale gash in the wood. She didn't know what was wrong with her. It wasn't up to her to analyze the information. Her job was to translate it. The branch chief had told her that, and it was true. "You're a damned good linguist, but that doesn't mean you know every-thing," he'd said. "None of us knows everything." And that was as close to an explanation as she got—more, she had to admit, than anyone owed her. If he was wondering too, he wasn't about to tell her. She could just imagine her next merit evaluation; crew chiefs didn't take kindly to linguists' going over their heads to a branch chief. And in this case, all it had gotten her was a rebuke anyway. She should have saved her time.

Alvin Jones saw the country crossroad up ahead and slowed to a stop. He looked at his watch. "Five minutes early," Anders said from the seat behind him. Jones nodded.

The car up ahead, facing them, also stopped. It shone its lights once, briefly, even though it was mid-afternoon and broad day-light. Jones opened the door on the driver's side and stepped out. Behind him, Anders stepped out as well. He walked around the back of the car and opened the other back door. "This is it," he said.

Yuri Klebanoff, still handcuffed, got out of the car. He shook each leg as if to loosen it, and then turned toward the car that was still fifty yards down the road.

Anders took Klebanoff's left arm and drew him around the front of the car until they both stood beside Jones in the middle of the gravel road. In the dusty grass at the edge of the road a single cicada chirped.

The three men began walking toward the car, and as if by some signal the car started moving slowly toward them. "Have you ever met this guy before?" Anders asked.

"Just talked with him on the phone is all," Jones replied.

When the car came up alongside them, it stopped again, and the driver rolled down the window. "Alvin Jones?" he asked.

Jones nodded and stepped forward and the man in the car opened the door and got out. He was tall and broad with a receding hairline, and he wore steel-rimmed glasses.

Jones took Yuri by the arm. "This is Yuri Klebanoff," he said.

"Yuri Andreyevich Klebanoff," the Soviet said, nodding curtly.

Klebanoff said nothing.

The Soviet reached out for Klebanoff's arm and directed him toward the car, opening the passenger door and letting him get in by himself before closing the door behind him. Then the Soviet looked back at Jones. "You have delivered the package," he said formally.

Molly stared around the store—one huge room lit by rows of fluorescent lights, some burned out and others flickering maddeningly. The walls, originally eggshell-colored, were scuffed now around the lower edges and dirty with handprints. Rows of chrome and brown metal clothes racks stretched all the way to the back of the store, some with bright-red *Vente/Sale* signs perched precariously above them or hung on wires from the ceiling. "How do you find a place like this?" she asked.

Gloria touched her forefinger to the end of her nose and wiggled it. "I have a nose for it," she said. "When you're an actress, you know how to find all kinds of places. A man's suit coat, don't you think? Maybe black or dark blue."

Molly fingered a housedress as they walked past a row of racks. "Mightn't it look too nice? Clean, I mean?"

Gloria shot a glance back at her. "Give me a break. We can dirty it up, if we have to." She advanced on the men's section and expertly shoved her way through a rack of suit coats. "What do you think about this?" she asked, holding up a navy coat with faint pinstripes.

Molly tilted her head. "Too classy."

"Hey," Gloria laughed, "she's going to be one classy dame. After all, it's the Cathedral, you know."

"How about this one?" Molly asked, pulling out a green-and-yellow check.

"We're going to have enough green. Besides, something dark would be better."

"Then this." Molly held out a shiny black serge sleeve.

"Good," Gloria said, nodding and moving closer. "Very good." She unhooked the hanger from the rack and looked at the coat, still nodding. "I like it. With the right dress, it'll be perfect. And some kind of hat. Don't let me forget the hat."

Cathy O'Neal walked into the car-rental agency. "I'd like to rent a car for a couple of days," she said.

The woman behind the counter smiled. "But of course, madame. We have—"

"I'd like a Honda, if you have any," Cathy said.

"Naturally, Hondas are quite popular."

"And do you have gray? I'd like a gray one."

The hotel room this time was small—one double bed and a rollaway that had to be kept folded up to allow movement from one side of the room to the other. Gloria sat cross-legged on the double bed, a game of solitaire spread before her. Cathy stood at the window gazing out, though there was nothing outside but the darkness and, ten feet from their window, the wall of a neighboring building. Molly sat in the one chair, a hard-backed leatherette-seated desk chair that could barely be pulled back from the desk without ramming the end of the bed. Ted, whose room was adjoining, had gone off somewhere to call Washington from a public phone. A minimal number of calls, they all had agreed, and never made less than a half mile from whatever hotel they currently used.

They had gone through the drill four times earlier in the evening; the first time with them all in the same car so that there was no mistake about the route, and other times just as they would do it tomorrow. None of them knew how much traffic there would be on a Sunday, but it almost certainly would be less than this evening.

Molly gazed absently at the cards as Gloria slapped them down in a slow rhythm. She had spent much of the day with Gloria, yet knew very little about her. Gloria was quicksilver, restive with darting eyes that took in everything one moment, languorous and dreamy the next, then loquacious and joking. If she and Gloria hadn't been living in each other's pockets for the last five days, she would have guessed Gloria was on drugs, but she knew now that it was just the way Gloria was. She had seen her spend twenty minutes applying lipstick; she had also seen her cover her own glorious hair with a dull brown wig and then wind the hair into a bun at the nape of her neck and slap on makeup that made her look ten years older and one tenth as attractive.

A knock sounded on the door to the adjoining room, and Molly, without having to leave her chair, reached over and opened it. Ted stepped into the room, carrying a paper bag. "They wanted to go with it tomorrow," he said.

Cathy turned away from the window. "And you talked them out of it, I hope."

"Do they have enough without Yuri?" Molly asked.

He let the bag slide to the floor and he raised a bottle triumphantly. "We deserve a celebration, don't you think?" He walked into the bathroom and brought out three glasses, carrying them upright, a finger in each glass. He set them on the desk and pulled a corkscrew from his pocket. "Oh, yes," he said, "I believe in coming prepared." Holding the bottle sideways, he gently worked the screw into the cork. Then, levering his thumb against the bottle's rim, he drew the cork out, swearing under his breath when a crumb of cork loosened and fell back into the wine.

He poured the pale liquid into the glasses, and then walked back into his own room. A moment later he returned, pouring wine into his own glass. Molly was handing out the glasses. He set the bottle on the desk with his right hand and with his left he raised his glass.

"Success," he said simply.

"Success," Cathy echoed and the others repeated the word. They all drank.

"Not bad," Gloria said, lowering her glass and looking at the wine in surprise.

"Hell, you think only California makes good wine?" Ted asked.

"No, but I never thought your taste in wine was all that great."

"They'll print it on Monday?" Cathy asked.

"Do they have enough without Yuri?" Molly asked again.

"They think so. The pictures are still the key."

"What if," Gloria asked, "just what if they really come ready to make a trade? Is Molly actually going to turn those pictures and negatives over to them?"

"If they're serious about a trade, yes," Molly said.

"And that throws Ted's story out the window," Gloria countered.

"No, because then we have Yuri. Yuri has seen the men."

"But without the pictures he can't identify them."

"He doesn't have to," Ted said. "We already know who the guys are. We already know what rocks to look under; and the guys in Washington have already begun finding stuff. They've already got enough to go with what they have."

"But they'll wait?" Cathy persisted.

"That was the agreement all along, and they'll stick to it. They're just not that crazy about it. You know, every day they wait is one more day for someone else to break it."

"How would anyone else know?" Molly asked.

"Washington's a small town," Cathy said. "Rumors generate faster than fruit flies." She looked at each in turn. "We're all set then? Everybody knows what they're doing?"

"I'm worried about Gloria," Molly said. "Are you really going to be able to make the change in time?"

"I had ninety seconds to age forty years in a play I did last winter at La Jolla. Next to that, this ought to be a piece of cake," Gloria responded, lifting her glass again.

"Yes, but you didn't have to make that change driving a car," Ted said.

"Just give me one thing," Gloria said, "give me one stoplight."

"Remember, Gloria," Cathy said, "don't start until you've fed yourself in onto Maisonneuve. That's the trickiest part, and if it doesn't work right, we might as well throw the rest of it out. If anybody's following you, you've got to draw them right into it. After we've got all the fish in the same barrel, you'll have seven short blocks and an easy right turn and then another quarter mile for the change. Don't push it before that.''

"The plan covers them in one car or two," Ted said. "Has anybody thought about what happens if they have three cars?''

"Oh, yes," Molly said. "I have. I'll bet we all have."

"If they have three cars, it isn't going to work," Cathy said. "Plain and simple. Nobody promised this'd be foolproof."

"And still we're doing it," Ted said, shaking his head. He took another drink and poured another inch into each of their glasses, finishing off the bottle. Then he sat down on the corner of the desk.

"I guess it's time for my little speech," Molly said. She looked at each in turn. "I've been wondering since last night—since Ted said he'd go along with it—what I'd say to you all. I guess you know by now that it's something I feel I have to do. I can't just walk away and not at least try to get Yuri back. It isn't only how I feel about him emotionally or anything else. It has to do with the fact that I'm the only one in the West who knows him and if anybody's going to do anything, it'll have to be me. It seems we all have our own reasons for doing this." She looked down at her hands, cupping the glass. "I just want you to know that whatever happens, he was worth our trying."

"You understand that if they do bring him and make the trade, or at least appear to make the trade, you're going to have to get him out of there as fast as you can," Cathy said. "Don't get so excited that you wait even one second longer than you have to. They won't do anything in the church, but you've got to be free of them when you're out the door."

Molly nodded.

"And if he isn't there, it's even more important that you get out. When Al Jones sees the picture, he's going to have only one thing in mind and that'll be to wrap you up right along with Yuri."

"I know that," Molly said.

"It's the CIA, goddammit," Ted said, shaking his head. "We're all out of our minds, there's no way—"

"You picked a fine time to think of that," Gloria said.

He leaned forward toward the bed. "Hell, I'm in this. I said I was, didn't I? But there's no way they're going to let Molly walk out of there. If they have to, they'll kill her on the spot— I'm sorry, Molly, but that's your life, that's your fucking life!"

"They won't kill her on the spot," Cathy said. "Not in the church. Not with so many people around. And it's not the whole

CIA. I don't know what it is, but I know Dennis wouldn't have gotten involved in what this is beginning to look like. He would have quit first.''

"Is that supposed to make it all right, that it's not the whole Agency?" Ted asked. "We don't even know how many guys they have up here, and for God's sake look at us. What are we? How can we let Molly walk into that? They know what they're doing; what do we know?"

Cathy smiled gently to herself and then reached over and touched his shoulder. When she spoke, her voice was soft. "Dennis was a very careful person. He never took anything for granted. I remember he sometimes used to talk about what he called the 'pro' factor. He used to think that professionals— any professionals, not just intelligence people—develop over time a sense of 'in-ness,' a sense that only they know certain things, only they understand certain things. The way doctors see themselves as healers, for example. So that it becomes very easy to begin to think that one has a special gift, and that only one's self and one's co-professionals have the gift. Or educators, thinking that only educators know about education. Or—you name it. And nowhere, he thought, was that kind of thinking more dangerous than for intelligence people. He used to say that the pro factor would give an inventive amateur a chance of pulling something off against a seasoned agent.''

"How good a chance?" Ted asked, laughing ironically.

"A very good chance," she answered, smiling to mask the lie.

"Then listen to this pro just once," Gloria said. "The key to acting is that you don't memorize lines and you don't memorize movements or cues. You learn personalities, ideas, situations. You learn them so well you could do them in your sleep, so that they are absolutely natural. Then when something goes wrong—and you can count that something will go wrong at the worst time—you can go on. You can make the scene come out right because you know the direction you have to go. Acting is a con job, and tomorrow we are all going to do that con job and make it work not because we've memorized it, but because we know how we have to make it come out and that's what we're going to be aiming for.''

"And somewhere," Ted said, "Alvin Jones and his guys also have a plan they think is going to work."

"If you don't want to do this, why don't you butt out?" Gloria asked.

He looked at her for a long moment. "It doesn't hurt to face reality, Gloria," he said finally. "That's exactly what they've got and we might as well remember it. That doesn't mean I'm ducking out on this; it only means I know what Alvin Jones is."

22

THE NAVE OF THE CHURCH WAS DIM AND COOL. AT the main altar a priest's voice rose with the ritual, sounding antiphonally against the slurry of lowered voices and the shuffle of moving feet. Candles flickered and worshipers knelt in the pews or prayed at the small chapels that lined both sides of the nave. Tourists moved along the side aisles, gaping at the stained-glass windows and gazing wide-eyed at carved wood and stone.

In a half-empty pew on the right-hand side was a blond woman in a blue denim skirt and a loose-fitting green blouse. Near her, in the same pew, an elderly woman bowed her head over a missal. She wore a red-and-yellow-and-black print dress, covered by a man's dusty black serge suit jacket, several sizes too large. On her head a navy-blue straw hat with red plastic cherries perched precariously over short gray hair. At her feet were two bulging plastic shopping bags. She held a large, grimy handkerchief to her nose and occasionally blew loudly into it. From time to time, the blond woman looked at her with concern, as if she were afraid that the woman might have a contagious disease. But the older woman, oblivious, bent her head and went on reading the missal and blowing her nose.

Molly looked surreptitiously at her watch. It was ten minutes to twelve. She'd been sitting there for forty minutes. She'd tried to concentrate on the replica of Bernini's Baldacchino that rose triumphantly around the altar. She'd let her eyes follow the undulating lines of the red copper columns, studied the gold leaf that decorated them, gazed at the crowning motif, with its lush winged figures. She'd stared at the cupola that crowned the sanctuary, painted in green with rose and tan and gold detail.

She'd looked at the tourists as they wandered by, oblivious to the service that was taking place, and at the worshipers, who sat or knelt quietly in the pews, oblivious to the tourists. But although she managed to keep her eyes from it, her thoughts had never left the gentle statue ahead and to her right—Saint Anthony, holding the Christ Child in the crook of his left arm, and a single lily stalk in his right hand. Before him, rows of red and white and green votive candles flickered. Let him come, she thought, let him be there.

"Any sign?" Cathy whispered softly, then blew her nose into the dirty handkerchief.

Molly didn't respond, and Cathy went on pretending to read her missal. To her left in the pew, near the center aisle, a man snored softly, his chin resting on his chest, his glasses almost falling off his nose.

Molly made a slight, involuntary move and the older woman beside her looked up slowly. Ahead and to the right, along the side aisle, a man was walking now toward the statue of Saint Anthony. She could see him in profile, his jacket open, his stomach protruding, his graying hair windblown and unruly around his face. She stared at him for a moment and then turned her attention to the open book on her knees. "He's alone," she whispered.

"I see that," Molly responded.

"One chance only. If he's not here, that's it," the older woman said. Her voice was firm and she took the chance of looking at the younger woman when she spoke.

Molly was facing directly forward, but her eyes followed the man to her right as he stationed himself beside the bank of candles and surveyed the congregation. *Dump him . . . dump him.* The words rolled around in her head. She closed her eyes. Until now, she had held out hope. He could still be here, she thought. Maybe with someone else. Maybe they'll wait to see what the pictures are. She could feel her heart beating in her throat as she rose from her seat, and she half-stumbled getting out of the pew. *Dump him. Dump him.*

Jones did not recognize her. She walked right up to him and he didn't recognize her until she spoke. "Do you have him here?" she asked in a lowered voice.

His eyes took her in, then flicked away in wary reappraisal. "Molly?"

"What did you expect?" she asked, reclaiming his attention.

"How stupid do you think I am? How many agents have you got here, anyway? Is he here or not?"

"Do you have the pictures?"

She pulled a photograph from her pocket and handed it to him. He looked at it—two men at relatively close range—and she heard his breath catch momentarily, but when his eyes met hers they were hard and cold.

"Yes," she said, nodding. "Did you think I was lying? There's more, but not until I get Yuri."

"What am I buying?"

"You're wondering about the negatives? You're buying them as well as the prints."

"Do you have them here?"

"Do you have him here?"

He looked at the picture again, as if weighing its importance. Then he slowly folded it over once and slid it into his coat pocket. When his hand came out of the pocket, it was holding a short-barreled .22. "It's small," he said, "but that only makes it inconspicuous. At this range, it'll do you just fine."

"Where is he?" she whispered fiercely.

He shook his head, but said nothing. *You don't trade with them,* Cathy had said.

She stepped back and he grabbed for her arm. He didn't see the woman in the man's jacket and the ridiculous hat until it was too late. She stepped up from behind him and shoved a disinfectant can in his face and pressed the plunger. He had half-turned toward her when the spray hit and his hands went up to his face in automatic self-protection, his eyes already watering from the spray.

Beyond, at the door to a small private chapel, another man in a gray suit only had time to see the movement of the multi-colored dress and the hands to the face, and then the blonde in the green shirt was moving quickly through the crowd. "Blonde, green shirt, blue skirt, like made of denim, coming out front. It's her," he said, knowing the microphone under the knot of his tie would transmit his voice.

Across the nave, moving toward the entrance in concert with the blonde, was another blonde, dressed identically. They exited the center doors at the same time without exchanging a word or even a glance, and paused for only a moment at the top step. Then each took off running down the steps, one turning right and the other veering to the left.

* * *

Two men in the brown Taurus parked across from the Cathedral saw two blondes in identical clothes at the door of the church. They paused just briefly and then one ran down the steps to her right, waited for a car coming up Mansfield, and then darted across the street. The other blonde turned to her left, ran down the steps to a gray Honda parked along Metcalf and got in.

"Clever," the man in the passenger seat said.

The two men exchanged quick glances, and then the driver pressed down on the accelerator. "What the hell," he said, "we're facing toward Metcalf. You know damn well the one's going to lead us to the other." He eased out onto Dorchester and turned almost immediately onto Metcalf as the blonde pulled away from the curb.

"License plate XRP 279," Anders said. "Hold back. Give her her own sweet space. Let her think she got away."

Hamilton, in the driver's seat, nodded and allowed a blue Peugeot to pull between him and the gray Honda. It annoyed him that Anders had felt obliged to give him instructions, as if he didn't know how to hang a tail. He was no hot shot just off the Farm, still thinking that smart operators played tag team with a target like they do on TV. He knew as well as Anders: the best tail is a single nondescript car—gray or brown—one that looks like half the other cars on the road. The rest is relatively simple: you just lie back and follow.

She drove down Metcalf to the first corner and made a right turn onto Gauchetiere. As Hamilton made the right turn behind her and drove under the viaduct, he noticed another gray Honda up ahead, just in front of the blonde's. At the next corner both cars turned left onto Peel, drove slowly for one block, then turned right onto St. Antoine, took it for one block and then turned right once more onto Montagne.

"She's looping," Hamilton said.

"Maybe not," Anders replied. "It may just be these damned one-way streets."

"No, if she weren't looping she could have gone north on Peel in the first place. What's the game she's playing?"

The car ahead drove faster now, and a block later it passed the other Honda. At the next corner, it turned right and the second Honda followed.

"They're together," Anders said. "Don't lose'em. It's the car in front you want."

Hamilton said nothing.

At the corner both Hondas turned left onto Peel. "What did I tell you?" Hamilton nodded. But now he saw that there were three gray Hondas ahead and he was no longer sure which was which.

Anders leaned forward in the seat. "It's the old ringer car trick, and you'd better get closer or we're going to lose track of her. I guess we can figure out what their game is."

Hamilton stepped on the gas. The three cars ahead turned onto Maisonneuve and they began moving in and out of the lanes, leapfrogging each other. He had lost track of which car was the one with the blonde. The car directly in front of him appeared to be driven by a man.

All three Hondas kept driving straight for several blocks, traveling right at the speed limit. Hamilton's eyes flicked to the rearview mirror. "Christ," he said, "look behind us."

Anders looked back and saw another gray Honda behind them. "Ignore it," he said. "She's got to be in front of us. Hell, it's probably one of the most common cars in the world."

"They've done their homework, you've got to hand them that," Hamilton replied. Ahead of him, the Hondas, one by one, were turning right at Guy.

"So far so good," Anders said. "We're still with them."

Almost as soon as he spoke, one of the Hondas turned off to the left, onto Lincoln Avenue. Anders read the license plate. "Keep with the other two," he said, "that's one of the ringers."

The cars were climbing now, toward the Parc Mont-Royal. This time, the Honda right in front of them—the one driven by a man—made a right turn. They already knew the license plate didn't match. There was one Honda left now and Hamilton accelerated to pull closer to it.

But the car ahead of them accelerated as if on cue, keeping well ahead of them, still climbing, the city now falling away beneath them. The woman pulled into the park drive, keeping her speed up as the park lay to her right and a cemetery to her left. She passed a car park, still accelerating as the car climbed. Finally, at the top of Mont-Royal, she pulled into an overlook. Three cars were there already, their occupants spilling out to look at the view. The brown Taurus drew right up behind the Honda, blocking its exit. Anders caught the license-plate number and grabbed for Hamilton's arm, but Hamilton was already stepping out of the car. He was at the door of the Honda before the woman had even opened it.

She opened the door and looked up at him, her brown eyes

wide in surprise behind horn-rimmed glasses. Her hair, dull brown, was pulled back in a bun at the nape of her neck. He guessed her to be in her late forties. She wore a blue skirt and an off-white blazer, buttoned primly, with a red scarf tucked in at the neckline. She stared open-mouthed at him for a moment. Then she unfastened the gold watch from her wrist and held it out to him.

"Eet is all I have of value," she said, her voice quivering, a French accent skimming over her words. "Please don't 'urt me."

Astonished, Hamilton took a backward step.

Then she blinked a couple of times and looked more closely at him, tipping her head back and holding her glasses up on her nose so as to see him through the half-moon part of the bifocals. "You cannot be a mu-gair weet such clothes."

"I'm sorry, but—" Hamilton started.

Still extending her hand with the watch, she tilted her head as if for a better look. "But pairhaps you are lost? Ah, you are tour-eest, no?"

Hamilton took another step back.

The woman glanced across the pavement and watched a young couple walking toward them. "But of course," she said. "No one would be so foolish as to mug a wo-man in plain daylight in such a public place. Do you need di-rec-tions?"

Hamilton looked at the young couple. Beyond them, a middle-aged man with three teenagers had just climbed out of a van.

"Never mind, lady," Anders said, having come up around the other side of the Taurus. Hamilton backed toward him. "Wrong license plate again," Anders murmured to him.

Both men walked back to their car and got in, still keeping their eyes on the woman.

"It couldn't have been the Honda behind us," Anders said. "There was no way she could have gotten back there."

"How much you want to bet she's one of 'em?" Hamilton asked.

"But not the one we want. The O'Neal woman, maybe?"

"We'll follow her."

"Is she the one you saw in the hotel?"

Hamilton cocked his head. "No. Wrong hair color."

"Ever hear of dyes? Ever hear of wigs?"

"Wrong eye color. Wrong voice. Not nearly as good-looking. And older, definitely older. But she still could be one of them."

Both watched the woman as she stood by the side of the car, looking around uncertainly. Suddenly her face lit up and her hand rose to wave a greeting. She ran toward a man who was running down the hill from the direction of the Wildlife Museum, and he, seeing her, sprinted forward and caught her up in his arms. He covered her face with kisses, almost knocking her glasses off. She laughed and leaned back to look at him, cradling his face in her hands. He pulled her close again and held her tight.

Hamilton looked at Anders. "Some romance. Or else a pretty good show."

"You think it's a show?"

Hamilton shrugged. The man and woman were walking away from the overlook, his arm around her waist and her head leaning on his shoulder. In a few more moments, they would be out of sight behind a clump of trees.

"Don't you think it's strange . . ." Hamilton began, "she didn't stop at the car park."

Without explanation, he stepped back out of the car and walked over to the Honda. Taking a slim blade from his pocket, he forced the lock and opened the door. He rummaged around under the seat until he found what he was looking for and pulled it out—a blond wig. He looked up; the man and woman were almost out of sight behind a hillock. He took off running.

The woman turned and saw him coming. She began running first, then the man joined her. They crested another hill and ran across another overlook until they came to another gray Honda. They opened the unlocked doors and climbed in, the man putting the car in gear and backing out even before the woman had her door closed. Another moment and they were gone, and the two men following them could only stand and watch in frustration.

Gloria pulled off the wig and shook out her hair. "You're not all that bad an actor," she said.

"Who said I was acting?" The tires squealed resistance as he banked a hard right coming out of the overlook. "Those two guys back there—it looked pretty tight for a minute."

She flung her hair back and laughed. "I accused them of trying to mug me."

"You didn't."

"I did. I learned long ago the old saw—the best defense is a good offense."

"I've got to hand it to you," he said, negotiating a steep downhill turn. "In your shoes I'd have been scared shitless."

"I was scared that the tape hadn't let go as soon as you said it would."

He grinned. "Your plate and Molly's dropped off within five minutes, just like I promised. Plop, plop, in the middle of downtown Montreal. Those guys never even noticed. You should have had more faith."

"It seems to me," she said, reaching into her bag for a hairbrush, "that faith in a person has to be earned."

He stared straight ahead, no longer smiling. "You're never going to forget that, are you?"

Molly followed Cathy and Gloria into the house. Its silence hung like a cloak around them. The other two women walked straight back toward the kitchen, but Molly wandered into the living room. She was thinking of O'Neal, of the last time she saw him. He'd squinted against the Roman sun and told her, if she had to, to dump Yuri. And she had.

A grand piano stood in the living room and family pictures hung on the wall above it. She guessed at Jason and Charlie, and the other one—she'd forgotten his name. There was one of O'Neal shooting baskets with the boys at a hoop on the garage.

From the kitchen she could hear Cathy on the phone with one of the boys. She hadn't wanted to call them until she was back. At first, they'd planned to drive straight through from Montreal, but as they came closer, they'd realized how late that would bring them home and how drained they really were. So they stopped in some little town in New York for the night. They could have flown back, but each for her own reasons had wanted the time that driving back gave them.

It was almost noon now, almost exactly nine days after she'd first called this house. The boys would be returning soon and the place would be full of people and noise again, the way it should be. Except that O'Neal wouldn't be coming back to play basketball anymore.

She turned away from the pictures and saw Gloria standing in the doorway.

"You okay?" Gloria asked.

"Yes."

"Well, will you go back to Africa now?"

"I don't know. I guess I need to think about some things." She turned and looked once more at the pictures. She didn't even have a picture of Yuri.

They'd stopped at a drugstore on the way into town and bought a newspaper. The now-familiar photographs had been spread across the front page. Ted had flown back to Washington yesterday afternoon, and the story had gone to press for the morning editions. The *Los Angeles Times* were part of the same syndicate as the *Post*—Ted had explained it but she hadn't really listened—and the *Post* had published the story as well. The paper lay now on the table in the foyer. Molly had scanned the story, but there would be plenty of time to read it later; and she knew it all anyway.

"It's not going to be easy, is it?" Gloria said.

Molly turned around again to face her. "What happened between you and Ted?"

Gloria shook her head. "That was a long time ago. It's over now."

"He came because he owed you, didn't he?"

"He came because he knew it was going to be a good story."

"But he stayed because he owed you."

Gloria shrugged. "It's hard telling why a person does things sometimes."

Cathy had walked through the dining room and stood now behind Gloria. "Father Jack says everything is going crazy. People are covering their asses like mad. He says we should have been here last night—the story broke on the eleven o'clock news. I'll bet the anchors all over town were going bananas. A story like this and it breaks on a Sunday night. Does anybody want lunch? I'm starved. God knows what the refrigerator looks like after all this time."

She started back toward the kitchen, but the telephone rang. She stopped to answer it and spoke for a few moments. Then she called, "Molly! It's Ted. He wants to tell you what you've stirred up. You can take it in the front hall."

Molly lifted the receiver. "Ted?"

"Listen, girl, have we got Washington going crazy, or what? It's absolutely wild around here; I wish you could see it. The phone has been ringing all morning. Before the story breaks, nobody will give you the time of day. But once the story hits, they come out of the woodwork with what they know—a piece here, a piece there. You can thank a CIA guy, friend of Dennis and Cathy—hey, I forgot to tell her about that—he really did a number for us from the very start. Plus, we got a call from some female who works for the National Security Agency who's been listening in on the Soviets talking about their end of it for the last year or more. Hell, that organization—they can listen in on just about every telephone conversation in the world. She was scared pea-green to be calling us, but, hell, at least she did. She linked Harbinger to what they call Phase II over there. She even knew that the Soviets had called their Embassy in Ottawa and given them instructions. Hell, *they* knew we were in Montreal, and they had half a dozen different sets of instructions sent to 'em in the last week, depending on who was sending them. The hard-liners in both countries have got egg on their faces over this. If anything will solidify Kalishev, this will. Yuri's grandpa might as well roll over and play dead, along with his buddies. And there's probably going to be a dozen different Congressional investigations. Molly? Are you there?''

"Sure, but you haven't given me a chance to say much of anything. Or even to think."

"Listen, Molly," he said, slowing down, "we got one more call. I should say *I* got it. My byline, I got the call, but it might as well have been for you."

He paused and she held her breath.

When he spoke again his voice was more serious, as if he wanted to make sure she would understand. "It was from somebody in the Soviet Embassy in Ottawa. It seems Al Jones offered to turn Yuri over to them last Saturday. The guy who called— Kostiouk is his name—had some very interesting things to say. God knows what he does up there; he's probably KGB. He told me that Jones wanted to turn Yuri over to him so that he could be sent back to Russia. Their problem with Yuri, of course, is that he defected, and on top of that he gave us materials that could have been damaging to the government—he's talking about the pictures. There's no way they could avoid trying him for treason and sending him off to Siberia for God knows how long. He—Kostiouk—made a point of telling me that's one of the differences between our government and his. We'd just bury the guy beneath something more sensational the next day, he says, and no one would even remember to ask about him. In the case of Yuri in Russia, there's no way that could happen. He's got a big name. His grandfather and buddies are in the soup. There'd have to be a trial. And that could be embarrassing in a number of quarters.

"So Kostiouk has made a unilateral decision. He didn't tell me about the unilateral part, but anyone can figure it out. After telling me all this crap about how things work in the Soviet Union, he informed me that Jones in fact did *not* hand Yuri over to him last Saturday. He says he went to the rendezvous as agreed upon, but Jones never showed up. He says that if Jones says he did turn Yuri over that he's most likely lying, and perhaps the Canadian Mounties ought to start looking in the ditches somewhere. He says, after all, that right now nobody can trust anything that comes out of Washington anyway.

"In the meantime, he says, maybe you ought to go meet the Air Canada flight that gets into Dulles this afternoon at five. He says there's going to be someone on that plane named Thomas Little and you might want to be there to meet him."

She was crying and she couldn't help it.

"Molly? Did you hear that part?"

"Yes."

"And one more thing. He says this Thomas Little says to tell you that he really does think he's going to like America. For real, this time. Whatever that's supposed to mean."

"Thank you," she said.

"Hell, you don't have to thank me. I'm just delivering the message."

"Thank you," she whispered again.

About the Author

S.K. Wolf is a former university librarian who has traveled extensively throughout Greece, Turkey, and the Middle East, and now lives in Livonia, Michigan.